Role Play

Susan Wright

107th Ave Press

107th Ave Press

Copyright © 2014 Susan Wright
www.susanwright.info

ISBN-13: 978-0692254004
ISBN-10: 0692254005

Trade paperback printing July, 2014

Acknowledgements

Thank you to Kelly Beaton, my Beta reader extraordinaire!

Cover art by Francisco Munoz

Prologue

Nine years ago
Tarrytown, NY

Sierra

I had to sleep with Lola on a fold-out sofa bed in our new apartment after our mom left our dad. I guess I was in shock from the split-up of our family and losing my brothers, so the memories of those months were blurred in my mind. I don't know exactly how long afterward it happened, the night Lola and I were woken up by the thuds coming from our mom's bedroom, and the loud voices.

Mom sounded shrill and slurred, like I always remembered, but then she cried out in a way that made my insides go hollow in fear. I was suddenly, completely awake.

I hugged my arms around Lola knowing I was no real protection for my little sister, who was eleven to my twelve. But it felt safer to hold onto her. To know I wasn't completely alone and scared. To feel a little bit okay because I had to be okay for her.

I listened as hard as I could even though I didn't want to hear it. As my mom cried out again.

What was happening? Would he come out and hit us, too?

Instead we heard the bed thump against the wall, and the sounds of springs creaking, fast and hard. Even in the midst of the creaking, it sounded like they were arguing.

I listened with all my might, ready to leap out of bed and drag Lola with me if he came after us, figuring that the stairwell in front of our new apartment complex, down under the first flight, would be the best place for us to hide.

And then... nothing. Lola snuffled and soon fell asleep. Our arms were still wrapped around each other, creating a tiny bubble we floated in together. I watched the lights flashing from the freeway onto the wall over me, afraid the man would come out to get us next.

But he didn't come out, not until morning when he hardly looked at any of us. He turned out to be just another random guy among the many my mom spent years hooking up with, some more memorable than others.

My mom didn't look any different the next morning, though I searched her face trying to find some hidden hurt. Mostly she was irritated because Lola pitched a fit over a skirt she wanted to wear but couldn't because it was dirty. Mom left early to go to work so I had to pour out the cereal and milk for both of us, and lock up behind us when we went to school.

I had lost everything. All I had left was Lola.

Chapter 1

Today
New York City

Sierra

My phone started to ring as I was walking down the block. I had to juggle two bags of groceries that I'd bought at the bodega by the subway as I tried to get my phone out of my purse. Naturally I dropped one of the bags and two oranges rolled onto the sidewalk and down into the dirty puddle against the curb.

"Crap!" I muttered. I didn't have anything to wipe them off, and I didn't want to put them back into the bag. Don't get me wrong, I loved everything about living in the city—it was my dream to move here for as long as I could remember—but it wasn't ever easy. Usually I loved the walk home between the row houses that lined the streets with all of the people going by. But I'd had a long day on my feet and another long block to go.

I let the oranges lie and found my phone. It was Dick. He only called me when there was a problem with Lola. "Hi, Dick. What's up?"

"Do you know what your sister's done?" Dick demanded in his gravelly voice.

"I'm too tired for guessing games, Dick. *What's up?*"

"She broke up with me."

I felt a pang right through the center of my body. The warning shot of worse to come. "Seriously?"

"You didn't know?" he demanded.

"No..." Sure, Lola and Dick bickered a lot, but that's because Lola was impossible to deal with sometimes. Somehow their relationship worked. In fact, the only bright spot in Lola's life right now was Dick. He was a NYPD detective and he had literally saved her a year ago, when she was flirting with drugs. It could have ended badly but Dick was the one who had pulled her out of it.

"I knew something was wrong." Emotion crept into Dick's voice, making him sound furious and freaked out at the same time. "I told you she's been avoiding me."

Dick had texted a couple of days ago asking me if anything was going on with Lola. I didn't tell him that she had stayed out all night several times last week—and again last night. Until I'd gotten his text, I thought Lola was spending more time than usual at his place. I had meant to ask her about it, but I hadn't seen her today. I wasn't even sure what her work schedule was this week.

"What are you fighting about now?" I asked.

"What do you think?" Dick demanded. "She hates her job and wants to quit. Her boss is an asshole. Blah, blah, blah... I told her I can't give her any more money this month. I thought she was pouting, but not like *this*..."

It was a sore spot for me, the money Dick gave to Lola for her share of the rent. I had protested the first few times—when she got fired last spring and again when she had to go to the emergency room to get stitches after she slipped on the icy snow piled at our corner. But after that, I don't know what we would have done without Dick. Our little one-bedroom place was a stretch, even living on the edge of Astoria among the industrial buildings.

"She doesn't mean it," I protested. Lola couldn't mean it. She relied on Dick. We both relied on Dick.

There was silence on the other end, which was somehow more unsettling. Finally, he said, "She's in big trouble, Sierra."

"Trouble? What do you mean?" My heart skipped a beat at the fear that Lola was pregnant.

Instead, Dick said, "Lola is a sex slave."

I wanted to wring his neck through the phone. "Dick! You scared the life out me. I thought you were going to say she's *pregnant*."

"I wish! We could get married if she had a kid. Maybe it would settle her down."

"Lola, a mom? Are you kidding me? She's a spoiled brat. She could never take care of a baby. She can't even take care of herself."

"You don't seem to be very worried about this," Dick said through gritted teeth.

"That's because I'm not. It's just another drama Lola can pull. Like switching stores at the mall—that was a stupid thing to do, but Lola wanted to show up her old boss. And now it's blown up in her face because her new boss doesn't trust her, because how can you trust anybody who would do something like that?"

"This isn't a job at the mall, Sierra! She's been

cheating on me."

I didn't doubt him for a second. I supposed that said something about my opinion of Lola. "I'm sorry, Dick. If it makes you feel any better, I'm sure she's been faithful up until now."

"Why is she doing this?" Dick demanded, sounding almost humble for him. "I love her."

"I know... but you know how Lola wants excitement in her life. All of her relationships before you were chaotic. This could be an old, bad habit rearing its head."

The situation reminded me a lot of when we had first moved to the city and Lola had quickly snagged two guys on her string. She pitted them against each other, so they would vie for her love. They had to grit their teeth and pretend it was okay as they competed with each other. It was so painful to watch.

But hope sounded in Dick's voice for the first time. "You think she's trying to make me jealous?"

"Lola wants you to rescue her," I explained. "She loves all of your arguing and making up... I mean, why else would she tell a cop that she's a sex slave, unless she wants you to save her? It's just another game in the never-ending game that Lola plays with life. If you play along, you could win. Unless you'd rather give up and let some jerk have your girlfriend?"

Again there was silence. I knew Dick was weighing his wounded pride against his love for Lola. "All right, I'll do whatever it takes."

I felt another pang, this time because of the

devotion in Dick's voice. I wished I had a man who felt that way about me. Lola was an idiot to mess with her relationship with Dick.

I realized that people were passing by me on the sidewalk, looking at me curiously as I talked about pregnancy and sex slaves to Dick. That was the city. You got so used to the crowds of people that you started to ignore them. There was always a show going on, and I guess I was the show today.

"We'll figure out something," I told Dick. "I'll call you later."

I abandoned the tainted oranges and hurried to my apartment. As soon as I got inside, I dumped the bags on the table and called Lola. It went straight to voice-mail. "Lola, call me when you get this. I need to talk to you," I said, hearing the irritation in my own voice.

Unloading the groceries, I got another nasty surprise. As I was putting away the Ziploc bags in the drawer, I found two unopened bills shoved inside. Slitting them open revealed the electric and cable bills.

I let out a shriek of anger. I had given Lola my half last week so she could pay them from her account. Now they were late.

I texted Lola right away: *Did you pay the bills because I just found them in the drawer unopened.*

As I waited to hear back from my sister, I did some homework and then made dinner. As the hours passed, I grew more worried.

If Lola went off the rails for real, she could take me down with her.

We had moved to the city three years ago from our mom's latest apartment in Peekskill. The only good thing about growing up in a series of upstate towns was New York City not far down the Hudson River. I worked my ass off to make it in Manhattan and finally landed a position in the Junior section of Lowenstein's on 5th Avenue. Lola's "fuck it" attitude hadn't gone over as well. She was lucky to have a job at the Forever 21 in Queens Mall.

I was planning on moving up, but Lola had refused to take college courses along with me. She said I was crazy—it was going to take me years to get my bachelor's degree because I could only afford one class a semester. But by the end of this summer, I would have my associate degree in business administration. The store always gave me the evening off for my class, so I was sure that with more seniority and my associate degree, I could make the move to supervisor. But to get a real career in merchandising, I would need a bachelor's.

I just wished Lola had more of my own determination to succeed. I couldn't carry Lola forever, and my sister had better learn that sooner rather than later.

•••

Lola didn't come home that night, and she didn't return my texts or calls. So I finally stopped trying.

I had a terrible day at work, and was even more upset with Lola because of it. I almost paid the bills myself when I got home, but I refused to let Lola off the hook. Someone always had to step up when my sister failed. It was getting really old.

I was still staring at the bills on the coffee table when my phone rang.

Dick said, "Lola's going out with that guy tonight. To some sleazy sex club."

"How do you know?" I demanded. "Did you talk to her?"

"Yeah, I went to the mall and met her as she got off work. She says she has a *master* now. She's helping him do shows."

"What kind of shows?" I asked in a hushed voice.

"Sex shows, what do you think?" Dick sneered.

"Just tell me what she said, Dick."

"She told me to get lost, that she never wants to see me again," Dick snapped. "She says she's got a new life. And when I said I wanted to meet this guy, to make sure he's okay, she flipped out. She says she trusts him with her soul, can you believe that? I offered to take her home, but she's on her way to do a show at the Chamber."

Everyone in the city had heard of the Chamber, the notorious underground fetish club. Hearing that Lola was going there sounded much more serious, now, especially since I found the unpaid bills and Lola had refused to return my calls.

But I couldn't help feeling suspicious after dealing with Lola's nonstop drama my whole life. "She wants you to go," I told Dick. "Why else would she tell you she was going there?"

"That's what I thought." Dick sounded madder than yesterday. "I don't need this shit, Sierra. Your sister is fucked in the head, you know that?"

"I know..." What else could I say? It was true.

"I'm going over there now," Dick told me. "I'm going to bust that guy's face when I see him."

"Dick, wait! You can't do that. Lola won't forgive you. She has to choose you. If you force things, she'll keep running away."

"*Sierra...* I'm not letting her go to that place with some strange dude."

I knew that Dick was too conspicuous with his shaved head and solid bulk that screamed "cop" to sneak into the Chamber without Lola seeing him. Then she might act out just to get a rise out of him. And if Dick saw another man touch Lola, there was no way he was going to be able to restrain himself.

"I'll do it," I told him. "Come and get me. I'll go in to keep an eye on her. The second I see something weird go down, I'll text you and you can rush in to save the day. A place like that is bound to get rough, and Lola won't like it."

"Maybe it will scare some sense into her," Dick agreed. "Good idea, Sierra. I'll be right over."

•••

When I got Dick's text, I ran downstairs and got into his car. "You took forever to get here," I complained.

"You need a disguise," Dick told me. "Otherwise Lola will spot you in a heartbeat. Then she'll make a scene and I won't get to save her."

I realized he was right. If Lola saw me, it would be no better than sending Dick in there.

"I went to get this at the precinct," he said,

pulling out a plastic bag. "We use it for undercover agents. There's some make-up in there, too."

I pulled out a bunch of maroon curls. "A wig? This is what made you so late?"

"Stop bitching and put it on."

Dick drove like a maniac to get into Manhattan, taking the Queensboro Bridge then across the park and down the West Side highway. It took a lot longer than I liked, not knowing what Lola was up to, but it gave me time to bundle my long brown hair up with the only two barrettes that were in my purse. Once it was on, the wig's curls felt strange and the vibrant maroon dye-job kept catching the corner of my eyes.

At the stop lights, I swabbed on the dark make-up, including the bright red lipstick. Dick kept sneaking glances at me. "That's better. But you should take off your shirt and just wear your vest. You look like a librarian right now."

"My skirt is short," I protested.

"Trust me, it's not good enough for this place. You need to blend in."

Turning my back to him, I took off my shirt and quickly shrugged on my vest. Buttoning it, I tightened the back strap so it didn't hang loose and show my bra. My breasts formed an impressive amount of cleavage in the plunging v-neck.

Dick kept eying me. My sister and I looked a lot alike, but our clothes were one of the biggest differences between us. I was always getting after Lola to not dress so provocatively, but my sister liked the attention she got. Even from guys hooting at her on the street. She ate it up while I shuddered every time it happened. I didn't want anyone to get any ideas that they could take advantage of us.

"This shows how much I'm willing to do for my sister," I muttered.

"That goes for both of us. She better appreciate it," Dick said.

Finally Dick parked his car on a strangely darkened street across from the dingy façade of the Chamber. The five-story brick building was narrow to fit the lot wedged between the busy streets that converged at 14th Avenue. In most places in the city, lights blared everywhere, but here the walls had solid faces of sooty bricks and the massive overhanging awnings cast dark shadows on the cars below.

It was not the sort of street I was used to. It hardly felt like I was in Manhattan at all.

"Okay," I said, putting down the visor to take one last look. "Here goes."

I adjusted my borrowed wig. The wig and my heavy makeup did the trick. I was unrecognizable. Even if I ran into my sister, Lola wouldn't know me.

"Ready?" Dick asked impatiently.

"I said I was going!" I flipped up the visor. "You don't have to keep asking."

His rough voice grated on my ear. "Look, Lola's been in there for more than an hour. There's no telling what's happening to her."

"You're the one who took forever picking up the wig."

Dick glared at me. "Are you going to get out of this car and do this thing, or should I go in myself and drag Lola out of there?"

I looked over at the dark maw of the fetish club. I refused to believe it was dangerous, because the city would shut it down if it was. Dick was a cop, for Christ's sake! He would know. He just hated playing Lola's game, and who could blame him?

I was pretty pissed about it, too.

"Okay," I said again. "You wait for my text, or you'll ruin everything. Got it?"

"I know," he insisted, more irritated than ever.

It would have to do. I could only help the guy so much. He had to give me space to deal with my crazy sister. With the right management, I could still make this whole sordid thing go away.

I crossed the cobblestone street. The guy at the top of the black stairs leading down under the sidewalk gave me a good once-over. He nodded appreciatively. "Looking for the Chamber?" he asked.

"Yes."

He jerked his head at the steps. "Downstairs."

It was seriously creepy going down the dim stairway. My toe slipped on the slimy edge, and I had to grab the railing to keep from falling.

My fear suddenly ramped up to anger again—this was all Lola's fault! I wished Lola was standing in front of me right this second. I would tell her a few choice things about herself. *Self-centered brat! Grow up already!*

At the bottom of the stairs was another door. Opening it, I heard voices around the corner. The New Jersey accent was unmistakable as the guy said, "I have to be in Montreal tomorrow, but I can find out and let you know next week."

I couldn't see the girl who answered, but her voice was husky like a smoker's. "You will? You're a life-saver, Victor. Why didn't I think of that?"

A low laugh drew me forward. From around the blind corner, the guy's voice went deeper with the classic come-on. "You can thank me *later*."

For some reason, it made me even madder. *I don't belong here!*

I never went to bars, and I hated pick-up scenes where the bridge-and-tunnel crowd pretended they were cool because they partied in Manhattan.

As I rounded the corner, I muttered, "Even I've got better lines than that, *Jersey!*"

And came to a full stop, face-to-face with a smoking hot guy. My eyes scanned upward, across his broad chest and arms that bulged as he crossed them. A strong jaw and cheekbones, tanned a golden bronze that matched his hair, just long enough on top to fall onto his forehead. It was too dim to tell what color his eyes were, but they were surprisingly light against his tanned skin. I could smell the money on him, the way his clothes fit and clung to his body. Only the best for a man like this.

He was standing in front of another black-painted door. In the wall next to him was an open window. Inside the window an emaciated blond sat at a cash box. Her mouth hung slackly. "Are you talking to *us*?" the blond cashier pointedly asked me.

Victor tossed the cashier an easy smile. "I know she's not talking to *me*."

"You're so funny, Victor!" The blond laughed, letting him know with her eyes that she was ready and willing. They were having a special moment right there in front of me.

It didn't help my mood when the gorgeous man completely ignored me, opening the black door and letting out the heavy thrum of music as he entered.

I shrugged. *So maybe I'm wrong, what's the big deal?* From around the corner I could have sworn he was your typical Jersey truck driver or construction worker. I had been careful to scrub the upstate New York from my own voice and stick to Manhattan-speak which had no trace of an accent. I learned quickly that girls who spoke well got the better jobs in the better stores.

"Read and sign this." The blond cashier handed over a clipboard.

It was a liability waiver. It talked about the risks involved in "BDSM" and had a lot of rules like "no intercourse" and "no oral sex."

I shook my head as I signed. "You have to tell people this?"

"It's a fetish club." The blond stared at me. "Are you sure you got the right place?"

"Unfortunately, yes." I handed over the money.

The blond looked at me like I was cracked in the head, as she handed over a wooden ruler, marked off in twelve inches with "The Chamber" and their website printed on it. "Tonight's theme is School's Out. You get a door prize for looking like a teacher."

"I do?" I glanced down at my short skirt and vest. "I never had a teacher who looked like this."

"A sexy teacher," the girl said.

I had to laugh at that, and it made me feel

better. I gave the skinny blond my first real smile as I opened the door.

It was too dark inside to see much but a lot of shadowed people packed into too-small a space. The ceiling was very low and everything—walls, floor and ceiling—were painted black. I couldn't shake the sensation that I was underground, in a clammy dungeon-like space with ancient brick walls.

The music was much louder, blanketing the voices except for a shrill cry that broke through every now and then. Men kept trying to crowd in too close to me, until I was practically vibrating with silent warnings to "Get Away!" I cut off every guy's attempt to speak to me with a tsst! and raised the ruler between us to shut them down. Like the dog whisperer, it worked perfectly. The last thing I was going to do was talk to a man in here.

The place was filled to the brim. People were standing all around me and blocking my way, as streams of men slipped by. Occasionally through the layers of watching people, I caught sight of a near-naked man or woman with their wrists chained above their heads or bent over padded benches.

Is this the kind of show Lola is doing?! I craned my head to see everyone, to make sure none of the women were Lola.

Shuffling along with the roving streams of people from room to room, I saw a lot more than I bargained for. The one thing I didn't see was Lola.

Wide-eyed, I came to rest against the wall in the largest room, as a line of guys shuffled past, not quite out of arm's reach. I was starting to think that Dick was wrong and Lola wasn't here. Or we had missed her because it took too long to get here.

Then I saw Victor again. He was so sexy that he didn't even have to try. With his golden good-looks, he stuck out in this crowd like a lion surrounded by black alley cats. I wondered what he was doing in this seedy place when he looked like he would be more at home in a Calvin Klein ad. With a perfect model hanging off him.

Next to me stood a curvaceous woman, also pressed against the wall. She was wearing a short plaid skirt and white collared shirt, like a Catholic school girl. She giggled and called out, "Hi, Victor!" as he came closer in the steady stream of men.

"Hi, Monica," Victor replied as he passed by, completely ignoring me even thought I was squashed next to her. "Having a good night?"

"It could be better..."

Monica turned to watch as Victor disappeared in the flow through a dark doorway to the back of the club. Her expression was wistful.

"You know him?" I asked.

Monica giggled again, and somehow it worked for the busty older woman. "Everyone knows Victor. He's super rich, travels all over the world in his private jet. Tricia says he has a loft on the lower east side that he stays at when he's not up at his house in Connecticut."

I was impressed. It was just my dumb luck to be a bitch to the most eligible guy in this dump. The one man who looked like he didn't belong here... like me.

"Is Tricia his girlfriend?" I asked.

"No, just a girl he plays with sometimes. Victor doesn't have a girlfriend. He says he's too busy."

"Not too busy to come here," I pointed out.

Monica was looking down the hall where Victor's back disappeared. "If I could have one night with him, I'd take it. They say he's a brilliant Dom."

"What's that?"

"A master, a man who tops." Monica looked at me more closely. "Is this your first time here?"

"Yes."

"Oh, honey, you should go to one of the BDSM groups. You're young, why not try the next generation? They call it TNG. That way you'll meet nice guys who are your own age." Monica glanced around. "Some of these men aren't even kinky. They're just horny. You don't want to get mixed up with them."

I turned to her to ask more questions, but that's when I saw Lola stand up on a stage in the far corner. "Thanks, Monica. I'll check it out."

Keeping my eye on Lola, I made my way carefully through the crowd to the other end of the long room. Lola was on a low stage, slightly elevated above everyone, standing next to a tall, thin man who had his hand on her shoulder. My sister was wearing cut-off shorts that I hated because they showed her butt cheeks when she bent over. It wasn't smart to expose yourself like that in the city. And Lola's tank top had been ripped off right below her breasts, revealing her midriff. Putting it all out there for everyone to see.

There were guys gathered around the stage, eyeing my sister hungrily. Clutching my ruler tighter, I almost rushed forward to help her.

But I realized that everyone was holding back, watching. Only the tall man was touching Lola's shoulder. Another man and a woman were on the stage next to them, packing up a duffle bag with bundles of fat white rope and what looked like leather straps.

Lola was standing there in front of the tall man, looking up at him, never taking her eyes off him. The guy was older, in his thirties. Too old for Lola, for sure. He had a serious, craggy face as if he'd led a hard life. His hair needed cutting. Even worse, he didn't look quite clean. He was definitely not the husky, manly man that Lola usually went for.

I waited with my heart beating fast, expecting something awful to happen. Like what I had seen in the other rooms.

But the man with Lola started talking to the other couple, and crowd that had been gathered around the stage began to drift away. I got the feeling that whatever had happened was now over.

I shuddered, realizing I must have passed by this stage earlier without seeing Lola because of the crowd of men around the stage. Maybe she had been lying on that padded table...

What did I miss?

I felt myself jostled, as a familiar voice said, "Excuse me." Victor slipped in next to me, waiting for the other men to pass by.

Victor literally made my breath catch, he was

so handsome. Standing next to me, all I could feel was how tall and bulky he was. He kept the other men away from us by his sheer presence. For the first time since I got into this place, I didn't feel like I was being pressed on all sides.

For a moment, I could breathe. It was a real relief. Everything had happened so fast, that I was glad to get a break. And he was the reason for it.

"It's crowded here tonight," I ventured.

Finally Victor looked at me. "What? No more name-calling?" He glanced over at the other end of the room. "I see you were talking to Monica."

"She said you were a good guy."

"I'm sure she said more than that." His tone was dismissive, as he went back to scanning the crowd.

I grimaced. "Whatever. If you're going to hold a grudge, then keep on moving."

Victor looked at me again. "You know, there's a difference between being rude and being a Domme."

"I only called you *Jersey*. That's not exactly an insult."

"It is in that snide tone."

I smiled. "Hey, at least I didn't call you Bridge-and-Tunnel. *That* would have been an insult."

I could tell I had gotten under his skin. His perfect poise was rumpled. I felt a little smug. I may not be much, but I wasn't nothing, even compared to a guy like him.

But I was too busy watching Lola to give Victor the attention he deserved. Now my sister was nodding repeatedly to everything the man was saying. Since when did Lola agree to anything without arguing it to death first?

"Do you know that man?" I asked Victor.

He gave the foursome a searching look. "I've never seen any of them before."

"I wonder if I could ask the casher. Do you think she would know?" Absently, I tugged on my red wig, making sure it fell over my cheeks to hide my face in case my sister turned around.

"She probably wouldn't tell you," he replied. "Confidentiality is big around here."

I considered that. "Do people hide who they are? That can't be safe."

"You can ask for references from someone who knows them. And use your common sense."

I glanced over at my sister. "What if you don't have any common sense?"

"Then you can get into a lot of trouble."

A chill went through me at his voice. He was serious.

But I shook my head. "How much trouble can you get into in this place? With all these people around?" No, my biggest fear was what was happening to my sister when she was alone with that ominous-looking man.

"Are you looking for trouble?" Victor teased.

Now he was using his come-on voice, the same way he had talked to the blond cashier earlier. Only now he was flirting with *me*, this successful, irresistible man who was so yummy I could hardly take my eyes off him to keep checking on my sister. Standing in Victor's protective zone I could ignore the crowd of men. I could swear his eyes were gray or green, some sort of arrestingly pale color. And he held my gaze now, like my sparring with him had made him notice me.

"I think I found trouble," I told him.

His smile deepened. "I'm Victor. What's your name?"

"Sierra."

"That's a beautiful name." His eyes traced the curve of my cheek and across my lips like a touch.

I was shaken from the spell of Victor's eyes as someone bumped into me from behind. Heavy hands fell on my hips, as a voice slurred, "Yeah, give me some of *that*, Baby!"

"Get off me!" I jerked away, but the guy behind me managed to hang on. I could smell the alcohol he was belching out with every heavy breath.

"Now that's what I'm talking about—" the guy started to say.

Victor was suddenly there, reaching over the top of me and wrangling the guy away. By the time I turned around, Victor had secured the handsy asshole with his arm twisted up terribly behind his back. Victor's other hand was bunched in the guy's collar.

"Hey, man—" the asshole started to protest, struggling ineffectually.

Victor marched him several steps over to the closest wall, through the shocked crowd that melted away in front of them. Casually he slammed the guy up against the bricks. The asshole let out a sick ooof! as he collapsed against the wall.

A couple of the guy's friends stepped forward just as the broad side of a bouncer appeared. Everyone took a step back at the sight of him. It all happened so fast that I was still settling my clothes from being rumpled by the guy, when Vic stepped away and let the bouncer take over.

"He grabbed her," Victor said

I quickly agreed, "He did! From behind."

The bouncer instantly took the measure of the guy and didn't need any more convincing. Even his friends faded away as the bouncer dragged him off towards the door.

Someone pushed past me in the bustle, and I realized it was my sister. Lola and her friends weren't paying any attention to the mini-drama Victor had created. Lola was following the tall man through the milling crowd. The other couple was close on their heels.

I moved fast, following the young blond woman who had helped load up the duffle bag. I had to stay close to them to keep the crowd from closing in and cutting me off. I didn't see what happened to Victor, lost in the sea of people behind me.

Now he would think I was even ruder, taking off without a word after he had helped me, but there were bigger things at stake here than a hunky guy. Even a guy like Victor, who could take down some jerk without losing a breath.

I followed the foursome that included my sister through an archway and into another long room. Here the crowds thinned and I hung back as they chose a table in the front, near a big empty stage. I found a nook where I could watch them unobserved, my belly knotting in anxiety. What would they do next?

They sat down and the other man went and got them all drinks. They relaxed back in their chairs as if their work was done.

I settled in to watch. Something had to happen, like that handsy guy who had grabbed me. But I was worried that I wouldn't be able to get Dick in here fast enough to "save" Lola. And now, having seen the whippings and heard the cries of pain, I worried that my sister's acting out could get her into real trouble.

Were these shows staged? Or was it for real? I wished I hadn't missed Lola's show. I wished Dick had come straight over to get me instead of getting fancy with the disguise. What was the use in coming to this awful place if I didn't find out what was really happening?

The longer I waited, watching the foursome casually chatting with each other, the more it looked like nothing else was going to go down. If I couldn't call Dick in to save Lola, he was going to flip out.

And then I realized what I already knew. Maybe it was the way Lola was talking so familiarly with these strangers who I had never met. I couldn't ignore the truth that was staring me in the face.

Lola wasn't doing this to get Dick to pay attention to her. She was serious. She had broken up with him and was moving on.

Had already moved on.

It scared me. Like nothing else had scared me in a very long time. We were barely hanging on by our fingernails right now, and Dick was the only reason Lola had any stability at all.

Not only that, it was frightening on a whole other level. Lola was always a step or two behind me. She didn't dash off into the unknown by herself. I'm the one who blazed the trail. I'm the one who made sure it was safe. *I'm* the one who pulled *her* along.

Now, I had the terrible feeling that I was watching Lola's back as she ran away from me, disappearing into the darkness ahead.

I had to find out why she was doing this.

"The one that got away...," a familiar voice teased.

Startled, I turned to see Victor standing in front of the nook. "What?"

Victor came closer. "I thought we were getting along in there."

I couldn't believe this was happening. The hottest guy I had ever met was hitting on me, and it was happening in an underground fetish club!

"I don't think we want the same thing," I tried to explain.

"Well, I am usually a top, but I'd be willing to bottom to you." Victor pointed to the ruler in my hand. "I mean it. If you'd like to try, I'm game."

"What, with this?" I held up the ruler.

"Why not? I'll give you one minute." His smile turned sly. "But then you have to give me a minute. Turn-about is fair play."

"A minute to do what?" I countered.

Victor pulled out a thick piece of cord about three feet long. "Nothing sexual or any groping. You can use the ruler on me. Only the ruler. But no touching my face with it. I'll use this rope on you."

"Just a rope? It looks like I've got the better end of this deal."

"You could try to whap me in the balls, but I'm betting I can block you." Victor smiled.

I had to laugh at that. Then he looked deeply into my eyes again, and I felt the tug of his confidence, and yes, his amusement, pulling me towards him.

You would think I would run screaming at such an offer, but no... I was intrigued. By his interest in me, by the intensity in his eyes.

He held the key to this world. The world where Lola was playing with fire. What was my sister up to with that odd-looking man? The foursome were still talking, revealing nothing, yet revealing everything about how comfortable Lola was in this place. With them.

Victor made me curious, not only because of my sister but because I kept looking at the rope in his hands and wondering how it would feel to let him touch me. I shivered slightly just thinking about it.

"How do I know you'll keep your end of the bargain?" I asked.

"You can go first." He pulled out his phone and punched in a few numbers. "Sixty seconds and counting. Are you ready?"

I felt rushed and unsure of myself. But I had to find out more. More than anything, I wanted to leap out in front of Lola, to figure out a way to stop her headlong flight into disaster.

Besides, what could go wrong in one minute? With all of these people around? Monica said Victor was the best. That was a glowing reference, if I ever heard one. I could handle anything for one minute. Then I would know what I was dealing with.

"Okay," I agreed.

Victor grinned and touched his phone. "Time's started."

I looked up at him for a moment, feeling the ruler in my hand. The edges were slightly rounded, but still sharp enough to hurt if I hit him with it wrong. But clearly he was expecting to be struck. I wondered why he wanted to feel pain, but if that was his thing, who was I to judge?

"Hold out your hands. Palms up," I said.

The way he stood there in front of me, his hands out, gave me a weird feeling in my stomach. I wished it was the other way around. I wanted to see what it felt like to be in his hands, the way he was in my hands right now.

I took the ruler and smacked it down on his upraised palm. He didn't even flinch. I had to admit, it made me smack his other palm a little harder. Still, no flinch. He was looking into my eyes, searching me, as if he could see everything I felt. It was a rush when I hit him because of how wrong it was, exciting because it was so taboo.

I wanted to laugh for some weird reason, and I couldn't stop my lips from twitching up.

Gradually men began to gather around us. I could see them moving in closer, fixated on us. It was creepy but the sexual charge in the air was also exhilarating. I didn't expect that.

I lost track of how many times I struck Victor's palms, hitting a little harder each time, expecting him to flinch. But he never did. He took my blows as if they were nothing, even as his flesh reddened and I knew I would have been shaking my hands from the sharp sting.

The alarm went off, rousing me. He dropped his hands, looking at me. After a moment, I said, "That was a long minute."

"Yes, it was."

"Did it hurt?"

"Yes."

I felt an odd thrill deep inside. It was so intimate, even though I hadn't touched him! Not really.

"Did it turn you on?" he asked.

"It was intense," I admitted. I liked that he let me do what I wanted to him.

"I think you've got a submissive streak, too," he suggested. "Do you want to find out?"

"What about them?" I asked, lifting my chin at the men who had gathered closely around us. They blocked my view of Lola. I craned forward to see my sister was still sitting at the table with the others.

"Come back here," Victor told me. He took me to the rear of the nook, keeping his back to the men who slipped in after him.

He gave them a glare over his shoulder, and they retreated to the front edge of the nook, forming a line. Squeezed into a corner, all I could see was Victor's chest and broad shoulders in front of me. But

I could feel the press of eyes on the other side of him, and was grateful for his protection.

Now I was even more curious. What would it feel like to stand there like he had done and take his blows? Was he going to hit me with the rope? Or maybe spank me? Wasn't that the usual thing that went on in a place like this? A little slap and tickle...

Victor pressed the button on his phone and pocketed it. "Okay, now it's my minute."

With a few twists of his fingers, he held out a figure eight that he had made from the rope. "Put your hands through here."

I stuck a hand through each loop, still holding the ruler. I wasn't going to let him take it from me for fear that he would use it on me. Now I was regretting how hard I hit him there at the end. But he had taken it without making a sound, acting like it was nothing. For some reason, I couldn't stop trying to get a reaction out of him.

Now it was my turn.

He tightened the loops around my wrists, drawing my hands palms together, like I was in handcuffs.

"Oh, I see," I said. I twisted my hands, trying to test how strong it was. I couldn't get free.

Victor lifted my arms over my head, holding onto the rope, and then pulled my wrists down behind my neck. My hands went to the back of my head, my elbows pointing upward.

Before I could grasp what was happening, he put one firm arm around my waist, walking me a step backward. My back went hard against the brick wall.

It didn't look that clean, so I was glad my own hair was tucked inside the wig.

Then he leaned into me, and I couldn't think about anything else. I was trapped, my wrists tied and pulled down behind my neck, as Victor pressed me against the brick wall. His big, hard body was against mine. I couldn't move, completely enveloped by him.

A rush of pleasure nearly overpowered me. It felt so good! With my head swooning, I almost didn't hear him.

"You didn't negotiate for a way to stop," he murmured.

As soon as he said that, I knew I was in trouble. I struggled against him, but he held me without any effort on his part. I couldn't pull my wrists from behind my head, and I couldn't budge his body against mine.

His eyes were hard and darkened. He looked like a completely different person, all sharp angles in his face, disgust oozing out of him.

It turned ugly so fast, I couldn't think.

"*This* is what happens to girls who let strangers tie them up," he growled. "What did you think was going to happen? You let some random guy do anything he wants to you? You throw your trust away on the first person who asks?"

I couldn't move; he was holding me too tightly.

Let me go, I wanted to scream. My mouth opened, but the words wouldn't come out.

"I could do anything I want to you," Victor told me. "You think the cops are going to believe a girl who goes to a club like this to pick up guys? They'll believe a man like me. I could shove that skirt up and take you right here in front of these men. They would lap it up. I'd be done before that bouncer got back here to break it up."

I knew he could. I was caught in his grip, struck dumb by my own stupidity. He had locked me up tight at his mercy with only a tiny piece of rope.

No, it was his words, the barely restrained fury in his voice that told me not to fight or I would unleash a monster.

"Or I could squeeze your throat until you see stars and start to black out," he said, rubbing his thumb along the base of my neck. "That's what happens to girls like you. Girls who think they're better than everyone else. But you're not better. You're crawling around in the filth with everyone else here, asking for something you don't even understand."

Suddenly something inside of me broke. He was right. What was I doing here? I put myself in his hands, so he could do anything he wanted to me. I had thrown myself into the dirt after Lola, thinking I could save her. It served me right.

Tears flooded my eyes. There was nothing I could do about it. After all these years of preaching at Lola for being careless, and I was the one who fucked up. With his words, he took all the fight from me in an instant, and everything I had used to sustain myself turned out to be a lie. The only thing holding me up was his body pressing into mine.

He saw it when I gave in. When I went limp

under him. His eyes grew brighter, like he had won something from me. Like he had taken some power from me, and now it made him stronger.

And still I couldn't do anything but let the tears spill down my cheeks.

Chapter 2

Victor

The phone alarm went off, cutting across my awareness. Cutting the ties that bound us together.

She was crying.

I pulled back to let go of her. I released her arms, letting her bring them down in front of her. The ruler fell with a clatter.

She was really crying now.

I seemed to come back slowly from the red hot haze that had burned through me since I had heard Sierra call me *Jersey* in that snide, condescending tone.

Like I was nothing.

But boy, she had changed her tune after Monica had gossiped about how rich and successful I was. Sierra was just that type of girl, the kind who came here looking for their 50 Shades billionaire master who would tuck them into the lap of luxury and blindfold them every once in a while when they had sex.

Sierra looked up at me in fear, tears trembling on her lashes.

I couldn't help it; I pulled her against my chest, holding her tightly. "It's okay. I'm not going to hurt you."

She melted into me and cried even harder, in relief or whatever was racking her right now. Maybe my mindfuck had triggered something, a memory of something awful in her past. No telling, since I knew nothing about her.

I liked her even better like this. Crying... vulnerable... My hard-on felt shameful, even as my dick throbbed harder for attention, urging me to grind into her again. Like when I held her helpless against the wall.

No use in lying to myself. I had done it on purpose. I wanted to make her feel bad after she made the darkness close in around me. I wanted to scare the living daylights out of her and bring her down a notch or two.

And she had handed herself over to me on a silver platter. Throwing the dice that I was her prince charming in leather.

As I cradled her head, I realized her wig was slipping off. I caught it before it fell, still holding tight to her. She bent her face into her hands against my chest.

Her real hair was silky soft, falling in a long dark cascade down her back.

It was like a mask had been ripped off her. The bold riot of magenta curls was gone, revealing a young woman with make-up smeared down her face as she looked up. Her dark eyes were huge, beseeching, the black lashes impossibly long. Her defenses were gone, that sassy tongue with a quick retort now stilled.

Suddenly I wanted to protect her—from guys like me! I felt like an asshole, and it was a serious rush at the same time, which made it even more fucked up.

My throat got tight as I stroked her hair. "Don't ever let a stranger tie you up," I murmured.

She sniffed. "I get that."

"I told you things could go wrong. But you wouldn't listen, chasing after that guy you don't even know."

Her eyes focused, losing some of that awful glazed look. "Was that supposed to be some kind of lesson?"

I wanted to say yes, but mostly it happened because I wanted it to. "Call it whatever."

"I don't know what that was!" Sierra managed to pull away from me.

The guys who had been watching were melting away quickly, sensing a scene gone bad and wanting to distance themselves from it. I felt even more conspicuous. I had lost my mind for a minute. What a stupid game to play with someone I didn't know!

I offered Sierra the wig, and she took it, watching me warily. As if unsure of what I would do next.

"Are you okay?" I asked. "I'll get you a cab to take you home."

She took a step away from me, warding me off. "I'm fine."

I watched as she stepped into the room, searching the crowd quickly. With a shake of her head as if disappointed, she headed to the exit.

I followed her. She was a little unsteady on her feet, and I had put her into that state. I couldn't let her wander off into traffic alone.

Outside, I expected her to hold up her hand to get a cab—they were everywhere around here. But she turned and went to the corner.

By the time I reached the top of the stairs, she was at the corner waiting for the light to cross the street. She was swaying a bit, staring off at one spot as if dazed. She was a slight form, closed in on herself in the moist summer breeze, pungent with the smell of the street. Slowly she pulled a tissue from her purse and blew her nose, wiping the smeared makeup off her cheeks with it.

I passed behind her and ran across the street in the middle of the block to get ahead of her. I figured she was trying to hail a cab going in the other direction.

But as Sierra crossed over and reached the other side, she turned and came towards me. I stepped back into the shadows of the doorway as she walked almost all the way up to me.

I thought she had seen me and was mad that I was following her, but she didn't notice me. She went straight to a black car parked at the curb and opened the door.

"What took so long?" a deep voice demanded. "Why didn't you answer my texts?"

Sierra sank into the seat, clutching the red wig. "Just go. Take me home."

"What happened?"

"Nothing happened. Now, go." She turned to the window, her fisted hand over her mouth. I didn't move, afraid she would notice me in the shadowed doorway of the shop.

The big blocky guy at the wheel kept complaining about keeping him waiting as he pulled out of the parking spot. He wasn't the kind of guy I expected to see Sierra with. He looked like an ordinary Queens schmo.

I had felt bad there for a second, watching her blow her nose on the street corner, but apparently she was pulling one over on that dude in the car, too.

What was Sierra's story? I couldn't figure her out. At first, when I saw her walking around the Chamber, I thought she was a wanna-be dominatrix hoping to make enough money to put herself through grad school. When she hit me with the ruler, she showed real promise—a genuine intensity and connection with me. But her dominance was mostly an illusion created by a sharp tongue, a wig and some makeup.

Really, she was a bedroom submissive looking for her sugar-daddy. She had judged me unworthy the first second she heard my voice. How could she hear the Jersey I thought I had buried deep inside of me? I would never know. But she did, and she had instantly rejected me for it, until Monica had gossiped about my wealth.

Then Sierra had been plenty ready to play nice.

So that made her fair game.

When I whispered those threats to her, now that had been the mind-blower. I still couldn't believe what a feeling it gave me. Power in the face of powerlessness. Not just because I was riding that dark edge that could swallow me up so easily, but because of her reaction, the way she gave in to me in the end. The way she looked at me as if she knew I owned her in that moment.

So where did that dude in the car come in? Did he know that Sierra was inside the Chamber?

I looked back at the Chamber. I could go back inside if I wanted to. Find another girl, have another scene, maybe take her home and fuck her.

The palms of my hands burned. Sierra had hit me hard.

I didn't want to go back to the Chamber.

I set off on foot down 9th Avenue. It would take forty-five minutes to walk home, but it would save me the fare for a subway ride. And nothing beat walking in the city.

...

As I entered my small loft apartment, I suddenly thought about Adrianne. She had put her stamp of style on my home: in the tiny kitchen, the exposed brick wall and the remodeled bathroom with the glass bricks that let in the sunlight. I could almost see her sitting at the tiny counter, her dark head thrown back in laughter.

I hadn't thought about her in years. On purpose.

I had added my own touches to the place over the past decade, imprinting myself on it with the black leather couch and stark photographs on the walls. It was spare and modern, like an interior designer had put it together. It gave exactly the impression what I intended.

Adrianne had left me the loft when she walked out all those years ago. Left me and our rocket-ship relationship for marriage to an investment banker. She had never taken me seriously because I was much younger than her, even though I dominated her in every way. Last I heard, she was living on the thirty-sixth floor of Beacon Court, a luxury glass tower on the Upper East Side. Her kid must be seven years old now.

I had tried to erase her from my life completely, but that was impossible considering I was living in her old loft. Ghosts of girlfriends past. But she had already been living there for a decade before I moved in with her, and that kind of stabilized rent couldn't be beat in Manhattan anymore. My neighbors were paying four times what I did.

Midtown rose beyond the Village, with its skyscrapers filling the view to the north. I dropped down on the couch facing the two large windows that filled the outer wall of the studio loft, over the tops of the surrounding low buildings.

I scrubbed a hand through my hair. *Why did I come home so early?*

Before things could get uncomfortably deep, my phone rang. I made a split-second decision and decided to go for it. "What time is departure?" I asked, by way of saying hello.

The girl was used to that and gave me the details. It would be tight, but I grabbed my bag that was always waiting and headed back down to the street to catch a cab.

It wasn't far to the Williamsburg Bridge and onto the BQE. It took only twenty minutes to make the trip to La Guardia airport, half the time of my usual commute by subway and bus.

The second I stepped into the corporate terminal at JFK, it felt different. The usual city noise was muted by the soft fabrics on the walls, and the lighting was artful and discrete. It was nothing like flying commercial with the long security lines and bus-station seating. Here, you knew you were special because they treated you that way.

When I got to the gate, I asked the flight attendant, "Anyone on board yet?"

She shook her head. "ETA twenty minutes."

"Cutting it close," I said.

She shrugged and went back to her pre-flight checklist of the booze and food on hand.

I ducked into the familiar cramped cockpit, one of dozens run by the private charter service I worked for. I'd been a private pilot for seven years—nobody knew the work I had put in, slaving as a mechanic out at Tetterboro, scraping together every flight hour from the time I was fourteen. But I had worked my way up tooth and nail.

And still it wasn't good enough.

I went through my preflight check, but I was dreading the moment that was coming.

The voices warned me. It was that time. When I had to present myself to the man of the hour, the bigwig who was writing the check for this exorbitant emergency night flight to Costa Rica.

I briefly shook his hand, noting his tired eyes, as his gaze slid back to the two men with him. Lawyers, probably. They always were.

Mr. Man went to sit down, negligently waving a

finger at the rapt flight attendant. Seeing the look in the woman's eyes, I knew deep down—Sierra had looked at *me* like that. Like I could give her the world if I chose to. Like I held it all in the palm of my hand. That I was irresistible.

That was the only reason she let me tie her up, even though I was a perfect stranger. Because she thought she already knew me, because of the fantasy.

I wasn't the one who had started the rumor that I was a billionaire. I had denied it in the beginning, but it must have made for a better story because it kept popping up in the sex clubs and fetish groups over the years. Maybe because I posted photos from the trips I took on my FetLife profile. Flying and seeing new places was the best part of my life. While Mr. Man was deep in business negotiations, I'd be sipping a drink on room service by the pool, working on my tan. Later I'd run along the beach and probably catch dinner at a hole in the wall in San Jose, talking to the locals and listening to the music.

So when women saw my loft and assumed it was my second home in the city, and that I had to be rich in order to have this lifestyle, it wasn't my fault if they threw themselves at me.

I put my headgear on, sitting back down to power up the engines. I was good at what I did—I could fly this plane and get us all safely to Costa Rica. By a lot of hard work and the sour luck of my break up, I had created a passable if modest life for myself in the heart of New York City.

But I knew Sierra wouldn't look at me the same way if she knew I wasn't wealthy. She may want to date me, sure, but she wouldn't give me the instant eagerness and respect she gave a billionaire. And that's what made me so mad that I could mind-fuck a beautiful stranger. I wasn't any different now than I had been in the club, but I could tell from the appraising way she had looked me up and down when she first saw me, taken in by my expensive shoes and shirt, that she *changed her opinion about me.*

Only that wasn't me.

That wasn't this hired gun. It was Mr. Man back there, probably earning a million dollars in this one deal. A man who could buy and sell girlfriends like they were candy. Even when someone else loved them and would have given them everything.

That wasn't me.

Chapter 3

Sierra

I put my head in my hands as Dick was driving me home. My heart was beating too fast, and I had to focus to breathe in and out. My chest felt so tight, it might explode.

Being completely overwhelmed—I hated it... but it was so invasive and intense that I couldn't help stop feeling it. I hated myself for it. Victor intended to scare me, so why was I still thinking about him and the rush it gave me when he was pressing against me?

I should hate him for doing that to me. I did hate him. But I also kept thinking about the way it felt when he pinned me against the brick wall with his whole body, and how turned on he obviously was as he whispered those terrible words to me. Then how gently he held me and told me he wouldn't hurt me.

I just wanted to turn off my mind and go home where it was safe.

"How did Lola leave without me seeing her?" Dick demanded.

"There must be a back door." I rubbed my neck where Victor's thumb had touched me. "You're the cop. Don't you know anything?"

He glanced at me again. "What happened in there? You're dead white."

"It's a meat market, a terrible place," I told him

dully. "I think it's dangerous."

"What was Lola doing?" he demanded, his voice rising.

"Nothing. She was talking to a man and another couple. I saw them sitting at a table."

Somewhat mollified, he glanced over at me. "Then what's wrong? What happened to you?"

I couldn't get into it with Dick. It was my own fault for being so stupid. I let Victor tie me up. I had taken the blind leap, for whatever reason, and I was lucky the guy wasn't truly rotten to the core because much worse than a few mean words could have happened.

"It's just a little shocking, is all, to see my sister in a place like that." I put my head back in my hands, hoping that would shut Dick up. I didn't want to talk to him about it.

I needed to talk to Lola. Desperately bad, I needed my sister.

•••

I lay on my couch feeling drained, like I had run for miles. Around eleven I got a text from Dick asking if Lola had come home. I ignored it.

Eventually I went to bed to toss and turn, thinking about what Victor had done to me and wishing I could stop. I felt anxiety, shame and even worse, like a fool.

So I was not in the best mood when Lola finally showed up after breakfast, looking radiantly happy.

"Where have you been?" I demanded, even though it was such a cliché.

"None of your business," Lola retorted with a

laugh.

I glared after her as Lola went into our bedroom. It was jammed with the two single beds and our dressers, and was dark because the window looked out on an airshaft. I had always shared a room with Lola—at least we weren't in the same bed anymore.

Lola was the baby of our big family and by the time we both had arrived one right after the other, our mom was done with raising kids. When we were girls, we relied on our older half-brothers to take care of us while our mom worked as a cashier and our dad got up early to go to the bakery. Lola and I stuck together and scrapped together to get our fair share of peanut butter and cereal. We always relied on each other, even before the divorce.

I waited impatiently for Lola to get out of the bathroom, the unpaid bills clutched in my hand. Lola was singing in the shower, like she didn't have a care in the world.

When Lola finally emerged, she stood in the doorway drying her long dark hair with a towel. I could have been looking in a mirror—people assumed we were twins all the time. Mutts, my oldest brother called us, but genetics had won out, taking the best of what our ordinary parents had to offer. Lola's skin was creamy pale, like mine, contrasting with her vibrant dark eyes and hair. We both were curvy in the right places.

"I found these two bills in the drawer," I said flatly. "I gave you my share last week, and you said you'd pay them. Now they're both past the due date."

"I paid those online," Lola tossed off.

"No, you didn't. I checked."

Lola shrugged. "Well, I thought I paid them. What are you getting so mad about? It's not like they make you pay extra if you're late."

"No, but you get dinged on your credit score if you wait too long."

"That's why you're yelling at me? Because of your *credit* score?" Lola snatched the bills from my hand. "I'll pay them now, if it makes you happy."

"Do you have enough money?"

Lola let out an exasperated sound. "Why do you always ask me that?"

"Because you don't have Dick to borrow from now if you need it."

Lola's eyes narrowed. "What's he been telling you? He made me take that money. He said it was a *gift*. Or I wouldn't have taken it."

"Why did you break up with him, Lola? I thought everything was going good."

"Lot you know!" Lola flounced over to pick up her lap top and flop down in the chair by the window. She looked at the bills again, checking the amount.

"What went wrong with you two?" I asked again.

Lola tapped into her computer, opening her account. "He's boring. He never wants to go out. And sex with him was like... snooze time. I never could get him to do anything fun. He's always so jealous and weird."

"Sex. Is that what you want?"

"It's not *all* I want. But I want something better

than *that*."

I was really worried about her. "Is that why you went to the Chamber last night? To find better sex?"

Lola sat up straight. "What do you know about the Chamber?"

"I know plenty. It's full of guys jacking off watching people beat each other. Why do you want to go to a place like that?"

"How do you know I went there?" She gave me a look. "Dick told you. What an asshole!"

"You went to that place with some guy you just met. What's wrong with you, Lola?"

Lola glared at me. "Wait, you're on Dick's side? I broke up with him!"

I tried to sound reasonable. "He's worried about you, Lola. Like I am. What kind of place is that for you to go to?"

"You don't understand. You don't want to understand."

"You haven't even tried to explain it to me."

"You've already passed judgment against me! Look at the way you're talking and you don't know anything about it."

I had to tell her. "Yes, I do. I went there last night looking for you. I was worried about you."

Lola's mouth fell open. "You spied on me?"

"Oh my god, Lola, I'm your sister. It's not spying when it's your sister making sure you aren't choked to death and stuck in a dumpster!"

Lola stood up, looking down at me. "And that's not judgment? You think I would put myself in that kind of danger? Seriously, how stupid do you think I am?"

I couldn't speak for a moment. My throat closed in, shutting off all words. *As stupid as me,* I thought miserably. Lola was madder than heck, but I needed my sister.

"It happened to me," I managed to say.

That stopped Lola, as realization slowly filled her eyes. "What happened to you?"
I clenched my hands together. "I let some guy tie up my wrists. But first I hit him with the ruler they gave me."

"You *hit* him?"

"Yeah. Pretty hard. On his palms."

Lola was staring at me. "And then what?"

"Then he tied my wrists. He said some things... I got scared because I realized he could really hurt me. But he didn't. Then it was over and you were gone." I tried to bring the subject back where it belonged. "That's how I know this stuff isn't just play acting. It can get serious. You shouldn't go to a place like that."

"Excuse me, big sister, but even I know enough not to mess around with a strange man. What got into you?"

"You went there with that old man you just met!" I hated to admit it, but I added, "And Victor is different. You must have seen him. Blond hair, taller than the rest of the guys, dressed really nice. People know him there—he's got a fancy job with the airline." I didn't want to add that he smelled good and his eyes were to die for. "Another girl told me he was really popular, and that she was dying to get together with him. I thought it was safe."

"Damn... you had a freakier night than I did. We went back to Martin's place and watched Hot Tub Time Machine."

"Is Martin that man you were with?"

Lola nodded, sitting back on her heels. "Did you see our scene?"

"What do you mean? You were talking to him. He had his hand on your shoulder."

My sister glanced away. "Nothing. But I think this proves that I know better than you what I'm doing."

"So you *are* doing this S&M stuff with Martin? You're letting him hit you? Why, Lola? I saw him— he's practically an old man."

"He's thirty-four!"

"And you're twenty-one."

"Well, he doesn't try to scare me like your random hottie did, I can tell you that."

I had no retort for that, because hopefully it was true. "I want to meet Martin. I want to make sure he's not a psycho."

"As if you're any judge!"

"I made a mistake. But I never would have been there if you hadn't gone."

"It's your own fault for following me around. Fucking hell, Sierra! It's time for you to let me live my own life."

With that, Lola packed up her stuff and huffed off to the bathroom. She blasted the radio and sang to it as she fixed her hair and makeup. She didn't say good-bye when she left.

Which left me feeling even worse. Lola was right. It was my own fault that I got into that mess. Why did I fling away all common sense? Because Victor looked deep into my eyes? Because my guts told me that I could trust him?

Maybe because I was sick of working so hard with nothing to show for it. Because I was ready for more, and was willing to take a short cut to get it.

But that was Lola, not me. It had never been me. Lola was used to taking whatever she wanted. As if she had the right. As if nobody else should care.

Maybe I wanted to feel that for just a moment. To feel that a hot, sexy man wanted me so badly that he would stand there and take my blows. And then feel him lose control over me. Because he did lose control. I had seen it in his eyes, the way Victor had blazed into pure aggression and desire. And then at the end, how his fierceness ebbed as he came back to himself, looking at me with concern. He couldn't have been sweeter as he held me as I cried, comforting me.

I smacked my forehead. *I am so messed up! Seriously fucked! Stop thinking about him!*

•••

I tried to talk to Lola over the next week. My sister wasn't very sympathetic about what had happened to me. At one point she yelled that it was my own damn fault. Lola said if I was going to be that stupid, I couldn't blame her for it. Lola kept saying she knew what she was doing.

I seriously doubted it.

Dick was super-pissed that Lola wouldn't talk to him after that. He kept texting and calling me, trying to find out what was going on with my sister. I didn't want to admit that I didn't know because Lola didn't come home.

But days later, because Lola wouldn't talk to me, I was finally driven to text Dick back: *Do you know where Lola is?*

A few moments passed, then Dick replied: *Meet me so we can talk.*

He was going to pump me about Lola and what she had been doing. But I didn't know anything. Lola came home a few times really late, after I was already in bed. And then she was still in bed when I got up to go to work.

Lola would hate it if I talked to Dick about her. But what choice did I have? I knew firsthand the danger she was flirting with. I had to do something. I couldn't sit by and watch my sister flush her life down the drain. Lola had nearly gotten into real trouble last year when she started dating a guy who did hard drugs. She called it weekend partying, but then she started staying out all night during the week, too.

Dick had busted Lola with ecstasy in her pocket last summer in the park. If he had arrested her, Lola's life would have been ruined. But Dick had taken pity on her, bringing her home in handcuffs, and releasing her to me as long as Lola promised to get into treatment. And she did, with Dick's help. He went with her to meetings, setting her back on the right path. It had been a real relief for me to have help with Lola. Lola had relied on him, and even though her drama continued, there hadn't been any real trouble over the past year.

Until now.

What if Lola started spiraling out of control again?

Finally, I texted Dick back: *Okay, after my class tonight.*

•••

After a long day at work, I got on the bus from Midtown to the Long Island Expressway that took me deeper into the island to Queensborough College. It was strictly for people getting their associate degree, and everyone worked while they were doing it, so it wasn't the college experience that I had always hoped for. But financial assistance was nonexistent, so I had to adjust my dream. The degree was a means to an end, not the end itself.

I would be glad when I never had to take the long bus ride again. I wasn't sure where I would finish my bachelor's degree, but I would make sure it was closer to home than Horace Harding Parkway.

By the time the class was over and I got back, I wished I had put Dick off until the next day. But he was parked up the street, texting me impatiently.

I got into his car as he silenced the radio that was mounted on the floor. There was a view down the sidewalk to the front door of our four-story tenement building. The light in the front window on the third floor was coming from our apartment.

"Lola's home," I said.

"Yup."

My sister knew I would be at class. So she was deliberately avoiding me.

"I wish I knew what was up with her," I said.

"You're not even trying. You're letting her self-destruct."

"How can I do anything when I never see her? She won't answer my texts. She thinks I'm judging her."

Dick let out an anguished sound. "She won't talk to me either. Did you find out anything about that asshole she's seeing?"

I was acutely aware that if I told Dick that his name was Martin, Lola might get so mad she would do something drastic. "Nothing. What about you?"

"I followed her to a couple different places—in Flushing and Red Hook. I haven't seen that guy around, though."

Now I was really glad I hadn't told him Martin's name. "You should stop following her, Dick. It's not right."

"I wouldn't have to if you would do something about it! It's just like last summer. You're sitting there watching her slide into hell."

That stung. "I'm trying to help her. She keeps pushing me away."

He looked up at the window where a shadow passed. "She needs a jolt, like last time. She freaked when she thought I was taking her to jail. She knew she was facing serious shit. That's the only reason she changed, because she didn't want to lose everything."

"How can we do that now? She won't be arrested for going to a club like that." I considered it. "Will she?"

"Nah, they keep it on the legal side of the line. I checked it out. No real sex happens in that place. No drugs. They keep it clean because they have to."

"It wasn't clean," I retorted, thinking of the sticky floors with a shudder.

"We need something." He turned to me, his voice softening. "You have to help me figure out something. I can't stand seeing her ruin her life like this."

"Ruin her life?" I asked. "Isn't that a little extreme?"

He jerked his head. "She has a profile on a fetish website. Kind of like kinky Facebook. She has a list of events she clicked as maybe-going. What if those places are worse than the Chamber?"

I stared at him for a moment, trying to wrap my mind around that. "This, I have to see." I pulled out my phone.

"It's a protected site. You have to make a profile to get on." He wrote down the name of the website. "Her screen name is Lollycat."

I took the piece of paper between two fingers.

Dick leaned closer, and I could smell the beer on his breath. "You can get hold of her laptop while she's sleeping. I've got a URL you go to and click download, and it will record what she's doing online—"

"I'm not going to do that!" I exclaimed. "You're crazy!"

"You better do something." He reached into the back seat and grabbed a plastic bag. Throwing it into my lap, it took me a moment to realize it was the red curly wig he had loaned me. I had left it on the car seat when he dropped me off last weekend. "You check out that website. You'll see! If you don't keep an eye on her, then I will."

I got out of the car. I didn't like the way he was yelling at me, almost threatening me, like he had a right to treat me this way. But I took the bag with the wig in it.

I headed to my apartment, determined to have it out with Lola once and for all.

•••

Lola was stretching on the living room floor when I came in. My sister had always been flexible and fancied herself a good dancer, but you needed lessons to be able to really dance. Not just copying what you saw on YouTube videos. Right now Lola was lying almost prone between her widely outstretched legs, with her long hair bundled up behind her head.

I could hear the deafening rap through the ear buds Lola was wearing. My sister gave me a wave, but didn't stop her rhythmic stretching.

I went into the bedroom to change into comfy night clothes, trying to figure out how I could make my sister talk to me. I went through my usual getting-home rituals, putting my clothes in the hamper, and washing my face and hands.

Walking back into the living room, I waved to get Lola's attention. "Hey, Lola!"

Lola only removed one ear bud. "What?"

"I wanted to talk to you about Martin."

"What about him?"

I flopped down on the couch, trying to send out

a relaxed vibe. "How's it going with him? You've been gone all week, and I wasn't sure if you were seeing him or doing something else."

"Both." Lola kept on stretching.

"Come on, Lolly!" The nickname came out without thinking, but it reminded me of the profile name that Dick said she had made. "Tell me what's going on. I'm so curious."

"Yeah, I know you're curious! Or you wouldn't have spied on me."

Irritation flashed through me. I had done it to try to understand her. But I couldn't tell Lola that or she would get even madder. "Well, I'd rather have you tell me. I just want to make sure you're okay. What if something happens that you don't like?"

"I have a safeword. That's what I say to stop whatever's going on if it's not working for me. But I've never had to use it. I got to trust Martin before I let him touch me."

"How did you get to know him?"

Suspiciously, Lola eyed me. "At the mall. He worked there for a while. We kept running into each other in the food court."

"And that made him trustworthy?"

"Sierra, I met him months ago. We were friends long before anything happened. He's a performer. He travels all over the world doing shows."

"What kind of shows?"

"Performance art."

I suddenly saw Lola's stretching as more than an idle exercise. "Like dancing?"

"Kind of. I want to be a part of his work. I'm

sort of on a trial basis right now."

"You mean you aren't having sex with him?"

Lola shot me a look. "It's none of your business, but I am."

My mouth opened. "How is it none of my business? I'm your sister."

"My private life is mine. Why do you keep acting like you own me? Like you can tell me how to live?"

"Lola! I'm just trying to help you."

"I don't need your help. And I don't need you telling me I should be doing *this* and I should be doing *that*. Go deal with your own shit and let me deal with mine."

"My shit is doing just fine. I'm getting my degree at the end of summer. And you could have, too, if you had taken classes—"

"Give it a rest, Sierra. For years you've ragged on me to go to school. I'm done with school. I'm never going back. I keep telling you that, but you won't listen to me."

I continued as if I hadn't heard my sister's protest. "My only problem is *you*, Lola. I'm afraid you're spinning out of control, again. Breaking up with Dick, who you love!"

"What's love?" Lola asked darkly. "He smothered me, like you smother me."

"I'm just trying to—"

"Help," Lola finished. "Which brings us back to that again. I don't need your help. It's none of your business."

"I'm family, Lola. We live together. If you spin out of control again, you'll take me down with you.

I'm living pay check to pay check here. And I know you relied on Dick for rent money. What are you going to do?"

Lola shrugged one shoulder, looking away. "I've gotten a couple of modeling gigs. I'm hoping this work with Martin will get to be a paying gig, too."

"Modeling." All of my doubts filled my voice. Lola may be pretty, but neither of us were fashion models.

"Bondage modeling." Lola lifted her chin. "And before you say anything, it's just pictures. And it's only topless. It's not like it's porn."

I stared at her, unable to form the words that were swirling around my brain. The first thing that came out was, "Are you kidding me?!"

"There's nothing wrong with it, Sierra." Lola got to her feet. "This is why I didn't tell you. Let me live my own life. Or I'll have to find another place to live!"

Lola stomped into the bedroom and slammed the door shut. I was used to that. Lola let everyone know when she was mad.

But the last time Lola told me to butt out of her life, she had been doing a lot of drugs with her ex-boyfriend. Lola was once again following some random guy to her doom. Just like our mother.

Even worse, Lola had never threatened to move out before. It was our unwritten rule, going back further than I could remember, that we stuck by each other. Through everything. No matter what else happened, we had each other's back. How could Lola forget that?

What would I do without Lola? The practical

side was a nightmare. I couldn't afford to live in the city alone. Not on my pay.

I was breathing faster, trying to figure out why Lola was suddenly threatening to move out.

It must be that guy, Martin. He had lured her away from Dick, and he was luring my sister into flashing her breasts and going to a fetish club. Maybe he was trying to get Lola to move in with him, so she would be dependent on him. Instead of me.

I must have sat there a full five minutes, running possibilities over in my mind. Then I reached for my laptop and punched in the website Dick had given me. I had to make my own profile to get in, so I signed up as Francisco29 to throw everyone off, and clicked at random on the buttons asking whether I was gay or straight.

As soon as I was in, with a question mark for a profile avatar, I searched for Lollycat.

I quickly found the profile and knew it was Lola because she had posted several dozen photographs of herself in her gallery. I clicked through quickly. Some were topless, all right. Lola was tied into unusual shapes, and was suspended by ropes. In several, she was held up by a thick webbing. A couple of them were stunning. I couldn't believe that was Lola, her profile so serene as she arched in a perfect circle, dangling from a crossbeam in an abandoned building.

Where on earth... did *that* happen?

She must have been doing this while I was sitting here worrying about her.

It was both better and worse than I feared. It wasn't quite porn, but it was a lot slicker and more professional than I expected. The names under the images were of different photographers, and I followed the links back to their profiles. There I found hundreds of photos, not just a dozen. My mind was boggled at the wide-ranging imagination of the photographers, and of the models tied up into beautiful contorted shapes. A few were graphic, but mostly they were otherworldly and haunting.

I took a deep sigh. Drugs, I could sort of understand. Lola was always so angry that it probably felt good for her to let go. But this stuff made no sense. Why would Lola want to expose herself like this?

Going back to Lollycat, I saw that there were events listed down one side that Lola had checked as "maybe going." In the text of her profile, she called herself a "new bondage model," and said that photographers could contact her about setting up a shoot with her. Under relationships, there were several names under "In a rope family with..." and Martin was the first one listed.

I poured over the profiles of the three names who were linked to Lola's profile. Their profiles had additional relationship links to other people. I could hardly get through it all, there were so many photos and comments posted, especially by the woman, JuneTime. She was the blond woman who I saw with Lola at the Chamber.

Under Martin's profile, there were hundreds of shadowy shots of swirling fire and bursts of sparklers partly obscuring the performers. None of them were of the high quality of the fetish photographers that Lola had posed for. They looked like snapshots taken at events, interspersed with startlingly ordinary photos of him hanging out with friends at parties or sitting on the back of a van between the open double doors. They chronicled several years of traveling around the country with his "performance troop" called Transcendence. They did "fire shows" and "freak shows" where he swallowed a sword and JuneTime twirled a baton lit on fire.

When I clicked on some of their hundreds of friends, things got a lot more graphic with photos of red marks slashing across people's backs and buttocks, and frankly explicit shots of genitals. Some men used a photo of their erection as their profile photo, of all things! As if that was appealing. I made sure to click away quickly from those profiles.

I was shocked to see how late it was when I finally put the lap top away, reeling at what I had seen. I had been in the fetish network for hours. I could hardly keep my burning eyes open, but my brain was buzzing in overtime.

I turned out the lights and lay on the couch in the dark, trying to absorb the riot of things I had seen.

I didn't understand it. And what I didn't understand, I had to figure out.

Dick was a jerk for suggesting I bug Lola's laptop. I would never do that.

But I could put on that red wig and go to the next event that Lola had checked as "maybe going." Pleasure Salon. It was being held at a bar on the lower east side.

There was nothing stopping me. And I might find out more.

The next day, yawning at work, I found the halter dress in a sales rack. It was black and when I tried it on, it fit my body like a glove. It was something I would never buy usually, so it was a real surprise to see how sexy I looked in it. In that dress, with that red wig, I could become a different person. Someone who could walk into a bar filled with fetish-lovers and feel right at home.

Then I could see for myself what Lola was up to.

Chapter 4

Victor

I was up the block when I spotted those distinctive magenta curls going into the bar. I got a sudden rush like I'd never felt before, the visceral memory of Sierra's body crushed under mine as I whispered those horrible words to her. Her rapid breath on my face, as I leaned so close to her cheek that I could feel her trembling.

I didn't like to think that it was nonconsensual, but it was a mindfuck she hadn't negotiated. I had set it up that way. And she, in her ignorance, had agreed.

It was wrong to take advantage of her. But I couldn't regret it, and that probably made me a bad man.

Then again, it wasn't my fault. I was always bad.

The fact that I went around letting people think I'm a billionaire proved that early prediction. But I only took advantage of women who were after me because of my money, so who was to blame for that?

Sierra was hiding something behind that gaudy wig. Now was my chance to find out what it was.

I went through glass door of the bar. It was once a Chinese massage parlor named Happy Endings, and the name had stuck when it was turned into a bar. Across the front of the building was the fuchsia awning with Chinese characters that proclaimed the services the massage parlor used to offer.

Inside it was sleek and modern, with glazed concrete floors and frosted glass partitions. I passed the stairs that went down to a big open space in the basement, and went to the main bar in the back. It was busy, like it always was for Pleasure Salon. People liked a low-pressure event like this where they could meet in public. Since it was a bar, and people were drinking, there was no playing allowed.

Sierra wasn't at the bar or seated in the two rows of banquets. I went downstairs to find the room filled with moving light. A show was going as two people twirled short ropes with balls of fire on the end.

I homed in on Sierra among the crowd along the side. The cocktail tables were filled with people standing around watching the show.

I worked my way through the crowd in her direction. Sierra didn't see me coming. She was focused on the performers. Her black halter dress clung to her curves, making an enticing package.

I noticed that Sierra never scanned the crowd or the stairs when more people came down, so she wasn't waiting for someone. Like last time at the Chamber, she was here alone. And she wasn't chatting up the men around her who kept giving her appreciative smiles in the rare times she looked away from the performers. She wasn't on the prowl.

What other reason than friends or meeting someone new would bring her to Pleasure Salon? The more I looked, the more it didn't add up.

The fire master up front started flogging the two girls with flaming whips. The girls squealed, probably more for effect than in real pain.

Now Sierra looked away from the show. With shaking hands, she dug out her lipstick and a tiny mirror, and quickly touched up her dark red lips.

I moved up next to her elbow. "Is that part of your disguise, Sierra?"

When she recognized me, her expression was shocked, angry and, yes, turned on. She was turned on!

I knew it. I couldn't have gone so far if she hadn't been right there with me. I hadn't mistaken the way her hips had ground into me, the way her eyes never left mine, the instant connection we had formed in the midst of our scene. All week I kept thinking it was a psycho delusion that rapists probably felt, but here was the evidence in her eyes.

She broke her gaze, turning her head away. "You have some balls coming up to me. After what you did."

Her voice was low and husky, like she was overwhelmed by the memory of it. I leaned in closer, wishing I could rid us of the barrier of her overly curly wig.

"I'll go upstairs with you," I murmured. "Turn myself in to the producers. We'll tell them how I scared you. I'll do whatever they say."

Her startled eyes met mine. "You wouldn't."

"They'll say I'm a jerk who shouldn't have done a mindfuck scene with someone I just met. And they'd be right." I leaned in to lower my voice. "But I couldn't resist you."

We seemed locked together, the rest of the bar disappearing. We were wrapped together in the darkness, as all the other eyes were focused on the flickering lights.

My fingertips brushed her cheek, silky soft.

She flinched. "Don't touch me."

"I won't until you ask me to." I clenched my fist, pulling away. I wanted to keep stroking her cheek, to smooth away the pain in her eyes. "So who are you hiding from in that getup?"

She raised her clasped hands to her breast, forming a barrier between us. "No one."

I gave a short laugh. "Don't try to bullshit me. I'm a master of disguise, and I see a snow job going on."

"Get lost." Without a backward look, she made her way over to the other side of the room.

It didn't bother me one bit that she was blowing me off. She was hot for me, almost as hot as I was for her. The fact that she was also pissed that I had scared her to death didn't matter. It might even be one of the reasons why she was so hot for me. Kink could be weird that way.

"Donations!" a girl announced, thrusting a top hat at me. She was wearing a bondage harness of black rope over a nude bra. Her dark hair was slicked down tightly and wrapped in a bun, with some sort of shiny stuff that likely repelled fire.

I pulled out a couple dollars, trying to place the girl. I had seen her recently.

Glancing over at Sierra, she was riveted to us.

Then I remembered. This pretty, if rather surly girl had been with the guy that Sierra chased after in the Chamber.

The same guy who was up front now packing away the fire gear.

"What's your name?" I asked the girl.

"Lola."

"What's the name of your group?"

"Transcendence." She gave me a mocking smile. "Any more questions and you'll have to give me five bucks."

I laughed at her as she moved on. From across the room, Sierra looked like she was dying to hear what we were saying. But as Lola circled around with the other girl in their ménage, Sierra managed to turn away just as she passed her table.

Sierra was hiding from Lola. *Interesting.*

I waited as Sierra watched the group finish packing up the gear. When they went upstairs, so did Sierra, with me following behind.

Lola's group was at the bar having a drink and celebrating a good show. One of the producers was talking to the guy in charge of Transcendence. In the brighter light, the performer's gnarly broken-down skin made him look older than he probably was.

I saw that Sierra had parked herself at a banquet along the side wall, where she could see the group through the glass partitions. A couple sat on the other side of her table, ignoring her with their heads very close in deep conversation.

I went up to the bar to say hi to the couple who produced Pleasure Salon, and got introduced to

Martin, the guy with the face. He had come to the city a few months ago, having traveled around the country for the past few years doing gigs. Lola was by Martin's side talking quietly to her other half in the show, June.

"Were all of you on the road together?" I asked, including the women in my question.

"June and Spike were. We met Lola here."

"What kind of shows do you do?"

"Anything we can," Martin said. "Party entertainment. Street fairs. Corporate hires. You wouldn't believe how they want to spice up a party, and we can keep it vanilla and still put on a slamming show."

Martin handed me a card that had their website and contact info. It was heavy on the flames, with the word Transcendence blazoned across it.

After I got the spiel, I went to the other end of the bar. When I caught Sierra's eye, I raised my drink to her. She looked away, mad.

What was Sierra's interest in Martin's group?

I waited for Sierra to make a move, but she kept watching from the shadows of the banquets. There wasn't much to see. Martin worked the crowd, handing cards out to anyone who would take them. A hustler, for sure. Pimping his thing, and shooting for the big brass ring by coming to New York.

But even when Sierra could have gotten a few words with Martin away from the two girls, she didn't try. She said hello to him when he greeted the other people at her table, and I could have sworn that Martin didn't recognize her. Which made it even weirder.

I nursed a drink until Martin and his crew finally made their noisy departure. Pleasure Salon was winding down and more people were leaving.

Sierra sat up straight as if ready to follow Martin out. But then she slumped back down.

I knew I couldn't walk out that door without trying once more with Sierra. How could any man walk away from a woman like that? Especially after what I had done.

I kept thinking about her. She haunted my mind, as I remembered little moments, a look or a motion that was seared into my brain. Why did she go to the Chamber? Why was she hiding behind that awful wig?

I had to find out more.

And I wasn't going to take no for an answer.

Chapter 5

Sierra

I looked up and saw Victor coming towards me. There was an inevitability about his approach that was inescapable, a train wreck that I couldn't avoid.

I wished he wasn't so bronzed and good-looking. It was bad enough he seemed to see right through me, but I could hardly look at him without feeling all sorts of things stir around treacherously inside of me.

Victor slid into the booth next to me. He didn't even have the grace to sit on the other side that the couple had just abandoned. I shifted over on the vinyl bench to get further away from him.

"Can you take off the wig now that they're gone?" Victor asked first thing.

I glared at him, angry and frustrated. I had accomplished nothing tonight, except for finding out that Lola was now walking around in her bra and letting her new boyfriend beat her with fire in public.

Even more surprising, the crowd had loved Lola. Her nasty wisecracks and that twisted scowl she made every time someone tossed her a dollar instead of donating more, only made them laugh. People gave her more because of it!

All evening I felt panic bubbling up inside of me, like things were slipping out of control. Like Lola was receding into the distance, beyond my reach.

So I snapped at Victor, "Are you always this much of an asshole?"

"Apparently with you, I am." His grin was rueful. "If you still want revenge, I can introduce you to the producers. They're bound to tell other people what I did, and then they'll warn all the newbies that they're taking a risk if they play with me."

I couldn't imagine telling anyone what had happened with Victor. Look at how unsympathetic my own sister was! "I could have told a cop about it, if I wanted to. But I didn't."

"You mean that guy in the car who was waiting for you? He looked like a cop."

Shocked, I finally met his gaze. "You followed me!"

"We had an intense scene, and you were wobbly. I had to be sure you got home okay. But then I saw another guy was already waiting for you."

"What's your problem? You follow me last week and tonight you've been watching me like a hawk."

"You're worth watching."

His tone was so honestly admiring that I couldn't be a complete bitch. Besides, the damage was done. He had seen everything tonight.

"Come on," Victor urged. "Tell me what's going on. Maybe I can help."

I gave him a sideways look. "Why would you help me?"

He shrugged. "After what I did, I owe you one."

He sat there looking so delicious that my hands twitched, wanting to touch his hair and his chest. It was traitorous, that feeling.

Sighing, I pulled off the red wig. It itched, and Lola was long gone. With both hands, I pulled out the barrettes that held my hair in place, letting it fall straight down.

"Much better," Victor murmured. He handed me a napkin. "Lipstick, too."

I bridled. "What makes you think this isn't my usual shade?"

"It's not."

He said it with finality, as if he had known me for years. He was right, but that didn't make me any more eager to do what he said. But the way he was stared made me feel like a clown. I slowly rubbed off the showy red color.

"Now we're talking." Victor looked pleased with himself. "Why are you hiding behind all that stuff?"

"It's my sister, Lola. The brown-haired girl."

"The one who looks like you! Yes, I didn't see it before under all those curls." He was nodding as if everything made more sense now.

"Something's going on with her but she won't talk to me," I admitted. "She's got this new boyfriend, Martin, and she's suddenly started modeling in fetish photos. She broke up with her old boyfriend, Dick, the cop waiting in the car. He's the one who told me she was at the Chamber. That's why I went that night. I was trying to find out what she's up to. I thought Dick could rescue her..."

For the first time, Victor looked less than self-assured. In fact, he looked a little sick for a moment. "That's why you were there?"

I nodded. I could swear he was feeling bad right

now. He shifted in his seat, suddenly unable to meet my eyes. "Did you think I was like Monica?" I asked. "That girl I met at the Chamber?"

"I thought you had *some* experience, a little at least. You were keeping those guys away with just your vibe, and let me tell you, that's not the place for newbies to go roaming around alone."

I took a deep breath, silently cursing Dick for tossing me in the deep end. "So you don't go around scaring every woman you flirt with?"

"No! Not even at the Chamber."

"But you couldn't resist me," I said, echoing him from earlier.

"No, I couldn't. I'm really sorry, I thought you were something else." He ventured a small smile. "But then again, you were wearing a disguise."

I had to admit that was true. "I guess it's more dangerous than I thought."

"It's actually pretty safe, if you use common sense."

He was reminding me of his first warning which I had ignored. Why did he keep trying to get one-up on me? It kept me on edge even while we were talking so friendly-like.

Victor pulled out a card. "Martin gave me this. It's got his website on it."

He opened it on his iPhone. The website was mostly black with vivid slashes of arching fire, and brightly colored wisps of costumes on nearly naked girls. It was nothing I hadn't seen on Martin's profile, but it had a more complete calendar of events where they were performing. Including a park in Brooklyn on Sunday.

I finally sat back, shaking my head. "Why would they do this kind of show in a park? There will be kids around!"

"Martin says they do vanilla events, more like a circus freak show, I imagine."

I considered it. "Okay, that's sounds more reasonable. But why did she let him hit her like that? That fire looks dangerous. I can't believe they allow it here."

"It's mostly cement down below."

"What about the girls? What if Lola caught on fire?"

"She had stuff in her hair and on her skin to keep the fire away from her."

I looked at him closer. "Really? So it's just an illusion?"

"I wouldn't say that. It can be dangerous if you don't know what you're doing. Like anything else. But from what it looks like, this guy Martin has a lot of documented experience. And that's good in the scene."

"You seem to know a lot about it."

"I dabble. I work too much to make it regular thing."

"Two Fridays in a row is sort of regular," I pointed out.

His expression was more serious. "I came tonight to ask the producers if they knew you. Most people come through here at some point. It's one of the main gateways to the scene. I wanted to find you to make sure I didn't hurt you. And I found you."

My face flushed. It was intensely flattering. Especially coming from a guy as successful and good-looking as he was. He could have any girl. Literally, any girl. But he came looking for me.

"Mission accomplished," I told him. "You actually proved to me how dangerous this is. I don't get why you do it. I don't get why Lola lets that guy hit her with those whips. It looks like it hurt."

"It also feels good."

"Did it feel good when I hit you with the ruler?" I asked.

"Yes, because I was thinking I would be able to do anything I wanted to you afterwards."

And just like that, my heart started beating faster. He was the golden boy when he was smiling, shining like the sun, but I preferred him this way, when he was intent and serious. Like we were sharing a secret together.

Victor held up his right hand, looking from it to me. "I used this hand on you last week. Just this hand, holding that rope around your wrist." His fingers flexed.

My mouth opened, looking at his hand. I wanted to pull away from him. But that would be giving too much away. Then he would know how much he had scared me. I had thought about what happened all week, and now here I was sitting next to him, talking about it like it was a perfectly natural thing. It felt like everything I thought I knew was splitting apart.

"I made you feel something real intense," he told me quietly. "Now I could make you feel so good you'd do anything for me. Without touching you sexually, of course. We *are* in a bar."

"Here? You want to touch me here?"

"You don't understand why people like kink, or why your sister is doing this. I can show you. And I can make up for the... extreme introduction I gave you last week."

I couldn't believe how tempted I was by him. "Look what happened last time I said yes."

"We weren't on common ground last time. Now I know where you're coming from. And you can stop me at any time. Just tell me if you don't like it."

"Like a safeword?" I asked, remembering what Lola had told me.

"Yes."

His hand dropped to the bench, straying closer to me. Like he wanted to touch me. He bit his lip as he looked down at my legs.

"Give me your foot," he urged.

"My foot?" I was wearing stiletto pumps.

"Yes, what harm could that do?"

We were sitting at right angles so it was easy to lift my foot up. He caught me by the ankle and carefully removed my shoe. I could just see my red-tipped toes peeking from under the table cloth.

His touch sent a shiver through me, just in the way he held me. So firm and confident, yet careful of me, like his hands were too big for my delicate ankle. The feeling reminded me of last time when he held me. And I knew that if he didn't want to let me go, I wouldn't be able to break free.

I looked around. The place had mostly emptied

out from the event, and a new post-happy hour crop of people were arriving. There were people at the nearby banquets and sitting at the bar. It felt safe enough, yet secluded.

Slowly, taking his time, he began to massage my foot. Pressing in at my heel and stroking up the toes—it felt heavenly! For a girl who worked on her feet all day every day, there could be nothing better.

He knew what he was doing. What wonders he could accomplish if he had lotion!

He moved up to include my ankle and I relaxed even more. His touch was so strong and sure, almost to the point of pain. But it's what I needed. I'd been strung tight as a wire for weeks over Lola.

Stop thinking about Lola, I ordered myself.

"Stop thinking," Victor said quietly.

Startled, I looked at him. He was making his way up my calf, and was giving my work-hardened muscles a good deep massage.

"You could tell that just from touching me?" I asked.

He didn't answer, so that was reply enough.

As he kept stroking me, I relaxed back again, focusing on how his hands felt as he mixed the deep massage with delicate stroking, running his fingers up to the inside of my knee.

He went slowly, and when he got to the hem of my skirt half way up my thigh, I was feeling like I didn't want to stop him. My entire leg was thrumming along with a few other things. Just from him touching my leg!

But he showed he could be a gentleman, and

he stopped at my skirt.

Gently, he picked up my hand. He leaned over and raised it to his lips. He didn't say anything, but he looked at me, and I felt his eyes pierce my heart. Desire and regret were in that look.

I know exactly how you feel, I wanted to tell him.

Looking deep into my eyes, he began to stroke my fingers. Gently at first, bringing the blood to the tips, then squeezing harder as he pulled on each one.

Suddenly, I was flooded with emotion, with tears rising to burn my eyes. Just being touched, so deliberately, with such care, was overwhelming. I rarely felt any touch. I avoided intimacy because I was too busy, and because I had seen Lola get into so much drama with her male protectors over the years. I was more concerned with building walls to protect us, but she was more impulsive. And not very careful. Lola had had two abortions, one when she was sixteen. That wasn't something I wanted for myself. So I waited for the perfect man to complete my perfect dream of the city.

But my first boyfriend in New York turned out to be a player that I mistook for a real man. He manipulated me into thinking he really knew me, that he cared about me. But all he wanted was to beat the challenge I gave him, and convince me to go to bed with him. Our whirlwind affair didn't last two months, before he was on to the next girl.

It certainly taught me a lesson.

But this man wasn't asking for sex. Victor was touching me to make me feel good. And it felt so very,

very good!

I sighed, my eyelids growing heavy. But I never took my eyes off him. It felt like I was in his hands completely again, only this time he was holding me like a baby bird, cupping me in his palms as he took care of me.

Chapter 6

Victor

I wanted to kiss her hand again, and trail my lips all the way up her lovely arm. But I had promised to use only my hands. But how tempting she was! I was leading this dance, but her shining eyes were drawing me in with her, exactly like last time.

Her skin was so smooth and creamy. And those soft sounds she was making made me want to lose my mind.

But I couldn't let go like last time. I couldn't believe she was letting me touch her after what I had frightened her. After she had seen the darkness in me.

Yet she was softening under my hands, going limp and languid. Trusting me. I could feel it pouring off her as she gave herself over to me completely.

My fingers stroked the curve of her shoulder, feeling the perfect arch and the curve at the base of her neck. She tensed again slightly, as I neared her throat, so I began to rub her shoulder, pressing one hand against the front of her should and the other on her shoulder blade until she relaxed in spite of herself.

I was still touching only her left side—I had a reason for that.

My fingers lightened, as I made swirls down along the top of her halter, under her arm and then back up again.

This time I didn't stop. I trailed my fingertip up her neck, feeling her sudden tremble. I continued up, gently forcing her head back, exposing her throat.

Her breath caught, and she stiffened, like she was going to protest. But I trailed my finger back down along her halter, and then back up, soothing her once again.

Then I stroked up with my whole palm, cupping her neck, feeling her fluttering pulse.

Then up to her face. She let out her breath in a rush, as I ran a finger along her jaw and up to the hollow of her check. I barely brushed her lips, feeling them pucker slightly under my passing fingertip.

I wanted to kiss her so badly, but I had to finish what I started. I traced the arch of her nose, and up her forehead into her hair. Massaging only one side of her head was impossible, but I concentrated on the left side. Her hair was so long it felt like a silk scarf in my hands, and was so light that it weighed nothing for its length.

Her eyes were closed as she leaned back against the cushion, making little moans at how good it felt with my fingers rubbing her head.

Finally, I honed in on her lips again and she stilled. When she opened her eyes, I was leaning so close I could have kissed her. But I held off by sheer will, remembering my promise to let her say no.

"I'm going to kiss you," I warned.

She lifted her face, reaching for me, silently saying *yes*. Her lips were so hot against mine, so ready and eager. I tried to hold back, to restrain myself, not wanting to scare her again. But I had to devour her lips, pausing to look deeply into her eyes, then kissing her face and lips again.

My cock was hard as stone, raging to take her. The sane part of my mind knew that wouldn't happen here. But I would make sure it did happen. Soon.

Her hands were on my face, as I pulled her against me. I couldn't stop kissing her! It was like a flash explosion had been set off, and nothing could stop it.

Until she broke free, pushing both hands against my chest and leaning back to get away from me. "I thought you said you were only going to use your hands."

"Scene's over. Now we're on to more important things." I tried to kiss her again, but she avoided my lips.

Pushing at my chest, she said, "I think that's enough PDA for now."

I didn't want to let her go. But I had to. She slid her leg off my lap and sat back into her seat. She ran her fingers through her hair. "That was a lot better than the first time."

I cleared my throat. I had to get a grip. But all I wanted to do was kiss her some more, and take her someplace where I could fuck her properly. "So you forgive me?"

She smiled a little. "Yes. But I think you only did half of me."

"The left side. Does each side feel different?" I asked.

She sat back as if considering it. "Yes—my left

side is alive! My right side feels like it isn't even there. It's dead, gone. But all my nerves are tingling on the left."

"You wanted to know why people do this kinky stuff. That feeling is why."

Slowly she nodded, as if finally understanding. "Lola likes to feel alive. She hates it when things are boring."

"Kink isn't boring, that's for sure. It can be anything you make it."

"Maybe. But Lola doesn't have the best judgment."

I felt the wall going up between us again, as she returned to her concerns. It seemed like nothing could come between this woman and her sister. And nothing would make much of an impression on her until she could stop worrying about Lola.

"Why don't I help you?" I offered. "I can go with you the next time. And get you a better disguise than that. I can find out more about this guy, Martin, for you."

Her eyes lit up. "Would you do that? I know you're really busy with your work. Monica said you travel a lot."

It washed over me like an icy flood. I recognized her suggestive tone, alluding to my jet-set, wealthy lifestyle.

I hated it.

I had almost managed to forget that she had rejected me until she found out that I was "rich and successful." She never would have done anything with me, now or at the Chamber, otherwise.

My raging hard-on was joined by real rage, making me want to take her and shake her out of her superficial mind. I wanted to force her to see who I really was, and make her want me with just as much panting, breathless need as she did now. Even though I was just a pilot for hire.

She must have seen my hardened expression because she drew back, not understanding. "If it's too much trouble…"

"No," I forced myself to say. "I'll help you. It's the least I can do."

"Transcendence will be at a park on Sunday."

"I'll be going to Morocco for a few days," I said. I didn't know why—I had stopped asking a long time ago. The destination and the departure time were the only things that mattered to me.

Her eyes lit up. "On business?"

"Partly. But I'm going to take some time to explore the city. Rabat." I was doing it again. Spinning the web and telling lies without telling them.

"It sounds so exciting," she said, leaning forward. More eager than she had been this entire time.

It made me freeze up. "Let's look at next weekend when I get back."

She looked a little hurt by my sudden cool tone. She probably thought I was being condescending. It was one of the easiest ways to make a beautiful woman do anything for you—treat her like she was nothing special. I had perfected the art, along with my rich playboy persona of "Victor." It was a rush every time a greedy little slut went to bed with me because she wanted something from me—and they all wanted something, whether it was clothes, money or a good husband who could support them in style. They thought they were taking something from me, so why not take something back?

I stayed in the role, taking Sierra's phone number so I could connect with her later. Then looking at my watch, just like I had seen hundreds of assholes do it to me, as if I had other places to go, people to see. "I can help you get a cab."

As we walked through the club, my hand went to her bare back, exposed by the halter top. I had to touch her one more time. I could feel her shiver slightly.

Before she got into the cab, I gave her a thorough, but quick kiss. Enough to top me off. But not enough to let her feel my desire again. I wasn't going to give her that satisfaction.

She looked confused and still turned on. It was a lot to process for a newbie. I felt awful that my first scene in the Chamber with her had been so harsh. But I couldn't lie to myself and say it didn't still give me a thrill to remember how close I came to losing it with her our first time, and how she gave herself over to me completely. In one minute flat.

She had seen my worst side, but she had come back for more.

As I watched the cab pull away, I was so whipped up I couldn't see straight. I started walking home real fast. I had the uncomfortable feeling that my dick would be hard every step of the way, until I could get home and jack off to the thought of her writhing under me as I took her. For tonight, the fantasy would have to be enough.

Chapter 7

Sierra

I was lost in a haze of lust for the entire cab ride home. Kissing Victor was different than kissing other men. He savored his kisses with me. It didn't feel like a means to the end of rushing me into sex. The way he looked at me, then leaned in to fervently kiss me again... it was deeper than lust, overwhelming my senses.

I considered asking the cabby drop me off at the subway station so I wouldn't have to pay a huge fare, but my outfit was a little too sexy to be riding around alone at night on the subway. Or walking home through the streets from the station. The fact that I dressed like this again and went there looking for my sister proved there was nothing I wouldn't do to help her!

I deserved this. So I lay back in luxury, wallowing in the memory of Victor touching me, like it was seared into my skin. It was so erotic, and he hadn't even tried to grope me as most men would have. Yet I felt how turned on he was when he pressed me into the kiss.

By the time I let myself into my darkened apartment, I was wondering why he didn't ask me to go home with him.

Not that I would have. But why didn't he ask, at least?

As my post-euphoric state wore off, I started feeling more confused. It was hard to reconcile the Victor of tonight with last week's Victor. I did understand a little better the assumptions he had made about me at the Chamber. Still, it was seriously twisted. For both of us. I hated myself for thinking about it as much as I did.

But I never felt such an intense moment in my life, as when I knew he could hurt me if he wanted to.

Under the strange bond formed by that, tonight had happened.

So here I was roaming aimlessly around my empty apartment, while he was probably off tickling some other girl's fancy. Maybe he had another date lined up for his Friday night. I was just his happy hour treat. A man like Victor had to have other girls waiting for his call.

That was probably why he had gone cold once I stopped him. He wasn't used to being denied by a woman.

I wondered if I would hear from him again. Now that things had been smoothed over from the first time, he might not see any reason to mess around with me anymore.

But he had offered to help me after I made him stop kissing me.

Around and around I went, coming to no conclusions. I had no basis for comparison for this sort of thing. I was too inexperienced with the games men played, and the last time I had been ensnared by a player, I had come out the worse for it.

•••

Once again, my sister was gone all night. I worked the early shift on Saturday, and found myself chatting with shoppers a lot more than usual. And I hung out in the break room with the other girls during lunch instead of going to eat in Bryant Park or on the library steps. Usually I loved to watch the world pass by, enjoying the city. But not today.

I was lonely. A girl could only study so much. Those nightly hours without anyone to talk to were getting to me. For weeks Lola had been staying away more and more, until she rarely came home.

Facing another empty Saturday night with nothing to do, I called my mom. Usually a text once a month was all she wanted, but mom was chatty tonight because my brother Mark was getting married and his fiancé got along well with mom. I had only met her once, but she seemed nice enough.

I wished I had girlfriends I could hang out with, but I had always hung out with Lola. As a kid, my best friend, Amy, had lived next door. Amy's mom had fed me and Lola, and done some of the things a mom would do if our mom had been around more, like putting on band-aids and helping with homework.

But when my mom and dad got a divorce, that house and that world had disappeared. My brothers moved in with their dad, while we lived in a series of small, stifling apartments as mom struggled to make ends meet. Lola and I needed each other to get through school—we went to several overcrowded, rough schools where the fights got physical far too often. We closed in on ourselves, always on the defense to survive. I barely spoke to anyone in my classes after I saw girls lash out at someone just for smiling or talking to them. It was then that I dived into books to disappear from my real life, and found out there were a lot of other ways to live.

Lola got by with a string of boyfriends who protected her to one degree or another. She had a few fights in school, again over boys. But she mostly stayed in the shadows like me. It wasn't until she graduated, with my help, and we moved to the city together that she busted out.

After another long night alone, I woke up to face my day off with no enthusiasm. It was a beautiful day, so I was determined to go out. I decided to check out Lola's performance in the park to see what my sister was up to this time.

I put on a baseball cap—which I never wore—and tucked my hair up underneath. With big sun glasses and a baggy shirt, I didn't think Lola would recognize me. It gave me a certain satisfaction that I could pull one over on her.

The summer festival in McCarren Park in Williamsburg was a home-spun affair. People from all around brought their dogs dressed up for the Pets on Parade contest. There was a marching band strutting around playing funky music accented by the tuba and rhythmic beats of the base drum. Kids were running around everywhere, and there were face-painters, balloon-twisters and street performers.

I felt happier as I wandered around. Anything was better than sitting alone. I bought an ice cream and actually laughed out loud at the dogs doing tricks in a corral for the judges.

When I found Lola, my sister was kissing Martin. They were behind a tree, making out for all they were worth. It reminded me guiltily of Victor, and how we must have looked necking in the bar. Just off to one side, June and Spike were sitting on a blanket sorting through their gear.

I backed away. Seeing Martin up close and in the daylight, his skin looked even more ravaged. He was too thin for his height, and his hands and feet were too big. There was nothing good-looking about him. But Lola was all over him.

When Transcendence began their show, Lola wasn't in it this time. Her sole job was carrying around a hat to cajole donations from the crowd. She was wearing a multi-colored taffeta petticoat with motorcycle boots and a black tank top, nothing like her usual clothes. June was dressed similarly in a camouflage skirt as she twirled a baton lit on fire, throwing it high into the air to admiring exclamations from the crowd. Then Martin juggled fire, first alone, than in tandem with Spike.

It was flashy and entertaining. And full of fun. Nothing like the dramatic sexualized atmosphere of their show at Pleasure Salon.

I had to keep circling to get away from Lola, and when I realized that my sister wasn't going to take part in the show, I retreated to the other side of the festival.

Pacing back and forth, I finally pulled out my phone and texted Lola: *Doing anything fun? Love to hang out.*

Maybe if I could get to know Martin and her

new friends, I wouldn't feel so worried. Or left behind.

It took a while, but Lola finally texted back: *Working. Be home later.*

I let out my breath in a long, low rush. I could kind of understand why Lola was hiding the more sexual stuff from me. But why did Lola want to keep me away from this? It was exactly the sort of thing we both liked to do. It was the perfect way to introduce me to everyone so I could get to know them.

Lola didn't want me to get to know Martin. Or her other friends.

That meant there was something to hide.

...

Later on, when Lola finally got home, she was carrying a big garbage bag full of something. When I asked if she wanted to watch a movie, she replied, "I have to do laundry."

"On Sunday evening?" We both hated doing laundry on Sundays. The Laundromat was always stuffed with people who had put it off to enjoy their weekend.

Lola shrugged. "You do what you gotta do."

It was another snub. Lola didn't want to spend any time with me. She knew I'd rather do anything than laundry tonight.

That was the last time I saw her for the next few days. I also didn't hear from Victor. Maybe he was still in Morocco, or busy with work. I was preparing myself for the possibility that he wasn't going to text me. And I wasn't going to text him. I was starting to feel like his sensuous touch-fest in the bar was just another way of using me. I couldn't understand why desire had overwhelmed me, and why I had kissed him like that.

But when I thought about him, a rush went through me, betraying me. I shouldn't want him, even though there was so much to want. A man like that was no good for a girl like me. But it felt so right.

I wished I had someone I could talk to. It was only because I was lonely that I had fixated on Victor this way.

Then coming in late from my class on Wednesday, I picked up the mail from our box in the hallway wall. There was a notice from ConEd that Lola's electronic payment had bounced.

...

Much later, I was already in bed by the time Lola got home. But I got up to show my sister the notice. "This is exactly what I'm worried about!"

Lola rolled her eyes. "It wasn't my fault. They deposited my paycheck a day late."

I shook the bill at her. "You need to keep more than $76.42 in your account. You can't let it go that low or things are bound to slip up."

"Don't tell me what to do!" Lola rounded on me. "Are you talking to Dick?"

I drew back at her sudden vehemence. "He texts me sometimes, but I haven't answered since last week."

"I just found him parked up the street watching our place. It's seriously creepy. You better not be talking to him about me."

"He's an idiot," I said, thinking about the Chamber, where he had tossed me inside without a care for what would happen to me. "I won't tell him anything. You can trust me, Lola."

But Lola didn't look like she believed me. I was so wigged out by the thought of Dick sitting out there watching me sit at home alone every night, that I didn't realize until I was lying in bed that Lola had deflected me away from the bounced check.

I felt like I was standing on a precipice, with no one to steady me as the wind screamed past me. Lola, on the other hand, fell asleep instantly and slept like a rock.

Chapter 8

Victor

With ruthless precision, I waited until Thursday before I texted Sierra. I wanted her. Bad. But I would only take advantage of her if she made it clear she was after me because I was rich.

I texted with no preamble: *You want to go to a party where Lola will be this weekend?*

After a few minutes, a text came back from Sierra: *Yes.*

I replied: *It's a private party. I'll wrangle us an invite and get back to you.*

Much quicker, her text came back: *Thanks so much!*

I tucked my phone back in my pocket. I had almost walked away, convinced by her behavior at Happy Endings that she really was interested in me as a potential sugar daddy. She was willing to spy on her own sister, so she was definitely the kind of girl who did whatever it took to get what she wanted.

I'd been trying not to think about her all week, but it was no good. I couldn't wait to see her again, as much as I tried to bury that feeling. In Morocco the thought haunted me around every corner—I could be wrong about her. I wanted to be wrong about her, and that wasn't good.

I had to see her again if only to convince myself of the truth.

To get an invitation to the party, I was going to have to do something I had been avoiding lately. Tricia was the one in-the-know who could get me into that party. She might even be going herself.

But I had to be careful about how I did this. If I texted Tricia, she would think it was a booty call and she would be mad if I didn't go through with it. I couldn't deal with Tricia right now; I was already on edge from Sierra turning into raptures over my luxury lifestyle on the heels of our passionate kisses.

There was no doubt in my mind that Tricia only wanted me for my money, and she would dump me in a hot second if she thought I was a lesser man. She literally begged me to take her to expensive restaurants and on trips with me. But I had her convinced that I wasn't into having a girlfriend, so she had been lingering in fuck buddy and occasional play partner status for nearly two years, longer than I had managed to string any other woman along. That was probably more a testament to her perseverance and determination to get what she wanted, rather than my charms.

So I waited until late that night and signed onto FetLife. Sure enough, Tricia was posting in some of her groups. She was networked into the BDSM community like nobody else. Even her profile photo showed her face, blowing a kiss at the masses.

I noticed that she had recently changed her relationship status to "In an open relationship with" some guy who lived in Brooklyn. Last year she had added me to her list as "Friends with benefits," and I was still linked to her that way.

I hoped her new relationship would make this easier. I sent Tricia a message through the website's kinky chat. *Hey sexy! What's up?*

Tricia replied instantly: *Nothing much. What about you? Cheeky said you were at Pleasure Salon last weekend.*

I hadn't even noticed Cheeky; I had been so focused on Sierra. Then again, I had only seen Cheeky around a couple of times, so she could have been standing right in front of me. It reminded me of how tight-knit the BDSM community was that Tricia was getting reports on me. I was very lucky that Sierra didn't want to make a big deal out of what I had done to her at the Chamber or my toehold in that world could have been jerked away from me.

I had never gotten more involved with anyone I met in the scene because I wasn't being honest about who I was. You could only get to be so friendly with people when you couldn't talk about what you did every day.

So my relationship with Tricia, and all the other girls I played with, stayed superficial by necessity. My only real love had been Adrianne. And she ripped my heart out when she left.

To Tricia, I typed: *I'm showing a friend around the scene. We want to go to Blain's party in Tribeca this Saturday.*

I'm going to be there, she said. *With my new boyfriend.*

Naturally Tricia would want some stroking before we got to the dickering. Since it was an open relationship, that meant she could still play with other people, meaning me.

I replied: *I saw that you were in a relationship, congratulations!*

I've been needing that in my life. I like having the emotional support.

It was typical of Tricia that she explained her relationship in terms of how it benefited her.

I texted: *I'd like to meet him. Can you get me an invite?*

You and your new girl?

Hardly that. I'm showing her the ropes.

I'm sure you're showing her everything you've got, she replied.

Now I was even more irritated. Getting the occasional bang from Tricia wasn't worth the hassle she gave me. I didn't reply to her overt jealousy. It didn't deserve to be noticed.

Our words lingered on the chat record. I knew Tricia would be looking at them, wheels turning around in her head as she tried to figure out the best angle for her. Did she want me at a party where her new man would be? Did she want to help me make time with another girl? Would she figure that making my life easy was a step in the right direction to being girlfriend material?

Finally her reply came through, as I knew it would. *I'll get you that invite.*

I smiled. She was still in the palm of my hand.

The next morning, I went to Purple Passion and found the perfect disguise for Sierra—a subtle leather half-hood that would cover her eyes and the top of her head, with a hole where her pony tail could stick through on top. I also bought a black cat-suit in heavy double-knit that flowed heavy and silky in my hands.

If she was a greedy little girl like Tricia, then she would expect to get beautiful gifts from men like me. Women like Tricia squealed and grabbed what you gave them, looking as eager as Sierra had in Happy Endings when we were talking about my trip to Morocco.

Her reaction when I gave Sierra the clothes would tell me what I needed to know.

Chapter 9

Sierra

When I got to the corner where Victor told me to meet him, he wasn't there yet. I waited in front of the Korean nail salon, trying to calm my jitters. I wasn't sure whether I was more nervous about seeing Victor again or seeing what Lola was capable of next.

I saw him coming up the street towards me, his hair blowing in the breeze. He looked so manly, his arms stretching the sleeves of his black T-shirt. I liked the fact that even though he was a busy businessman, he kept himself fit. For the first time, his clothes didn't reek of money—he wore faded jeans with holes in the thigh and motorcycle boots. The casual look made him look even sexier.

"Hi," I said. "How was Morocco?"

"The usual," he tossed off, looking me up and down. "Your outfit's no good. You look like a waitress."

I looked down at my black button-up shirt and skirt. "You said you were going to help me with a disguise."

Victor patted the messenger bag slung over his shoulder. "I've got it in here. You'll have to change at the party."

"What if Lola sees me first?"

"I'll make sure that doesn't happen."

His tone was final, like I shouldn't question his

judgment. I wasn't used to men who were so definite about things. Is that what it took to be successful? Telling everyone the way it was?

"Are you ready to do this?" he asked. "Once we're in there, you'll have to play the part or we won't blend in."

"What kind of part?"

"As my submissive."

A flow of people were walking past us on the sidewalk, within arm's reach. But nobody was paying any attention to us. Still, it was a weird place to have this kind of discussion.

"What do I have to do?" I asked.

He raised one brow. "Whatever I say."

He wasn't smiling or joking about it. This was the serious Victor, the one who had devoured me with his eyes as he lured me into letting him touch me again.

"That's too open-ended for me," I finally said.

"What are your limits?"

I licked my lips nervously. "What will people be doing?"

"Some will have sex. Others will do BDSM."

"So it's even more extreme than the Chamber?"

"It's completely different. It's a private party. You have to know Blain to get an invite. You can be more open at a party because it's safe. We'll see all sorts of things."

"No sex for me," I managed to say. "No way."

"Okay, no sex. What else?"

"I'm not getting naked. Your disguise better be more than two scraps of material or I'm not putting it on."

Finally he smiled. "You'll be completely covered except for your chin and your beautiful mouth." He reached out to lightly stroke my chin. "Any more limits?"

"Can I add more things as we go along?"

"You've become a better negotiator, Sierra. Yes, feel free to add things to the 'Do not' list."

I looked at him for a few seconds longer, trying to figure out my own feelings. He wasn't being very warm. In fact, the cool, restrained man I had left at the bar last week was standing right here in front of me. Not the man who had looked so guilty when he found out why I went to the Chamber. Not the man who made it up to me by touching me so sweetly...

But this was my only chance to see Lola. And I couldn't deny that I was fascinated by Victor. He could mesmerize me with a look, or dismiss me with just a turn of his head. I never knew how he would react. It was frustrating, but also exciting.

Like I was going to leap off my lonely precipice holding his hand. *Who knows where I'll land?*

"Okay, let's do this," I said.

•••

In the elevator, I sneaked looks at Victor on the way up to the penthouse. He seemed perfectly relaxed, while I was jittery and nervous. What could possibly be more extreme than the Chamber?

There was a burly dude with a clipboard at the door. "Victor and Sierra," Victor told him. The guy checked off something and gestured to the door.

"Where's the closest bathroom where she can

change?" Victor asked.

The guy gave me a quick up-and-down look. I felt like a piece of meat that had been assessed and approved. "Down the hall to the right."

We stepped into a foyer that was fairly well lit. Ahead was the living room that was much darker, where shadowy forms of people were walking around.

Victor turned and took me down the hallway to a half-bath. He handed me the messenger bag. "Once you're dressed, call me and I'll help you put on the mask."

Inside, I pulled out lots of black material, glad to see such a concealing costume. I stripped down to my black sports bra and boy shorts—the barest I had decided I could go while I was still at home and not under Victor's spell.

The cat suit was skin tight from the ankles on up. I had a hard time zipping up the zipper in the back, but there was no way I was calling Victor in to zip it for me. Contorting myself, I finally managed to get it all the way up. The high collar was so tight it was barely tolerable.

Looking in the mirror, my eyes widened at how big my breasts looked. The stretchy nylon really accented my waist and hips, too.

When I opened the door, Victor stared at me hungrily. I didn't know what to say to the naked lust in his eyes, so we silently stood there looking at each other.

Then a guy passing by strained to see in, and Victor stepped between us, glaring at the guy. He stepped into the bathroom, looking mad.

"I hope it's not too tight," he said.

"I can barely breathe. But it will do."

He looked at me as if waiting for something. So I dug into the bag and pulled out a fold of black leather with lacings. "Is this the mask?"

Victor took it from me. "Yes. Put your hair up in a ponytail. Right about here," he said, touching me on the top-back part of my head.

I pulled out my brush and managed to get my hair into a ponytail despite the vacuum suit I was wearing. Victor kept looking at my gyrations, but he didn't smile or say anything until I was done.

"Turn to me." With gentle hands, he fit the head piece across my eyes and forehead, and over my head. "Hold up your ponytail while I tighten the lacing."

He was right behind me, breathing on my neck as he concentrated on the lacings. The headpiece tightened on my head and across my face as he pulled. Every part of my body except for my jaw and hands were bound tightly by him. It was comforting and warm, almost too much. Every movement reminded me of my constraint.

My vision was cut off on the sides, like a horse wearing blinders. I hadn't realized how hobbled I would be in the mask.

But when I looked in the mirror, I was unrecognizable. Even my sister wouldn't know it was me if I was standing right in front of her. I looked like a plastic fetish doll with exaggerated curves and a high arching pony tail.

"I guess that works," I told Victor.

"Yes, it does," he agreed fervently.

It was considerate of him to lend me the disguise. I just hoped I didn't bust out a seam and ruin it.

Victor waited a moment, looking at me in the mirror. But when I didn't say anything else, he abruptly took hold of my hand and led the way as we explored the sprawling penthouse. There were at least six bedrooms on the two floors, and two large living rooms that had views north and east. But the place was sparsely furnished with only a few black couches and chairs, and plain mattresses with white sheets for beds. There were also black padded benches and tables, plus towering wooden X's like I'd seen at the Chamber.

The glass doors were open to the terraces with incredible views of Manhattan and New Jersey. The buildings were stacked so close together that only a dip in the height showed me where Greenwich Village was. Beyond, the rooftops rose again to the skyscrapers of Midtown, with the Empire State Building taller than the rest.

I felt like I was in a movie.

Victor got plastic cups of wine which we sipped as we watched an older man paddle a squealing, writhing girl. The girl was cute with broad hips and an infectious laugh. I couldn't understand why she kept laughing in between her cries that begged him to stop.

"Is he tickling her?" I asked.

"Among other things. That paddle is wood so it's pretty heavy."

The girl seemed to like it, throwing herself into it with abandon. The skin on her buttocks was blotched dark red amongst the pink.

I looked sideways at Victor, who was watching the scene with detachment. "Is that what you do?" I asked.

He finally smiled. "I'd rather use my hands when I spank a girl."

I was feeling warmer, just thinking about it. "Does it hurt?"

"It doesn't have to."

His hands reached for my waist, pulling me into him. His palm slid down the curve of my ass, cupping my cheek. My hands were against his chest, as his face bent close to my ear. "Like this."

He smacked my butt cheek firmly.

"Oh!" I exclaimed.

I could tell he could have spanked me a lot harder. He was holding back.

He smacked my other butt cheek, letting me absorb it. My rear end was tingling as the warmth spread through my lower body.

It felt like I had been shaken. Briskly.

"That woke me up," I said.

"There's nothing like it when you're having sex. It makes everything more intense."

He was still holding me close, rocking back and forth slightly as his hand rubbed my butt, soothing away the sting. I could feel his rigid hard-on pressing against my belly.

"Men are also submissive," he said. "Look over there."

A man knelt in front of an elegant woman, sucking on her toes. The woman was watching him critically, tapping him with her riding crop to emphasize when she spoke to him.

"The subs also serve their Doms. They do things to make their lives easier, or to please them."

I suddenly wanted to please him, for all sorts of complicated reasons. Not the least was the way his hands felt on me, rubbing and caressing me. I was loving all of this touching. I'd never been touched this much even when I'd had sex, and up until now I never thought about it. But sex was breast squeezing and hip thrusting, and that was it.

I moved against Victor. "What pleases you?"

"*You* please me," he said very low, both hands still running up and down my back to my butt, pulling me into him.

Soft moans and cries urging for more filled the air. Everyone wore a secret smile, like we were getting away with something just by being here. I saw naked people, topless people, people fully dressed or even wearing business suits. But they were all letting go of the roles they usually played and exposing something deeper, rawer in themselves.

It felt so right, seeing these things while feeling his hands run freely up and down my body. Feeling him awaken my body in a way I'd never felt before.

And I could feel my own power, moving slowly, feeling him react to my response to his touch. Hearing his hiss of indrawn breath. Feeling how aroused he was, rubbing himself against me.

Then he spanked my ass again, making me

gasp at the sudden, sharp sensation. It sent a shock wave through me, making me jerk in his arms. His hands soothed my skin, running down, stroking me, sending waves of pleasure through me.

Like it was building to a moment suspended in time. I had to let go.

The swoon had already started, the dive and rush of ecstasy, of relief. He pressed his whole body against mine, shamelessly rubbing his thick rod against me. I couldn't breathe, didn't care.

It was such a perfect moment, the heady atmosphere carrying me along in the same ecstatic wave with everyone else. And all I could think about was *this* was what I wanted. To feel his desire. To let go in this moment, and get swept up along with him.

There was the proof in his burning eyes and how tightly he held me, how firmly he ran his hands over my slick bodysuit. In his harsh breaths, marking every touch.

"Yes, that's it," he urged, feeling me tense in a new way as his fingers sank between my legs.

I grasped his arms, holding on as the waves went through me, driven by his insistent fingers. He saw everything in me. He touched me in a way I'd never felt before.

His acceptance made it easy for me to let go, to let him drive me forward with just his touch.

"That's right," he murmured. "You're going to give it to me."

His husky demand took me over the edge as I cried out, colors bursting behind my clenched eyes. He was rock solid, giving me something to hold onto as my climax ripped through me, spinning my mind away.

Chapter 10

Victor

I loved watching Sierra come in my arms. I loved it that I had taken her there, with only my touch. My voice. She was so responsive to me. She didn't need the showy scenes that some women demanded in order to be the center of attention. I liked it that she preferred to let go in a quiet corner, unobserved by anyone but me.

She was breathing fast, looking in my eyes. Then I realized she was very flushed. And couldn't quite catch her breath.

"Can't," she said faintly. Her fingers hooked into the high collar of her suit, trying to pull it away from her throat.

I swept her up in my arms and carried her onto the terrace, where a cool breeze was wafting over the bricks. Taking her all the way out to the railing, where the air was moving the most, I asked, "Are you okay?"

"Hot. Can't breathe," she panted.

I tried to set her down, but her legs collapsed under her. I lowered her to the flagstones. "Let me," I told her, reaching for the zipper at the collar.

It stuck coming down, the material was stretched so tightly. No wonder she couldn't breathe.

"You'll be okay," I assured her. "I'm just opening this up."

I was ready to go for my rope cutter to slice through the nylon, but she took a deep breath as I jerked, and the zipper came down to her waist. Her hands started clawing weakly at the sleeves, as if she had to get them off. I helped her. They were so tight. Her skin was sheened with moisture and flushed red.

She collapsed against me, and I leaned against the outer wall of the terrace, holding her. "Catch your breath."

"I'm still hot." She pulled away to peel the cat-suit off her legs. That left her in a black sports bra and boy shorts. And the head mask.

It was more covered up than a lot of people here, but she had said "no nudity" in her negotiations. I pulled my T-shirt off with one motion. She saw what I was doing and let me slip it over her head. "Better," she said.

I pulled her back into my arms, loving how her silky hair felt against my bare chest. Her fingers rested against me, as I stroked her hair, relieved that she was okay. Things kept going wrong whenever I topped her. I hadn't meant to hurt her, but the way that cat-suit had peeled off made it look like a torture device.

"I hope I didn't ruin your suit," she murmured into my chest. "The next girl you lend it to better be smaller than me."

My hand stilled. "I got it for you."

She peeked up at me. "Maybe you can get it cleaned and take it back."

I suddenly wanted to laugh. "Spoken like a woman who's done that before."

"Hey, it was a dress for a date. And I didn't have anything nice enough to wear." She took one look at my face and we laughed together. "Girls do it all the time. I'm always charging back credit for pretty dresses."

"You work in a store?"

She raised her brows. "At Lowenstein's on 5th Avenue."

"Do you like it?"

"I'll like it even better after I get promoted. I'm hoping that happens this fall, after I get my degree. It's just an associate degree, but it should help."

I was on the verge of telling her that I knew what it was like to work hard, having worked my way up as a ramp rat as a kid. I knew how tough it was to make ends meet. But then Sierra added, "It's nothing compared to your job. It must be so exciting to be able to fly anywhere you want. What is your work exactly? I don't think you've ever said."

The longing in her voice was unfeigned. She thought I was rich and successful. She had struggled hard for years. Of course she wanted someone who could make things easier for her.

I couldn't do that for her.

In a burst of anger, I was ready to tell her that.

But a familiar voice cried out, "Victor!" from over by the door. Suddenly Tricia was rushing over to us, dragging a guy along with her.

"Incoming," I murmured to Sierra. "Let me help you up."

Tricia came to a screeching halt in front of me. "Am I interrupting? Are you having a scene?"

"Aftercare."

"Sor-*ry*!" she sang out. "Should we come back later?"

Tricia was so used to being wanted that she stomped all over everyone without a thought. I used to think her long black hair and almond eyes were the most exotic thing I had ever seen. But now I just saw... crap.

I wanted to snap at Tricia for standing there so smug. If she was going to be polite, she never wouldn't have barged over while I was cuddling with another girl. She knew she was interrupting an intimate moment.

"Sierra, this is Tricia," I said flatly.

"I got you the invite for this party!" Tricia told Sierra. She gushed too much, introducing her boyfriend as Craig. He was a nothing kind of guy, slender and slouched with his long black hair falling in his face. But Tricia clung to him adoringly, like he was a Greek god.

But her eyes also kept straying to my bare chest. Sierra noticed. My arm tightened around her. Tricia was a game-player at heart.

"Are you having fun learning the ropes?" Tricia asked Sierra pointedly.

"Yes." To her credit, Sierra wasn't playing back. Between her ability to freeze people and the head mask, which put a barrier between her and everyone else, Tricia was stymied.

Suddenly Craig spoke up. "You're Victor. *That* Victor."

Tricia slapped his arm. "I told you, Baby.

Victor."

Craig jerked his chin in my direction. "Huh."

So Craig had finally put it together that I was Tricia's "friend with benefits." And he looked like he wasn't too happy about it.

Tricia was smiling, pleased to get a rise out of her boyfriend. He was probably feeling outgunned by her and looking for a way out. But that spark of jealousy meant it wasn't over yet.

Happily, Tricia let her gaze drift down my body. "Your boot has a smudge on it," she told me.

I didn't even look down, refusing to play whatever game she had going now.

Without warning, Tricia knelt down at my feet. Sierra stiffened at being so close to her. But I kept my arm tight around Sierra so she couldn't move away. I didn't look down at Tricia.

Deliberately Tricia buffed the top of my boot, as if removing something. I could feel her fingers press my foot through the leather, making a secret connection with me. Craig started to bend down to pull her up but gave up, clearly aware that he couldn't make Tricia do anything.

Then she slowly stood as if she knew every eye was on her. "All fixed now. See you later!"

With that, Tricia took Craig's arm and dragged him away. He looked back at me a couple times, as if warning me.

Finally Sierra asked, "Um, what was *that*?"

"She's trying to make her boyfriend jealous."

"I could see that. I meant, what is she to you?"

How could I admit she was a fuck buddy?

"She's completely disposable."

Sierra frowned. "That doesn't sound good. Are all your women disposable?"

"All of them, but you."

I hadn't meant to say it, it sounded so corny. But it felt true. Just touching her made me feel good. I had been hard since I saw her in that cat-suit, and when she had nearly fainted, I was ready to do anything to help her. It wasn't lust, it was something more. Like when I touched her, and she looked at me, she really saw me. Not the part I played.

"I don't believe you," she said, pulling away. "Why would you want a salesgirl like me? You *should* be dating a woman like Tricia. Did you smell her perfume? That's Flowerbomb. $180 a bottle. I wouldn't be able to eat for weeks if I bought perfume like that."

"I don't want her. I like how *you* smell."

I was looking deep into her eyes, and she seemed to be just as mesmerized. I was thinking we should go inside and find someplace private to finish what we started.

Then a flare of fire lit everything around us.

It was Transcendence. Martin and his troop had set up on the larger terrace around the corner. Spike was blowing fire to scattered applause.

"That's Lola!" Sierra exclaimed.

Without another thought, she pulled away from me. I followed along behind as she hurried over to that side of the terrace.

The troop had a big fire pit going, with the flames illuminating three people dancing around it.

They were all topless, wearing black clouts, with dabs and slashes of black paint decorating their bodies. Martin was beating a rapid rhythm on a deep, reverberating drum.

Sierra went right up close to them, unafraid in her mask.

"What's that hanging on them?" Sierra asked me.

"Jingle bells." I wasn't sure if I should tell her, but she was here to find out what was going on. "They're hanging from strings pierced through their skin."

"What!?" She stared at me as if I had to be kidding. "Isn't that dangerous?"

"They know how to do it safely."

It was a good thing other people were starting to dance, drawn in by the drum. They weren't paying attention to Sierra. Most people in the scene were sensitive to acceptance, and didn't like it when someone showed too openly that they were squicked.

Sierra was staring for all she was worth, until Lola circled around. Lola's head was thrown back and she was in the throes of subspace from the piercings. She had a dozen large jingle bells hanging from her back, arms, thighs and chest. Spike had twice as many and was even more enthralled than Lola. June only had a few and was banging on a much smaller drum to complement Martin's beat.

Then Lola turned, and Sierra let out a squeak, quickly muffled by her hands. Lola was so far gone she didn't hear it.

"What's that on her back?" Sierra demanded.

I had to wait until Lola circled back around. This time I got a good look. Wings were outlined on each one of her shoulder blades.

"That's not a tattoo!" Sierra breathed.

"Yes, it is," I said. "A brand new one." Lola's skin was shiny from Vaseline, used to keep irritants away from the raw skin.

"It's huge!" Sierra was seething. She looked like she was going to explode.

I put my arms around her, stroking her back, alarmed by how rigid Sierra had gone. "There's nothing you can do about it now."

"How much does something like that cost?" she demanded.

"I don't know. It's only the outline. Maybe $500."

Sierra was vibrating in my arms. "She bounced our electric bill this month! To get wings! Permanently on her back. Like she's some kind of demented angel!"

"Okay, girl, let's take it down a notch." I began walking her away from the fire. I didn't trust that wild look in her eye. This was the woman who had insulted me the first second she saw me. She was capable of anything.

Sierra resisted. "What are you doing?"

"Getting you away from your sister."

She struggled harder. "I have to talk to her."

"Now is not the time."

I lifted her up and carried her back to the other terrace, where things had been going so well. Until Tricia came and blew up our moment.

"Put me down!" Sierra exclaimed, as I was putting her down.

"You don't want to go back there," I told her.

"Why not? Lola can't keep getting away with everything."

I gestured to the growing crowd around Transcendence. "This is their *job*. You can't make a scene and ruin it for the whole group. Or for Blaine—he doesn't want drama at his parties. He let us in with the understanding that we'd behave ourselves."

Sierra stopped trying to peel my hands off her. She may not want to admit it, not yet, but she knew I was right.

"Your sister would hate you, if you busted up their show. Not to mention, she's deep in a scene right now, and the last thing you should do is mess with her flow."

I tried to draw Sierra back in, to hug some of that terrible tension away, but she was too angry. She grudgingly promised she wouldn't do anything rash, and then spent the next hour perched on the periphery of the crowd around Transcendence, watching her sister dance until she happily collapsed into Martin's lap.

It was only when the performance group left the party that Sierra went off her guard. She finally pulled off the head mask, wincing as it tugged on her pony tail.

"Here," she said, handing it over to me. The cat-suit was already folded up back in my messenger bag.

"You can keep it," I told her.

She shrugged, insisting I take it by holding it

out. "You can lend it to me if I need it. I definitely won't be doing this alone again."

I realized that my test had been flawed from the start as I tucked the mask in my bag. Of course she didn't care about presents of fetishwear. Sierra was here to watch over her sister. She was curious about kinky stuff, but that impulse wasn't driving her down this path. Not yet.

Right now, Lola was the only thing she was thinking about. Like Sierra's entire world had been blown apart by a pair of tattooed wings.

I couldn't imagine what that kind of love felt like, where everything another person did could affect you that much. My own sister couldn't care less about me or what I did. I hadn't spoken to her in years.

My whole life would have been different if she had been a sister like Sierra.

For now, I could tell a losing battle when I saw one. I stood guard while Sierra got dressed and then took her downstairs and put her into a cab. I didn't even try to kiss her. I was surprised by how much I wanted to. But she was so upset and closed in on herself, that it wasn't an option.

And I still didn't know the answer to my question. I knew she was attracted to me. But was it because she thought I was rich and successful? Or because she saw beneath the Victor-persona to the man I was inside?

Chapter 11

Sierra

Things changed after the party. I no longer wandered aimlessly around our apartment, missing Lola. The best I could do was make a nest on the couch and curl up there. Doom was inevitable. Everything had changed—Lola's new wings proved that. Now I had to wait it out to see where this titanic shift left me.

Then I would figure out how to deal with it.

Through my misery ran darker veins of anguish. The way Victor had shoved the cab money in my hand and then closed the door would haunt me for the rest of my life. Like he was getting rid of a problem. It must be nice to be able to shove money at a problem and make it go away.

But I couldn't blame him. I was such a monumental drag at the party. Look at the way he had to carry me off so I wouldn't make a fool of us both! He was probably regretting letting Tricia leave with that awful boyfriend of hers.

So on Wednesday, I was surprised when I got a text from Victor. *Found out more info re Lola. Want to know?*

It was hardly a love letter, but it made me sit up and take notice for the first time in days. Victor was still helping me! He wasn't completely turned off by how I had acted at the party.

I wasn't completely alone.

Yes! I texted back.

Lola had been MIA ever since the party, except for a text about the electric bill. She said she had finally paid for it. The end of the month was in ten days, and I was not confident that Lola would have her half of the rent. I had enough to cover it if she didn't. But it would take most of my savings to do it.

I wasn't sure that there was anything Victor could tell me about Martin that would stop the madness, but it was worth a try. And it was worth getting to see Victor again.

I have to show you online, he texted. *Can you come over tomorrow?*

I couldn't help myself. I danced around the tiny living room with my phone. *He's into me!* He must be, or he wouldn't ask me over to his place.

It made my insides turn to mush whenever I thought about the way he had stroked me through the cat-suit. He had made me come using just his fingers, while I was covered from head to foot. It sure felt like sex to me. But I didn't regret doing it one bit. It pleased him, and that was intensely satisfying, almost as much as the orgasm itself. It felt even better to daydream about it now and wallow in the sensation of being held by him.

He had been so sweet to me after I nearly fainted. I couldn't have imagined how genuinely caring he could be. His eyes had been filled with concern. But in unsettling flashes, I also kept seeing his eyes from our first night at the Chamber, when he didn't care if he hurt me.

How could the same man look at me so completely differently?

When Victor texted his address, I checked it on Google and clicked on street view. The building was nice, made of gray brick with new, oversize windows. His apartment number was 606 so he was probably on the sixth floor, near the top. There were two garages beside it and on the other side a tenement building. But there were a couple of mopeds parked out front in the Google image, giving it a swanky look.

And this was just his pied-à-terre in the city! No telling what kind of private castle he lived in out in Connecticut.

It felt too good to be true. My life was falling apart, but this amazing, hunky guy had suddenly appeared, eager to help me. Eager to touch me and make me feel good.

All night and the next day at work, I let myself dream big. What would it be like to be that rich? To never have to worry about money again? To be able to buy every sublime jewel or dress I wanted? To have a gorgeous house or two or three where my friends came for dinners and my husband waited for me in bed...

But I couldn't believe in my own daydreams. Even when I nearly convinced myself it could be true. I knew I was just getting my hopes up for nothing.

My life isn't a Lifetime movie, kept going through my head.

I was still telling myself that as I walked up the sidewalk to Victor's building. No mopeds were parked outside the building at the moment, but everything else looked the same.

It was only mid-afternoon. Victor had asked me when my shift ended and told me to come over right afterward. So I chose a dark blue wrap dress for work today. It could translate into evening, if he asked me to grab an early dinner with him. I hoped I looked classy enough to take anywhere. Bev at the makeup counter had touched me up before I left work.

Two rows of silver buttons were set in a plate by the glass door. I pressed 606 and was buzzed inside. The lobby was not very big, but it was elegant. The floor and half way up the wall were tiled in marble, with the ceiling very high overhead.

The elevator was tiny and smoothly took me up six floors. I couldn't remember the last time I had been this nervous about a guy. I was used to first dates, but it rarely went beyond the second date when they realized I wasn't going to just fall into bed with them. There were too many sure things out there for most men to waste time with me.

But Victor and I were already far beyond our first date... even though we hadn't gone on an official date yet.

I took some deep breaths and tried to calm myself.

Victor had his door open, waiting for the elevator to arrive. He was wearing dark suit pants with a pale gray button-down shirt. His collar was open like he had pulled off his tie. When I went inside, the dark suit jacket was draped over the back of a chair.

Oh, my!

All I could see were the windows dominating the room. Two big windows, at least ten feet across. The view was west towards Soho and Chinatown. The taller buildings rose on either side of us.

"Oh... wow." I couldn't believe it... my dream view! I went right up to the windows, drinking it in. "Look at your view!"

His smile was a little forced. "I've seen it."

"I wish I could wake up to *that* every morning. It must make your whole day better."

Victor didn't say a word. He must be used to women raving over his view. I took a quick tour around, checking out the small galley kitchen with a stainless steel tile backsplash and black marble counter. The bed was tucked in by one of the windows, in the nook formed by the bathroom.

"Glass brick!" I exclaimed. "I love that look."

I went inside the bathroom. The light filtered in, a lovely bluish-green color. The tiles in the shower were also blue, aqua, green and white. It was the prettiest bathroom I had ever seen.

When I came out, he was staring at me glumly.

"I'm sorry for showing myself around," I said. "It's just that your place is *amazing*. I can't get over the view."

"You get used to it."

"Maybe you do. I wouldn't."

His eyes narrowed even more. "I suppose it's what everyone wants when they come to the city."

"And you've got it," I pointed out. "I would give anything to make my dream come true."

"Anything?" he asked.

I instantly caught his sexual innuendo. For once, my doubts were silent. In this beautiful apartment, with this amazing man, it felt like anything could happen. Like my future could be anything I wanted.

The tension between us leaped higher as I slowly walked back towards him. Now he was smiling, in response to me. I let my gaze sweep over him slowly. His eyes were even greener against the gray of his shirt, and the sunlight slanting through the windows lit up his hair like gold.

I went right up to him and put my hand to his cheek. I kissed him, letting all of my passion connect with him through my lips. He took hold of my waist, pulling me in, taking control of the kiss.

He was so strong! I felt small and fragile in his grasp, as if he had to be careful not to bruise me. I knew how tightly he could hold me.

My hands roamed from his silky hair and the back of his neck down to his chest. I remembered nothing felt as good as cuddling against his bare chest when we were at the party. When he was holding me on the terrace after I almost fainted, I wanted to be held by him forever.

His lips were soft but firm, growing more eager as he bent me back slightly, pressing in to take what I was giving him. As if he wasn't satisfied with just receiving.

We stumbled to one side, engrossed in each other. Victor steadied himself on the couch, still kissing me. He grabbed my legs and picked me up, sitting me on the back of the couch. I wrapped my legs around his hips, and he pressed himself against my lace-covered crotch.

One of his hands slipped down, his sure fingers finding just the right spot.

My breath hissed inward. "How do you know?"

"I pay attention."

He kept on kissing me, rubbing me with the heel of his hand, his fingers curving under me, pressing against me. My panties were already damp.

"Umm...," he murmured. "You love it, don't you?"

I loved it that he was touching me, making me feel so good. I loved being in his place; it was how I always wanted to feel. Like everything would turn out okay in spite of all the shit.

"You love it," he whispered. His hand kept pressing against me, sending me higher.

"I do," I managed to say.

My head tilted and I arched back into his arms, every muscle straining. He bit down on my lower lip, his teeth sinking into the thick pad. The pain made me gasp, but somehow it drove me even higher.

My legs wrapped tighter around him, squeezing him with my thighs. He groaned, his other hand holding me up by my waist. But I was twisting so hard that he had to pull his fingers away and grab onto me with both hands on my hips.

He pressed his hard-on against my panties, bucking against me. It felt even better than his hand! I turned my head back and forth, my hips grinding against him.

He broke away from ravaging my lips to look

into my eyes. "I must have you," he said.

"Yes!" I panted.

His eyes lit up. He picked me up and with a few steps around, fell down on the couch with me. His hands were at the waist of my dress, pulling at the strings. "Like opening a present."

He pulled open my dress and gaze down at me for a few moments. "*Yum...*" His hand stroked my waist and down my hip. Then up to my breast. "I could eat you up..."

A shiver ran through me at his firm touch. He bent down and kissed my belly, then up between my breasts, pushed together by the cups of my bra. He lightly licked, then bit the fleshy top of my breast.

A noise broke from my throat, almost a protest. But I let him bite me again, all over my chest. As he devoured me.

I helped him get off my bra, and unbuckled his belt with shaking fingers. He ripped off a couple of buttons getting his shirt off and they went flying. His muscles bunched as he jerked it away, and I had to touch his chest, had to feel how glorious hard he was, yet soft enough to sink my fingertips into.

It was like we were caught in a tornado, whirling around and around, clinging to each other. As if I would die if I didn't join with this man right this second.

He ripped open a condom and put it on with a practiced expertise that I would only remember later. Right now, I was glad to spread my legs as he settled between them, urging him closer, so I could feel his body against mine.

"You're so wet," he growled. "Say you want me."

I barely hesitated at his demand. "I want you!"

He pushed the tip of his cock into me, biting his own lip as I lifted my hips to let him slide deeper. I loved the wash of ecstasy over his face, then how he looked into my eyes, letting me see how he felt.

As he thrust in deeper, I pulled him down against me. He was so heavy, pressing me into the cushions as he pushed into me. Flashes of the Chamber went through my mind, of Victor's eyes as he took possession of me, how he comforted me there and on the terrace, when I felt safer than I ever had before.

Only now I was euphoric, flying higher than I had ever had before.

He lowered his mouth to my throat, kissing me. I gave into the inevitable as he buried his face and bit my neck.

It sent me right over the top. I couldn't withstand the battering waves that drove me out of my mind. I had never felt so good...

"Yes!" I cried out. "Victor!"

Chapter 12

Victor

"Yes, give it to me," I growled.

I couldn't get enough of feeling her moving underneath me, drawing me in with her hands and legs, riding me as much as I rode her.

I greedily watched her face as she came, knowing that pleasure was because of me. It felt so good that I almost climaxed instantly, as I plunged in and out, never ceasing.

I could feel everything! Usually it was like I was watching myself when I fucked a woman, watching how she let me inside of her. Taking my own satisfaction, separate from hers.

But Sierra drew me in and there was no wall between us. She threw herself with abandon into me, and I couldn't hold back.

I wanted to keep feeling her skin, so firm and smooth, and hear those little sounds she made from the back of her throat, like purrs and growls, urging me on.

The room spun around me as I raised up, trying to breathe. Trying to separate, to delay. But there was nothing like that now. There was only the sensation of rocking together, like we were alone in the world.

I came in a long slow buildup like I never felt before, as a tidal wave rushed through my soul, wiping out everything I had carefully built over the years. Washing me clean with her. Destructive, yet purifying.

As I slowly swam back to life, I realized I was squashing her into the leather cushions of the couch. The smile on her face, the way she languidly stroked the hair at the back of my neck, said she didn't mind.

"The bed is right there," she laughed. "We couldn't even make it."

"That was... wild," I agreed.

This was supposed to be the usual kind of conquest. I had seen plenty of women get turned on by my place before. But Sierra had prowled around in delight, assessing the loft like she was a real estate agent. She had been completely open about her enthusiasm.

So I figured I was right about her after all. She was on the hunt for a sugar daddy. It gave me the green light to keep lying to her.

I had been surprised when I kissed her that she jumped me instantly. Maybe the sight of my view had overwhelmed her usual caution.

But something else had happened as we had sex. She had drawn me in unawares. I started to believe in her again. Like she could be real, not a selfish bitch like the others. Like Adrianne.

I pushed myself off her, detaching myself by degrees. She looked like she didn't want to let me go. And I didn't want to let her go. But the contrast between reality and what I felt was giving me a mind-warp.

I avoided her eyes as I gathered up my clothes. My shirt was messed up, with the fabric torn by two of the buttons when they came off. I crumpled it up to throw it away. I couldn't afford to waste money like that. I made do with putting on my suit pants, the best I owned, which I had kicked off as heedlessly as my shirt.

She wasn't smiling now, not after I pulled away so abruptly.

Sierra went into the bathroom and was in there long enough that I was able to calm down and regain my wits. I wasn't sure why I had reacted so strongly to her.

When she came out, her own polite mask was firmly in place. It was almost like the whirlwind sex hadn't happened. Almost.

I'd never seen a girl detach as quickly as I could. Usually a woman would be trying even harder, touching me even more to break through.

"You said you found out something about Lola?" Sierra asked.

Glad to be reminded, I went back to the desk where my laptop sat. I clicked on the saved website and entered Lola's full name into the database. It was easy to find out stuff about people online. You just had to know where to look. And I had gotten very good at researching the background of the women who pursued me. Tricia came from a wealthy family and she was a manager at a big insurance company. She also had too much credit card debt that her daddy paid off every so often. And a previous marriage that she had never mentioned to me, or as far as I could tell, anyone else in the scene.

Sierra was from upstate New York and had

taken the SATs twice, scoring well but not high enough for any scholarships. She had a credit card that she used sparingly and paid off immediately.

That information had given me hope, but then she had come in gushing over my apartment, and the doubts had taken over again.

"What is this?" Sierra asked, squinting at the screen.

"Lola is getting food stamps. She applied last month."

"Food stamps!"

"It says here from her income that she qualifies."

Sierra stared at the number, as if adding it up in her head. "Yes, that's what she makes."

I gave her a sideways look. So it wasn't a complete scam. She and her sister were that poor.

Then Sierra caught sight of something. "Wait a second! Is that supposed to be her address?"

"Yes, it's the one on her driver's license."

"But that's in Brooklyn!"

"Bed-sty, to be exact," I said.

"Lola and I live in Queens."

I turned the laptop to myself and called up the DMV. "The last time it was updated was five weeks ago."

"She changed her address?"

"That's also Martin's address of record," I told her.

Sierra looked very pale. One hand was steadying herself against the desk. "She's leaving me..."

"Most likely she's giving her boyfriend the food stamps. Martin can't get them himself because he's only been a New York resident for a few months."

"She's barely slept at our place for weeks."

I hesitated, hearing something in her voice. "Is that such a bad thing? It's not very good between you two."

Her lips pressed together as she turned away from the computer. "I've always had Lola. I've never been alone."

I watched her walk over to the window and stare out at the view. It gave me a pang to see her take solace in it. "I've always been alone," I told her.

That got her to turn around. I felt like I had said too much, but the concern in her eyes was reward enough.

"What about your family?"

"None to speak of."

"No mom or dad?" she asked. "Somebody must have raised you."

"Barely."

I wanted to believe in her, but all evidence pointed to the contrary. I needed to find out the truth once and for all. I couldn't stand the way my gut told me to trust her, but objective observation told me to cool it, pull back and take charge.

There was no other choice. I had to keep moving forward. I was committed now, so I had to play the game as I had always played it. And see what kind of person she turned out to be.

"Lola's profile says she's going to the Festival this weekend," I told her. "It's north of Baltimore. It

will be two whole days where you can see her. Maybe
if you talk to Martin, you'll feel better about the whole
thing."

"I don't know... what if she's angry that I
followed her there? That could be the last straw for
her."

"If you don't want her to see you, this will help."
I reached into the desk and pulled out a camouflage
face mask. It was silicone with holes punched into it,
and looked like a steampunk version of a face mask.

She put it on and went to look in the mirror by
the door. "Wow, you can't even tell it's me! And my
voice... it sounds different."

"With that, she doesn't have to know you're
there. And we can have a fun weekend besides.
Everyone should go to Festival at least once in their
lives."

"I have to work tomorrow."

"We can leave after you get off."

She pulled off the mask and considered it.
"How would we get there?"

"I'll fly us down."

Those were the magic words. Her eyes were
shining. "You'll fly us? I didn't know you could fly."

"I do it whenever I can. So what do you say?"

I had already arranged to rent one of the puddle
jumpers out of Tetterboro. My company kept a full
fleet there, and they gave us a ridiculous deal on
them to keep the flight miles up on the smaller prop
planes.

"What if I can't get off work on Saturday?" she
asked, as if afraid to get too excited.

"Call in sick," I said. "You won't regret it."

Chapter 13

Sierra

Of course I agreed. I hoped that we would end up kissing again. This time in the bed, by that glorious window. I wanted to snuggle with Victor for a long time, and ask him more about his childhood. I never met anyone who didn't have family. It was my biggest fear, losing Lola. But he lived with that reality all of the time.

So I was ready to settle in for the evening, but Victor looked at his watch and told me that he had a business dinner to go to.

I ended up on the sidewalk much quicker than my mind could process. My body was still throbbing from our first time making love, as I walked to the subway entrance. I had barely been at his place for an hour.

That's not right.

I couldn't understand how something could feel so right and so wrong at the same time.

Looking up at Victor's window, I thought about how wonderful it was going to be to go away with him. Our relationship had taken a huge leap forward really fast. Maybe I should have played harder to get, but that bus left the station when I let him touch me again at Pleasure Salon, after that awful scene in the Chamber. And then I let him stroke me until I came at the party... that was practically sex, no matter how kinky it was.

So why not do it right? And it was so right....

I was ready to fall into daydreams again, but something else was bothering me. I didn't like the idea of calling in sick for work. I rarely called in sick, and only when I had to. If I could mask the symptoms, I showed up with a smile. Lola called in sick whenever she wanted to, and that's why she could barely keep a job for six months. The one thing supervisors wanted was no surprises and a warm body on shift.

I got onto the subway and on the way north, made up my mind. I got off at 34th St/Herald Square along with the mass of rush-hour commuters. I was jostled and quick stepped it to stay up with the pack. By 5 PM, I was normally still working or long off, so I usually didn't have to deal with this crush.

I managed to peel away from the crowded rush headed for the track change, and took the stairs to the street. I had to fight the inward flow as everyone else was getting off work and heading down into the subway.

I walked straight to the store to make my plea to my boss. Kalisha was a girl on the rise, in her late twenties and that much further along in her career than me. I found her in the big storeroom. She was checking the packing slips on a load of boxes that came in against the list on her clipboard.

I realized it could blow the whole weekend away if my supervisor refused to let me off. But I had gotten this far by playing it straight. I couldn't change now.

I explained to Kalisha that my new guy wanted

to whisk me away for the weekend, but I would need to take Saturday off. Kalisha grumbled and checked the schedule, and for a second I thought I made the worst mistake ever. But then my boss relented. I had always been good about taking other girl's shifts when they couldn't make it into work, a fact that Kalisha remembered just in time to be gracious about my request.

By the time I got back on the subway, I wasn't even seeing the rush hour traffic anymore. All I could think about was going away with Victor, worry-free! I almost didn't care how Lola thought she could afford a weekend in Baltimore when she was bouncing checks and getting tattoos. I was too excited about Victor to give Lola much thought.

But when I reached my darkened apartment and saw the few remnants of Lola scattered around, reality rushed in.

When I opened Lola's closet, it was nearly empty. Lola had a habit of selling her clothes when she needed cash. Maybe that explained the drought, but more than likely her clothes were living in her new home now. In Bed-sty, a trendy neighborhood, but I'd heard it wasn't really safe in spite of the influx of hipsters and artists looking for cheap digs.

I didn't think spying on Lola at the Festival would solve anything. At this point it was more a reflexive action, trying to stave off the inevitable. I had to take any chance I could—maybe I could learn something that would keep us from flying apart like a nuclear explosion. At the very least, I had to take the chance when it was offered.

I couldn't imagine my life without Lola. We had grown up twined together like two trees, and I still needed that support. Lately I had found myself thinking more about the rest of my family, the fact that other than Lola, I had no one else I could turn to. My tired, uninterested mom. My older brother who was about to get married and hadn't even bothered to text me about it. I had to hear from my mom and then like his Facebook status. It made me felt rootless and exposed.

That's why I was going to the Festival with Victor. The breath-taking, confusing Victor. The man who had made me feel better than I'd ever felt before, and who touched me like he couldn't get enough of me. The man who had gone completely cold once the sex was over and couldn't rush me out of his place fast enough.

But he asked me to go away with him.

I spent hours packing the overnight suitcase I usually took up to my mom's for Christmas. It was too small to fit everything I wanted to take. I checked Lola's profile and found the link to the Festival website, but it didn't give much information unless you were registered, including where it was located.

I wasn't sure what kind of clothes I would need but the descriptive words on the website like "rustic" and "woodsy" gave me a clue. I packed for a series of picnics, with shorts and peasant skirts, plus my slinky halter dress in case I needed something sexy for evening. Shoes were the hardest, and I finally decided to take a huge tote that I could carry on the plane with extra shoes and toiletries.

The next day at work, I got the text from Victor: *All set. I'll pick you up at your place at 4.*

I texted back my address, while Kalisha and the other girls began calling me out for getting whisked off by my rich boyfriend. It was exciting to be dating a man like Victor. *This* was why I had worked so hard to make it in the city. To see more, do more and make the most of my life. To be surrounded by people who were trying to better themselves, who weren't satisfied with just getting by.

I wasn't satisfied with just getting by.

I was ready and waiting on my stoop when Victor pulled up in a cab. I didn't want him to see my shabby little place, not when he had such a magnificent apartment. He must already think I was low-rent. I didn't want to prove it to him.

He was in another immaculate suit, looking very sharp. I felt like a movie star, wearing my summer dress and stiletto sandals, heading off to the airport for a late flight.

The glamour continued as the car took us across the Triborough Bridge and the Washington Bridge, offering panoramic views of the city. Then we were in New Jersey and it was all grey and industrial again.

Victor instructed the cabby to avoid the main terminals when we reached the airport. When we pulled up, a man in a sky-blue uniform took our bags from the trunk before Victor could reach in. Victor smiled and tipped the man as he told him, "Gate D-12. Thank you."

I was reaching for my tote, but the guy grabbed

it and slung it onto the cart. I was so embarrassed when several shoes fell out and hit the sidewalk, scattering. A couple passing by looked down as if they were escaping rats.

"Oh, no!" I started to go over.

But the guy picked up my shoes and shoved them back into the bag with a grin. Maybe it was the way his brow raised when he glanced down at my open-toped pump, but it made me feel a little cheap. I wished Victor hadn't seen it.

Unnerved, I followed him into the grand round room of the terminal. The ceiling soared overhead, with a plane hanging in the center. A huge mural was painted around the bottom of the ceiling forming a band of figures exploring different ways to fly, including silver rocketships.

I finally lowered my gaze to find Victor watching me. The corner of his mouth was turned up. I wasn't sure if he thought my gawking was cute or pathetic.

I scurried after him to the vast sweep of a desk interspersed with terminals. It was all Greek to me as he checked us in.

The woman at the counter smiled at him. "Nice to see you again so soon, Victor. Taking a short flight today?"

"Just a weekend in the country," he said easily.

"I'm jealous," she tossed off.

She was jealous? No, I was jealous. The blond girl was pretty in her uniform. It seemed like Victor knew her well, and I wanted to ask about her, but it was impossible without it sounding awful.

Even though I had never flown before, I thought

I was faking it okay until we got through the cursory security check to the waiting room. It was a plush room, much like the designer section at my store. You knew when you walked in that this place was meant for rich people—people who wanted exactly what they wanted, when they wanted it.

There were a few groups of people lingering near the gates that studded the outer wall. They were all in business suits, like Victor, or a uniform like the blond woman at the desk. Suddenly I didn't feel as comfortable wearing my backless dress. It felt like they were all looking at me curiously.

Maybe it was inappropriate to wear a sundress on a plane. What did I know?

It was nerve-wracking, and I felt completely out of my depth. Soon the announcement came that Gate D-12 was open. I followed Victor through the door into the suddenly blinding sunlight. I couldn't see anything.

I made it down the steps by clutching the railing as hard as I could. Definitely heels weren't a good idea. And the wind whipped around and blew my skirt up so that I kept having to hold it down with my hand.

It wasn't until we reached another set of steps that I looked up. "Is this your plane?"

"Yes. I learned to fly on a plane like this one. It has sentimental value." Victor reeled off its name and designation number.

"It's so small," I said doubtfully.

"No use taking the jet out for such a short trip. Besides, this way we can stay lower to the ground.

You'll see more that way."

I shakily climbed up and had to duck to get through the doorway after him. It was tiny! I could barely stand inside, and there were only a handful of seats.

Victor took off his jacket and hung it in a narrow nook. "Come sit up front."

I followed him as he settled into the left-hand seat. Once again high heels were no help as I gingerly lowered myself into the confines of the other seat. There was a complicated board in front of me full of lights and switches, and nothing above that but a windshield.

Victor put on his headphones and started powering up the plane. It was so hot that I forgot to be afraid even when the props sputtered into motion and the sound ramped up. He knew exactly what he was doing, and his hands... those hands that worked wonders on me, now controlled the plane. The vibrations from the plane shook me right to the core.

I squirmed a little on my seat as we taxied out onto the runway. Just moving across the ground, it seemed fast. His little plane joined a line of bigger ones waiting to take off. We were dwarfed, which didn't help my fear. A rumble and whosh made me turn to see a giant airliner taking off on the runway on the other side of the terminal.

"It's so loud!" I said. But anything was better now that the rich-persons' terminal was behind me.

Victor seemed exhilarated. "This always reminds me of when I was fourteen and got into a plane for the first time. It was right before 9/11, when things were much looser. A pilot I got to know took me up while he was getting his hours. There's nothing like it..."

As he revved up the engines and we began dashing down the runway, I pressed back into my seat holding on as the plane shook so hard it felt like it would break apart. Then we leaped into the sky and the bumping stopped.

"We're up!" I exclaimed, then laughed out loud. "That was wild!"

Again, he looked at me with curious eyes, as if trying to figure me out. "Haven't you ever flown before?"

"No, this is my first time."

He shook his head slightly, as if he couldn't imagine that. I felt even more low-rent. But I had never had the money to spend on a vacation, or any reason to fly.

"Take a look at this," Victor said.

I looked past him as he banked over the Hudson River. The buildings of Manhattan were nearly within reach, their upper floors right below us.

"Fuck, yeah!" I blurted out. Then winced. Maybe that wasn't the right thing to say, but... *fuck, yeah! "This is amazing!"*

It was like that for the whole flight. Victor kept pointing out things and I kept oh'ing and ah'ing. It was the most exhilarating thing I'd ever done. By far.

Landing was the cherry on the cake. It felt like we came in so fast that I wanted to crawl through the back of my seat. But Victor set the plane down with a feather touch, and we were bumping and shaking all over again as we rolled over the tarmac.

I couldn't get enough of him. His sure hands on the controls... his voice as he spoke to the air traffic controllers... and his sharp glance as he maneuvered through the huge, bewildering maze of an airport. I felt like I was safe with him, that I could relax and he would be able to take care of me.

That's what came of dating a man who knew his way around the world.

Maybe it was a let-down after such an intense few hours, or maybe my body believed my emotions and suddenly decided to let go and relax.

I was drooping by the time we reclaimed our luggage, tired and a little dazed. And very glad that Victor seemed perfectly capable of handling everything. We were waiting on the curb for only a few minutes when a long passenger van pulled up. A bunch of people were already seated in the van, but they good-naturedly made room for us. It was hot and humid, even as the sun was setting.

We drove for what felt like ages. I let my head fall onto Victor's shoulder and dozed. I'd gotten up early for work and stayed up late last night packing.

It was dark when we finally arrived, and I couldn't see much of anything but a few telephone poles with lights at the top.

When my feet hit the ground, my high heels sank into the dirt. It was soft from the recent rain. "Oh, no!" I exclaimed, trying to scrape the mud off my heels. But there was nowhere to step.

I climbed back into the van to change my shoes, glad that I had another pair handy in my bag. I resolved to not wear heels when traveling again. I just hoped there was another time.

Everyone else from the van was gathered around the back grabbing their suitcases. By the time I joined Victor, wearing sneakers without socks, the others were disappearing down a gravel path.

We went past a few wooden buildings with front porches, overlooking a sunken meadow. Our way ran along the ridge next to the buildings.

Solar lights that people used to line driveways were stuck along the path and where other paths intersected. There were few overhead lights, and it was much darker than the parking lot.

"This one is ours," Victor said.

I was ready to collapse in a chair by the fire—I could smell wood burning—and have a tall, cold drink. I needed bucking up for what lay ahead. If the fancy airline terminals were any indication, I was not going to feel comfortable visiting the other side of the class divide any time soon.

Victor pushed open the screen door and held it for me. The room was much bigger than I had imagined, with high beamed ceilings. But then I saw the beds. There was nothing inside but a row of cots down each wall, with a rough partition in the middle that formed cubbyholes for our things. Towels were hung on two wires along the back, and someone had set up a window fan to try to stir the stifling air.

I stared at the cots that Victor claimed. He unzipped the duffle and pulled out two sleeping bags. "Here's yours."

We were in the middle of the row. The prime

spots by the windows were already claimed.

"Rustic," I murmured, looking up and around.

Victor grinned. "It's camp."

"I never went to camp when I was a kid."

"Neither did I," he admitted.

Camp had been a distant dream for me as a girl. As distant as an apartment with a view was now. In my young mind, camp had stood for the ultimate in freedom and fun. Getting away from your parents and the same old street and the same old people. Swim and play all day and sleep under the stars at night.

I wouldn't have to struggle to pretend to be something I wasn't. I could do camp. Probably much better than I could do glamour.

Suddenly I wasn't nearly as tired as before. I wanted to get out and see what the Festival was all about.

Chapter 14

Victor

I was surprised by how Sierra sprang to life once we reached the Festival. As we wandered around the extensive grounds, she practically danced along with the music that filled the air. There were bonfires going here and there, and a big one in the center of the sloping meadow. She got hold of a glow stick at some point, and forever after my memories of that night were etched with glowing green streaks and swirls.

That night, I dropped out of my jet-setting role with Sierra. I wasn't pretending to be someone else. I was just myself, enjoying being with her.

I loved the loose camouflage tank she wore over a tight white one that showed the curve of her breast when she moved. Her long legs were even more mesmerizing in her little shorts, flashing as she ran down the dirt paths. Her steampunk mask looked perfect, giving her the air of an action figure instead of an ordinary girl.

There were clutches of tents in lines along the paths and in big clusters near the tent-cabins. Each of the different areas had a theme—at one, everyone was naked. I noticed that Sierra stared for all she was worth as we passed by, but she didn't say anything.

She also didn't say anything when we saw a man casually spanking a woman as they sat on the front steps of a cabin. Inside a couple of tents we could see people having sex, and one couple was openly fucking over the railing of one of the bridges that crossed the creek. It was a heedless, anything-goes kind of place.

For dinner, we bought big bowls of stew sold from a folding table outside one of the tents. We sat cross-legged on the grass as a mock-battle raged in the dark meadow. One side was wearing camouflage, and several of them urged Sierra to join before the fray broke out. She laughingly declined, but I thought she regretted sitting it out once the nerf-ball engagement got underway. It turned out that they needed the extra man because the other side that was dressed as little kids went in with a wild scatter-formation, and whipped the camo-dudes' asses.

When we reached the bandstand, people were dancing on a large concrete floor to techno-music. The flashing lights made it the brightest place in camp. We danced for a little while, before pushing on.

At the bottom of the meadow, we crossed another bridge over the winding creek, lured on by the sound of drums. Several poles were erected in a giant teepee skeleton over the path at the entrance to a clearing. A bonfire was going in the center and people were dancing around it to the beat of at least eight drums.

I looked at Sierra, remembering the tiny drum circle at the party. The night she saw Lola's back tattoo.

Sierra settled the mask over her face as we went in. It was easy to spot Lola in the crowd—there were feathers in her hair, sticking up and dangling from long thin braids. She was nearly naked, with only a black clout, like the kind Transcendence wore at their drum circle. This time it didn't look like the group was working.

Lola kept bouncing up and running over to talk to people, gesturing a lot with her hands, more animated than I had ever seen her. Then she ran back to Martin and plastered her nearly nude body against his lanky frame. He seemed patient with her, slightly paternal with his reassuring pats and nods. He was always watching her.

Sierra had gone silent, the mask over her face. We sat on logs where we could see Lola's crew. Martin finally settled onto the ground next to June and Spike, leaning back on a log. Lola rushed over and plopped down on the ground, snuggling against him.

"I hardly recognize her." Sierra's voice was muffled by the mask.

I took another look—Lola's resemblance to Sierra was remarkable. I would recognize her anywhere. Plus there were those wings that she was flying in all their glory now, with some color added. I didn't know if Sierra could see that in the flickering light.

"She's smiling," Sierra added.

I realized she was right. That was the difference. The surly sneer was gone, and Lola was laughing and relaxed.

"Do you think she's doing drugs?" Sierra asked.

I watched more closely as Lola hung out with her lover and her friends—it looked like she knew a lot of the people here. She occasionally got up and danced around the fire, then flopped on the ground against Martin again. I had the feeling Lola had already danced for a while and was riding a post-euphoric high. Martin kept checking her back, so maybe she had been pierced again.

"I don't see any drugs," I finally said. "The producers are careful about keeping things like that out. I don't even smell marijuana."

Sierra nodded. "She's just having fun."

We stayed there for a long time, watching the dancers circle in front of us, as new people joined and others dropped out. Eventually Lola and Martin left, arms wrapped around each other, with Martin calling back something to Spike about breakfast tomorrow. They headed into the darkened area beyond, where camping tents were pitched.

Sierra let out a long sigh. I wasn't sure what she was thinking, but she looked sad.

"Do you want to go?" I asked.

She stood up, but she turned to the dancers. "Just a minute."

Sierra took a few steps toward the fire circle, picking up the rhythm of the beat. First she circled outside the dancers, but soon she melded in seamlessly, skipping and twirling in her own orbit. The others gave way, hungry for more dancers to feed the frenzy.

I sat down again, as I watched Sierra loosen up, raising her arms, and finally smiling again. I was so glad to see her feeling better that I didn't mind sitting on the bumpy log while she circled again and again.

There was something touching about her abandon.

As it went on, I wished I could feel the same way. But I knew even if I stood up and moved my body to the beat, circling the fire, it wouldn't work for me. I could never let go like that. I had never felt that childlike innocence that allowed you to trust that everything would be okay.

Because I knew it wasn't okay. There were times you were cold and hungry and nobody cared, and if you couldn't do something about it yourself, you were screwed.

But for a while I could almost feel it by watching Sierra, as she threw all care away and danced.

...

When I got up the next morning, Sierra was still face-deep in her make-shift pillow made from a towel I had brought. She had danced around the fire last night for over an hour, and I had to support her as we made our way back to our cabin. She was weaving and trying to kiss me as we walked, almost as if she was punch-drunk. Dancing in the circle had raised her endorphins, like a long-distance run, or exactly like a good scene did.

So I had tucked her in bed, kissing her smiling lips. Her eyes were already closed, and despite the noise coming from the still-partying Festival and a guy snoring over in the corner, she fell instantly asleep.

I went to breakfast alone and left a message for her, but when I got back, she was still sleeping. Two others in our cabin were also still asleep. It showed how hard she must work so that when she finally released that tension, she passed out for this long.

When she finally woke smiling, and I heard her singing in the bathroom next door in the common showers, I realized Sierra didn't have any problem with the inconveniences of camp life. Luxury wasn't a necessity for her. Unlike Adrianne, who would have hated the Festival for its bugs and noise and most of all, the other people rubbing elbows with us in the cabin.

I had expected that Sierra, with her high heels and pretty dresses, wouldn't like to be without a fully-stocked private bathroom and her own plug for her flat iron. But she twisted her hair into two knobs on the top of her head, like perky ears, and was ready in minutes, sans makeup. I liked that about her.

We spent the afternoon in the giant pool outside the mess hall. It was busy and people came and went, while we lay in the deck chairs or bobbed in the water on noodles. The sun moved in and out of clouds, keeping it from getting too hot. Her swimming wasn't very good—it was actually dog paddling. She said her brothers used to take Lola and her to the public pool a few blocks away when they were kids. I could tell the pool was a place she remembered fondly.

I would have been perfectly happy, but she made a few comments about how wonderful it must be to swim in the fancy hotel pools when I traveled. And how great it must be to be able to get away from city heat whenever I wanted to. She also asked me more about places I had visited, like Thailand and

Peru, and had I ever been to Egypt to see the pyramids? I usually liked to talk about my travels—it was the best thing in my life.

But I didn't like the eager way she asked, like she was imagining herself going along with me. And that wasn't something I could give her. Only a client could invite people onboard.

I also noticed that even though she wasn't high-maintenance, she never once offered to pay for food or drinks, and she happily accepted a chain rope bracelet I bought for her when she admired it on the marketplace row where vendors were selling toys and clothes. For me, this weekend was blowing my entire savings. Renting a plane to impress my girl was not in my budget. But she didn't think anything of it because she assumed I was rich and could give her this trip with a snap of my fingers.

Keeping a running tally on her kept me from thoroughly enjoying myself like I did the last night. There were times when I caught her looking at me curiously as the black thoughts consumed me, making me frown or turn away from her.

One thing was undeniable—I couldn't keep my hands off her. In the pool, my fingers slid over her wet waist, cupping her curves, supporting her butt as I held her in the water. We kept kissing each other, long and slow, as people splashed around us.

She didn't suggest that we go back to the drum circle where Lola was camping. I didn't suggest it either. I didn't want her distracted from me.

When we finally tired of the pool, and were wandering back to our cabin, we were drawn to the cool shade of the barn that had been converted into a giant hall with a stage across one end. Play furniture was set up here and there, along with giant pulleys that riggers used for suspension bondage. This was one of the places that had been packed last night with people playing, but Sierra had taken one look and turned away. She wasn't a voyeur and the sounds of people crying out seemed to be too much for her.

But today it was empty. The late afternoon sunlight slanted through one door, catching motes in the beam.

This time when we kissed, there was a new urgency. The long teasing caresses all afternoon suddenly exploded between us, now that we were away from the watching eyes. We strained against each other, as if we couldn't get enough.

She ran her hand down to stroke my cock through my swim shorts. It stiffened from turgid to rigid under her fingers. I groaned as she encircled it with her hand, sending a shiver down my spine.

"I wish we had someplace private to go," she murmured between kisses.

I backed her up to the stage. "This looks private enough to me."

"Here?" She looked around. "Look at the doors. They're open."

Through the doors, we could see people outside walking back and forth. Dinner would be starting soon in the mess hall.

"I don't care if anyone sees. People are having sex all over."

"I care!"

I shrugged. "Then we won't."

I kept kissing her, drowning in her, losing myself in the smell of her skin and the soft fullness of her lips. I dared to hope this could be real, that it wasn't just my promise of wealth that turned her on.

I kissed down to her neck, and she arched back against the stage. Her lips opened with a moan. The luscious softness of her made me crazy.

Putting my hands at her waist, I lifted her up so she was sitting on the stage. It was the perfect height for me to press my cock against her crotch. Her legs wrapped around me, holding on. It wasn't sex—we still had our swim suits on—but it was as close as you could get. I loved the flair of her hips under my palms, as she ground herself against me.

Then I realized she was taking quick looks through the doors, wary of someone walking in on us. I pulled off my bandana and held it between us in both hands.

"Let me put this over your eyes," I said.

Nervously, she checked the doors again.

"It will help you relax," I told her. "And heighten your other senses."

She looked into my eyes. I couldn't see where the pupils ended and her irises began, they were one dark pool. I felt like I was looking inside of her. I knew I could hurt her because I had done it before. But it would be worse now because she trusted me.

Then she let go, like she did last night at the drum circle. Her shoulders relaxed, and she nodded, gazing deep into my eyes.

I kissed her, holding her cheek. Like a promise that I wouldn't fail her.

I placed the blindfold over her eyes and tied it at the back of her head. She touched it, sightless. It made me feel bigger to see her go helpless in front of me.

Slowly at first, I began to grind against her again. Now she felt every motion, no longer distracted. I always wanted her this way, completely focused on me. I knew it was just a game, but it meant more than that somehow.

She arched back in my arms, her legs tightening around me. Though constricted by my trunks, I rubbed the length of my cock up against her, right against her pussy.

We rocked together, like we were resting on the ocean waves, lifted up and down together.

"Yes...," she breathed.

"Yes," I agreed through clenched teeth. "I want you."

"Yes."

Her hips moved back and forth, urging me on.

"Yes?" I asked. My fingers went down to her crotch, feeling the slick dampness on her inner thigh. My fingers shifted aside the fabric of her suit, pressing against her silky lips.

Her inward gasp drove me higher. By sheer force of will, I held myself on the edge of sanity. I couldn't go further, though every fiber of my being was screaming at me to get inside of her. To pound her and never stop—

"Yes!" she exclaimed. "I want to."

"You do?"

"Yes!"

Shoving down my trunks, my cock was out and pressing against her pussy. As I pushed the tip inside of her, she tilted back, letting me in deeper. That was all the encouragement I needed.

I pumped into her, lifting her off the edge of the stage and holding her hips. Possessing her completely, feeling every breath and clenching muscle in her body responding to me...

And suddenly I was stripped bare again, feeling like nothing could come between us.

She rode me, crying out as she came. It went on for longer than I thought possible, as she arched and strained against me.

As she gradually went limp in my arms in a post-euphoric daze, I laid her back on the stage and lifted her legs so I could dive even deeper. She was laid out for me, open for me, giving herself to me.

As I pumped into her, I leaned over. My lips were close to her ear, as I murmured, "They love watching you."

Her body tightened as she gasped. "Watching...," she repeated breathlessly.

Her hands went to her blindfold, as if to take it off, but I blocked her. "Leave it."

She slowly dropped her hands to my shoulders.

"They love how you move, like I do," I whispered. "Like your whole being is being consumed."

I kept thrusting into her, loving how she let me do it, even when I told her people were watching us.

She wanted to give me that. She wouldn't stop me, even though she could. Because she wanted to please me.

"I'm letting them watch you," I growled into her ear. "To prove to you that you're *mine*. I can do whatever I want with your body. Because it's *mine*."

Her back arched and she began to come again, surprising us both. It sent me right over the top. I had never felt so connected to anyone, like we were both feeling everything together. My breath was her breath, and we needed each other to survive.

As my climax overtook me, crimson waves ran over my sight. The last thing I saw was Sierra, her hair fanned out on the old wooden stage floor, her skin glowing with life and sunlit fire. Her eyes covered because I wanted her to only see me.

I collapsed on her, weak-kneed, my strength sapped by this beautiful woman. I only knew that I had completely opened myself to her.

Maybe this one is for real.

Chapter 15

Sierra

I wanted to lose myself in the wonderful feeling of Victor lying on top of me, a welcome comforting weight. My fingers idly twined in his silky bronzed hair at the back of his tanned neck, cherishing the softness of him there. If we had been in bed, I could have laid there forever.

But I kept thinking about the people watching me. Like he said.

Sneaking one hand up to my face, I lifted the blindfold. Only to see... nothing

Nobody was in the barn. Through the closest door, people were walking past outside in the meadow, but there was nobody inside.

"There's nobody here," I said with a laugh. "Why did you say that?"

"It made you come." His smile was wicked.

I put my hand to my mouth. He was right—I had come like being struck by lightning. Only it wasn't the thought of being watched. It was him, his hands, his voice in my ear, telling me that I belonged to him.

I felt almost shy with him, as if I had revealed more than I intended. When he said "mine" my heart had sung. I felt giddy and happier than I had ever felt before. Could I really be this lucky? To find a man like this, in such an unlikely way...

But Victor wasn't easy to read. There were moments when he was so distant that it seemed like he wished he wasn't here with me. Like when I reminded him of the differences between us. I knew I wasn't like the usual kind of girl he dated. I had a feeling he wanted me to forget about that, but how could I? He was way out of my league. The more I saw of him, the more I realized that. Maybe he was okay with camping once in a while, but if I wanted this to be more than a wild fling, sooner or later I was going to have to go into his world and see if I could get by on his terms.

But for now, making love to him made it nearly perfect.

If only I didn't have to deal with Lola. But camp had shown me something I hadn't realized before. No wonder Lola would rather hang out with her grubby nudist friends rather than with me. She looked happy with them. It looked like it was playtime for her, like I was having playtime with Victor. But I knew it wasn't real. How long could this last for both of us? In the back of my mind, I kept thinking about our bills coming due next weekend.

I looked for my sister at dinner, but Lola was nowhere to be seen.

Afterwards, Victor pulled me into a hammock on the edge of the meadow and we watched the Festival flow by in the slowly fading twilight.

With my head tucked onto his chest, he rocked us with one foot. I knew it was a risk that he would pull away again, but I had to find out more about him.

"So who did raise you, Victor?"

His body went very still. I realized he had been nice and relaxed, and with one question I had destroyed his mood. I had been hoping for a better reaction than that.

"Family is important to me," I tried to explain. "I wouldn't have survived without Lola and my brothers. My mom could barely keep a roof over our heads."

After a few moments, he said, "My grandparents raised me." As if realizing that wasn't giving me much, he added, "They weren't exactly thrilled about it."

"What happened to your mom?"

"She's out of the picture. At least it taught me that you can't depend on anyone, not even family."

I lifted my head to look at him. "That's not true! We all depend on people."

"You only get let down." His voice roughened. "We're alone in life. The sooner you rely on yourself, the better off you are."

A jolt of panic went through me. I depended on Lola. But Lola had never been what you call reliable. And now most of my sister's things were gone. Could Lola really abandon me?

I sat up, wondering if I should go down to that primal camp and confront Lola right now. But she would hate that. She wouldn't like it that I was here. Especially after what had happened with Dick.

"What's wrong?" Victor asked me.

I sat on the edge of the hammock looking down at him. "It's what you just said. I'm not sure I'd be okay alone—"

I stood up and came face-to-face with my sister. Lola's eyes went wide and she could only point at me for a few moments, speechless.

My mask was hanging around my neck, forgotten. I figured there was nothing to do but face it. "Hi, Lola."

"You! What are you doing here?"

Martin was with Lola, so I held out my hand to him. "Hi, I'm Lola's sister, Sierra. I've been wanting to meet you."

Martin smiled. I had a hard time seeing past his scarred skin, but his eyes were very sharp and knowing. Like he had seen my kind of reaction to his face before and was used to getting past it. "Lola's told me a lot about you," he said. "She says you're finishing your degree this summer."

Lola stepped between us. "Why are you talking to her?" she asked Martin. "Can't you see she's here spying on me?"

"I'm worried about you, Lola," I said. "I never see you. You never talk to me. You're off doing... kind of *extreme* things. What sister wouldn't be worried?"

"I can take care of myself."

"Can you?" I shot back, losing my cool for a minute. "Because I seriously doubt it. You haven't ever been on your own."

"I am now," Lola declared. "I'm moving out at the end of the month."

I stared at her, shocked. "But that's next weekend! What about the rent?"

"I'm not living there anymore."

"Lola, you can't just leave. I can't afford our

apartment without you."

"Get a roommate."

"It's a one bedroom!"

We glared at each other. Martin was right behind Lola, looking really concerned now. Victor was standing next to the hammock, awkwardly watching our battle.

"How could you do this to me?!" I exclaimed.

"All you care about is yourself," Lola flung back. "It always has to be your way. I'm done with it. I'm doing what I want, now."

I could hardly think, I was so angry. I did everything for Lola. I took care of our place and made sure we survived on our own for the past three years. And this was how she treated me?

I appealed to Martin. "Don't you think Lola should have told me? How am I supposed to find the money on my own? I'm going to get kicked out of my apartment if I don't pay the rent."

Lola pointed to Victor. "Why don't you ask him? You made me ask Dick enough times. Now it's your turn to make your boyfriend pay."

I realized Lola was pointing at Victor. I wanted to die. It was bad enough that I was fighting with her in front of him, but that was a really low blow. "I don't care how you get it, Lola. Just get me your half of the rent next week. You have to give me a month to find another place."

"You've been spying on me. I don't have to do anything." Lola grabbed Martin's arm, and dragged him down the path heading back to the primal camp.

I stood there breathing fast like I had just

dashed across the meadow. It was all blown up, scattered in pieces around me. The beautiful life I had built in the city was gone along with my sister. I had never realized on what fragile ground I had built my dream of living in New York.

I didn't know what to do. I didn't even have the option of moving in with my mom. I would never go back to sleeping on that sofa bed and watching the weekly parade of men. Besides, the commute was deadly.

I had no other options.

Then I turned to look at Victor, and my heart sank. His eyes were cold. Brawling with my sister in public, airing our dirty laundry for everyone to hear... I felt like a Jerry Springer reject.

While he was a Rolls Royce.

And to top it off, Lola had called him my boyfriend. From the expression on his face, there was no way he was liking that.

I was just a hot piece of ass to him.

I had lost him. Before I ever really had him. I knew it was far-fetched from the beginning that a man like Victor could want a girl like me, no matter how many romantic movies pretended otherwise. But to see him draw away from me only hours after the best love-making of my life, made me tear up.

Chapter 16

Victor

"Everything okay here?" a deep voice asked.

I turned to find Josh had come up behind me. Josh was even taller than me, a real bear of a man. I had played with his girlfriend a few years ago, before they got together, and she had introduced us. To give him credit, I never felt an ounce of jealousy from Josh over the fact that I had been with his girl first.

"The sisters were having some words," I explained.

Sierra was watching Lola storm off, but she turned back to Josh. "I'm sorry. I know you people don't like drama."

"Not a problem." Josh had a sweet smile for such a big man. "Just making sure everything is okay."

Josh was wearing a walkie and had a yellow ribbon on indicating he was part of the volunteer staff for the Festival.

I wondered if Sierra knew. She looked sorry enough.

"It's okay," she told Josh. "We've got nothing else to say to each other."

"Is she your twin?" Josh asked. "You two look a lot alike."

"I'm a year older."

Josh grinned. "Could of sworn you were twins."

Josh gave me a warm pat on the back of my shoulder before walking away. His last admiring look was for Sierra, but she didn't notice.

As I glanced around, I realized a lot of people were dispersing, having watched the fight. I recognized Pierce, an English guy who was living in New York, hanging out on the periphery of the scene. His accent was his magic ticket, like my faux-millions were mine. Pierce gave me the nod, looking appreciatively at Sierra. He was exactly was the kind of man I didn't want Sierra to end up with.

A man like me.

We were left standing there by the hammock, looking at each other.

Seeing Sierra's eyes bright with tears had a weird affect on me. I wanted to put my arms around her and tell her everything would be all right. But I knew it wasn't true. Sometimes it wasn't all right. Sometimes it sucked big time.

Sometimes it crushed you.

And from what it sounded like, her sister was leaving her high and dry.

But how could I comfort her with Lola's words ringing in my ears— *Now it's your turn to make your boyfriend pay.*

They had lived off Lola's boyfriend, that sad-sack cop. Obviously Sierra was comfortable doing that. And I was just starting to be convinced that she wasn't liking me because I had money.

After a few moments, Sierra said, "I'm going back to the cabin to lie down for a while."

"Sounds good," I managed to say.

Without another word, she walked off into the growing darkness.

I felt like a heel. I should go after her and tell her the truth about myself, so I wouldn't have to play a role with her anymore. Then I would know. She would probably reject me soundly, and that would make getting home very difficult.

The last time I told a girl the truth, it had gone very badly. It was many years ago, before I knew how powerful kinky sex could be on the psyche. For people just starting out, especially. I had a whirlwind affair with a girl called Cherry, training her to serve me exactly how I wanted, and before I knew it, she expected everything from me. She knew me as *Victor*, a successful, powerful businessman, and with the formal rules of a master, I was able to keep the perfect balancing act going for longer than I imagined possible.

But what I thought was devotion turned into obsession. And neediness. When I realized she was in love with me, and it wasn't really *me* she was in love with, I finally told Cherry that I was just a pilot, not a millionaire. She thought she could make me marry her by holding the lie over my head, but I refused to play along. So she told people the truth. But anyone could see by that time that she was spinning out of control. She had a wild look in her eye that made people nod cautiously and turn away. I shrugged it off whenever someone asked me about what she was saying—about my job, about me promising to take care of her for the rest of her life. Nobody took her seriously.

Cherry finally dropped out of sight and I hadn't heard of her in the years since.

Sierra liked *Victor*—she didn't know anything about Vic. She may not be high-maintenance, but she liked the illusion I had created for her.

Right now, when she needed help, I couldn't bear to see her turn into another Cherry. Clinging to anyone who could save her. I was so afraid it would happen with Sierra that I couldn't let it.

I checked on her a couple times that night, but she was sleeping. Several people stopped me as I wandered around the camp and asked about the "twin fight." It was the hot gossip of the Festival. Some people claimed they had heard the girls were rolling around on the ground and pulling each other's hair like in a real catfight.

I didn't like being this notorious. My gig worked because I kept as low a profile as possible. But now, looking around and recognizing people, I realized there were at least a dozen people I knew from the city. Without being aware of it, I had become friendly with a lot of people, under false pretenses.

If I told Sierra, she would tell others here and it would blow up in my face. The spotlight was already on us. I was going to be lucky if I got out of this intact.

But part of me wanted to tell her, just to blow up all of my lies once and for all.

Then what? This was my life.

I wished it was possible to have a repeat of last night, when we both were so free. Or this afternoon in the barn when she made me feel better than I had ever felt before, like she was in the palm of my hand. Like I could do anything because I could blow her mind.

But I couldn't do that in my role anymore, not while I was lying to her. So I was okay with finding, every time I checked, that she slept the night away.

As I wandered around the Festival, I felt oddly displaced, like I was watching myself watch everyone else having fun. A few girls tried to flirt with me, but I was so tightly wound that I couldn't respond. It was like the Festival had turned into a completely different place, with everything flat and devoid of meaning and color.

When I woke in my cot the next morning, Sierra was already gone. Her sleeping bag was neatly rolled and her cubby was empty with her bag ready to go. The other cubbies were still spilling over with personal stuff.

I found Sierra in the mess hall. Her laptop was plugged into the wall and she was searching the screen intently.

"Morning! What's up?" I asked her.

"Morning," she said with a smile. "I'm searching Craigslist for a room for rent. Do you know where Canarsie is?"

"Brooklyn."

"I see that." She tilted her head at the screen. "It's on the other side of JFK airport. I bet that's some commute into the city. How long does it take on the subway?"

I realized she was looking at me expectantly. "I usually fly out of LaGuardia. I don't know, maybe forty-five minutes."

"Plus there's a transfer at Broadway Junction," she said thoughtfully, her eyes back on the screen.

Since Sierra was absorbed in her computer, I went over and got some breakfast and coffee. When I came back to sit across from her, she barely looked up at me as I ate.

"Here's one," she would say occasionally. "Room in single family house in Flushing." Or "$500 for a nook off the living room. That doesn't sound reasonable, does it?"

Finally she said, "Here's an okay one, but it's not available until next month. If only Lola would pay for her half of August rent, then I would have options."

"Just don't pay rent," I suggested. "You won't get an eviction notice the first month. They'll use your security deposit."

"I hate it, but if she bails, I might have to do that," she sighed. "I don't want trouble. But everyone expects first month and security deposit, and some of these people want last month's rent, too. Then I would need at least $1,500 to get into a new place. I don't have that."

Her money talk was making me feel very uncomfortable. I couldn't shake the feeling she was fishing. Like she expected me to help her out. If I had $1,500, I probably would have given it to her. She was worth it. I had already proven that by blowing nearly that much on this weekend.

But it still seemed hollow compared to our first twenty-four hours of Festival, when we had truly meshed together, with no ulterior motives other than having fun.

Or so I thought.

The feeling of watching myself continued throughout the morning as Sierra sent out emails asking about rooms for rent and talked to people on the phone. During the long van ride back to the airport, she sat silent for the most part. The others chatted happily about the things they had done at the Festival.

In the airport, I took her to the sky lounge which had a great view of the airport. But this time, instead of losing herself in the experience, she promptly plugged in her laptop and continued her search.

Finally I couldn't hold it in any longer. "If you need help, I can loan you some—"

Sierra gave a short laugh, cutting me off. "No, I'm going to have to do this myself. Like you said, we're all alone in life. And the sooner I face that, the better."

My heart sank. I knew for a fact that she wouldn't be here with me if Monica hadn't told her that I was rich. And now she felt abandoned by me. She was right, but for the wrong reasons. There was nothing I could say about it other than confess the truth, so I sat there silently.

We barely spoke during the plane ride. When I dropped her off in front of her stoop and got out to get her bag from the trunk, she gave me her practiced smile and said, "Thank you for taking me down to see Lola. Even though it turned out so badly, I'm glad it's finally settled. I couldn't have done it without you."

"I wish I hadn't suggested we go down there. You wouldn't be in this position."

"I think Lola was going to stiff me no matter what I did. The way she talked to me... I've never heard her say those kinds of things to me before."

"I'm sorry." I wasn't sure what else I could say.

"You've been really sweet," she said sadly. She was trying to smile, but I could tell it was too difficult. "Thank you for everything."

Sierra turned and carried her bag up the steps before I could pick it up again. I had expected a hug, at least. I stood there staring up at her as she let herself into the building. With a little wave, she disappeared inside.

I wanted to call her back out and say everything that had stopped up my mouth all day. Confess everything. But I knew what kind of girl she was, and she wouldn't be forgiving to find out I had lied to her from the beginning. Since I couldn't be the man she wanted me to be, my only other option was to leave.

Chapter 17

Sierra

I stepped into my apartment feeling like a stranger. It was so drab and sad-looking, exactly like I felt. A month ago it had been wreathed in golden rosy colors, a necessary step towards my vision of living a successful life in the city.

Shabby or not, this would be gone soon. Victor was so right—I had to depend on myself, or the rug would be pulled out from under me again. It was stupid to rely on Lola when I had seen over the past year that she wasn't capable of pulling her own weight. I should have made a change sooner instead of waiting until Lola self-destructed.

The situation with Victor made it even worse. We both were in sad, distant moods on the flight back. I would never forget the tone of his voice as he reluctantly offered to lend me money. Humiliating! Like he had been expecting me to try to leech off him, and I had proven his suspicions in one fatal day.

I had hoped he would see that I was taking care of myself by organizing my room-for-rent hunt, but honesty about my situation had gained me nothing with him. His good opinion had already been thoroughly blown. He didn't want anything to do with me after my fight with Lola.

It was especially humiliating because I was falling for him. I could hardly think about him without flushing, remembering how he knew my body so well. His voice in my ear would linger with me forever. His touch was seared into my skin—how he had lifted me to the stage like I weighed nothing, kissing me like he would never stop.

That was passion I had never imagined before. It wiped out everything else in my past like it was dust. If I still had that with Victor, I wouldn't be nearly as upset about Lola's bombshell. With a man like that by my side, I could get through anything.

But he wasn't by my side. He had a whole other life. And I had no place in it. It felt like I wasn't good enough, and I hated that. I prided myself on being competent and knowing I was making good things happen for myself. I didn't need someone looking down on me. Especially right now when I was barely treading water.

A knock on the door interrupted my unpacking. When I went to the peephole, Dick was standing outside.

Irritation flushed through me. None of this would have happened if Dick hadn't thrown me in the deep end at the Chamber.

I flung open the door. "What do you want?"

"I want to see Lola."

I kept blocking his way. "She's not here."

"I can see that. I want to know where she is."

"I don't know. She hasn't given me her forwarding address."

As soon as I said it, I realized my mistake. His hand gripped the door, pushing me inward. When we were both inside the tiny kitchen, he shut the door behind us.

"You mean Lola's moved out?"

"Yeah." The way his eyes shifted made me uneasy. "So you might as well stop trying to stalk her here."

"Where is she?"

"I told you, I don't know!" Actually, I did remember the address in Bed-sty that Victor had shown me on the computer. But I wasn't going to tell Dick that.

He looked at me with hard eyes. "You better not be lying to me." With that, he strode into our bedroom.

"Hey! Wait a minute, Dick—"

He opened Lola's closet and saw the empty space, with the discards left behind. Then he went into the bathroom and rifled through the medicine cabinet. "Gone, it's all gone!" Whirling on me, he took my arms in both hands, giving me a shake. "Where is she?"

I tried to get away, but he was too strong. "You're hurting me, Dick!"

His fingers eased, but he didn't let go. "Tell me, where is she?"

"She's living with Martin!" I exclaimed. "Don't *you* know where? You've been spying on her for weeks."

He finally let me go. "She quit her job. I've been hanging around here but she never shows."

I rubbed my arms. I was suddenly glad that I didn't have to care that Lola had quit her job. That was her problem, not mine. "Take the hint, Dick.

She's moved on. She's left both of us behind."

"Not you," he protested.

"Yes, *me*. She won't talk to me anymore."

"Where were you this weekend? I know where she was because she puts it out there for the world to see. She was at a pagan bondage festival down in Maryland."

"Lola's a big girl. She's taking care of herself."

"She's just twenty! What does your mom think? I'd be furious if I was her."

"I don't know." In fact, our mom knew nothing about what was going on. And I doubted she would care. She would be most afraid that one of us would try to move back to her place. But Dick didn't know about that. He had only met our mom once, and he had dominated the conversation with his insistence that he could take care of Lola for her. He didn't realize that our mom had never taken care of Lola. I did.

"So you don't care about Lola anymore?" he demanded, like he was reading my mind.

"Lola's made her choice. She's on her own. Like I'm on my own."

"You're making a huge mistake. You're going to regret it when your sister pays the price."

I didn't like the sound of that. But Dick was sweating and flushed and I didn't want to rile him up any further. I moved toward the door. "I'll let you know if I get a forwarding address from her, Dick."

He hesitated. "You better not be lying to me."

"Why would I lie? I'm mad at Lola. If I could, I'd sic you on her in a heartbeat."

He must have heard my very real anger because he finally backed down. "Make sure you do."

It was tense going until I got him out the door and bolted it behind him. I had never been scared of Dick before, but he had scared me when he grabbed my arms. I rubbed the reddened skin. Lola had said he wasn't a nice guy sometimes. Maybe she had seen this side of him, too.

It was not good.

I wished I had someone to talk to about this. When I turned out the light on the empty apartment, with the sounds of the city pressing in on all sides, I had never felt so lonely. I almost looked forward to the idea of moving to an apartment where I had roommates. At least I wouldn't be alone anymore.

•••

Over the next few days, all of my free time was spent on the subway going from room sublet to roommate shares. So many people were desperately looking for a place this close to the end of the month that I started to run into the same faces—like the red-headed guy on the bike and the girl who wore a black watch cap even though we were going through a hot and humid spell.

The entire city stank in the summer heat wave, as if warning me that New York was going to pound me into the ground before it was done with me. Any illusion I had that hard work would be enough was destroyed by this dismal come-down from my apartment to a measly room share.

It was heartbreaking to be judged and dismissed by the people showing off their apartments, sometimes before I opened my mouth. I didn't know whether it was because I was young or because my income was scary and nobody wanted to trust it. They were eyeing me like I was a potential Lola, and it was infuriating because I didn't get into this state by my own doing. Unless you considered trusting my sister to be a fault.

The apartments were not good, and the ones that were barely acceptable had serious flaws, like a very long commute or weird roommates. I started to think I didn't want to room with men. The way they looked at me was not right. Not if I wanted to be able to get milk from the fridge at night.

Working the pavement brought back memories of when I was eighteen and had just graduated from high school, and was eager to get started with my new life in the city. I had hoped for a studio apartment of my own, but that cost too much for me. So I had looked at roommate share situations and found that nobody would rent to me until I had a job for six months.

That started my year of commuting from Tarrytown to Midtown. A lot of my paycheck went to paying for the train. The rest I saved up, and once Lola was free, I found our little one bedroom that barely had space for two single beds. It was on Ditmars Blvd with traffic always crisscrossing on it, so it was noisy even at night. And when the wind was from the north, I could smell the sluggish East River in the industrial bays.

Maybe Lola was right and I had used her to afford our place in Astoria. Even though Lola didn't have the same dream as I did about making it in the city.

I sure hoped Lola was doing what was best for her now. Because I wouldn't be able to help if she couldn't handle the shark-infested waters.

The worst was, I never heard from Victor. Not once.

It was impossible not to think about him. I thought of him constantly in my long trips to the distant corners of the city. I kept thinking about how I had messed up with him, and the way his eyes went gray and flat as he withdrew from me. It hurt so much. So I pushed that away to remember how his hands had taken hold of my waist, pulling me in close to him. How strong and big he was, lifting me with ease. His warm breath against my face as he was deep inside of me…

It took me back instantly to those moments, and I was lost in the pleasure again, as the remembered sensations washed through me. It was the drug I used to get through the pain. When I was lost in those moments, everything else receded: the faces on the subway or bus, the confusion of new streets, of being afraid and trying to deal with suddenly being uprooted.

My own neighborhood felt strange because I knew I no longer belonged there. Soon I wouldn't be buying my morning coffee at that corner deli or shopping for groceries in the bodega by the subway station. It really hurt that I wouldn't be able to walk in the park along the East River anymore and watch the tugs go by.

Doggedly I went through my days, going to work and even making it to class on Wednesday. At that moment, making it to class felt pretty heroic. Every other second was spent trying to find a new home.

I normally would have kept my troubles to myself at work, ever mindful of my need to rise in the ranks. But I couldn't pretend that the weekend went great when it had been a complete disaster, resulting in the need to find a new apartment and the loss of my potential most-sexy boyfriend. The girls were sympathetic, including Kalisha, and they agreed that the only thing rich men wanted from girls like us was sex on the side with no strings attached.

It didn't occur to me to go to my family with my complaints. They had their own problems to deal with. My older brother had helped me out before, but according to his Facebook updates, he was also searching for a new place to rent upstate where he could live with his fiancé.

Besides, it wasn't so much money that I needed. I needed a room in the city that wasn't awful, where I could try to rebuild my life.

At one point I found myself sitting on a bench, not sure where I was. The search had overwhelmed me. People streamed by in a sea of scissoring legs, nobody noticing me.

I was lost.

Nobody cared. Nobody came to help me. I don't know how long I sat there until I realized that if I didn't pick up my own butt and get on my feet, everything I had worked for would be ruined. I couldn't let myself slide back into living in Peekskill or Tarrytown or wherever my mom had landed this month. I had to fight, even when there was no fight left in me.

Standing back up from that bench, I felt like was in a deep, deep hole. And I would have to claw my way out one step at a time.

The first step was the worst. But after that, I went into auto-pilot, turning off my mind as I smiled at the next prospective roommates, ignored the rejection and refused to get my hopes up. It was easier that way, to go numb. Numb was better than feeling so awful.

After work on Friday, my first appointment took me on the 7 train only one stop into Queens to Long Island City, where I got a bus to go over the Pulaski Bridge into Greenpoint. It was one of the closest places I had seen advertised, but the big disadvantage was that it was nowhere near a subway line into the city. Waiting for the bus among a crowd of stoic commuters was no fun, and I could tell it would be freezing in the winter with wind blowing off the river. But as a bonus the city skyline was practically within arm's reach.

The bus let me off on McGuinness Blvd, a very busy 6-lane artery that carried truck traffic along the industrial corridor west of the Brooklyn-Queens Expressway. Greenpoint looked a lot like my Astoria neighborhood with two-family houses mixed in with tenement buildings and small warehouses. There were lots of trees, which I liked. Even though I was tired, I perked up on the two block walk from the bus stop.

The address was for a big blocky building, three stories high. The brick wall on the ground floor had a large bay door. A mural covered it like graffiti writ large. I had to check to make sure it was the right place. It looked like a warehouse.

Buzzing the 2nd floor, a scratchy voice told me to come up.

The black-painted stairs reminded me unpleasantly of the Chamber, but here light poured down from the ancient skylight in the ceiling. Several bikes were chained to the pipes running up the walls, and the garbage cans smelled terrible.

At the top of the first flight of stairs was a table piled with envelopes, so many they were spilling off. A guy opened the door and saw me looking down at them.

"We need to toss all that. Mostly it's for old tenants and junk mail. Every few months the landlord throws it away." He smiled at me. "Are you Sierra or Lucy?"

"Sierra." Strike one against the place—he was a guy.

He opened the door for me to come in. His black hair was so curly it made corkscrews falling around his bony face. He was smiling a lot, and had that overly-relaxed bohemian air. "I'm Jake. This is it!"

His hand swept out to encompass a large room with three battered couches of various colors and sizes, with tables scattered among them. A large plain dining table was closest to the door with eight assorted chairs pulled haphazardly around it.

I was kind of appalled, especially when I saw the large bathroom created by drywall to create an open-air nook, exactly like the kitchen area. There were two refrigerators in the kitchen, and Jake showed me the cabinet that would be mine and the empty shelves in one fridge waiting for the new occupant.

"How many people live here?" I asked faintly.

"There's five bedrooms."

Strike two—I couldn't imagine sharing an apartment with that many people.

Lining one long wall were a series of doors. One of them had a padlock on it. "Marky is out of town. He travels with a touring company. I think he's in Phoenix this week."

Near the back, Jake flung open a door to reveal an eight by ten room. A sturdy wooden loft bed filled the end wall over the window that had lots of small rectangular panes. It was actually half of a window with the makeshift wall cutting it in half so it was shared by the room next door.

"You can open this part," Jake explained, turning the handle so one pane of the window swung outward. "You have two in here. I almost swiped this room when Sheila left, but I like being on the front end. It's quieter than back here by the kitchen."

"That's some sales pitch you have there."

Jake laughed. "It is what it is. You want to see the roof? We like to hang out there in the evening."

"Who's we?"

"The folks on our floor and the third floor.

There's eight rooms up there. Ours is smaller because the landlord lives in the back, through that door."

I looked at yet another black-painted door between the kitchen and the last room. "His place is through there?"

"Yeah. It's handy when the toilet stops up."

"I'm sure."

I followed Jake up the stairs, but I didn't know why I was bothering. This was *not* the place for me. Most definitely.

Then I was on the tar-paper roof looking at one of the best views of the city I had ever seen. Manhattan stretched north and south, the golden glow of the afternoon sun catching the windows.

"Wow!" I exclaimed. "You can see all of the bridges!"

"You should see it at night," Jake told me. "We watched the fireworks from here on the Fourth. We have a huge party every year."

From the trio over in one corner, an obnoxiously loud voice called, "She's invited next year! Jake, tell your pretty friend she's invited."

The invite came from the heavy-set guy reclining in the folding chair next to some boxed soil where vegetables grew. The man and two women were sitting under the shade cast by a big umbrella.

"She's here to see Sheila's room," Jake explained.

I followed him over. The man was wearing beaten-up shorts and a T-shirt, and his cheeks had four days stubble on them. But his head was perfectly smooth and bald.

"Keith, Candice and Devi, this is Sierra," Jake introduced.

The three of them nodded at me, looking me over. It was every horrible experience I had gone through in my room search, all rolled into one. I felt judged and dismissed in seconds.

Devi turned to Candice and asked, "Why is she smiling weird like that?" Devi was all softness: soft white flesh, soft beige clothes, and soft washed-out hair.

"I don't know." Candice's blunt voice much lower than I expected. After a moment, I realized Candice might be a guy. Or a very manly woman who was rocking a black chiffon blouse.

"This isn't a job interview, honey," Candice told me, raising her voice like I was a little slow.

I realized I *was* smiling. It was my at-work face that I wore without thinking anymore. The pleasant approachable face I put on around people I needed to please. It was the trick that Lola could never learn, or never wanted to learn.

That reminded me of how happy Lola had looked at Festival, before our fight.

My smile vanished.

"That's better," Devi said in her high wispy voice.

Jake was still standing there, and he was grinning from ear-to-ear. I asked, "How come he can smile and not me?"

"Jake means it," Devi said.

I had no defense without my smile-shield, so my feelings of loss and unhappiness lapped over me.

"Most people don't want to rent a room to someone who's a downer."

"Are you a downer?" Devi asked curiously.

"Not usually. But it's been a bad week. That's why I'm looking for a place."

Candice sat forward eagerly. "Divorce? Cheating boyfriend? Murdered roommate?"

"Uh… no." I gave her a look. "My sister left and I can't afford my apartment without her."

Candice and Devi sat back, clearly disappointed that I didn't have a juicier story. I had failed to impress the owners of yet another apartment I didn't want. It was demoralizing.

But Keith finally spoke again, declaring, "You look like you need a beer."

He popped open the cooler next to his chair and held out a Corona. "There's limes on the cutting board."

It was barely four in the afternoon, a little early to start drinking. And I had three other places to see, so I really didn't have time. But the breeze on the roof was cool, and the empty chair in the shade looked inviting.

Candice and Devi started talking like they were carrying on a conversation that I had interrupted by my arrival. Something about an ex-boyfriend, and a new girl he was seeing.

"Sure," I agreed, accepting the beer from Keith. "Why not?"

Jake went back down to wait for the next applicant, while I fixed my beer and settled into the chair. It was even more comfortable in the shade with the fine breeze lifting my hair off my forehead. The city was spread out in front of me like I could pluck anything I wanted from it. But that was an illusion. The city dangled the possibility of amazing things, but how could I get any of that for myself? I was stuck in a low-end job and would live in a low-end dive. It had been that way for years and would continue that way for years to come. I knew it wasn't easy working your way up, but I hadn't expected that every rung would be this herculean effort.

I leaned my head back against the chair, hoping Keith wouldn't try to talk to me. I was glad for a moment of peace before I had to hit that bus ride back to the subway and civilization.

I only got half way through my beer when Jake spoiled it by bringing Lucy onto the roof. Lucy was a bouncy girl who reminded me of a terrier with her shaggy hair and constant yapping.

"I love it!" Lucy exclaimed, rushing over to us. She included me in her fawning, mistakenly thinking I was one of the roommates. "It's perfect! I've always wanted to live in a commune, where everyone shares everything and eats big meals at the table together. I can cook! I make eggplant to die for. You have to let me make eggplant for you!"

Candice looked appalled, one hand on her chest, as Lucy got in her face, talking about the fresh veggies and fruit she got from her job in a health food coop in Bushwick. Devi was shaking her head slightly, looking down her nose at the flow of one-sided talk.

I smiled. Seeing it from this side, Lucy's

eagerness was definitely off-putting.

Lucy looked around. "I'll get a chair and sit down and tell you about myself—"

"You don't want to live here," Keith suddenly said. "The landlord's an asshole."

Lucy hesitated, as if she might not have heard correctly. But Candice and Devi were nodding. "He is," Candice agreed, lowering her voice. "He comes and goes as he pleases from next door, so we have to lock our rooms to keep him out. There's no way a pretty girl like you would be safe."

Lucy was frowning at her. "You're joking."

She looked at Jake, who lifted his hands in a wide shrug, still smiling. "I've heard the stories," he said, "but it's not a problem for me."

"What happened to Sheila, the last girl who had my room?" Lucy asked.

They all shut their lips and looked at each other, obviously unwilling to talk about it.

Lucy's pretty face was now twisted in doubt. "I think you're lying to me. What kind of people are you? I wanted to live here."

"You can get an application on your way out," Jake assured her.

"I don't want an application," she said as she left the roof.

As they disappeared, Candice made a derisive sound. "Next!"

"Weak," I agreed. "Very weak."

Devi laughed out loud, a startlingly beautiful sound.

"Some people are too sensitive," Keith agreed.

"High maintenance is a real drag. Now you didn't run off when we busted your chops, Sierra. You sat down like a real human being and had a drink with us."

I felt better than I had since my fight with Lola. "I'm glad I did."

"You want the room?" Keith asked. "A thousand bucks gets you in. Five hundred due the first of next month."

My eyes opened wide. "I can have it? Don't I have to talk to the landlord?"

Keith took a swig of beer. "I am the landlord."

"*You* own this building?" I asked incredulously.

"You don't have to sound so surprised," he said in mock-offense. "But in fact, no, I don't own this building. I've rented these two floors for the past fifteen years from the owner, a sweet old lady. She likes having me rent out the rooms and take care of the place."

"So you were calling yourself an asshole," I realized.

"Yeah." He laughed and tossed his beer bottle in the big garbage can.

Devi leaned closer to me. "But he won't molest you unless you ask him to."

"I figured that," I assured her.

I looked at Jake, Candice and Devi. Suddenly it wasn't so hard imagining living with them. It would sure cure my lonely blues! It was nothing like what I had envisioned for myself in the city, but maybe that was a good thing. Maybe my own judgment wasn't to be trusted. So I would trust theirs. They thought I fit in, and pray to god, I could.

"Yes, I'm in," I agreed.

Chapter 18

Sierra

Things moved quickly after that. I signed the new lease and called to let my old landlord know I was going to be out by Monday, the first of the month. The guy at the management company was snappy about the short notice and warned me that they would "recover" money for any damages. But Keith assured me that New York was very tenant-friendly, and unless there was damage or I left the place dirty, I would probably be let off my lease with no additional penalties. After all, they could rent the place for more now.

I texted Lola that she had two days to pick up the rest of her stuff before the keys were turned in. I wasn't sure if Lola would bother, but she showed up with Martin, June and Spike, and cleaned out the apartment of everything I didn't pack into the van I rented from Man with a Van. Between me and the Man, we managed to get my twin bed down the stairs along with a dozen boxes of my stuff, including some nice kitchenware I had accumulated.

Lola took our turquoise couch, the kitchen table, her own bed and dresser, and everything else. Lola didn't have much to say to me, and she wasn't even apologetic about blowing up my life. She just asked me where my new place was, and said, "Huh, that's near Williamsburg!"

I checked the map online and realized that Williamsburg was about twenty blocks away from my room in Greenpoint. Williamsburg was the epicenter of coolness in Brooklyn. True, there was no good way to get there but to walk or take a cab, but I had walked further for less. It was funny that I had no idea when I had rented the room. It felt like Siberia at the time. No wonder Lucy had been so enthused.

My first few nights in the huge echoing loft were not easy. There was even more traffic on McGuinness than Ditmars, and the constant rumble of the nearby BQE freeway never stopped. Plus I had to fit myself into my roommates' routines. Jake went to work in the morning, so when I had a day shift, I had to time my shower carefully or I was screwed. Devi played her guitar every evening in her room, but the sound came clearly through the adjourning wall. I started going up to the roof to soak in the view whenever Devi played to avoid her hippy-dippy voice. And Candice was loud in the kitchen, as Jake had warned me, grinding her coffee and giving great hacking coughs as she puttered around in the morning.

But there were unexpected rewards, as well. A smile and a friendly hello when I came home. Someone to sit with on the couch when I watched a movie at night. All of my roommates were good company, though I didn't have much in common with any of them. Jake worked at Home Depot in Middle Village, while Candice was a bartender in Chelsea. Devi was technically attending film school, though Candice said she had been at it for over six years with nothing to show for it yet. Devi's parents sent her a monthly check and she worked part-time at a used clothing store, where she got her flowing old-fashioned clothes. The others said Marky was a quiet guy who had gotten his first break as a dancer in a touring company. He would be returning at the end of the month.

Yet even as I settled in and got used to everything, I felt disjointed and out of place. It was like a knife had cut off my life behind me, and everything was now different. Mostly I missed Lola. I had never realized how much I relied on my sister as my companion. Lola was my best friend. We used to always be together. Since Lola had started seriously dating Dick, that had naturally lessened, but as a detective he worked long, irregular hours so we still had plenty of time to hang out.

I wondered what Lola was doing now. But I knew if I texted her, Lola would resent it. Lola wanted a clean break from me. She wanted it to be this way.

And that hurt.

It didn't help that Victor had rejected me at the same time.

No wonder I decided to move into the loft. At least they wanted me. I felt like I had crawled into a hole, wounded and bedraggled, where I could lick myself into order again. These people might be a little weird, but they were nice to me, and suddenly that was the most important thing. To be around people who liked me.

So when I got home from a late shift on Friday night, I was happy to sit on the roof with Keith and Devi and a few of the others from the third floor who were partying at home. I was still there at two in the morning when Candice got home from the bar.

The next morning, I had a vague memory of Candice helping me down from the roof. The way her strong arms supported me reminded me of Victor.

As I woke up, I could hear Candice hacking away in the kitchen, banging pans around. Instead of irritating me, I smiled and put on my robe to go out. Candice looked as rumpled as I felt, with her short black hair sticking up in several directions. She was making her coffee.

"Thanks for being so sweet to me last night," I told her. "I drank too much."

"How do you feel? Want some coffee?"

There was a strict no-taking rule in the loft, and sharing was by invitation-only. So I was pleased by the offer. "Yes, I'd love some. I've got a couple of cheese Danish in the fridge I picked up from the bakery yesterday. You want one?"

"It looks like we have ourselves breakfast. Pass it over!"

We sat down and ate our Danish and drank coffee. I asked about the neighborhood, and Candice told me, "If you're looking for a nice place where you can meet people, go to the Pencil Factory with Devi tonight. It's just an ordinary bar, but that's where the young people are going."

I shook my head. "I've got another late shift, so I'll probably just come home again like last night."

Candice gave me a closer look. "What's your story, Sierra? Do you have a boyfriend?"

"No."

"Why not? A pretty girl like you. I'd die for hair like yours. You must have guys all over you."

I shrugged. "Not really. I'm too busy."

"Hmm... now that I think about it, you do have a real distinct 'get away' aura about you. Are you gay?"

"No." I gave a short unfunny laugh. "There was a guy I was interested in. But it barely got started, and it blew up when my sister left. We got into a fight right in front of him a couple weeks ago." I was a little surprised at myself for spilling everything out there, but it felt better to admit it. "He couldn't get rid of me fast enough. I think he was afraid of being saddled with me, bag and baggage."

"You like this guy?" Candice asked.

I drew in my breath. "Oh, Candice, you should see him. Gorgeous eyes, a beautiful smile, and he made me feel better than anyone ever has before. I keep thinking about how he touched me, and whispered to me."

You're mine...

"Damn... why'd you let a man like that go?"

"He let me go."

"You can't give up that easy, Sierra. You have to go out there and take what you want in life. If you want this man, then *take* him."

I started to smile. Candice made it sound so simple. "How do I take him?"

"By storm, honey! He saw you at your worst, now show him your best. You hit a rough patch, but you're on top of your game again—living in a stylish loft not far from Bedford Street, the envy of all the hipsters, with fabulous roommates like *me*. Put on your red dress and show him what he's missing."

"I don't have a red dress."

Candice gave me a look. "Honey, every girl should have a red dress."

...

It was almost too easy. Before I went to bed, I logged onto the fetish network and went to the Pleasure Salon profile. Sure enough, under the list of their friends, I found an avatar that showed the sunset from Victor's window. I recognized it instantly. His profile was minimal, saying he lived and worked in New York City. Most of the photos were of exotic places he visited with comments underneath. Lots of women commented on his photos.

Under events he was going to, he had listed "Leather Pride Night Auction." The auction was tomorrow night.

The next day at work, I found a sexy red dress that I must have hung up a dozen times, but never considered buying for myself. Kalisha agreed to let me pay for it on layaway. The other girls said the ruby red set off my skin tone. Bev did my makeup again, and I never looked better. The girls were a hundred percent behind Candice's plan for me to show Victor what he was missing.

I had to admit I was scared when I arrived at the Sanctuary where the auction was being held. But it turned out to be an old church with stained glass windows and stone archways over the doors. It was so bizarre that I was reassured. How could I be afraid walking into an old church?

Inside there were a lot of dressed up people, some in evening gowns with their partners in black tie. The event was a charity auction, but I hadn't realized how dressy it would be. Thankfully my red dress was longish but it didn't hide much with the slit up my thigh. For once, I actually felt like I fit in.

My only worry was how Victor would react when he saw me. Candice's advice was good but putting it into action could be disastrous, as I had learned from Lola. I didn't kid myself. I was ready for the cold shoulder from Victor.

But when it came right down to it, I didn't want Victor's last memory of me to be fighting with my sister at Festival. I was determined to leave a completely different impression on him. Even if he rejected me, I would have the satisfaction of knowing I went out with style.

So I got a glass of wine and slowly mingled with the crowd. Up on stage, the auctioneer was cajoling everyone to buy a corset dress made of deep blue satin modeled by a lovely woman with coal black skin. The bidding was fierce.

That's when I saw Josh, the big guy who had come up to us at Festival to make sure the fight was over. He was the last person I wanted to see.

But Josh gave me a huge grin and called out, "Sierra! Is that you? I called your sister *Sierra* at Festival, but I'm starting to see the difference."

I smiled back. Maybe I would never be able to shake my awful mistakes. "It's nice to see you again, Josh."

"It's great to see you!" He was so enthusiastic that I briefly worried what his intentions were, until he looked around. "I want to introduce you to my girlfriend. Anna! Come meet Sierra."

A voluptuous girl with a sweet smile joined us. "Hi, Sierra."

"She's one of the twins," Josh told Anna.

I bit back my retort. Josh wasn't trying to be mean. He couldn't help it if I was haunted by my past.

But Anna saw that I was irked. "They aren't twins, you silly. You said so yourself." Then she added, "Don't worry, Sierra, everyone's got a story floating around about them. It means you're part of the family."

That made me feel much better. Acceptance was my preferred drug right now. "I'm glad. I hope Victor is happy to see me tonight," I blurted out, without thinking.

"You're not here with him?" Josh asked, looking around. With his height, he could see over the heads of everyone in the room. "He's over that way, by the bar."

I strained to see where he was looking. "I think I can find it."

Anna was looking at me, but now concern filled her face. "Be careful with Victor, Sierra."

It was like a cold wash of water went through me. All I could think about was that first scene at the Chamber, when Victor had scared the life out of me. "Why?" I asked.

"I used to play with him once in a while. But he

only does casual sex. He doesn't have girlfriends." Anna shrugged. "I couldn't handle it. It's got to be more for me, and it wasn't fun being rejected by him. I just want to warn you. He's broken more than one heart around here."

"Oh..." It felt like the air had been let out of me. It was my worst fears confirmed. By a woman who knew better than anyone. I could hardly look at Anna now, knowing she had sex with Victor.

Josh had his mouth closed tight, but he was nodding slightly, as if he agreed with his girlfriend's assessment. "Victor's a great guy. But... yeah."
I realized after a few moments that I was standing there with a stunned look on my face as they watched me sympathetically.

I'm a real hot mess, no doubt about it.

So I put on my fake salesgirl smile and raised my glass of wine. "So here's to some casual fun!"

Josh and Anna laughed along with me, but Anna didn't believe me. How could she when she knew exactly how thrilling Victor was?

When we parted, I headed in the opposite direction from where Josh had spotted Victor. I had my pride. No way was I going to approach him right now.

I needed to sort out my feelings. I knew better than to give up just because his friends didn't think Victor had it in him to really care about a girl. I had to find that out from Victor himself.

Or I would always wonder if these feelings we had shared when we were making love did mean there was something more between us.

But as I wandered around the charity auction, the words played over in my head, "He only does casual sex."

Chapter 19

Victor

When I saw Sierra in the Sanctuary, I was blown away. She stood there in a slinky red dress that cut high on her thigh and low in the back. It clung to her body, and I could almost feel how the silky material would slide over her breasts, with her nipples hardening under my hand. My cock stiffened painfully fast, and in the swimming haze of lust, I almost went over and grabbed her.

Like it was my right.

But it wasn't. I hadn't spoken to Sierra for two weeks, ever since I had dropped her off at her apartment after we got back from the Festival.

So I forced myself to stay back, to watch and find out what she was up to, rather than be an idiot and rush in.

Every man in the place looked Sierra over at least once as she roamed around the former sanctuary of the 19th Century church. The Leather Pride Night auction didn't allow play, but a small trail of men followed in her wake. She still had that untouchable air about her that drew them in, yet kept them at bay.

But there was something else about her. Something new.

For one thing, she wasn't hiding behind a disguise. It was the first time Sierra was out in the scene as herself, and there was an added confidence that I liked.

And instead of the pleasant expression she tended to wear, there was intensity in her eyes and determination in the set of her jaw. She was a woman on a mission, and she didn't mind letting everyone know it.

I wanted to go up and talk to her more than anything. Over the past two weeks, I kept thinking she would text me to ask for help, since she obviously needed it. But I after her first hasty rejection of my offer, I didn't want to chase after her and insist she take my money. That was too perverse even for me.

Every day I dreaded getting that inevitable text from her, pleading with me for help. I was angry at her for being like the others even though it felt different when we were together.

Also I felt bad for her because it wasn't her fault that life was hard and women sometimes needed help from their boyfriends to get by.

But I wasn't her boyfriend. I was the guy who was lying to her about who I was.

And having mind-blowing sex with her...

Sierra had ruined everything for me. I surveyed the fetish scene bustling on one of the biggest nights of the year, where tens of thousands of dollars would be raised for charity. I counted eight women here tonight who I had played with, and all of them thought I was rich and successful. Including my date for the night, Karla, a pale blond woman who was nearing thirty and on a constant search for a husband.

Instead of feeling exhilarated, it made me want to run. That is, before I saw that Sierra was here.

Karla approached me, laughing at something a friend had said, as she rapidly downed another cocktail. Alcohol was served because no playing was allowed at the auction.

"There you are!" Karla sang out, long before she rejoined me.

She had texted me yesterday that she had an extra ticket after breaking up with her boyfriend. Like with Tricia, I had been Karla's booty call between boyfriends for over a year now, and she fully expected to go back to my place tonight.

But she left me cold; her staccato laugh, her exaggerated flirting and the way she made it clear she was available to me again. She was hoping for more than friends with benefits, like they always ended up hoping for more.

"I keep losing you," Karla complained. "Where do you keep going?"

I had my eye on Sierra at that very moment. So far she hadn't seen me. But faced with the sudden choice, it was easy.

"I see woman I need to talk to," I told Karla. "She may tell me to get lost. You may tell me to get lost, now that I've told you this. But I have to apologize to her."

Karla considered me. "Which woman?"

I indicated Sierra. "In the red dress."

"What do you need to apologize for?" Karla slurred her words slightly.

I did not want to be having this conversation,

but I needed to talk to Sierra without Karla drunkenly shoving her way in and asserting her "rights." "I took her to Festival and haven't called her since."

Karla was astonished. "Why not? She's really pretty. And young. Too young for *you* to be playing mind games with."

"I think she likes mind games. At least I hope so. Maybe she'll talk to me again."

Karla was shaking her head at me. "I should be mad at you. But I'm really not surprised. You're bored with me, aren't you?"

I smiled sadly. "You want a boyfriend, Karla, and I'm not that guy for you."

"I keep hoping you'll realize what a great thing we have together…"

I knew she was thinking about my loft in the city and my supposed house in Connecticut, and a life of leisure as my wife. I could hardly feel bad when I wasn't really the man who was breaking up with her.

"I'm sorry it didn't work out." I only had to stand there and look sad, and eventually it would be over.

"Whatever! I'm going to hang out with my friends." Karla waved across the room at them.

I tucked twenty dollars in her palm. "Here's cab fare so you can get home okay."

It was a typical move for my role, and I did it without thinking. Because that's the only thing my relationship with Karla ever was.

She actually smiled, liking it. Which made me feel a little sick inside.

It was even worse when I turned to face Sierra. She was far enough away that she couldn't hear anything, but she must have seen me talking to Karla.

I walked directly over to her, feeling as if the sticky mess of my life was falling away as I neared Sierra. I had never had a better time with anyone than our first night together at the Festival. Not even with Adrianne. And I had never felt so close to a woman than when we made love in the barn and I told her "*You're mine...*"

And in this moment, I felt it again. *You're mine...*

I reached out to touch her waist, to lean in to kiss her gently. It was only after I pulled back that I realized she could have withdrawn or turned away to stop me. She smelled delicious, and I drew in a deep breath, my face lingering near her hair.

"How are you?" I asked, all of my pent-up concern spilling out in those brief words.

Her smile was easy. "I'm doing great."

I took her hand, unwilling to lose contact with her now that she was near me again. She flooded my senses—I couldn't think for wanting to pull her close and kiss her again, this time for real. But some distant, sane part of my mind was screaming at me to slow down.

"Is your sister here?" I asked.

"God, I hope not," Sierra said fervently. "I don't think this is her kind of thing."

I looked around, realizing that was true. This was a high-end event in the kink community, with not a drum to be seen.

"You're here alone?" I asked.

She held her hands out slightly, as if that was self-evident. "I had such a good time at the Festival, before the bad stuff happened. I wanted to see more. I ran into Josh over there. He introduced me to his girlfriend, Anna. She said she dated you a couple of years ago."

"Yes." There was nothing positive to say about my "relationship" with Anna, so I quickly added, "What's happening with your apartment search?"

"I got a new place. It's in Greenpoint."

"Already? When do you move in?"

"Last weekend," she said with a laugh.

"That was quick." I wasn't sure what to think about that. "You could have waited out the month. Saved the rent."

She shrugged lightly. "I found the place I wanted. And now I'm settled in. I really like my roommates. We have a rooftop view of the city that's to die for."

"Greenpoint, huh?" Now I felt like an even bigger asshole for not texting her. It turned out she didn't need me after all. She had been busy taking care of herself.

Sierra talked about her new neighborhood and the Polish bakeries and the novelty of taking a bus ride as part of her commute and being able to see where she was going rather than always being underground in a subway.

It wasn't what I had been imagining. Sierra wasn't begging for my help. Maybe that last day at

Festival, she wasn't trying to shame me into helping her. She had been taking care of things and figuring out where she would live.

It made everything feel so real, that frankly, it was all I could do to listen to her. I was looking at her mouth as she talked, adoring the slight dent in her full bottom lip. And her lovely face, the way the curve of her cheek caught the light. And her dark eyes that dragged me in whenever I dared to look into them. It made me want to reach out and caress her bare arms and draw her close to me.

Then I realized she had stopped talking, but I was standing there caught by her eyes. After a moment, I smiled. "I'm sorry. It's just that you're such a beautiful person, so strong and... luminescent. I'm getting distracted."

I ran a finger down her bare arm that felt like silk, and then lifted her hand in mine. I didn't want to let go. She was fragrant and warm, and it was all I could do to keep from taking her in my arms.

"Why didn't you text me?" Sierra asked quietly.

This was the moment—when I should come clean and admit I wasn't rich or successful. That I was a liar.

But if I confessed now, she wouldn't let me keep touching her. And at this moment, touching her was the *only* thing that mattered.

"I saw how bad it was with your sister," I said. "I didn't want to encourage you to keep following her around. I felt responsible for suggesting you go down there. I knew if you asked me, I'd do whatever you wanted."

"I agree with that. I'm not following Lola anymore."

I shook my head, my throat suddenly tight. "I really hoped you could work it out with her. I never was able to make things right with my sister. So maybe I pushed you too much."

Her eyes met mine, disarmed by my confession. "I talked to her last weekend when she moved her stuff out. Lola's doing what she wants. And I've moved on."

"Good," I said, stroking her arms. "So you forgive me? I'm sorry I wasn't around to help you move."

"I got a man. With a van."

I laughed. "So you didn't need me."

"Not for moving," she agreed.

My smile deepened. "Maybe I'm good for something else..."

I leaned in and kissed her. She raised her face, as eager as I was. The agony of holding back finally eased inside of me. My arms encircled her as I pressed against her body. She molded to me, melting soft in my hands.

But from the corner of my eye, I saw a guy pass by too close to us, straining his head to watch us kiss. All of the sharks who had been following Sierra were now circling us, watching me hold her and hungrily eyeing the way her skirt rode up on her thigh.

I grabbed her hand and glared at the watching men to back off. I didn't think this would be such a problem at a classy event. But our PDA was getting out of hand.

Sierra didn't ask where we were going. She looked just as dazed and turned on as I was.

I saw the old confessionals along the back and made a bee-line toward them. The first handle I tried was locked, but the second one was open.

I pulled her inside with me, and there was barely enough room for us to stand next to the bench seat. But my arms were around her and I was kissing her again, this time letting go completely.

She reached up to touch my face so tenderly that I turned to kiss her fingertips. Her hand was small in mine. It felt right, as if I could be her rock and she could be my light.

The faint cries of, "Ah, ah, ah..." filtered through the wooden screen behind her. She heard it at the same time, and we broke off our kiss to listen. The rhythmic rustle and the cries were unmistakable. A couple was fucking in the box next to us.

I leaned down and could see the faint shadow of people through the wooden screen. The woman was getting louder, losing herself in the pleasure.

My hand slid down to Sierra's thigh, drawing up her dress. "They have the right idea."

The bumping from next door made her eyes widen. Her hands were pushing on my chest. "They're having sex!" she whispered, finally realizing.

"Yes." I leaned in and kissed her again, lingering over the sweet taste of her lips. My hand drew up her skirt again.

But she stopped me. "No."

"But this is perfect," I murmured, pressing into

her. "Nobody can see us."

She pushed harder at my chest. "People are right on the other side of this door! All dressed up. I'm not having sex with you in here."

I realized she meant it. For a moment, I hesitated, and then leaned forward to kiss her. Hoping she wouldn't cut me off completely.

"I need to get out," she said quietly before I could touch her lips.

I unlatched the door so she could leave. She settled her dress, glancing around uneasily. A couple of the guys were still hanging around watching us.

I felt bad for letting my dick stampede ahead of my brain. But even now, part of me wanted to draw her back inside the confessional and kiss her into oblivion so I could do anything I wanted to her.

"Let's go back to my place," I said. "You'll love the view at night."

She looked tempted, which perversely irritated me. It was my usual line, and she was responded to it.

"I don't know," she said. "I think you have the wrong idea about me. I'm not the kind of girl who has casual sex with men. I know we fell into this because I was freaking out over my sister. But I want a man who's part of my life."

I was brought up short. The last thing I expected at this moment was the Ultimatum.

Here I was thinking she was different, but she was still angling for the same thing as all the rest. *Give me everything,* was the constant demand I heard from women. They were willing to settle for far less, my pathetic relationships had proven that, but they still demanded everything and made me miserable knowing that I could never give them enough.

"Don't look like that," she told me. "I didn't hear from you for weeks, and now you're all over me. What am I to think?"

"You don't want a relationship with me. You don't even know me," I snapped. "You want the fantasy—the billionaire hero who sweeps you off your feet, while you save him from his dark pain. Well, it doesn't happen that way in real life, Sierra."

She stared at me, hurt and growing angry. "You don't know what I want. I don't expect anyone to rescue me. I've always taken care of myself, and Lola too—"

"Victor!" a woman called out. Karla staggered up, smiling apologetically at Sierra. "'Scuse me, *dear*. Victor, can I have another twenty? I lost my cab fare, and you promised to get me home."

Sierra backed off, letting Karla move in to hang off my arm. I could tell Karla was exaggerating her drunkenness, playing it up to take a poke at Sierra and get revenge on me. I should have known that selfish Karla wouldn't leave me alone without squeezing more than twenty bucks out of me.

Sierra turned around and walked away without a word. I tried to peel Karla off me, but she was laughing now.

"Boy is she pissed at you!" Karla exclaimed. "Did you see her face? She was mad when you came out of that confessional. What did you do to her in there?"

I had a terrible sinking feeling.

"I misjudged her," I whispered, more to myself than Karla.

I knew that Sierra had the right to be mad at me. She wasn't a gold-digger. Lola might have been living off Dick, but that was Lola. Sierra didn't do that.

In fact, I couldn't imagine her doing that, now that I knew her better.

I should have confessed to her at Pleasure Salon, or even at the party. If Sierra was angry with me now, how would she react when she found out that I had been lying to her? She actually deserved a rich successful guy, not a liar like me.

It was all fucked up.

Chapter 20

Sierra

I grabbed my cover-up from the coat check girl, and ran out of the Sanctuary. I paused at the top of the steps leading down to the street. People were still coming in, and a small crowd of smokers hung out on the flagstones at the bottom.

I got my bearings and went down to 6th Street that fronted the church. The subway station was seven blocks away. I had worn a light coat on purpose so I wouldn't have to pay for a cab ride home. But apparently Victor was used to giving cab money to his girls. He had done it for me once before. It must be nice to be able to buy any woman he wanted.

I felt awful, like I had a hole pierced through my middle. Like something important was missing. The hope was gone.

While it was flattering to be desired by a man like Victor, I couldn't stand being just another number in his phone. I wasn't like Karla, okay with getting cab money from a man after he decided there was another woman he preferred for the night.

When I realized that he intended to have sex with me in the confessional, within minutes of seeing me for the first time in two weeks, it suddenly felt wrong. He was attracted to me, but that wasn't enough.

Like I thought, *we don't have a relationship.* He was on a date with another woman tonight, and he ducked out on her to mess around with me.

I was done with Victor. I didn't do casual sex, and he didn't do relationships. There was nothing else to say.

It wasn't exactly the great last impression I had intended to leave with him, but it would have to do. I didn't see any way forward for us.

My eyes stung as I turned the corner and hurried down Avenue B. I felt safer on the brighter lit avenue. But if I stayed the course heading south, I would pass Victor's place a few blocks south of Houston.

Right now, I wanted to avoid Victor. When he touched me, I lost control. It was too seductive to fall into the pleasure he gave me. To let everything else go and surrender to him.

I had to hold it together and get out of here. When I was safe at home, I could fall apart.

I turned onto 5th Street and headed toward Avenue A. I didn't want to risk running into him. That was a scarier thought than the darkened street.

But it was creepy in the shadows, cast by the trees blocking the street lights. I was hurrying along when a hand grabbed my arm. "Sierra!"

"What—" I exclaimed, thinking it was Victor.

Turning, I saw it was Dick. "Dick! What are you doing here?"
He pulled me deeper into the parking lot. I took a last look down the block, but Victor was nowhere in sight.

"I'm looking for Lola," Dick said. "Was she at

the auction?"

I was shocked. "You followed me to find Lola?"

"Don't you play all high and mighty with me, Sierra! I know you moved, and you didn't tell me."

"I don't owe you anything. You're not dating Lola anymore."

"She needs help. She's losing it. She didn't quit her job—she was fired. There's clothes missing, boxes of them. Her boss wants to find out where she is, too."

A familiar surge of protective fear starting to rise. Lola was in trouble again... she needed me...

But I forced myself to say, "There's nothing I can do. Lola won't talk to me."

"I can't find her, Sierra. She left that flophouse she was staying at in Bed-Sty. Since she doesn't work in the mall anymore, she's dropped out of sight. She's not updating her profile to say where she's going to be. I was hoping you knew."

"Seriously, Dick? You are a terrible detective. There were two vans parked outside our place last weekend when we moved out."

"I was working Saturday. If you'd told me what was happening, I could have been there!"

"It's none of your business where Lola is living," I said flatly.

Dick stepped closer to me, grabbing my arm again. "It is my business. Even though she's going through a psychotic break, probably because of drugs, that doesn't mean you give up on her."

"Let go of me, Dick!"

I tried to wrest my arm from his grasp, but he

had hold of me tight. "I know you have her address. Give me your phone."

"No!"

He shook me. "Give it to me!"

I tried to hit him, but he was so much bigger than me. I cried out as the pressure on my arm sharpened.

He held me off and ripped my bag from my shoulder.

"Give that back!" I cried out.

He shook me hard, bringing me close to his face. "Shut up! Or I *swear*!"

He shoved me away hard, and I stumbled in my high heels. My ankle twisted under me and I went to the ground with a cry. Pain shot through my bare knees as I landed on the asphalt, scraping the skin on my hands, too.

Dick stood over me, rifling through my bag. He pulled out my phone and threw my bag to one side.

I tried to reach out for it, but when I moved my leg, my ankle screamed in pain. My hands clutched at my ankle, but it didn't help. I didn't know what to do.

He was frozen, staring down at my phone. "Last text eight days ago. You've barely texted her this month! Are you calling her?"

"She won't talk to me! Don't you get it?" Dick grabbed me by the arm and hauled me up. My ankle gave out with a hard stab of pain, but he was holding me up.

"You're hurting me, Dick," I panted.

He got right into my face. Suddenly I was afraid of him, really afraid. He didn't look like the man who had dated my sister for over a year. He smelled of alcohol and his eyes were reddened and watery. If he wasn't holding me up, I would have sunk to the ground in fear.

"Tell me what her address is," he demanded.

"I don't know!"

"You do know! Don't lie to me." He gave me another hard shake.

"I don't know! I thought she was living in Bed-Sty," I cried.

Dick was in my face again, leering at me. Fear spiked through me as he raised his hand. "You're just like your sister. A lying little cheat!"

I cringed back, knowing he was going to hit me.

Suddenly an arm caught Dick's upraised hand, and jerked him back.

The three of us stumbled together. Dick wouldn't let go of me, and I cried out in the pain as I put my foot down.

But Victor had control of Dick's other arm, and was slowly wrestling him away from me. Dick was a big guy, but there was nothing he could do against Victor except huff and puff. "Get off me!" Dick demanded. "I'm a police officer."

But Victor took him down, right down to the ground, until Dick's face was pressed against the asphalt. "Cops aren't supposed rough up women. That's stuff the Post eats up!" Victor said through his teeth.

I shakily sat back down on the ground. My face was wet with tears. I didn't realize I was crying until that moment.

"Call 911," Victor told me.

Dick started thrashing harder under Victor. "I know this girl! I'm dating her sister. She's withholding important information for my investigation. Let me go! You don't know who you're messing with, buddy!"

Victor ignored him, looking only at me. "I can hold onto him until the cops get here. Look at your knees! You're bleeding."

"I just want him to go away," I managed to say. My lips felt numb, and I could hardly speak.

I needed Victor to help me, and there he was, helping me.

Thankfully I sagged against my outstretched arms. I was breathing fast like I had just sprinted for my life, and was dizzy with relief. Dick mugged me!

But Victor had saved me.

Chapter 21

Victor

I wanted to pound Dick slowly into the ground, but the security cameras watching over the parking lot would be merciless on me. Calling 911 was a distant second choice, but still much better than letting the jerk walk away.

"He hurt you," I told Sierra. "I can't let him get away with that."

Even Dick heard the barely-contained rage in my words. Smashed into the asphalt, completely at my mercy with his arm twisted up painfully, Dick's tone finally started to change. "I didn't mean to hurt you, Sierra. I'm going out of my mind with worry. You know that."

"Get him away from me," Sierra pleaded.

"Are you sure?" I said through clenched teeth.

"Yes..."

I hauled Dick off the ground, not caring how rough I was on his shoulders. Dick yelped in pain.

I walked him back to the sidewalk and thrust him away from me hard. Dick nearly fell to the cement, but he managed to keep his feet. His hand went to his shoulder, and he winced, bending over.

"Try it," I ordered through my teeth. "Just *try* it."

I hoped Dick was stupid enough to take a crack at me. I would enjoy beating the shit out of him in "self-defense."

Dick didn't look like he was ready to try anything. He hobbled off, still holding his shoulder like he couldn't move it.

"Don't you go near Sierra again," I called after him.

I waited to make sure Dick was walking away before I went back for Sierra.

She was struggling to get up. She favored her right leg, limping forward to get her balance.

I stopped her by picking her up in my arms. "Do you have your purse?"

"Yes. Not my phone. He threw it away."

I turned and walked around still carrying her, until we found her phone which thankfully wasn't broken. Tears were shining on her cheeks.

I held her close, her face nestled against my shoulder and her arm clutching me around my back. I carried her back to Avenue B and started down the block before she faintly said, "I can try to walk."

"That's the worst thing you can do on an injury. If I see an empty cab, I'll grab it. But that's not likely this time of night."

I carried her six blocks down to my apartment, keeping a sharp eye out for Dick. Sierra held onto me tightly, her eyes closed. Her breathing was ragged. I wished I could do something more for her, and I didn't even notice the ache in my own arms as I neared my place. I would have carried her to Brooklyn if I had to.

In the elevator, she said into my chest, "You can let me down."

"Not a chance." I adjusted her in my arms. I didn't want to let her go.

I carried her inside my place and sat down with her on my couch, holding her in my lap. I needed a moment to feel like it was finally safe. Dick wasn't going to jump out from behind a car and attack her again.

"Thank you," she murmured into my chest. "I don't know what I would have done without you."

My heart twisted. What would have happened if I hadn't kept searching for her after she ran out of the Sanctuary?

My blood boiled at the thought of that piece of shit hurting Sierra. I wished I could go back in time and punch him good. Dick was already facing enough trouble, a cop roughing up a civilian, and a pretty girl at that. I could have gotten away with punching him in the eye.

But Sierra had already seen enough of what I was capable of. Somehow her frantic eyes had reminded me of when I had threatened her, silently begging me to stop. I couldn't do that to her again, even to satisfy my powerful urge to fuck Dick up.

Rocking slightly with my face pressed against her hair, I took in the fact that she was okay. I had reached her in time. Now it was over.

She shifted a little, looking up at me. Her eyes looked even bigger shining with tears.

Was it sick that I loved her like that? When she was so vulnerable and open to me? I knew I could reach into her heart and rip it out right now. She was completely in my power. I had saved her, so I owned her now.

She's mine.

But I couldn't say that to her. I didn't have the right.

I stroked her cheek. "I'll take care of you."

I slid her off my lap onto the couch. She winced a bit when she moved her leg. "My ankle. It twisted when he pushed me down."

Once again I regretted not pounding Dick into the ground. She drew back slightly at the intensity in my eyes.

I turned to her ankle, unstrapping her high heel to look at her pretty slender foot with toenails painted bright red. There was something very arousing about the red tips. Just touching her foot, feeling her soft skin, made my hands linger and soothe her even as my cock stirred.

I forced myself to focus on her ankle. Two blue streaks were deepening on the outside. I moved her foot gently. She hissed but didn't cry out, so it wasn't broken.

I had dealt with enough injuries from my job so I knew exactly what to do. I got her foot elevated with an ice gel pack draped over her ankle. With a hot wet towel, I washed the blood from the scrapes on her palms and then her knees.

"Ouch," she said, trying to pull her knee away.

I held onto her. "You don't want it to get infected."

I washed methodically until slowly my hand with the towel stilled, as I remembered when I was a kid and the school nurse had cleaned a cut on my knee. Nobody ever touched me as a kid. Nobody ever gave me hugs or lay on the couch with me like I saw other families do. So I vividly remembered the nurse's touch, and the kind look in her brown eyes as she smiled down at me and took care of me.

It had filled my heart then, though I had forgotten it until now. Remembering it, I felt that same sense of crushing emptiness suddenly filled with a golden light—a simple touch and kind brown eyes. For a moment, everything was good.

"Are you okay, Victor?" she asked.

I realized I was looking into her brown eyes, feeling safe and happy like I did in that rare moment when I was a kid.

Instantly I pulled back, looking down to gather up the bloody towel and bowl of soapy water. I was revealing too much, feeling too much. I had to get control of myself—

"Don't..." She reached out and put her hand to my cheek, pulling me towards her. "Don't leave me."

That decided it. I couldn't deny her. I held onto her tightly, not wanting to let go either. It wasn't a sexual thing, which was unbelievable considering how I had reacted in the Sanctuary, when I was all over her.

This was more. I needed her comfort, and she needed mine. And for some reason, it was okay for her to need something from me. Because she was giving back to me wholeheartedly.

We lay together on the couch for a long time, and I got up only to remove the ice pack for twenty minutes, then put it back on again. Neither of us said much. It felt as if she was drifting out of reach even as I held onto her tightly. I knew it was only a strange illusion that made it feel as if she was sliding out of my grasp. But it made my body tense as she moved against me, molding herself to me. As if I was resisting a hurricane wind that threatened to tear us apart.

Even when it was late, I didn't want to let her go. "Do you want to stay the night?"

She glanced over at the bed, biting her lip.

"No sex." I couldn't tell her that was impossible now. The only way I could make love to her was if I was honest with her. And I couldn't be honest right now, not when I felt torn open already. Not when I was realizing what kind of words I would have to say to admit the life I'd been leading.

But I couldn't let her go.

She put on one of my old T-shirts to sleep in, and I carefully climbed into bed next to her, taking her in my arms.

And then nothing else mattered.

Then everything felt real and solid. Then I knew this was right. I was exactly where I was supposed to be, holding her close and protecting her. I realized then how much I had hated going to bed every night these past two weeks, when I didn't know where she was or what she was doing. That I had walled in my own feelings so I couldn't hear my own longing for her.

But now I couldn't deny it.

Chapter 22

Sierra

It was heaven cuddling with Victor on his bed, looking out at the lights of the city. Even though everything else in my life was seriously messed up—with Dick's mauling smack on top of the awfulness—I wanted just one night off. One night of peace, lying in Victor's arms. One night when I didn't have to care about anything else. When I didn't have to care about what this meant or where it might be going.

I could just feel happy.

Every time I opened my eyes I saw Victor and beyond him the open windows with lights of the city, like we were at the bottom of a bowl of buildings that rose up gradually on either side of us.

It was the first thing I saw when I woke up in the morning.

Victor was still holding me, moving sleepily as I woke him by shifting. His hands tightened on me for a moment before he was fully awake.

"Now that's a view to wake up to," I murmured, looking down at his naked back and curve of his buttocks in the shorts.

"It's too bright," he murmured.

I realized he was right about the sunlight. Checking the time, I saw it was nearly 11. A jolt of panic shot through me. "Oh, no! I can't believe it's so late! I have to be at work by 12:30. I can barely get out to my place and back in time."

Victor propped himself up on his elbow, looking adorably tousled. "Are you okay to go to work? What about your ankle?"

I carefully stood up. A sharp twinge went through my ankle when I put weight on it. "I need to wrap it, but I think it's okay. I really hate to call in sick when Kalisha was so cool about letting me off for the Festival."

"You can get ready here. I have an ace bandage. That would save some wear and tear on your ankle traveling back and forth."

"I guess I could..."

He leaned over and snagged my red dress from the floor. "It's wrinkled."

"I can't wear that. But I do have the dress I wore yesterday. I bought that one at work."

He grinned. "So you decided to go to the Sanctuary at the last minute?"

Actually I had started planning it the moment Candice suggested that I go out and get what I wanted.

But I wasn't going to tell him that.

"Can I take a shower?" I asked.

"First you have to pay for your overnight stay." He drew me closer and kissed me. It was nothing like our passion-laden kisses at the Festival, or even last night at the Sanctuary. It was more like a girlfriend kiss, a loving morning kiss.

As I showered, he made breakfast for us. There was French toast waiting for me when I got out. I sat down at the black granite counter and looked out at the view as I ate my French toast with maple syrup. His coffee was divine—it came from a one-cup dispenser that probably cost a fortune.

"This is the life!" I said. "I feel like Cinderella. Only I'm still at the ball."

"It's way past midnight," Victor reminded me.

As I took a bite, I asked, "Are you going up to your house in Connecticut or staying here for the rest of the weekend?"

He wiped his mouth. "Staying here."

I looked out at the view with a sigh. "I wouldn't want to leave if I had this place. It's small, but it's perfect, if you know what I mean."

"I do."

We ate in silence for a few minutes. I asked, "Are you leaving town this week?"

"I'm going to Miami tomorrow."

I almost told him how much I'd always wanted to see Florida. I wondered if palm trees really looked like that.

But the familiar wall was rising up between us. He looked preoccupied, like I had sparked some train of thought that was taking him further away from me.

"What do you do exactly?" I asked.

He chewed and swallowed before he answered, "I'm in transportation services."

"And it's your own company? When did you start it?"

"I bought into an established business." He went to the coffee machine. "Another cup?"

I was so envious of him. He had made it, and he was only twenty-eight. In seven years, hopefully I would be in a much better place. But some people were lucky—they got a boost in life. It would take a lot to bring me up to his level of success.

After that I stopped asking questions, and he stopped talking. He did give me a lingering kiss good-bye at the door, but he didn't say anything about getting together again. It was an odd way to leave things after such an intimate night.

Maybe it was intimate, but what exactly was it? He didn't try to have sex with me, not even this morning when it would have been natural for a man to make a move, waking up in bed with a woman he supposedly couldn't keep his hands off.

I couldn't complain because he respected my decision to not have casual sex. But I was disappointed that *casual* sex was the only kind of sex he had.

Yet nothing felt *casual* about the way we made love. It was all-engrossing, over-whelming passion that swept us up and dashed us both against the rocks. There was no faking that, no ignoring what happened between us.

By the time I got to the department store, it felt like a safe haven. I knew my place there, and what I had to do. As I clocked in, I felt more like myself than I had in days.

But the second Kalisha saw me, my boss exclaimed, "What happened to you?"

"What's wrong?" I asked, putting my hand to my hair.

"You look all bright-eyed and glowy." With a narrow look at my outfit, Kalisha added, "Isn't that what you were wearing yesterday? Don't tell me! The red dress worked? I *told* you that was the one."

I laughed and blushed. I never would have imagined sharing my personal life with my supervisor. But Kalisha seemed to like it.

And I would take friendship in any form it came, and be grateful.

Eight hours never passed so quickly—it was always busy in the store on the weekend. When Kalisha found out I had strained my ankle, she let me switch back to wearing my sneakers on shift. It was the only thing that got me through.

As I limped around helping customers and stocking merchandise, I tried not to think of how badly our morning had ended, or the way he had kissed me last night at the Sanctuary. Being with him was more erotic than anything I had ever experienced before. It was like I never knew what passion was— that true desire that made two people want to dive into each other and never come up for air.

But I knew my limit, and this was it. I would have a real relationship with him or nothing. I couldn't do anything *casual* with Victor.

•••

When I got home from work late on Sunday night, I limped straight up to the roof. Looking at the skyline of the city bright with lights, I picked out the low dip over the east village, nearly at the base of the Williamsburg Bridge, where Victor lived.

He was probably there right now. Unless he was out with someone else.

Candice was on the roof drinking a beer with a

few of the other roommates. "I think that dress is a repeat," she said.

I pulled out a bit of the red dress from my bag. "It worked. My boss helped me pick it out yesterday."

Candice's eyes lit up. "I saw you didn't come home last night, and I wondered... tell me!"

I settled into a folding chair next to Candice looking out at the skyline. At Victor's place, it felt like we were inside the view, surrounded by buildings. Here, the city was barely out of reach on the other side of the river.

"He was all over me at first," I said, "but then I found out he was there with someone else. A terrible blond woman who was drinking too much."

"Sounds awful."

My expression fell. "It got worse. After I ran out, my sister's old boyfriend grabbed me and tried to get me to tell him where Lola is living now."

"Honey, are you okay?" Candice asked.

The concern in her voice made the whole thing wash over me again with a sick feeling.

"I've known him for a long time, but he went crazy. He hurt me." I showed Candice the fresh scabs on my knees and the bandage on my ankle. "He would have hurt me more but Victor stopped him. You should have seen him. Victor carried me all the way to his place, blocks and blocks. It was like we were both possessed."

"And you made love all night," Candice finished. She must have seen the doubtful expression on my face. "Or did you?"

"I told him that I didn't want to have casual

sex. But after Dick attacked me... I didn't want to leave his place, and he didn't want me to go. So we cuddled all night."

"Cuddled?" She gave me a hard look. "That is *so* romantic. Nothing like a near-death experience to wake a body up."

It was true. I was not in my right mind last night, and I ventured to guess that Victor wasn't either.

"Yeah, well, in the cold light of day, things definitely looked different," I said. "On his side. As soon as I started asking him what he was going to do today and what's up with his work, he shut right down." I sighed. "I think I am just a booty call."

"You weren't last night," Candice pointed out.

I sat back and put my foot up on the rickety table to elevate it. I had tomorrow off, so it would give my aching ankle a chance to recover. So many hours standing up had taken a toll.

Right now, all I wanted to do was sit with my new friends and enjoy my beer.

I knew exactly where I stood with Victor, and that was *nowhere.* If he wanted a relationship, he knew where to find me. I had gotten one text from him today, close to dinner time, asking how my ankle was. I had replied: *Doing okay. I should get through the day.* And after that, nothing. Not a word.

After a night like last night.

He was keeping his distance from me. Otherwise he would have texted more. He had done the bare minimum that human decency demanded, and that was it.

I had no idea when I would see him next. Would I see him again? I wouldn't track him down again like I did last night. I couldn't stand having to drag him away from another date.

"I feel like I'm not good enough for him," I sighed.

"Don't you *ever* say that! You should bite your tongue before you say that." Candice smacked the back of my hand. "You're good enough for any man, Sierra."

"This one is complicated. He has casual sex with girls like me who he meets in fetish clubs." I laughed when Candice's eyebrows went right to the top of her forehead. "I was following my sister! I was worried about her."

"I would have pegged you for vanilla all the way," Candice said.

"Not so much anymore," I admitted. "But Victor doesn't take me seriously because of the way we met. He's never taken me out on a real date. I haven't met any of his friends. He probably saves that for potential girlfriends while I got slotted into the slut category."

"Well, honey, it's up to you what you want to do."

I nodded. "I've already decided. If he doesn't care about me the same way, then I can't keep seeing him."

Chapter 23

Victor

I was in agony. I should have confessed this morning, but Sierra woke up talking about my *amazing* view and kept right on gushing through breakfast about my *amazing* life. I lied to her face. Along with different kinds of evasions of truth I usually justified as "not really lies" even though they most definitely *were* lies.

I was caught in a nightmare of my own making. I should have told her. But I couldn't form the words. I couldn't face the slow disbelief that would spread across her face, and the disdain and disgust that would follow.

I needed more time, to figure out how to say it. Suddenly I knew why people broke up by text message. They didn't want to see *that* look. Of shock and pain.

Beating my head with my own hands, I paced all day, trying to figure a way out of this mess.

My feelings had grown beyond desire, beyond passion for Sierra. As a kid, I had learned I couldn't trust the women I was closest to, not my grandmother, not my sister. They let me down every time.

But last night I felt such deep trust for Sierra, such simple comfort in her arms. I was sure that she cared about *me*. She was holding *me*.

She understood me, and saw the real me through the lies. She had been through hard things, too. I could tell. It was like we were made for each other.

I regretted that I hadn't told her the truth weeks ago, blurted it out when she came to see my place that first time, or at Festival when we were so close. Maybe then she would have understood. I could have helped her look for a place and helped her move, and shown her I was a good guy in spite of everything.

All night, I had planned to tell her the truth this morning. But her enthusiasm for my *amazing* view and my *amazing* job threw me off. I was accustomed to thinking that without my faux-riches, no woman would want me. It was hard to think otherwise and too easy to slip into that role.

I had hated letting her go like that this morning, but I was paralyzed by indecision, the words admitting that I had lied to her, had lied to everyone, were on the tip of my tongue.

But I couldn't pull the trigger.

What if she didn't forgive me for lying about being rich and successful?

I either had to give her up or tell her.

I couldn't keep lying to her so I could keep on kissing her. That wasn't an option anymore. Last night had proven that to me. And this morning. I wanted her so badly, but my lies stood in the way. Apparently I had enough decency left to stop me.

All evening long, I kept an eye on the clock, and knew when she should be home. That's when I realized I had forgotten to ask her something.

Grabbing my phone, I texted her: *Are you home okay?*

She answered: *Yes, hanging out with my roommates on the roof.*

I forgot to ask. How did Dick know you were going to the Sanctuary last night? It was the question that had niggled at me the entire time I carried her home, but in the overwhelming feelings of last night, it had been pushed aside. Then the crushing lies had clogged my mind.

There was a much longer pause before she replied: *I don't know. He said Lola wasn't posting on her profile anymore. Maybe he hoped she would be there.*

I wanted to believe that was true. But it didn't feel right. None of this felt right.

Before I could ask her, another text from Sierra came through. *Or maybe he followed me there from work. He was watching our apartment before I moved.*

I took a ragged breath. *Bingo!* Dick was a nasty guy. Only a shithead would stalk his ex and then hurt a girl like Sierra.

I should have asked these questions last night, but she had shaken me to my core.

I didn't want to scare Sierra, but this wasn't good and it needed to be dealt with. So I texted: *He may have followed you home tonight. You have to be careful.*

The silence was telling. Finally she texted back: *Yeah.*

That wasn't enough for me. *We should report*

him to the police review board. Cops can't do that. It will stop him from attacking you again.

Her text protested: *I can't get him in trouble. He helped me with Lola for a long time.*

I tightened my lips. *I'll do it. What's his last name?*

She didn't answer, and I wanted to reach through my phone to take it from her. How could she protect an asshole like that?

I texted again: *Don't let him get away with this. You can't. Do you always want to be afraid when you're walking home at night? They'll slap him on the wrist and he'll leave you alone.*

After a few moments, she finally answered: *Dick Langstrom. He's a detective.*

I smiled, glad that she listened to me. I had to be sure she was okay. She trusted people too easily. Once again, I had that odd feeling of wanting to protect her from guys like me.

She deserved better.

I'll let you know after I report it, I texted back.

Thanks!

I wanted to be sweeter to her. She deserved that. But it was all tangled up in my lies.

First, I would make sure she was safe. Then I would deal with the mess I had made of our relationship.

I called the 800-number for civilians to complain about cops. I was surprised that even though it was nearly ten on a Sunday night, I got a response instantly. I described what had happened to the investigator on the line.

Then I waited on hold for a long time before the investigator came back, and said, "There is no Dick Langstrom or Richard Langstrom who works for the NYPD as a detective or a police officer. Nor as support staff, in any capacity."

"He isn't a cop?" I demanded.

"No. Did he show you a badge?"

"No. But my... he may have showed a badge to my girlfriend." It wasn't the right word for what we had, but it was the best word that fit.

"Do you have his phone number or address?" When I admitted I didn't, she said, "Have your girlfriend report it. Impersonating a police officer is a crime. Give her this number. We'll need his address or phone number."

I hung up, my heart pounding.

Dick had lied about his job. What did Sierra say—he had helped her with Lola for a "long time." The whole time he had been lying to them.

It was scary and awful, and yet I couldn't shake the knowledge that I was doing the same thing. The exact same thing. I lied to women to get them to sleep with me.

Dick had probably lied to Lola to get her to sleep with him. And then he built an entire relationship on it. Like I was doing with Sierra.

I tried to tell myself that I was different—I hadn't roughed up Sierra. Only I did, in the guise of a scene. I had scared her and took advantage of her naivety because I could. It was only words, but sometimes words were terrible enough.

I should know that better than anyone.

I found myself clutching my hair and staring at my hateful view. My lying view that told women so much without me saying a word. A rumor and a lucky apartment had helped me slide into becoming a monster.

Who was I kidding? No kid as unloved as me could grow up and be able to act like a real human being. It didn't take beatings and starvings to warp a kid. It just took people who had better things to do than pay attention to you.

So I decided to be something I wasn't, so that women would want to be with me.

Including Sierra.

As much as I wanted to run far and fast from all of this—my usual solution any time it got too real—this time I was worried about Sierra. I knew my own motivations. But what was Dick capable of? What if Dick was outside her place right now, hoping she'd come out and he could intimidate Lola's address out of her?

I had to tell her about Dick. I had to see how she took it when she found out that Dick was lying to them.

I couldn't wait because she might be in danger from that asshole. She had to know what she was dealing with right now so she could take steps to protect herself.

I was on the street and nearly at the subway before I realized I needed to let Sierra know I was coming. I texted: *Stay there. I'm coming to see you.*

Instantly, she replied: *Why, what's wrong?*

I couldn't tell her by text. I had to see her when

I told her. *In subway now,* I texted back.

Only three stops in, I got out of the station and ran two blocks over to the G train in Broadway station. It was only six stops in all—ridiculously close—except for double fair and the need to go outside in a dicey neighborhood to change stations.

Still, it was fast even though it was inconvenient. I was eager to tell Sierra about this easy way to get to her place from mine... and then realized that she probably wouldn't be needing it once I confessed.

When I got out of the underground G train, she had texted me her address. I didn't like the looks of the five blocks between the subway station and her place. The trees blocked the street lights so there were lots of shadows. Cars were parked along the streets where anyone could lurk.

I didn't see anything suspicious on her street. But the address she had given me was a giant warehouse with a mural splashed across the lower half to discourage more random graffiti. I checked the number again, sure it must be wrong. But it wasn't. I couldn't imagine Sierra living in a place like this.

The black door wasn't latched closed, so I was able to walk right in from the street. That meant Dick could get in.

I pulled it shut firmly behind me, making sure the automatic bolt engaged.

Music floated down from the top floor. It was too dark in the stairwell, another strike against the place.

The door to the second floor was locked,

thankfully. I knocked.

Sierra opened it. All I could see was her, as I gave her a tight hug. I hadn't meant to touch her, but I couldn't help myself. The short, floaty dress she wore with her bare feet was intoxicating. But it made the ace bandage on her ankle even more noticeable.

I hadn't banked on the affect she had on me. How could I tell her that Dick had betrayed her sister, knowing I was betraying her right now?

When I released Sierra, a tall, black woman came closer. I realized she was trans. Another guy with crazy cork-screw curls was lying on one of the couches in the big room, grinning and waving as Sierra introduced them as Candice and Jake.

"Did you know the door downstairs was stuck open?" I asked. "I was able to come right in."

"The jamb swells in the heat sometimes," Jake said, still grinning.

It irritated me that he was taking it so lightly. "Anyone could get in. Sierra was attacked by a guy last night who's trying to find her sister."

"We know." Candice gave Jake a hard look. "Go put a sign up reminding everyone to pull the door shut."

Still smiling, Jake went to do as she ordered.

"What did you find out?" Sierra asked me. Candice crossed her arms, listening.

"Dick's not a cop," I said. "The NYPD has no record of him working there."

Sierra's dawning horror was even worse than I had imagined. It went over her in waves as more and more of his lies came back to her.

"He brought Lola home in handcuffs!" Sierra exclaimed. "He said he could arrest her."

Candice didn't seem to be as surprised. "Cops take people to *jail* in handcuffs. They don't take them home."

Sierra's mouth was still open in shock. "Are you sure, Victor?"

"The civilian review board is sure," Vic said.

"I have to tell my sister." Sierra started texting as she said, "I don't know if she'll listen to a message from me. I'm telling her: *Dick isn't a cop. He followed me last night and jumped me, trying to get your address. Call me.*"

Sierra pressed send, then clutching the phone silently, walked over to the couches. Candice watched after her, as did I. Sierra stood there staring into the other end of the loft, waiting for her sister to respond.

Her phone rang and she answered it on the first ring. My heart sank at her broken voice as Sierra said, "Lola, I just found out that Dick isn't a cop!"

Like one, both Candice and I stepped closer. We couldn't hear every word, but enough of Lola's high pitched cursing came through to make it clear how mad she was.

I felt like I was taking body blows, watching Sierra remember that first night when Dick had brought Lola home in handcuffs. Actually in handcuffs! And threatened her with jail. Sierra's voice broke again at how she thought it was the most romantic thing that love at first sight had kept Dick from ruining Lola's life.

"He's a jerk!" Lola shouted, loud enough to be

heard through the phone. "I *told* you he was a jerk, but you kept telling me how *nice* he was to me. He wasn't nice! He was jealous and he never wanted to do anything but keep me locked up in his crappy apartment."

Candice's brows were raised high listening to them. Even Jake returned, and a washed-out blond woman was peeking out from the middle door in the row along one wall, as if drawn out by the noise. Sierra was so aghast by Dick's betrayal that she didn't know she was sharing it with everyone.

"Lola, you have to report him to for impersonating a cop," Sierra said into the phone to her sister.

"No way!" Lola shouted, again loud enough to be heard. "I'm done with that whack-job. And you better be, too!"

"Lola! What if he comes after you?" Sierra listened for a moment. "Lola? Are you there?" She checked the phone. "She hung up on me."

"Honey, that is one dysfunctional relationship you have with your sister," Candice told her.

"I know," Sierra agreed, stealing a glance over at me. "It's better that we're not living together anymore."

I didn't know what to say. There was nothing to say that wouldn't make me the hugest hypocrite alive. It was already choking me, wrapping its monstrous tentacles around my throat, the knowledge that I was betraying her even worse than Dick. I was betraying myself by lying to her when I cared so much for her.

I couldn't take advantage of her anymore. I had

to fix this.

But I couldn't confess now. Not when she was reeling in pain from this blow, and frightened of what it meant. Not when she was looking at me with such mute appeal to help her.

I couldn't hurt her now.

I would make sure she was safe. I would help her through this. I would be a good friend, and show her that I cared. And I wouldn't touch her again until I fixed this mess and I could kiss her with an honest heart.

Chapter 24

Sierra

I suddenly realized that everyone was staring at me like I was a freak show—the Idiot Child on full display. Bound to destroy everything I touched through sheer stupidity.

The fact that Victor looked so sorry for me, so distantly untouchable and full of pity, made it worse. I knew better than to talk to my sister in front of him. Didn't our fight at the Festival teach me anything?

No wonder Victor was just standing there. The litany of shit that was my life was spread out for him to see. Who wanted to take on that kind of mess? Especially a guy like him who could have anyone.

To give him credit, Victor was honest about not being the savior type. He never liked me better than when I was taking care of myself. The way he had reacted to me at the Sanctuary had told me that.

So I raised my chin, trying to shake it off. "I guess that's all there is to it."

"We should report him for hurting you last night," Victor told me. "He said he was a cop. I heard it."

That raised visions of the police arriving at the loft with their flashing lights as I gave them a statement. I could only imagine what Keith would say about that. He was a practical man and he wouldn't like the new girl bringing the cops down on us the second week I was living here.

I couldn't be the kind of roommate who caused trouble. I didn't want to make an awful situation worse than it already was. Dick was a by-product of the Lola implosion. I needed to put that safely in the past where it could burn to the ground without me. I didn't want to drag it into my present, which was finally getting better.

"No, I don't want to report it," I said. "Dick practically crawled off last night after you took him down. He's out of my life."

Victor appealed to Candice. "Don't you think she should take it more seriously? Dick was shaking her last night—look at those bruises on her arms!"

Candice took a long look at me. "Do you have pepper spray, honey?"

"No."

"I'll get you one of mine," my roommate said, heading toward the second door from the front.

As Candice left, Victor told me, "I think you should reconsider this."

"I'll think about it," I said quietly, glancing after Candice. "But not now."

He grudgingly accepted that. "How's your ankle? Shouldn't you sit down?"

"Yes, I should. Why don't I show you my room now that you're here?" I drifted over to my door, the second to the last in the row.

Victor joined me, but he still seemed a bit reluctant. I was ready to get past the bad news and concentrate on the fact that he had run over here to tell me I was in danger. Surely that proved he cared about me! My body was thrumming, remembering how it felt when he carried me to his place, literally sweeping me off my feet last night.

I opened the door to my room, showing off its compact neatness. I had placed the single bed under the loft and lined it with cushions to make a wide couch against the window. The red chair was in the corner in front of the sheets that marked off a narrow closet. A little table along the wall served as my desk.

I retreated inside to sit on my make-shift couch. I carefully massaged my ankle through the bandage. "That feels better. My day off is tomorrow, so I can rest it all day."

I had wondered what it would be like to have Victor here in my room. He dominated the space, making it seem even smaller.

He was looking around in disbelief, even worse than I had feared. "Are you okay living here, Sierra?"

"Sure, my roommates are nice. I'd show you the view from the roof but I don't think my ankle could handle another climb."

Instead of coming to sit beside me, Victor came to kneel in front of me, gently picking up my foot. His hands scnt a shiver up my body. He looked at me so tenderly, and his hands were careful.

"How does it feel?" he asked.

"I was going to put ice on it again before bed."

"I'll get it," he offered, standing up again.

"I got a new ice pack on the way home. It should be cold by now. It's in the freezer in the door."

I unwrapped the ace bandage from my ankle, realizing I should have done it as soon as I got home.

It was throbbing from being bound all day.

Victor brought back the pack and pulled up the little stool for me to rest my foot on. He wrapped the ice pack onto my ankle with a towel. It reminded me of last night when he cleaned me up. The scabs on my knees were still fresh. I was in pain in half a dozen different ways, but the feel of his hands on me, so tender and knowing exactly how to touch me, burned through my body. This was true masochism, loving the pain because of the pleasure that came with it.

He looked up at me like he had a million things he wanted to say, but he couldn't.

I reached out and took his hand, drawing him close to sit next to me. I leaned in, fully expecting he would kiss me. I felt the pull between us. I wasn't imagining it. We were breathing together, poised to close the separation between us.

I savored it, knowing it would make the kiss that much sweeter.

Victor stopped. "I have something I need to tell you."

The tone of his voice made me sit back slightly. "What is it?"

"I can't tell you now, not while you're dealing with all of this."

"Why not?" I cocked my head. "Dick's an asshole, forget about him. It's my own fault for being gullible. And Lola's, for being so stupid. How could she believe him for that long? You get what you deserve, right?"

Victor stood up suddenly. "I've got to go."

"Victor?" I couldn't understand what was happening. "Wait! I thought you wanted to tell me something."

"I'll call you tomorrow, after I get back," he said, heading out of the room.

Candice ran into him at the door, making me wonder how long my roommate lurked outside listening to us. "I've got the pepper spray, honey!"

"Thanks, Candice." I was looking at Victor. Suddenly my room felt chilly, and I shivered, wrapping my arms around myself.

"Hold it in your hand when you're walking," Victor ordered. "It's no good when it's in your purse."

I nodded. How could he sound so concerned when he was rushing to get away?

"Say it," he demanded in a low voice. "Say you'll carry it."

"I'll carry it," I repeated, feeling that tug between us in his order and my obedience.

Candice was looking between us with her eyes wide, like she could feel it, too.

I started to stand up, but Victor said, "Don't get up. That ice needs to stay on for twenty minutes." He took the pepper spray from Candice and handed it to me. His fingers were hot. "Make sure and lock up after me," he told Candice.

With that, Victor was gone. Candice stared wide-eyed at me like she also couldn't believe it, before following him.

I strained to hear the sounds of Candice letting him out and locking up behind him. Then my roommate came back into my room. "What was *that* about?" Candice asked.

I let the air out of me. "I wish I knew! I thought he was going to kiss me, and then he jumped up and left."

"I can tell he's worried about you," Candice said. "He couldn't have been sweeter. Or more protective."

I shook my head. "I think my life is too messed up for him. He's successful and going places. I'm sure he doesn't want feuding sisters and psycho ex-boyfriends around."

"I wonder what he wants to tell you?" Candice asked.

I gave her a narrow look. "I knew you were listening. What do you think it is? Nothing good, or we'd be making out right now. Maybe that's all I am to him—hot sex. But he respects me enough to not push it when I said I don't do that."

"Maybe he has a girlfriend already."

"Someone told me he doesn't do girlfriends. Just casual sex."

"I don't know... rich men always have arm candy. What did you find out when you Googled him?"

I shrugged. "Nothing, really. There's hundreds of Victor Johnsons, but I couldn't find his Facebook or LinkedIn profile. Just his pilot license registered to his NY address."

"What's the name of his business?"

"I don't know. He doesn't like to talk about his work, so I kind of avoid it." I felt bad about being so suspicious, but Victor had brought it on himself by the way he was acting. Why did he run off like that? From the way he stroked my leg, his fingers lingering on my ankle, I knew he wanted to keep touching me.

"Maybe he's a private man," Candice said doubtfully.

"He definitely doesn't like to talk about his family. He tenses up whenever I ask him questions. I take it his childhood wasn't good."

"There's a mystery here," Candice agreed. "Maybe he sucks at relationships because of his bad past. Some people can't handle intimacy."

"We sort of fell into this because he was helping me spy on Lola. And you heard for yourself how that ended." I took a deep breath. "I wanted to talk to him about it last night, but then his date came up and I ran out. Then after Dick... we were both so high on what happened that I don't think either of us were thinking straight. We just sort of clung to each other."

"And now he wants to talk to you."

I sighed. "This isn't good."

Candice didn't agree out loud, but she looked it. I fell back against the cushions, letting the fear wash over me.

A lot of things had gone wrong in my life. There was no reason to think this would be any different.

Chapter 25

Victor

My mind was made up—I would tell Sierra the next time I saw her. I didn't set out to deceive her. Sierra had scorned me first for my New Jersey accent. She only started talking to me at the Chamber because she thought I was a fantasy billionaire. She had sex with me that first time because of my *amazing* view. She wasn't having a relationship with me, she was making love to Mr. Master of the Universe himself.

She would hate me when she found out the truth.

I had to get up early to make my flight to Miami. It was a drop-off—the client was staying for a week so someone else would do the pick up.

I would be back by this afternoon and would have to face the music with Sierra. It was her day off and she planned to stay off her feet because of her ankle. I could drop by and destroy the best thing I had ever found.

I was deep in a funk waiting for my gate to open in the familiar Terminal D, when I saw Blevins.

Normally I wouldn't go near the guy. He was a braggart and an asshole, but he called out, "Hey, Johnson! You taking out the Falcon at Gate 9?"

"Yeah, jumping to Miami and back."

"I didn't know you flew those." Blevins gestured

behind him. "I've got the Gulfstream again."

"I heard you're working for La Vista now." It was a newish company that was started by two pilots backed by venture capitalists. I saw them on the board a lot lately.

"I'm buying into Vista," Blevins said proudly. "They need pilots, so they're giving me equity in the company as part of my pay. I'm going to be a partner."

I stared at him, amazed that such a great opportunity had gone to such a jerk.

"Hey, you should check it out," Blevins said. "They're on the lookout for another jet man. Ever flown the Boeing?"

"Sure." I couldn't believe what I was hearing.

Blevins fished a card from his pocket. "Give Tom Benson a call, man. He was just saying he was looking for another jet guy."

I held the card. "You don't need to put in any money?"

"I didn't," Blevins said smugly. "Catch you later, buddy!"

With that, he sauntered through his gate to the little Gulfstream.

I knew Blevins was a blowhard. But this business card was legit.

What if it was true? I would take a cut in pay to buy into a growing company like La Vista. It could mean serious money down the road.

It could mean everything with Sierra.

I let myself hope for a minute. If I could take a stake in La Vista, then I hadn't lied to her yesterday when I said my business was transportation services. I would be a partner of an already established business!

The only thing missing was the house in Connecticut... and a few millions. But with La Vista there was every hope of making that dream come true.

For the first time, I had an eerie feeling that my double life could merge ahead with my real life. I could be the man Sierra was looking for. Maybe not as rich as she expected, but a man on his way up.

For her, I could work harder than I ever had before.

For myself, I would never give up.

I called the number and asked for Tom Benson.

···

By the time I arrived back in La Guardia, I had my answer. La Vista was interested in exploring an equity-in-kind for a partnership. I would have to submit my flight records and go through a psychological exam, and the cut in pay was not to be sneezed at.

But it was worth it.

When I asked how long it would take to finalize the deal, Benson assured me the one with Blevins was finished in less than 30 days.

I wanted to rush over to see Sierra and tell her the good news. But the fact was that until it was completed, I was just a gun for hire. And I had lied about everything.

If I was a partner in La Vista, then I only had to admit that the degree of my success and riches wasn't as high as I had led her to believe.

It was almost too good to be true.

I mulled it over all day, and realized the only way was to stop seeing her until the deal went through. I would have to stall her for a few weeks. That would be my atonement, my way of marking a pause in our relationship, of letting her know how serious I understood my lies were. That way, I might come out of this with Sierra in my arms.

I passed by the 7 train station, knowing it would be impossible for me to put on the brakes if I saw Sierra in person. Last night it had taken sheer will-power to leave her room, when I wanted nothing more than to lie down with her and hold her all night. My senses were overwhelmed as I sat next to her, and I had come close to tossing away my good intentions and kissing her.

But I couldn't be a Dick.

So I went home. The first thing I saw was the photo of my so-called Connecticut house. I ripped the back off the frame and tore the photo to pieces. That lie was over.

With my feet firmly on a new path of honesty, I called Sierra.

She picked up quickly, like she had been waiting for my call. "Yes?"

My heart twisted—she sounded so scared. She was afraid of what I was going to tell her. I wished I didn't have to do this. But I had to.

"Are you okay?" I asked.

"As much as I can be. What did you want to tell me?"

I took a deep breath. "I know you want to have a real relationship. I do, too, believe me. I never have before, but with you... it feels right."

"Oh, Victor!" she exclaimed, so happy.

"I only need a few weeks, and then I'll be able to explain everything."

There was a few moments of silence, then she asked, "Do you have a girlfriend?"

"What? No! I don't have a girlfriend. I want to be with you... but I need a few weeks." I realized I was sweating. "Is that too much to ask, Sierra? After everything we've been through. You know this isn't easy for me to ask."

She took a deep breath. "No, it's not too much."

"Okay." I was relieved. "Good. Let me know if you see Dick."

Faintly, she repeated, "Okay..."

"Promise?" I insisted.

"I promise."

When I hung up, I felt like shit, but at least it wasn't the end of the world. We could wait a few weeks, and then when I confessed, it wouldn't be such a sharp come-down for her. She wouldn't lose all respect for me.

She'd see that I hadn't meant to lie to her, and hopefully she would be able to forgive me.

Chapter 26

Sierra

I felt awful. Even Candice didn't know what to make of it.

There was something going on that was bad enough to keep Victor away from me. The natural conclusion was some other woman was in the picture, and he needed to be off with the old before he was on with the new.

At first I kept remembering the concern in his voice, and the way he said, "I want to be with you..." It was enough to make me patient. I also got a text every day from him asking about my ankle, and if I had seen Dick. By the end of the week, my ankle was healed, but his *How are you?* texts kept coming.

It felt weird to be in touch but not really talking. That felt wrong on a gut level. Either he cared enough to want to see me, or he didn't.

Gradually I began to think this was a stall, and he was slipping away the easy way. But why not just tell me it was over?

Maybe because he was conflicted. Part of him wanted me while another part of him didn't. There was nothing false about the passion that flared between us whenever we got close. But I could see how he tried to hold back from me.

It made me feel judged, and it was so unfair! My life had been smooth sailing for the past few years. I had everything under control, even though I walked a tightrope to make it that way. It wasn't my fault that everything happened to come unhinged when I met him.

His feelings were written in his texts as clear as day, in how short and blunt they were, asking if I was okay. Whenever I texted back that I was getting off from work soon, or it was my day off, or I was out with Devi or on the roof, he always texted back one word: *Good.*

I didn't trust a man who wouldn't talk to me. So I couldn't trust this forced separation.

Another week later, and I had had enough. I didn't answer his text, so he texted his question again: *Are you okay?*

A couple of hours passed before he tried again. *Is Dick bothering you?*

Irritated, I finally texted back: *Don't worry about Dick. He's long gone. You don't have to text anymore to ask.*

His quick response came back: *I'll stop asking if you promise to let me know if you see him.*

I flung up my hands, at a complete loss for understanding. Why did he care? It wasn't like Victor wanted to be with me. I didn't answer him.

A couple hours later, I got another text from Victor: *Promise me.*

What would he do if I kept ignoring him? Would he come see me again? Maybe talk to me about what was really going on?

I could passive-aggressively force the issue by ignoring him, but I had told him he could have a few weeks.

So I finally texted back: *Ok.* I even added the period to let him know it was settled.

After that, I heard nothing from him. Not for days. I almost regretted telling him to stop texting. Those little daily signs that he was thinking about me had kept me going. Now, without them, I felt like it was really over.

Candice stopped asking about Victor around then, like he was old history.

The only good thing was my final exam, which I did well on, having nothing else to do but study after Victor went on silent running. I expected to get my degree in the mail in the next couple of weeks. For such a life-changing event that I had worked hard for years to achieve, it felt completely flat. I texted my mom to let her know, but I didn't bother telling my brothers.

I wasn't even sure when to celebrate. After my exam? When I got my final grade? Or when I opened the envelope with my degree?

It was that random. And typical of my new life, which was unpredictable in so many ways. It felt odd to finish that huge effort and have nothing to devote my evenings to. Study had filled a lot of my spare time. I had spent so long doing nothing but keeping my head down and plowing ahead with my work.

Now I was bobbing alone in the ocean, with possibilities opening around me. Except for the one I wanted—Victor.

So I felt perfectly justified in going to the one source where I could find out about him—his profile on the fetish community website. It was the one I had found the night before I went to the Sanctuary.

Victor's profile wasn't updated, and neither was Lola's, when I checked. For the whole summer, since he had known me, there were no posts or new photos added. The wall messages posted by women had been left hanging.

I knew Lola was hiding from Dick. Who was Victor hiding from?

I followed the various messages back to their owners until I found KoalaKarla. I was pretty sure that Karla was the woman Victor had been with at the Sanctuary.

Karla was barely active with a few posts in groups and on friends' photos. But under events she was going to, she had listed Pleasure Salon on this upcoming Friday night.

I was really tempted to go. Even though spying had gotten me into trouble with Lola, it had also clarified things and let me finally confront the problem. No matter what the downside was, moving into the Greenpoint loft was the best thing I had done for myself in a long time. It had shaken me out of my complacency and opened up new friendships. Lola was right—we couldn't rely only on each other for support.

I had grown to love the nights on the roof more than anything I had ever done in the city. The conversations never stopped, the energy was incredible, and I liked the crazy struggling hopeful people who lived so closely together. We were a family in a way, loose-knit and independent. But someone was always there when I got home. It made me feel like I wasn't alone.

I was also mulling over Candice's advice, to go out and take what I wanted. To stop waiting and letting life pass me by. So why not take control of the situation with Victor again? Seeing him at the Sanctuary had brought us closer, for that night anyway. I could tell I had broken through something as we lay in each other's arms all night.

But then he retreated again. It made me think that more was going on, whether a woman was involved or not. Victor had a serious block, and I needed to find out what was behind that block.

So that's how I ended up going to Pleasure Salon again at Happy Endings. I reasoned the bar wasn't far from Victor's place, and if he was going out, that was the most likely spot he would be going tonight.

I decided to bring Devi just in case Dick was still lurking around. I would have preferred Candice but she was a bartender and always worked weekends. Devi was fun to hang out with, and was outgoing and could carry on a conversation with anyone who caught her eye, using her whispery voice to dramatic effect. According to Candice, Devi's parents were musicians who lived in a big loft in Soho. They had been supporting their daughter's "independence" for years.

Devi's privileged background gave her confidence like I had never seen before. She even showed me the secret way from Greenpoint to the Lower East Side, taking the G train to the J line. The two blocks where we had to get out and walk on the streets between the stations were scary. We were in the barrio down under the elevated tracks. Some of the stores were shuttered closed, and there was trash ankle-deep in the gutters.

But Devi marched along like she belonged here. A true child of the city.

If I hoped to blend into the crowd at Happy Endings, I was mistaken in taking Devi. My roommate was wearing flowing black sleeves with giant ruffles at the wrist. Her waist was cinched by a wide elastic belt over her jeans, and she wore black stiletto heels. All that black made her pale soft skin and hair disappear, so she had compensated by putting on bright red lipstick and dramatic smoky eyes.

I looked around at the men in suits and women in business wear. Clearly a lot of people came straight to happy hour from work. Devi hadn't listened when I warned her what I was wearing based on what I saw last time—my midnight blue suit with my hair down. Victor liked to stroke my hair...

Devi led the way to the bar where she ordered us both a pink cocktail. I wasn't sure what was in it, but it was delicious. Then Devi led the charge downstairs where the first act for the evening was taking the stage. Old-fashioned burlesque music greeted us, and on the stage a woman was slowly stripping from behind giant feathered fans.

The place was packed, like last month when Lola and Martin's troop had performed. I didn't see Victor. Or Karla, for that matter.

Devi drank and flirted with everyone around us,

as several bump and grind acts took the stage. They all included some kind of twist on the usual strip-tease, with one girl twerking to Beethoven. I laughed and clapped along with everyone else, and really enjoyed myself, despite a sinking feeling with every minute that Victor wasn't going to show.

I wasn't sure if I was relieved or not. I didn't exactly want to see Victor out cruising for women while he had put me on hold.

After the acts were done, the crowd slowly dispersed around us. Devi had two guys glued to her side competing for her attention, so I was happy to wait as the place emptied out.

Then I saw Josh, the big bear of a guy who had been so nice to me at the Sanctuary, and whose girlfriend Anna had told me Victor only did casual sex.

"Hi, Sierra!" Josh exclaimed with his usual enthusiasm.

"Hi, Josh." I introduced him to Devi, who dismissed him with one look and went right back to her guys. "Where's Anna?" I asked.

"She couldn't get off work in time. I'm meeting her for dinner later." He glanced around. "Is Victor here?"

"I don't think so."

"Are you still seeing him?"

I had to shake my head at that. "No, not really."

"Yeah, well... he's a stupid man!"

I laughed at his compliment, given so lightly that I couldn't take it seriously. "He did see me at my worst. So did you. That awful fight with my sister..."

"It's going down in history. The twin fight at Festival. I keep telling people you never touched each other. But rumors fly, you know." Josh laughed and made scratching motions with his fingers like he was a cat.

Another guy came up to our cocktail table. Josh turned and introduced him, "Sierra, this is Liam."

Liam was dark-haired with an easy smile, very good-looking. Devi's attention perked up on the other side of the table, distracted from the two men she had already captivated.

"This must be your first time," Liam said to us, by way of greeting. "I've never seen either of you here."

"I came last month," I told him.

"I'm glad we were interesting enough to bring you back again."

Devi leaned on the table, her hand at her chin. "Are you the producer of this event?"

"No. Just a participant."

Somehow Devi managed to grab Liam's attention as the other two guys watched sullenly. I smiled and turned back to Josh.

"Speaking of your sister, I saw her last week," Josh told me. "They were doing a performance at P.S. 121. Martin suspended her from one ankle."

"Sounds fun." I hoped it was fun for Lola.

"Victor was there, come to think of it. He likes that place. It's tamer here because of the liquor license. There the performers can really let loose."

I thought about how Lola had walked around in

her bra here, while she was topless at the Festival and the private party. Apparently topless was her preferred style.

And Victor's.

So I had the right idea, wrong event. If I had gone to P.S. 121 last weekend, I would have run into Victor there. He was out cruising for women, while I was waiting for him at home.

I had a hard time paying attention to what the others were talking about after that.

When we said good-bye, Liam openly gave each of us his card, saying, "If you want an introduction to BDSM, then get someone reputable. You can ask Josh, ask anyone, I play safe and follow limits. I won't do anything to you that I haven't done on myself."

Devi tittered and pushed on his arm. "Whips and chains! I'm not doing that."

"It's not just whips and chains," Liam said. "But since you mention it, whips and chains can take you places you've never gone before..."

I slipped Liam's card into my purse while Devi kept flirting with him, insisting that bubble baths were her fetish. Liam was laughing at her.

But Josh was looking at me, and at my questioning lift of my brows, he agreed, "It's an incredible rush. Like jumping out of an airplane."

I remembered how Victor had frightened me, and for a few moments, I thought it was for real. That he was going to hurt me.

It was perverse, but I had never felt more alive.

I knew that there were dark places inside of Victor, and things got ugly when that darkness came out. Maybe he was trying to protect me from himself by pushing me away.

Maybe I should listen to him.

Then again, maybe I shouldn't give up on him. He made me feel better than I ever felt before. It sounded like he had led a lonely life with people always giving up on him.

We said good-bye to Josh and Liam, then Devi and I headed down Delancy Street to the subway station. Usually I didn't like taking the subway this late, and I wasn't looking forward to that frightening two-block walk through the barrio. What if Dick was ready to ambush us? Or anybody?

But Devi tripped along Delancy Street heading to the subway station like she had no second thoughts about it.

Naturally when I stopped thinking about it, I finally saw Victor. He was coming out of the subway station at the corner of Essex.

We saw each other at the same moment. I wasn't sure who was more startled. He was wearing black slacks and workshirt. For a moment, before he saw me, he looked exhausted.

I felt sorry for him for a split second, and then I remembered what Josh said about seeing Victor at P.S. 121 last weekend. He didn't deserve my sympathy.

He was either going to step up or I was stepping out.

Chapter 27

Victor

"What are you doing here?" I demanded.

"We were at Pleasure Salon," Sierra said coolly. She looked at my clothes. "Where are you coming from?"

I hesitated. This was why I didn't want to see her until my deal was settled. Everything was in place, I was just waiting for the contract to sign. "I just flew in from Chicago." Then my brain caught up with what she had said. "You were at Pleasure Salon?" I asked.

The washed out blond with Sierra laughed. "Yeah, it was a lot of fun. You should have been there."

"You've met my roommate, Devi," Sierra said, watching me carefully.

I wasn't happy about the news that they had been at Happy Endings. I never expected Sierra would be going out and about in the scene without me.

I drew Sierra aside to get out of the stream of people on the sidewalk. The swooping lights of the Williamsburg Bridge were anchored a block away. The lights of the traffic coming and going filled the sharp slope of the bridge and spilled into the wide street in front of us.

Devi stepped away from us, idly looking into the window of a shoe store. It was hardly private, but it would have to do.

"Are you looking for Lola?" I asked.

"No." Sierra stayed at arm's distance, not giving me any signals to come closer. "I heard you saw Lola last weekend at P.S. 121."

"Did she tell you that?" I asked, surprised that Lola had noticed me in the crowd.

"Josh told me. He was there tonight."

Quickly, I assured her, "I was only there to make sure Lola was okay. I saw a post about Transcendence performing and I knew Dick might see it."

"Lola has her own friends to watch out for her," Sierra said with a frown. "Is that what's come between us? Lola?"

"What? No!"

"How well do you know my sister?" she demanded.

I felt like this was spiraling out of control. Devi was watching us with open interest as Sierra didn't bother to lower her voice.

"I don't know her at all!" I protested.

"Then what is it?" Sierra demanded. "It's been three weeks. You go watch over my sister, but you can't hang out with me? What's going on, Victor?"

I hadn't counted on making her this angry. Sierra was so mad that if I blurted out the truth now, she would never forgive me.

And the thought of Sierra running around loose in the scene made me see red. I couldn't let any other man touch her! Or dominate her...

I almost reached out and dragged her into my

arms right there. Maybe that would have been the smart thing to do.

Instead I said, "If you want to go out, I'll take you to the Masquerade next weekend."

One more week, that was all I needed. My contract was bound to come through this week. I could spend the whole weekend with her, wooing her back, and then break the news to her that a house in Connecticut was only a dream right now. But I would work hard to make it a reality.

My invitation caught Sierra off guard. "A masquerade? Like a ball?"

"It's a big fetish event, high protocol. You'll have to play the part of my slave. Call me master. Do everything I say." I ran a finger down her arm, taking up her hand. So glad to finally be able to touch her. It made everything worthwhile. "Can you do that?"

Sierra thought about it, her chest rising and falling rapidly. I rubbed her fingers lightly, feeling them go warm in her sudden flush.

"I don't know," she said doubtfully.

"You went to Pleasure Salon to make something happen," I told her. "It worked. Do you want to go with me or not?"

Suddenly, she met my eyes. "Yes," she said. "I do."

A satisfaction so deep swelled inside of me. I didn't care what it took, I was going to keep her for myself. I wasn't going to let her be used and discarded by the dogs that ran around the scene. If she was determined to experience submission, then I was going to take care of her and make sure she was treated right.

···

Emboldened by the thought that I was doing this to come clean with her, I sent Sierra a new text every day. First I told her to wear a garter and stockings. Then I asked if she had shoes with an ankle strap. No bra. A long, full skirt. Dangling earrings.

I told her to wear no perfume or scented lotion. I wanted to smell only her skin. Her luscious body.

Each day another command, and each day I was more eager to possess her completely.

Each time, she responded with: Yes.

Open-ended, a freely-given consent to do as I wanted with her. Like the way she had handed herself over to me in the Chamber, so innocently sure that I could be trusted.

How wrong she was! But I would make it up to her. And dominating her through my texts was one of the most erotic things I had ever done. Because I wasn't plotting out my moves and playing a part to woo a woman into surrendering to me. Every word was exactly how I felt. I wanted to own her and show her off so everyone would see that she belonged to me. I wanted to touch her, take her and keep her for myself. Men would lust for her yet know that she had given herself to me.

But each day, there was no word on my contract. Benson wasn't returning my calls, and even the lawyer stopped getting back to me.

Finally on Friday, I'd waited long enough. I went down to the address on the card Blevins had given me and forced my way in. From the first sign of resistance, I knew something bad was happening. And when I held my ground, Benson finally sent the lawyer to tell me.

The deal was off. The stuffed shirt attorney wouldn't tell me why—probably didn't want me to sue them. I wondered if it was the kink. Or my fucked up family. Maybe my psych evaluation didn't go as well as it should have.

All of my big plans fell to earth with a crash. I knew it was too good to be true, but I had wanted it too much.

I was fucked. I was face-to-face with it. I was going to have to confess my lies to Sierra that I was a hired hack at the beck and call of the real deal millionaires. There was going to be no nice shading of the matter. No, the come-down was going to be complete.

I should have gotten the pain over with weeks ago.

I returned home with my mind far away, trying to imagine Sierra coming to my place as I had arranged, expecting to surrender to my masterly commands, her emotions built to an erotic peak by our text-play.

And I would have to sit her down in front of my view and confess my lies.

It was too cruel. Like adding insult to injury to break it to her after making her wait for weeks to hear the news. Especially after I had her keyed into an erotic high, and excited for our big evening out together where she would finally be dominated as she clearly longed to be. I had ruined her first time, at the Chamber, and now I was going to ruin this experience.

She would never forgive me.

That certainty settled in my core, darkening my night and the next day. I found myself getting ready to go to the Masquerade, going out to buy Venetian masks for both of us in gold and red. And a short corset in bronzed gold. I wanted to cinch her into it so she would feel like my hands were clenching her around her waist all night. I didn't ask the price—I would have paid twice what it cost to be able to corset her.

I was going to do it. I was going to take the role of her master and make her my slave. None of it was real, anyway, except for the feelings that we both craved. She would know exactly how I felt about her by the end of the night.

Then I would tell her everything tomorrow morning, and if she couldn't forgive me after that, then she never would.

Chapter 28

Sierra

I couldn't refuse to go to the Masquerade after Victor asked me, even if it came out of left field. He was right—I went to Pleasure Salon to make something happen with him. He was so upset, threatened even, that I went to Pleasure Salon without him that he asked me to go to the Masquerade.

I wanted a real relationship. But it looked like the only way Victor knew how to connect was in the fetish world. And right now, I was prepared to use any key I could find to unlock his mysteries.

Maybe I should have been annoyed by his texts telling me what to wear. But instead, the transgressiveness of it was thrilling, like I was walking on the edge where I shouldn't be. Where no good girl should be.

My anticipation built all week as I discussed the texts with Candice and Devi, who helped me create my costume. Candice lent me the black lace garter belt and white gauze skirt with deep ruffles. Devi lent me the white silk peasant blouse and the shoes with ankle straps. They were only half a size too big. I was so broke I had to put the sheer black stockings with a back seam on my charge account at the store.

Then I got the text late Saturday afternoon: *Car*

will be waiting downstairs at 9.

Victor was sending a car for me. Once again, I was reminded of how nice it was to have money. It made it so easy to solve the everyday problems of living in the city, like how to get to a party without spending a fortune on cabs.

My roommates were impressed when I told them. Candice had been suspicious at first when Victor suddenly popped up again after his long silence, but the car won her over. It was thoughtful and showed class. I told them, "*See...?*" and they did start to understand the roller-coaster ride I'd been on with him.

It didn't take long to drive into Manhattan. I had the spacious interior of the car to myself, with nothing to do but wonder what would happen. I didn't know what to expect as the town car pulled up in front of Victor's apartment building, with its large blank windows glinting in the street lights.

When Victor opened the door to let me in, I had the same feeling—as if his polished exterior was the only thing visible.

I was supposed to consider Victor my "master" for the night. Could I do it? I told him I could. But everything about him put me on edge. He didn't kiss me as I entered. He stepped aside as if carefully deflecting me away. He only smiled slightly, keeping me at arm's length as he examined my costume.

"Turn around for me," he said.

I felt embarrassed as I slowly spun in place. Was I wearing what he asked for? I thought the details were correct, but there was a slight frown between his eyes as I finished my pirouette.

Victor was wearing black—button-up shirt, pants and boots with a deep sheen. It set off the golden triangle of skin at his throat and his sun-bleached air. I had never asked him what sports he played to get so tanned. I knew it only went to his shirt sleeves, leaving his chest and shoulders a paler tawny. All of his tones were golden, and the black set his rugged beauty off to perfection.

I wished I could ask him questions—I had a lot of them! But his scrutiny was silent. And I remembered what he had said about the roles we would play. Perhaps he was already toying with me.

"You said I have to be a slave tonight?" I asked. "Shouldn't we negotiate first?"

Now he smiled. "You've learned from the best."

"How can I trust that you won't take advantage of any loopholes I might miss?" I asked.

He considered that. "You can't. Finding loopholes can be fun. But if you truly want me to end what's happening, you can say 'safeword.'"

"How do I know you'll stop?"

He leaned closer. "If you don't think I will, then don't play with me."

He meant it. I didn't even hesitate. "I think you'll stop if I want you to."

"Good."

I shivered. It was that word again, the one he used to respond to my texts when he didn't want to get into a discussion. That word ended the conversation.

This was his ride, the only way I could go deep

with him. To find out what lay beyond his glossy façade and why he was so isolated and alone. I could ask him, Why don't you have a Facebook page? Why don't you have a girlfriend? A man like him should have a girlfriend, one that wore Flowerbomb perfume.

But questions always made him push me away.

"Will you do as I say?" he asked.

Ah, such a question! I thought. He was standing so close to me, but not touching me. We had barely moved from the door, as if the tension between us was so thick that we weren't able to walk in normally and sit down on the couch to have this discussion like two ordinary people. Because it wasn't ordinary. There was a charged electricity between us, barely held in check by his way of distancing himself from me.

"Yes, I want to please you," I said honestly.

"Good. What are your limits?"

I drew in my breath, my eyes on his. "I don't want limits tonight. I want to see where we can go together. Where you can take me."

In response, he reached up to touch my cheek with his fingertips, caressing my face to my chin. With a slight pressure he raised my face to him. I thought he was going to kiss me.

Instead, he whispered, "Stay like that."

He stepped back, and I was poised, my face lifted, my lips slightly puckered as if to kiss him. I had started to lift my hands, so I clasped them at my waist, my weight still shifted forward on my toes in eager anticipation.

I almost broke from my pose, feeling caught

when he stepped away rather than kiss me.

But... *I want to please him.*

So I stayed as he had placed me, watching with my eyes as he slowly circled me, taking another long look at my costume. This time, bound by his word, I felt every glance fall against my body.

"So beautiful," he murmured, behind me now. His hand trailed along the back of my arm below the ruffled cuff. "The white sets off your skin, like a sun-kissed goddess rising from the foam."

I trembled, unable to see him. It was so naked, so honest. His admiring voice, the longing that roughened it, and the lingering way his fingers touched my arm. Like he was barely restraining himself from throwing me down on the bed and taking me.

But that's what always happened between us. Either the spark combusted and we exploded together, or he threw up walls and ran away. Anything but exploring this tug of war between us.

He circled around to the front, looking down into my eyes. "You belong to me."

I felt it then, with a wild hope. *Yes, I belong to you!* It was what he'd said in the barn at the Festival, when he had played with my mind as we made love.

"Yes," I agreed. As I had agreed all week to his demands.

Now he really smiled. "I think there's too much of you covered up."

"There is?"

He reached for his back pocket and pulled out two gold cords. "Don't move," he reminded me.

I was swaying from holding my pose, leaning forward on my toes. But his warning kept me still as he knelt in front of me.

He touched my ankle, feeling the strap around it. Then he trailed his hand up my leg, up my outer thigh to my hip. He passed the cord under my skirt and waistband, then tied it at the bottom with a knotted bow. It pulled the skirt high up on my thigh, nearly to my hip.

Brushing my skin, he did the same with the other side. The skirt looped down in front, barely covering my panties. The rest of my skirt trailed off to the back.

I could feel the air on my exposed legs. The bare skin at the top of my stockings got goose bumps.

Victor stepped back and examined me. "Better."

He turned to the desk and picked up a tissue-wrapped package. He pulled out something bronzed. "It's a corset. I want you to remember all night, with every breath, that you're bound to me."

He stepped close to me. "Lift up your arms, over your head."

I slowly lifted my arms over my head and clasped my wrist in my hand. As he fit the bronze corset around my waist and clicked each hook shut, I felt a deep blush spreading through me to be dressed like someone who was helpless. He was taking possession of me, reducing me to this state of utter dependence on him.

I knew it wasn't real. I took care of myself every day, worked harder than I ever thought possible to make my dreams come true. But in this moment, putting myself into his hands, I felt light and free of all worry. I was safe with him. Protected by him.

So even as he loosened my peasant blouse so it fell off my shoulders, and he tightened the corset to the point where I gasped, I felt a warm and happy buzz growing. The luxury of being able to stop struggling! To relax and let him decide everything. To let him tie the lovely Venetian mask over my eyes.

When he led me to the mirror, I was transformed. A Victorian courtesan with a tiny waist, my nipples poking the silk of the blouse, and a naughty peek of garters showing.

Victor's Venetian mask was similar to mine. He looked like he could rob a bank in style, a study in red and gold.

When Victor put his hands on my bare shoulders, looking at the two of us in the mirror, I shivered in delight. I could have stayed forever, looking at our new personas in the mirror. We could be anything we wanted tonight.

"Our car is waiting," he said.

"Do you have a coat I can wear?" I asked.

"No."

My eyes met his in the mirror. I knew there was no reason to deny me. He must have something I could put on to cover my shoulders and the bunched up dress between my thighs.

I had fought Lola over this for years. It was a hard thing to ask of me, much more challenging than Victor may have realized. I had protected her with every ounce of my being, and look what she was doing now—showing her body off to anyone who wanted to see it. So my constant efforts turned out to be pointless.

Maybe it was okay for Lola, but that didn't mean I wanted to expose myself, even at Victor's order.

He didn't say a word to convince me, silently waiting for me to comply. He let me slowly form my own arguments in his favor. I wasn't revealing anything—it was risqué but not indecent. And the mask made it clearly a costume while hiding my identity. Even if someone took my photo and put it on the Internet, nobody would recognize me. I didn't even recognize myself.

I started to smile. I could walk around Manhattan in disguise as an old-fashioned slut if I wanted to. If Victor wanted me to. It wasn't hurting anyone, not the least myself.

Yet I felt terribly exposed as we stepped into the hallway. Thankfully nobody else was in the elevator, but we passed one of his neighbors in the lobby. Victor nodded to the man and said hello as if everything was perfectly normal. I could hardly look at the guy. All I got was a confused impression of a big grin before he turned away.

On the street it was worse because there were more people walking by, but better because it was dark. Somehow my costume was not nearly as awful away from the mundane brightness of the lobby. I was grateful Victor didn't have a doorman.

As we got into the same town car that had brought me here, I gave a sigh of relief. Maybe this wouldn't be a big deal for another girl, but for me, it felt like I had already been put through my paces before we got into the cab.

Victor grasped my hand and abruptly brought it to his pants. He was thick and hard beneath the soft twill. He stroked himself using my palm, without looking at me, idly watching the traffic and pedestrians outside our windows. I kept looking at his face, as he settled back, his expression softening as he continued to stroke himself with my hand.

He was using me to pleasure himself. But he was so detached. Here in the car, where I finally admitted to myself that I would have done so much more if he had asked, he never looked me in the eyes.

When I ventured to ask him, he stopped me before I could finish. "Don't speak."

So I continued to stroke him, putting my attention completely to the task, rubbing and dragging my nails across his long thick hard-on through the twill. But he held firmly onto my hand, setting the pace and rhythm he wanted. I struggled inside of myself—he was using me, objectifying me with every command.

Why did I love it so? Why did it make me more eager to please him? Why did it make me hang on his every word, every turn of his head. Like I existed only for him. He made it that way, with his attitude and hardly any effort on his part, as if this was the natural state of things between us, that I should serve him without question. That he should be the center of my world, while he cherished and took care of me.

"We're here," he murmured, rousing me from

the erotic haze I had fallen into. As I shifted, I realized I was damp between my legs. Just from stroking him!

Victor smiled at me, his eyes piercing me, knowing exactly what he had done.

I tried to pull myself together to face the sidewalk, but I was stripped bare by this point. I felt so naked anyway that skin hardly mattered anymore.

Besides there were plenty of half-dressed people on the street outside the venue. It looked like your typical Chelsea dance club with no sign, only ropes and bouncers by a nondescript door in a black facade. But the scattered bunches of people arriving or waiting to go in were dressed in black tulle like dark ballerinas, or vampires in long coats and high-necked dresses, or sheathed in brightly colored rubber so that every curve showed.

As we entered, I mostly saw the masks that everyone wore: tufted by feathers, sparkling with spangles, some with long noses and some full-faced and painted in delicate designs.

There was an exhilaration in the air, as if everyone felt the same abandon. As if anonymity made them freer to be whoever they wanted to be.

Now Victor's attention was on me, very different from his aloof demeanor in the car. He made sure I wasn't jostled in the crowd, ushering me through as if I was made of glass. He held my hand, watching my reactions to everything, kissing my palm and putting his arm around my shoulder to guide me.

In the lobby and the dance floor beyond, where the buzz from the crowd was the loudest, there was typical techno dance music. Little clots of people were dancing around the edges, with the main mass in the middle, their arms pumping overhead.

Victor took me straight back to the open stairwell. On the second floor, a more soothing electronic music without vocals played in the long darkened loft. Plush chairs and sofas were arranged in groups around the pillars. Pools of light picked out one spot from the next, while the outer edges were in darkness, giving the illusion that the room was much bigger than it was.

I was panting from the climb and my tight corset, and I couldn't quite catch my breath for the sudden fear that Lola would be here. Maybe it was the underlying drum beat of the music that reminded me of Lola. It was the first time I considered the possibility, and I was glad about that. It was about time I stopped thinking about my sister all the time.

Victor was watching me, smiling a little too smugly. "Transcendence won't be here. They don't book entertainment for the Masquerade. *We're* the show."

"Now you're reading my mind?" I asked. "Am I that transparent?"

"Yes."

Again he said it with such finality that I couldn't say anything more.

And with that, my apprehension faded away like it never existed. I didn't have to be afraid of showing too much of myself to him, whether it was too much skin or my insecurities. Victor already knew, and here he was, still with me despite the odds against us.

As for the others, being masked was freeing in a way I never imagined it could be. It didn't matter what I did because they didn't know it was me, so I didn't have to play by my usual rules. I could throw all of that away, and be someone new. Someone who experienced every moment without fear.

Victor slowly led me by hand through the clusters of furniture, past the dim forms of couples in various positions. The rainbow upholstery turned out to be white slipcovers that turned colors under the lighting. Exposed skin had a red or blue or green cast. With the masks, everyone was alien, like we were no longer on Earth.

The sounds of flesh being smacked, the low cries and groans, filled the air with their lust. Then I saw bared buttocks pumping and legs kicking high, or people humped over each other as they knelt on cushions in front of the chairs. Other people were wound in ropes and were being flogged or spanked as they bent over the backs of the couches.

Victor stroked my arms while we watched the various scenes, a methodical rise and fall that mesmerized me with sensation. Even the people making love were fair game, as we drifted by to pause and watch their ecstasy.

It was a heady thing to see people being intimate in real life. Much more so than watching a video. I could feel their passion, and knew it was real.

At the other end of the long room was a frosted wall that cut off the bathrooms. The glow through the wall served to light most of the area near it.

Victor led me inside the bathroom. The light

was bluish, like I was underwater in the stainless steel and white bathroom. Both men and women were using it and washing their hands in the long silver troughs where water ran continuously.

Victor pushed me up against the frosted wall, face-first. My palms splayed against it to brace myself.

He leaned into me, pressing me against the wall.

With my eyes so close to the glass, I could see the dim shapes through it. On the other side, the hazy forms of people were turning and pointing. They could see the shadow of my body through the glass wall, our hands pressed against it.

Into my ear, Victor murmured, "I want to see how well you followed my orders."

People were coming into the bathroom behind us, going into the stalls and washing their hands next to us. But Victor didn't pay any attention to them. He leisurely bent down and circled his hands around my ankles. "Straps. Good."

His hands trailed upward. "I like the seam, that's a nice touch."

He was lifting my skirt as he raised his hands. I bit my lip, knowing I'd be exposed.

Tugging on the garter, he added, "Black lace is always a good choice."

With his thumb still hooked around my garter, he circled his arm around my chest, pulling my back into him. "Keep your hands on the wall," he ordered.

I held on for my life as his hand slid to my breast. His fingers tightened, gripping my breast until

I hissed my breath inward. He was rougher than I expected, as if he felt the right to treat me however he liked.

His fingers pinched my nipple through the silk. "No bra. But then we all knew that."

I jerked, but he wouldn't let me budge. "She doesn't like to be teased?" he asked, his voice mocking.

"No!" I exclaimed. But I could hardly complain, not when his fingers were doing things with my nipple that I had never felt before, like there was a live wire connected to my core.

"No...," I repeated more weakly, twisting in his arms.

He kept pulling and twisting on my nipples, one then the other, as he held me against him with one arm wrapped around my waist. I felt engulfed by him, hidden yet exposed as his fingers pressed harder and harder.

I wanted to protest, "We're in a public bathroom!" But that was part of the crazy weirdness of the whole thing. That he was holding me and torturing my nipples in here. But people were doing much more out there.

Writhing in earnest to get away from the sharp pains and tugs he was giving me, I finally cried out, "Victor!"

His face buried in the back of my neck, taking a deep breath. "No perfume. Excellent."

"Was that another test?" I panted.

Abruptly he released my nipple, pressing himself against my back, his hands braced against the wall. His breath burned hot against my ear. "What was the one thing I didn't tell you to wear?"

I arched my back, loving the feel of him up against me. His rigid cock pressed into the cleft of my buttocks, rubbing into the curve of my lower back. With hardly any effort, he could slide himself inside me, and I would cry out in pleasure.

I knew what he was talking about. "My panties," I breathed.

"I didn't tell you to wear underwear, did I?"

"You... you said no bra."

His hand slid down to my thigh, up and under my skirt. His hot palm caressed the bare curve of my butt. "You're wearing a thong."

"Yes."

"Are they over your garter or under?"

I flushed, remembering how Candice instructed me to put my thong on last. "That way he can take it off and you still have your garters on," my roommate had explained.

I had tried it that way, but it was too slutty. And it wasn't comfortable.

"Under."

The disapproving murmur filled my ear. "I can take care of that."

He dug into his pocket and pulled out a curved black hook about the size of his palm. "Do you know what this is?"

"No..." The glint of steel at the heart of it looked sharp. My voice got louder. "What are you going to do with that?"

"No questions." His voice was calm, but

determined. I knew I couldn't stop him, whatever he had decided to do. It gave me a weak feeling in my knees, like the way he had destroyed my illusions about myself in one minute flat the first night we met. I thought I was so smart and had everything under control, but that turned out to be laughable. I was flailing and barely keeping afloat, and it was no use kidding myself otherwise.

Letting go and letting him decide was so much easier. Even if it was only for one blessed night of relief.

I sighed and relaxed, and he rewarded me by hugging me tightly from behind. He knew the mental struggle I had just gone through. He knew he had won.

Victor ran his hand up under my skirt, up to my hip. Slipping the hook under the side of my thong, he gave a tug and it separated with hardly a sound. He changed hands and did it to the other side. "It's used for cutting rope quickly when something goes wrong."

He reached around to my front and put his hand over my mound, rubbing his fingers down into the silky hair. The thong separated and fell. With a flick of his hand, he dropped the cut up thong to the floor. His fingers were slick from the priming he had done to me.

My thighs separated slightly, inviting him in further. He sank his finger into my cleft, drawing a moan from me. My clit slipped under his slick fingers as he rubbed it, and my moans turned into cries.

I didn't care anymore what he did to me in the

bathroom. I wanted him inside of me *now*. "Please, Victor! Please..."

"You want me to fuck you?" he asked harshly, his mouth against my ear.

"Yes! Please, Victor!"

I felt I existed only to please him, to be filled by him. That the only thing that mattered was being his.

He pulled back, and I thought he was going to satisfy me.

Instead he said, "Come with me."

Chapter 29

Victor

I had to tear myself away from her. I wanted nothing more than to give her what she asked for right there between the sinks. But that's what I always did. I fucked her instead of truly possessing her.

So I did what I had to do. I pulled away again. Leaving her vulnerable, confused, under my control. I had toyed with her all night, delighting in her reaction.

I had her in the palm of my hand. She was glassy-eyed from arousal, and driven to the peak of frustration. I had to steady her as I led her from the bathroom.

I took her over to a couch in a darkened corner, but before she could sit down, I grabbed a cushion and dropped it on the floor. "Sit," I quietly ordered.

She looked down at it for a moment, but I didn't have to urge her. She sank gracefully down to sit at my feet.

I pulled her head against my knee, stroking her hair as I tried to cool myself off. I wanted nothing more than to drag her up on the couch and bury my cock inside of her. But I couldn't share that with everyone here. She belonged to me alone. And while I would show her off, I would only give others a taste of her.

But she nuzzled her way between my legs, her breath hot through my pants, turning so her mouth was against my cock that strained against my pants. With the mask over her eyes, she was still completely Sierra. I never imagined her as someone else.

I twined my fingers in her hair as she pressed her hot mouth against the mound of my hard-on.

"You would suck me off here?" I asked hoarsely. "With everyone watching?"

"Yes." Her eyes glinted through the mask in animal hunger.

"You would do anything I say?" I asked.

"*Yes.*"

My voice hardened. "Then kiss my boot."

Her mouth opened in a gasp. I knew that it wouldn't be easy for her to kneel down to me and kiss my foot in the middle of the Masquerade. It would be even harder than giving me a blow job.

That's why I wanted it.

With her breasts heaving, she backed up slowly. She glanced down at my polished boots, then back up at me. I waited on edge, knowing I was asking a lot of her, maybe too much. If she resisted, the spell would break. She was not one to fight against her submission. She needed to dive into it like someone who was fearless in leaping off a cliff.

But I had to know if it was true. Did she belong to me?

She pulled back her cushion and settled her knees, leaning over with her entire body. In one graceful motion she placed her lips against the top of my boot. I could feel her press her mouth into the leather to feel my foot inside. Then before I could say anything, she rose and sank again, kissing my other boot.

My heart swelled as she sat up on her heels, smiling shyly up at me. She was giving herself to me, no holding back, no second thoughts. She trusted me...

Even though she shouldn't.

I had a golden collar in my pocket, but I suddenly knew I couldn't put it on her. Not while the lies were still between us. It would make a mockery of everything we had done if I collared her while she didn't know the truth about me. Even if it was only for one night while we were masked.

My finger touched her mask. Why was it easier this way? Maybe it was the barrier between us that allowed me to let go completely.

I took her by the hand and led her through the Masquerade. I had to get out, to run off with her alone. Every vaguely familiar face was threatening, was someone who could break the spell I had woven between us. So I rushed off into the night, my only desire to get her home.

She dashed after me, her hand outstretched in mine as I drew her along. I ducked into a cab with her, giving my address, and then turned on her with a voraciousness that surprised us both. I kissed her mouth, her face, her neck, biting and pulling her flesh with my teeth until she cried out. I didn't care about the cabbie, I was barely restraining myself from doing more.

She drowned under my assault, her fingers

pressing against my chest as she tried to breathe. I pulled her across my lap, holding her tightly as I kissed her. The noise of the cars, the honking and sounds of the city disappeared in her lips.

I pulled it together long enough to make it into my building and up the stairs with her. I had been mugged before, and I wouldn't let that happen while I was with Sierra.

But we were barely through the door of my apartment before I was kissing her again, my hands popping the hooks on her corset. She was pulling up my shirt and unbuckling my belt, as I jerked down her skirt.

She raised her hand to swipe off her mask, but I stopped her.

A little more time, that's all I needed. Before I had to tell her the truth.

She stopped, her eyes questioning, stilled by my refusal.

The mask hid what she was thinking. For the first time that night, I wasn't sure about her. She stood there wearing only her long peasant blouse and her stockings, while I had on my pants with my shirt off.

And our masks.

My hand cupped her neck, and I drew her closer. "*You're mine.*"

Her chin jerked, as if instinctively denying it. She was fighting me.

I brought her forehead to meet mine, my hand still around the back of her neck. It was vivid in my mind how she had surrendered to me the first night I had met her. It was wrong to get so turned on from frightening her, from convincing her that I held her life in my hands. But she had given herself over to me completely, and I took her.

Just like I wanted to take her now, and plunge into her, claiming her for my own.

"You're mine," I repeated hoarsely.

"No...," she barely whispered.

In surprise, I drew back to look into her eyes, that were suddenly swimming with tears. She was crying! She couldn't be crying now, but she was!

But I didn't hurt her.

She was crying and looking up at me as if I had. "I wish it was true," she managed to say.

My fingers tightened on her arms. "It is."

"No, it's not. And you know it."

I stared at her.

"This is just a game you're playing with me," Sierra told me. "This isn't real."

I felt the ground drop beneath my feet. It was true. I had created the Victor persona for her to fall for, the millionaire master every girl wanted.

Is this what it had come to? I would have to confess at the height of our scene? Destroy everything I had built for her throughout the night?

I reached for Sierra and slipped the mask up to wipe her tears. I felt the familiar jolt in my cock at seeing her so vulnerable, as the knowledge burned along my nerves, setting me on fire.

Maybe I was torturing her for my own pleasure. Maybe I was that messed up, needing to see her suffer to prove that she would stick by me. But she could sense the walls between us. Instincts couldn't be denied.

And neither could my raging hard-on.

Touching her face, separated by a wall between us that I couldn't ignore, I had to admit the truth. "I'm not really Victor. I'm Vic."

I pulled off my mask, letting it drop behind me.

She blinked up at me, her eyes enormous from the tears. "What do you mean?"

"You were right the first night we met. I was born in New Jersey. It's what did this to me. I was so mad that you called me on it, in that snide way, and that's why I scared you. Because you reminded me of all that."

"All what?"

I raised my eyes to the ceiling. "I wasn't beaten or abused. Maybe you'd understand that. I was ignored. I didn't exist. I still don't..."

"You don't exist?" Sierra asked slowly.

"I know it doesn't seem possible, but this man you've gotten to know isn't me."

"In some ways, I do feel like I hardly know you," she agreed.

"What is there to say? I grew up dirt poor and abandoned. My sister is... really my mother. Until I was thirteen, I thought my grandparents were my parents. Until I found my birth certificate, and then it all made sense. Why none of them liked me or wanted me around. I was shame to my grandparents, a mistake to be erased from my sister's life. My *mother's* life. She was fifteen when I was born. They should have given me away. Maybe then I would have had a fighting chance."

I never expected to make my confession this way. Never imagined telling her my darkest secret. But I had been longing to be honest with her, to find a way to open my heart so she would understand. And it spilled out.

"I'm Vic, not Victor," I repeated more firmly. "Nobody, really. I got no education, had no hope of bettering myself. I had to do it all on my own. I never thought I would succeed at anything."

Sierra put her hands on my chest. "Vic, I do understand. I had to fend for myself as a kid, *and* take care of Lola. But at least I had my older brothers to help me when I was little. I wasn't completely alone. It must have been awful."

I shrugged, finally putting my arms around her. "It's the only thing I know, being alone. The one time I tried, that I fell in love, it was a disaster."

This was it, time to confess it all. That this was Adrianne's old place, and that I wasn't rich or successful. That I had lied to her from the beginning. Time to turn that shining love in her eyes to disdain. And she would look at me the same way my grandmother looked at me when I came through the kitchen door, as if she wanted to take the broom and sweep me back outside with the garbage.

"Sierra, I'm sorry... I'm so fucked up. I've done horrible things to you. I don't know how you'll ever forgive me—"

My chest twisted as I strangled on the next words I had to say.

"It's okay," she told me. She reached up to kiss

me softly. "I'm glad you told me. I've been longing for this moment, when you opened up to me. Vic..."

I kissed her back, feeling that unbearable tightness begin to ease. I knew I should say the next words, to admit everything. I had jumped over the present and suddenly bared my soul to her. I never planned on doing that. But I trusted her so much that it had burst out of me.

And now I was filled by her acceptance. That empty place inside of me overflowed with the love in her eyes. For her to know I was nothing, unwanted by the people who should have wanted me the most, unlovable and unable to love... yet somehow she cared about me even more.

So I kept on kissing her. In a distant part of my mind, I knew it was wrong. But it was too much for me. I had woven a spell around her all night, keeping myself on a razor's edge to give her the exhilaration she was seeking. With my emotional release—telling the truth about what twisted me into this man—came a relief so great that I couldn't control myself anymore.

I hugged her tight, kissing her with abandon.

Chapter 30

Sierra

I felt Vic holding back at first, but then he let go and I let go with him. I felt so bad for him. Now a dirty tow-headed boy replaced the snotty rich kid I had imagined him as a boy. Why didn't he realize that people would respect him more to know he had made a success of his life despite such hardship? The rejection he suffered from his family had cut him deep.

Our kiss quickly caught fire. As he picked me up and carried me to the bed, taking his time to strip off my stockings and kiss my legs all the way from my toes to my lips, I threw away restraint.

I couldn't get enough of the way his skin felt, the hardened muscles shifting underneath as I clung to him.

He was insatiable, and so intense in the way he watched my every reaction, and drank in every moan and gasp. He seemed to take the most satisfaction in giving me pleasure.

The beauty of his eyes, pale gray-blue, so clear it was like I could see inside his soul. It made me feel as if I was saving him, like the romantic movies that I loved.

That feeling was more than pleasure as we rocked together, him quickening and then pausing to plunge as deep inside of me that he could, making me moan to be so filled. Building slowly, our bodies moving together, never stopping until pure sensation was rippling through me.

I wanted him with a fierceness that I'd never imagined. All of him, not just his body and the feel of his hands on me, but his thoughts and emotions, too. I wanted to know everything about him, and it felt as if we balanced on the verge of something grand, tipping over into a passion that would unite us as one.

He looked into my eyes, brighter than tears, as I arched my back. He started to come, and I knew it was because of me, that I was giving him that pleasure.

It sent me right over the edge.

•••

When I woke up in the morning, the sunlight was streaming through the big windows even though the loft faced west. I could hear the sleepy holiday traffic and distant sirens through the glass.

Vic was still asleep, his thick bronzed lashes fringing his closed eyes.

I looked down at him as he slept, and felt a swelling of love like I had never felt for anyone. I wished I could wipe away the past that haunted him. But I also wanted to talk to him about it, so that he would know he was finally understood and loved. I was ready to dive into the abyss with him if it would help him heal.

It was a miracle that I had finally broken through to him. It hadn't been planned, my sudden burst of tears last night. But when he said, "*You're mine...*" I knew it wasn't true. I could feel it in my heart, a sudden sharp pang, that there was something terrible standing between us.

Our masks said it all. I wanted to take mine off, but he wanted to keep them on. At first it was so freeing to wear my mask to the Masquerade. It let me get beyond myself, enough so that I had let him cut off my thong in the bathroom in front of everyone and begged him to have sex with me right then and there.

He touched me in ways I didn't know existed, playing with my mind and emotions as much as my body. I would have done anything for him last night, and that's why I kissed his boots.

Why did the thought of it make me squirm and throb between my legs? It was so wrong, but it felt so right.

But in the end, I couldn't make love to him with our masks on. Not when he called me "mine." Not when I wanted desperately for it to be true.

So he had to be honest, and he did it for me. Because he wanted us to be together.

I was reluctant to wake Vic, as much as I wanted to talk to him—I had tons of questions stored up for him. But he was sleeping soundly after our late night last night. I sneaked into the bathroom and then into the galley kitchen. Going quietly through the cabinets, I saw that Vic had run out of nearly everything. There was nothing I could throw together for breakfast, not even eggs.

I picked up my discarded costume from the floor and untied the gold cords so it was an ordinary long skirt again. And I tightened the neck of the blouse so it didn't fall over my shoulders. Picking up the bronze corset, I carefully folded and smoothed it with the cords, laying it on his desk. Vic's place was so compact there weren't many places to put things.

I took his keys and quietly let myself out of the loft. It was a beautiful morning, with the hottest weather of the summer safely past. The street was empty, probably because it was the long weekend, the last of the summer when so many people left the city. But things like holidays didn't matter for a girl like me. I would be working tomorrow on Labor Day.

The corner deli had nice-looking lox, so I ordered two toasted everything bagels with lox and cream cheese. And two large coffees.

I was returning with our breakfast when I saw Dick. He was lurking between two cars, looking up at Vic's windows.

I stopped short.

A surge of anger made me clench my fist in the bag. That asshole lied to me! Lied to my sister, too. Took advantage of us both. I remembered Lola in handcuffs with mascara smeared under her eyes, standing in the door to our apartment with Dick holding onto her arm. Confessing that she had been doing drugs and the cops caught her with them. I was so scared that Lola was going to be arrested and ruin her life. I was so grateful to Dick, so pathetically grateful that he wanted to take care of Lola.

"You! Dick!" I marched toward him, juggling the bags while pulling my phone out of my purse and dialing 911. With my thumb poised over *send*, I ordered, "Get the *fuck* out of here! Or I'm calling the police."

Dick raised his hands, caught off guard with my approach from behind. "Sierra! Hey, wait... I tried to text you but you didn't answer."

"So you come here to stalk me?"

"Your rich boyfriend will pay me back. Lola owes me two thou. You know she does. Hell, I handed it over to *you* some months to cover rent."

"That's between you and Lola. I don't live with her anymore." I pushed past him. "You better go now or I'm calling the cops. And I'm telling them you impersonated an officer. You handcuffed my sister and threatened to arrest her."

He blanched. "Hey, wait a second... You can't do that."

"Oh, yeah? Consider it done."

I punched the number and when the operator came on, I said, "I want to report I'm being harassed by a man who identified himself—"

Dick eyes went wide. He turned and abruptly ran off. His bulky body swayed back and forth as he scuttled around the corner. It served him right to run like a scared rabbit.

The dispatcher was asking for my location. "I'm sorry," I said. "He heard me and ran off. I don't know where he is."

As I hung up with the dispatcher, I saw Vic standing in the doorway of his building. His hair was standing on end and he was wearing sweats and no shirt or shoes, like he had run down six flights of stairs to help me.

"Are you all right?" Vic demanded, coming up to

me panting and flushed.

I was shaking. "Did you see Dick run when I called the cops? Like I lit a fire under him!"

Vic was shaking his head. "I saw you two from the window. What happened?"

"He asked for two thousand dollars. He says Lola owes it to him."

"Then he better go ask Lola," Vic muttered. "Why's he here looking for you?"

"He wants me to pay it." I wasn't going to tell him about that "rich boyfriend" crack Dick had made. "I called him on lying about being a cop. The coward ran off!"

Vic had his arms around me. I couldn't tell what he was thinking. But he looked like he had been punched, like he was in pain.

As we went upstairs, I was proud of myself for confronting Dick and calling him on his shit. I was talking too much, keyed up, but Vic didn't have much to say. At first I thought he was worried about me. I expected him to tell me to call the cops as soon as we got inside his place.

Instead, Vic said, "I have to tell you something, Sierra. I should have told you last night."

The pit of my stomach dropped. It felt same way as when Dick told me Lola had broken up with him. Like another disaster was about to hit.

I had known it all along. I wanted to believe in the fairy tale last night. But the Great Wall of China that separated me and Vic couldn't be as easy to surmount as a revelation about a selfish teen-aged mother who refused to acknowledge her own son.

"What is it?" I asked.

"I'm not rich." His voice was flat, his eyes cold. "I'm not a partner in my own business. I'm a pilot for a charter company. I fly rich people around the world, but I'm barely scraping by."

My head shook slightly. "What do you mean? You're not... what about this place?"

"I inherited it from Adrianne, my first girlfriend. She was living here for ten years before I moved in so the rent is cheap. She married an investment banker the week before she turned thirty, and she said it was because I wasn't good enough for her. That I'd never be good enough." He tightened his lips briefly. "I don't have a house in Connecticut."

Shocked, my eyes went to the photo on the table behind his couch, but it was gone. I didn't notice that last night.

Like it never existed.

Vic stood there, only wearing sweatpants hanging low off his hips. He looked gorgeous, but it was fake.

"You lied to me," I realized.

"I lied to everyone," he agreed. "I give girls what they want—the billionaire lover who rocks their world."

"It's a *lie*."

"Of course it is! Do you really think you can start a relationship the way we did? You were wearing a disguise, and I was *Victor*."

I backed up a step. "You scared me because I called you *Jersey*. Because I saw through you."

His chin jerked. "Yeah. But then Monica told

you I was rich. Then you were interested in me."

My heart was pounding too fast, and I felt like my world had been cut out from under me. I was hanging in midair, waiting for the hard drop.

Everything had changed. But mentally I couldn't catch up to figure out in what ways—except the shock that this man I trusted was not who he had pretended to be.

"No..." Panic ripped through me, as I hoped that there was some way this could be fixed and everything could somehow go on. I didn't want it to be true.

I was falling in love with him...

"Sierra, please." He tried to reach for me, but I retreated to the door.

Slowly it was sinking in—he had been lying to me all along. Every time he talked about his life. Every times he looked into my eyes, he was hiding that lie. That's why he didn't take me out to dinner. That's why he arranged it so we never talked. That's why he kept disappearing.

I had been making allowances for him, while he was taking advantage of me.

Everything was founded on lies. Not some little lie told last week, a mistake in judgment, an aberration from the norm. This was the original lie, the game he had played with me from the start.

He made me feel like I wasn't good enough for him! Those times he withdrew, and I thought it was because I didn't fit into his life. It was because he was lying to me. Manipulating me!

He used me, while he had the nerve to act

superior to me.

"You're *worse* than Dick," I told him, pulling open the door.

"Sierra, don't go." He stepped forward as if to stop me, but I glared at him.

"Stay away from me," I said flatly. "Don't call me. Don't text me."

I ran when I reached the sidewalk. I couldn't get away fast enough.

...

Later on, I couldn't remember a thing about that subway ride. The next thing I knew, I was sitting on the edge of the bed in my tiny room. I wasn't even sure if I had seen any of my roommates when I came into the loft—it was a terrible blank.

Everything Vic had ever said was suspect. What was true? What were lies?

You are mine...

My heart felt pierced, literally stuck right through, and it was pounding too fast. It felt like I was still finding out, still realizing the extent of how terrible this betrayal was.

It showed me what Vic really thought of me. He thought that I liked him because he was rich. He knew I talked to him in the Chamber because Monica told me about his Connecticut house and great job, so I thought he was different from the others.

While he thought I was a shallow gold-digger.

My day dreams about Victor were shattered, dead and gone along with his imaginary house. And now I also had to feel bad about myself because I was mercenary enough to like the idea of a man like *Victor* who could make my life easier.

The last thing I wanted to do was tell Candice and Devi the truth. It was awful. If it was only one lie, even one big lie, it would be different. But there was something awful about a continuous lie. That every time we were together, he was lying to me about who he was, pretending to be something he wasn't, and laughing at me for believing him.

Even last night, when he sort of started to confess but not really. What was that about?

It reduced everything to a game, and I was the prize. Whether by trickery or deceit, it didn't matter. *I* really didn't matter, only the fact that I had surrendered to his lies, to the phantom man he had created that no girl in her right mind could resist.

That was the worst part.

···

Later that afternoon, the sounds from the rest of the loft finally reminded me that a big Labor Day bash was being held on our roof tonight. Everyone else didn't have work on Monday morning, but I did. Not that it mattered.

It was going to be a long night.

I hoped to avoid everyone, but a girl had to pee. I had to leave my room to get to the bathroom.

Devi came running out of the kitchen to intercept me before I reached the bathroom. "What happened last night? Did he like your outfit?"

"He loved it," I told Devi. "He gave me a corset..." That I had left behind on his desk. Along with the bagels and coffee. "And a beautiful mask with gold trim..." Also left behind with the rest of my future.

Devi tilted her head. "What's wrong?"

Candice poked her head out from the kitchen, watching us.

It was the downside to living in the loft. The lack of privacy. I wanted to crawl off and cry alone, but I couldn't.

I had gotten the support I needed from them since I moved in, and I was grateful for it. I couldn't turn on them when I didn't want them up in my business.

"It's awful," I admitted. "You're going to die when I tell you."

That brought Candice out of the kitchen. "What is it?"

"He confessed last night. He's been lying to me. He pretends to be a multi-millionaire to trick women into sleeping with him."

"What?!" Devi exclaimed. "Who does that?"

"Someone with serious issues," Candice said, her lips pursed up in disapproval.

"Yeah," I agreed. I wasn't going to break his confidence and go into his tragic family background. But it qualified as "serious."

"But... he's so cute!" Devi protested. "He could get any girl. Why is he lying?"

"It's New York," Candice pointed out. "Most beautiful women like Sierra want a man with money."

I frowned. "I'm a salesgirl. I don't care if he's a garbage man, as long as he's good to me."

"Come on, Sierra," Devi chided. "You have to admit he would be the total package if he actually did have the goods."

I drew in my breath. "I know that's what *he* thinks! And yes, maybe I did move faster than usual because of it. But I was attracted to him as soon as I saw him, and that's when I still thought he was a schmuck from New Jersey. Which is exactly what he turned out to be!"

Devi raised her hand as if to dismiss all of that. "It doesn't matter. Any man who does that is not worth your trouble."

Candice shrugged. "People do make mistakes. It seemed to me like he really cares about Sierra."

"So what does he do?" Devi asked.

"He's a pilot. He said he works for a charter company, flying rich people around."

Devi made an exasperated sound. "A glorified chauffeur."

"A pilot is a noble professional," Candice protested. "I bet he makes good money. And benefits. What's the guy lying for if he has all that going for him?"

"Yeah," I agreed. "It's the fact that he lied to me. And made me feel like I was less than him because I'm working class."

Devi lifted her fingers and fluttered them. "But you *are* working class. That's what made it such a Cinderella-story."

At that moment, it felt like I was standing on the other side of a distinct class divide. Candice rolled her eyes at me as if to say that on some things, Devi was impossible.

Suddenly I was done making nice. "I'll get your blouse back once I've dry cleaned it, Devi. Excuse me,

I'm on the way to the bathroom."

Candice called after me. "You can toss the skirt in my room. I'll wash it with my other whites."

An sad ending for a costume I had loved so much. Yet it seemed fitting considering everything else that had happened.

...

I did my best to avoid everyone that evening as the party prep picked up in pace. Music blared from the roof long before the party started, and with my open windows to catch the nice weather, there was no way to avoid it. Eventually Candice completed whatever creation she was making in the kitchen and finally took it upstairs.

I ducked out to grab my stuff from the bathroom. Likely friends of my roommates would be coming down all night to use it. I could hardly imagine the state it would be in tomorrow morning when I would be trying to get ready for work.

Living in the loft had its negatives, that's for sure.

As I was returning to my room, I noticed that the door on the end was sitting open. Our other roommate was finally home. Marky, a dancer who had been on tour for the past couple of months.

Feeling distinctly anti-social. I hurried into my room and locked the door behind me.

I was determined to sit out the party there. And wallow in my misery.

But people kept gathering down on the sidewalk below, calling out to tell the roof partiers to buzz them in. And by sunset the sound of talk and laughter finally melded with the music, and the smell of the BBQ on the grill made my stomach rumble.

It was hard to wallow when there were so many distractions.

I knew I looked awful, with my hair stuck up in a pony tail and my old shorts and tank top, but what did I care? I slipped on a pair of flip flops and went into the living room. There were two people who I didn't know grabbing a bag of ice from our freezer.

I followed them up the two flights of stairs to the roof.

It was packed with people. Some dancing, most just hanging out. A lot more chairs had mysteriously appeared. Yellow police tape was draped along the top of the walls on the long sides to keep people from sitting there.

Keith was in his usual spot, guarding his potted garden with a beer in hand. The grill was belching out smoke under Jake's smiling eyes. Jake called out a greeting to me and offered me a hamburger, which I devoured like I'd just crossed the Serengeti. Keith saw me standing there and ordered one of his friends to get out of the chair so I could sit down and eat.

I got by without talking much. It felt good to be among people who liked me, a balm on my soul. I felt pummeled by the city, by those I cared about most.

I wonder what Lola is doing now? I thought. I had spent my whole life knowing exactly what Lola was doing. It was weird having my sister disappear so completely from my world.

On a sudden impulse, I texted Lola my address

and said: *We're having a roof party. Bring Martin if you can.*

After a few minutes, my phone dinged. Lola replied: *Busy now but next time yes.*

I took a deep breath, trying not to feel hurt by the blow-off. Lola might not be ready to try, but I wasn't a quitter.

Still, I might have to accept the fact that I wouldn't be able to have a relationship with Lola anymore. *If that's her choice, I can accept it.* But I wasn't going to give up trying.

"Hi, there," a guy said, standing above me.

He was dark-haired and smiling. It took me a moment to recognize Liam from Pleasure Salon. Josh's friend.

"Hi," I said. It was a little weird. The last time I saw him, he was offering to show me and Devi what kink was all about.

"Devi invited me," he explained. "But I came because I wanted to see you."

"You did?"

"Yes. I saw you at the Masquerade last night. At least, I think that was you. Wearing a white dress?"

Before he was even finished, I got up from my chair to close the distance between us. I didn't want him talking about that in front of everyone.

Liam immediately caught on, lowering his voice and moving aside with me, away from the clutch of people around Keith. I noticed that Keith kept glancing at me to make sure I was okay. I must have been radiating my distress.

"Sorry about that," Liam said. "I didn't realize

you weren't out. But I have to warn you that Devi is telling everyone that you both went to Pleasure Salon and that's where we met."

I closed my eyes briefly. "Great. Just what I need right now."

Liam shrugged. "Most people don't care. But you have to be careful with your job. Sometimes supervisors can get all moralistic on you."

"I'll keep that in mind."

His smile was so easy and relaxed, his eyes admiring. "You looked beautiful last night. It was the best scene I saw in the bathroom all night."

I blushed hard and fast. I could hardly bear to look at him. Everything I had felt last night surged up inside of me, along with the memory of my burning need to give myself to Vic completely.

To think that other people like Liam had been watching us...

No, that wasn't *us*. It was *Victor* who had master-minded that scene, not Vic. It was Victor, the fake millionaire who was designed to bring women to their knees. Literally.

"I don't mean to embarrass you," Liam said. "Unless you like that sort of thing..."

I put my hands to my head. "I really can't deal with this tonight."

"I'm sorry. Is something wrong?"

My throat began to close. "Yes."

"Do you want to talk about it?"

I shook my head. It was too raw. How could I tell him that last night was an illusion? That I didn't really know the man was I was playing with.

Liam patted my arm, his smile turning sympathetic. "I understand completely. You have my number if you want to talk to someone. It can be confusing sometimes, exploring this side of ourselves. I'll go now and get out of your way."

"You can stay," I said. "Enjoy yourself. It's a party."

"I came to see you. And I've done that." He gave me a very sweet smile. "Hopefully I'll see you again sometime."

With that, he nodded pleasantly and threaded his way through the crowd. I watched him leave, so I caught his last wave from the doorway to the stairs. I lifted my hand in return.

I was almost sorry he had left. Thinking about Liam was better than thinking about Vic, but everything was a reminder of Vic.

Now that Liam was gone, I was able to relax back into silence, letting the party flow over me. I felt as if I was floating above myself, stunned.

After a while, I went back downstairs and locked myself in my cubicle. The party raged on overhead, showing little signs of wearing down.

It was the worst night ever. I had lost more than Vic. I had lost my trust in myself, in my own judgment. First Dick, then Vic liked to me for months. If I couldn't take care of myself, then I was seriously screwed. And I should have known from the warning signs and red flags that Vic was not what he claimed to be.

I lay awake for most of the night and had to get up early for work. I wanted to curl up and protect myself before I was fully awake. Aware of the pain before I was aware of anything else.

I stumbled through my morning routine in a half-dazed state, appalled by the mess left behind in the loft by the revelers, but still so absorbed by the fact that the best relationship I'd ever had was nothing but a sham. He had been using me and laughing at me for being so gullible the whole time. I could hardly keep myself moving through my shower and morning prep, getting myself to work step by step. I got a lot of practice doing that the week I was looking for my new place, so I knew what it took to endure.

That's how I doggedly went through the next couple of days, getting my work done one step at a time. Until I came home on Tuesday afternoon to a large envelope addressed to me, left carelessly on the table in the stairwell.

I opened it up to find my Associate Degree certificate. The one thing that hadn't let me down. My family had told me for years that it was a waste of time, but I did it, one hard class at a time. Like I had done everything clse in my life.

For four years I had worked for this moment.

I walked into the loft, but it was strangely empty and quiet. No music thrumming upstairs or coming through the back door from Keith's apartment.

There was nobody I could call. My mom? She would be proud for a moment but the moment would pass quickly, and I didn't want to deal with her abrupt hang-up right now. My brothers would make a joke about my obsession with books and schoolwork before they thought of congratulating me. Lola? It was too rife with recriminations—she would think I was crowing over her.

No, it felt like I was embarking on my new life the way I should be, alone with only my own sorry wits at my command.

Chapter 31

Vic

I shuddered every time I thought of Sierra's eyes after I had told her. Shocked contempt, and more. I deserved every bit of it.

I should have told her before the Masquerade, or even weeks ago. At least after the Festival. When I knew I couldn't keep lying to her. But I had run away rather than tell her the truth. She was the brave one, tracking me down at the Sanctuary. And at Pleasure Salon.

While I was busy running away from life.

And now I had lost her. Lost her for good.

How could she forgive me? I couldn't even try to contact her. Her last words were final—*don't call or text*. After what I did to her, she deserved the right to set her own terms.

I'm so sorry...

The unsaid words choked me.

I did an overnighter in London on Tuesday, and came back to an empty feeling. I had to fix this with Sierra.

It was a tragedy that I had ever started lying about myself in the first place. It had started so small, such a stupid toss-away thing for toss-away girls. But it snowballed into something more, until it had taken over my life.

On Wednesday morning, I made up my mind. She said don't call or text, so I wouldn't. I couldn't go by her apartment because that was creepy after Dick's stalking.

But I had to see her. I couldn't leave things like this between us. I needed to say *I'm sorry*.

I thought it would be better if I met her in public, but I didn't want to make her feel unsafe by "running into" her at her bus stop or one of her local shops. I wanted her to feel in control.

So I went to Lowenstein's. It was a risk she would think I was messing with her work. The only way was to be a legitimate customer and back off the instant she wanted me to.

I had to try.

Lowenstein's was a big department store. I went to the Men's section and bought a couple collared shirts and a pair of pants. I charged them to the store credit card the helpful salesman filled out for me.

Armed with a large shopping bag, I combed through the store looking for Sierra. I finally found her in the Junior section hanging up clothes.

She looked serenely beautiful, concentrating on her task. Her hair was tucked up in a twist, and she was wearing a striped blazer with navy blue pants. Every time I saw her, I seemed to see more in her. This was the serious Sierra, the woman who had worked hard to make something of her life.

She looked up and saw me as I closed the distance between us. "What are you doing here?" she demanded, her voice strained.

"I needed some new clothes." I lifted the bag slightly. "And I had to say I'm sorry to you. I'll be on the steps of the Library if you want to talk."

"I'm working."

"When you get off."

"That's in three hours."

I shrugged. "I'll wait."

Sierra frowned. "I told you not to contact me."

"I haven't texted or called. But I've wanted to tell you that I'm sorry. Face to face. I feel awful about this."

She considered me for a moment, and then turned back to the rack. "I'll think about it."

I nodded and backed up. One of the other employees was staring over at me, so I said a little louder, "Thank you."

Sierra saw where I was looking, and replied with a bright fake smile, "You're welcome."

I went downstairs and considered what to do. I could get back home with my bags and return in plenty of time. But what if she ran out during a break to see if I was there, but I wasn't?

I turned north and marched up to the Library and sat myself down in the very middle of the steps, the bag beside me. I had nothing more important to do right now than wait for Sierra.

Chapter 32

Sierra

The shock of seeing Vic in the store shook me. I had trouble listening to people after that. Their mouths moved while I was thinking—*what could he possibly say that would change anything?*

Nothing. There was nothing that could explain this away.

But I couldn't stand him up. Now that I knew he was there, waiting to talk to me, I had to hear what he had to say for himself.

The man knew me too well. All those mind games were paying off for him. He knew how to make me do what he wanted.

I went to the bathroom after punching out, and looked at myself in the mirror. The affects of the past few days showed. I looked tired and bruised, but there was something in my eyes I liked. I hadn't been beaten.

I walked up to the Library and from the corner of the block, I could see Vic sitting in the midst of the mid-afternoon crowd. He was looking my way, as if watching for me. He picked up his shopping bag and met me halfway.

"Thanks for coming," he said.

"I'm ready to be stunned and amazed by your explanation of all this," I retorted.

Vic let out a derisive sound. "I have no

explanation. No excuse. It's as fucked up as it looks, sorry to say."

"You should have told me!"

"I started to. A few times. At our first party, I was about to tell you but Tricia barged up. And then the Dick thing happened... but I should have told you much sooner. I was falling for you, and didn't want to ruin it."

"No, you were testing me. To see if I was a gold-digger," I said.

He grimaced. "Yeah, at first, it's true. I tried to tell you after the Masquerade, but all that stuff about my sister spilled out. I never told anyone about my sister being my mother, not even Adrianne. I hid it from her because I knew she wouldn't like it. I knew she couldn't be trusted."

I stared at him, seeing him blanch at his own words. It was so raw. But people were bumping past us on the sidewalk, practically jostling us aside.

"Let's go sit down," I said reluctantly.

We walked around the Library to Bryant Park in the back. It was a polished park, the jewel of midtown. We found an empty bench and sat down. Vic was turned towards me, but I faced resolutely forward.

"I told you I was messed up," Vic said.

"I thought you were a hot sexy mess. Not a pathological liar."

"Can't I be both?"

"No."

Vic grimaced. "I'm sorry. I can't believe I ruined the best thing that's ever happened to me."

In spite of myself, I felt a thrill inside. "You spent the whole time making me feel like I wasn't good enough for you."

"No! I didn't. I never meant to. If I was distant, it's because I wanted to tell you the truth but I knew you would hate me for it."

"So why didn't you tell me if you wanted to so badly?"

"It was always the wrong time. There was the fight with your sister, and you needed money for a new place but I didn't have any. And then... I had a chance to buy into a charter company. I thought it would make it better if I was a partner in my own business. I knew you wouldn't care about the money. But then that fell through, and when Dick came to my place, I finally realized there never would be a right time. So I told you."

"You didn't include me in your life. Or take me out on a real date. I thought you had other girls for that. Rich girls who were more like you."

He looked appalled. "You thought that? Truth is, you saw my life. Work and a little fun on the side."

"Good luck with that," I said shortly, staring into the bushes across the way. A woman and three tiny dogs went by, trotting so fast their legs blurred.

"I want to have fun with *you*, Sierra. I'll take you on dates. If you want to travel, we'll travel—"

I put my hands over my ears. "I can't believe you because all you do is lie."

"I'm not! I want to start over with you, Sierra. We can get to know each other for real."

I wished I could believe in him again. But how?

His foundation was rotten at the core. It must be to allow him to do this, to lie to everyone, even at their most vulnerable. What kind of hardened asshole could pull that off year after year? Girl after girl?

"I don't know," I said. "I doubt everything about you now. What kind of man does this? Do you have *any* morals? Is cheating off the table? I mean, you must be an expert at self justifications."

"I know I don't want to hurt you again."

"I don't buy that. You knew you were hurting me when you were lying to me. You did it to manipulate me, start to finish."

"No, that's why I stopped seeing you after the Festival. I couldn't keep lying to you."

"But you still believed I was after you for your money. Or you would have told me," I pointed out. "While you were having sex with me! You were lying to me and laughing behind my back about how you tricked me into it."

"Not laughing—"

"How could you do this to girls if you don't feel contempt for us?" I was getting madder by the minute. "I could tell everyone that you've lied."

His expression was impassive. "I expect you to. I don't care."

"Oh, really?" I glared at him. "You're full of shit! Obviously this Victor-charade means everything to you."

"No, it's over and done with. Never again."

I shook my head. "I have no reason to believe you."

"I can prove it to you."

"How? You've already proven yourself to be a liar." I stood up, still shaking my head. "I should have known better than to talk to you again. You tricked me in our first scene when I thought you were going to hurt me. And you tricked me the whole time we were together. I'm done with you."

With that, I turned and walked away. All I could see were the lies. I wanted to call him *Victor* because that's who I had fallen for. Not this new man, not *Vic*. The man I made love to wasn't lying or manipulating me. *Victor* knew me inside and out, and I trusted him.

How could I trust Vic? I couldn't.

I mean, I know he's twisted. But this is really twisted. Seriously twisted.

I didn't look back as I left the park.

Chapter 33

Vic

I couldn't believe it. In spite of everything, Sierra walked away. I could talk my way out of hell if I had to. But she up and walked away.

She had stripped me of my powers, unmasked me for the man I was. And judged me unworthy.

I sunk my head in my hands, wishing I could start all over again, go back to the day I met Adrienne and walk past her. During our relationship, I was still working towards my pilot's license, and she was the one who confirmed my grandmother's words that I would never amount to anything. That's why she left. And even when I finally did get my license after she left, and started to fly for a living, I should have been proud of myself. Why did I keep on with the charade I had invented? Because I couldn't let myself believe in my own success?

I had sabotaged myself. Looking back on the years, they were so empty. At the time it had been exciting, getting away with something, having sex with the most beautiful women in the city, watching them chase after me and beg for my attention. Degrading themselves in all sorts of delicious ways to win my love.

But that was nothing now that I had met Sierra.

From now on, I would be the kind of man she

could admire. No matter what.

Chapter 34

Sierra

I fumed all the way home. Now I was really mad. Maybe it was the proper sequence for the stages of grief, and I was grieving for the loss of my *Victor*. The man who had seduced me into submitting to him, until I begged him to take me in front of a hundred strangers. Then I kissed his boots in gratitude.

I made a disgusted sound, making several people on the bus look over at me. I was getting heartily sick of my train-to-bus commute, with the long wait in between at Hunter's Point. But what choice did I have? I didn't make enough to live in a proper apartment. My bank account was nearly zeroed from the money I had hemorrhaged over the past month, including the gone-forever security deposit my old landlord had officially claimed because I hadn't given him thirty days notice.

Vic had baited his trap with the lure of money and an easy life. And I had been stupid enough to fall for it, and to think I wasn't good enough so I wouldn't protest when he didn't take me out or introduce me to his friends.

I was so gullible! How could I have dropped my guard so much? Because I wanted to believe that an irresistible man found me irresistible?

It was the memory of his touch that I couldn't shake. I really wished I could stop thinking about our last scene at the Masquerade. But it haunted me, that feeling I had craved to finally become one with him. He had hardly touched me, but it was embedded in my body and heart and mind, the ways he had touched me. As if he had claimed me, and because I had given myself to him, I could never take it back. In spite of everything, I dwelled on our moments together, every look from his eye, every caress of his finger across my skin.

I would never forget his face when he told me about his mother, like he was showing me the ugly scars he kept hidden from everyone else. The walls in him had fallen, and his eyes pleaded with me to understand, no longer closed off. It was exactly what I had longed for, and it was even better than I had imagined. The way he had made love to me... as we gazed into each other's soul...

I realized I was sitting on my bed in my cubicle room, and couldn't remember how I got home. Again.

It was really stupid to walk around the city in a daze. I was a hazard to myself.

I was overwhelmed because I couldn't separate Vic from Victor, the con artist from the master, the lover from the liar. Maybe they were one and the same, and the feelings he had given me at the Masquerade were part of the con. Maybe it was nothing but manipulation and I was eroticizing my attacker.

Sick, sick, sick...

It made me worry for Lola. Was my sister going

through something like this with Martin? If anyone fit the con man label, it would be a grifter like Martin. An older man taking advantage of a young, flighty woman who was alone in the world for the first time...

What if Lola was going through the same mental and emotional manipulation, as Martin softened her up for some devious reason of his own?

I put my head into my hands. I had come full circle. Only I was a lot worse off now. I had gone to the Chamber to find out if Lola was in danger, but it had taken the whole summer to find out the truth. It was even worse than I had feared.

And Lola still wasn't speaking to me.

I opened up my computer and took a look at Lola's profiles. Her Facebook page hadn't been touched in a couple of months, with only sporadic updates before that. Her profile on FetLife was exactly the same as the last time I had checked.

On the other hand, the Transcendence page had lots of events listed on their calendar. It looked like they were doing more gigs than before. Maybe the addition of Lola to the mix had helped give their troop a boost.

They were booked for the second and fourth Saturday of the month at P.S. 121, the place Josh had told me about. When I checked out P.S. 121 online, it turned out to be a performance space and art gallery with recording studios and rehearsal rooms on the upper floor. On the ground floor was the gymnasium and cafeteria of an old school that had been revitalized by the local community in Alphabet City, back when nobody wanted it.

The calendar listed Transcendence among several acts for next Saturday at the performance space, and in the gallery in the former cafeteria space there was a show of leathercraft and steampunk art.

It also said the TNG was going to have an outing to P.S. 121 this Saturday to take in the art show and performances. The word "TNG" caught my eye, and it took me a moment to remember Monica, the woman I had met that first night in the Chamber. Monica had suggested that I go to TNG because that's where I could find real kinky people my own age, not just horny guys.

Poor Monica was also being duped by Vic, along with so many other girls.

There were lots of reasons for me to go to P.S. 121 this Saturday. Not the least was to find out why my heart was still calling out for the things Victor had done to me, no matter how much I told myself that *Victor* didn't exist. That man who held me in the palm of his hand was a figment of my imagination.

But if I did go, I had to do it right this time. I picked up my phone and texted Lola: *I want to come to P.S. 121 this Saturday to see you and TNG. Is that okay?*

Hours passed before Lola finally responded: *It's my work. I can't have drama.*

I felt unjustly accused. I almost fired back an irritated response, but then remembered that our last encounter at the Festival had been dramatic enough to spawn legendary rumors of a twin cat-fight. Lola was still mad about that.

So I swallowed my pride and texted back: *No*

drama. I promise.

Lola must have been waiting because she replied: *It's open to the public. I can't stop you.*

It couldn't have been clearer. Lola wanted nothing to do with me.

But my effort was my own. I wasn't going to give up on my sister, and if she didn't want to talk to me, that was fine. She would know I was there if she needed me.

I also had questions that needed to be answered about Vic.

...

I had a tough time figuring out what to wear on Saturday night. I didn't consult with Devi and Candice this time—things had cooled between me and Devi since our Labor Day party. I didn't like it that Devi had told everyone we went to Pleasure Salon together. One of our 3rd floor roommates was being weirdly friendly now when I said hello in passing on the stairs.

Finally I settled on black leggings and a chiffon blouse that looked like a runny water color in dark blue and purple. And high heels, of course. Josh had said that you could go topless at P.S. 121 so that meant people would be dressed sexier than at Pleasure Salon, but that wasn't my style.

I wasn't playing a role or dressing to please anyone other than myself tonight.

I took the short-cut subway route and braved the two block walk alone between the stations. It would suck getting back home, but what choice did I have? Twenty-five bucks for a cab was too much when I also had to pay to get into the event. Getting out at the first station, I clutched Candice's pepper spray in my hand as I hurried along, keeping up with the stream of passengers who were also heading into the city on the same awkward route.

P.S. 121 was as close to the river as you could get on the East Side without getting wet. From the outside, it looked like an old-fashioned four-story block school building with the words Boys and Girls chiseled into the stone over the doorways at each end. I went through the open door under Boys.

The first thing I saw in the anteroom was Lola, painted bright pink. I didn't realize it was Lola at first. All I saw was a naked pink girl greeting people who were coming in, and then my brain caught up with my eyes.

Lola scrunched up her face, which was also a uniform pink. "I told you not to come," she said defiantly.

"I didn't say anything," I protested.

"I can see the judgment all over you." Lola stood back and waved her hand in my general direction. "All you do is criticize me."

"Lola, everyone is looking at you," I pointed out. And it was true, everyone coming through the door stared at the naked pink girl. "It's not just me."

"It's worse with you. They think it's interesting and fun to see a pink girl. You make me want to hide."

I couldn't believe I was being lectured by my naked little sister. "Back up, Lola. I just came in. You didn't even give me a chance to say hello to you." I turned to Martin who was hovering unhappily nearby, wearing a ring-master's black tail and top hat. "Hi, Martin. How are you?"

"I'm fine. We're psyched about our performance tonight." He rubbed a soothing hand against Lola's back as she subsided into a sullen silence. "The girls are going to be wild creatures caught in our nets."

"Really?" I asked. "That sounds interesting."

In a low voice, Lola told Martin, "She's being sarcastic."

"No, I'm not." Irritated, I turned back to Martin. "I can't wait to see it."

Without another word, I walked into the large auditorium. I was really pissed. Why was Lola being so awful? Sure, I had messed up by spying on her. But it was done out of love, and it didn't make sense that Lola would cut me out of her life because of it. Besides, Lola had been pushing me away even before I spied on her. That's why I had been forced into desperate measures in the first place.

I wandered around and looked at the leather and steel bondage contraptions that were scattered around the outer edge of the room. A couple of people were being tied up or spanked, but it was nothing like the Masquerade where bodies were writhing in every darkened nook. Mostly it was people standing around talking—civilized like. Some were wearing fetish gear, but most people were in business or casual clothes including one guy in shorts and sandals.

A performance was in progress onstage—several women were wearing black bodysuits and prancing around with bits in their mouths. Their harnesses were held by a man in a western hat. I realized they were supposed to be horses, and remembered the listing on the calendar said there would be a Pony Girl Exhibition.

I was shaking my head in wonder at the vivid imaginations of these kinksters, when I saw Josh and Anna.

Smiling, I made my way over to the towering man and his diminutive girlfriend. "Hi! You go everywhere, don't you?" I asked them.

"Pretty much," Anna admitted. "Josh has a lot of commitments."

I shook my head slightly, not understanding.

"He volunteers for a lot of groups and events," Anna clarified.

"That's me," Josh said. "Overextended."

They both gave me a hug, which surprised me but made me feel warm inside. They were so friendly that I hung out talking to them for a while, wandering around and watching the pony girls up on stage.

"I saw that TNG is supposed to be here," I said.

Josh looked around. "They met at the diner a couple blocks over. They'll be here any minute. They do an intro there to explain safety and negotiation, and to answer any questions. Then they come here to have fun."

"Oh." So I had missed the question-and-answer portion of the evening. Things weren't going as I had planned.

When did it ever?

"I can introduce you to the couple who run it," Anna offered. "TNG would be a good place for you to go. I send all the young newbies there."

A shot rang out, making me jump. I looked at the stage where the guy in the cowboy hat was now cracking a long whip, making what sounded like gun shots. He wasn't hitting any of the pony girls with it, but they were trotting faster in a circle.

"Why do they do that?" I asked.

"It's a fetish," Josh explained. "There's something freeing about taking on an animal role. You can let go and release your primal self."

"At least they're being honest about it," I said.

Anna laughed. "There's no hiding it if you're doing pony play. Or puppy play."

I was about to ask her more when I suddenly saw Vic. He was over near the door as if he had just come in. That meant he had seen pink-Lola in the anteroom.

A flash of jealousy shot through me. Vic had seen Lola naked again. Why was he sniffing around after my sister? Was he trying to get one of us, and it didn't matter which one it was?

Vic was standing there so confident and easy, in his black jeans and T-shirt. Even his simple clothes screamed "quality" and wealth. Maybe it was his model-good looks. Or maybe because he spent more money on his cotton shirts because he knew from experience that a woman could spot the difference.

Was it wrong that I couldn't take my eyes off him? Wrong that he held such power over me? All I wanted to do was hug him and let him hold me until the nightmare went away. Until I could believe in the man I had thought he was.

Anna followed my gaze and realized, "There's Victor."

"I know," I said shortly.

Another woman went up to Vic and greeted him. He smiled in his charming way, a little reserved in the face of her eagerness. She was practically on her toes, leaning towards him, and standing too close.

It took me a moment to recognize Monica. Instead of the Catholic school girl outfit, Monica was now wearing jeans and a tank top that barely contained her bust.

Vic was smiling easily down at Monica, talking to her, oblivious that anyone was watching them.

Anna gave me a sympathetic glance. "He's like a meteor, Sierra. He passes through women's lives. He doesn't stick around."

"He's been seeing Tricia for almost two years," I pointed out.

"That's because she's fine with being a booty call in between her real boyfriends." She gave Josh a glance. "I wanted more from a relationship. And you do, too."

"Yes."

It strangled me, this terrible knowledge I had. I should warn everyone that Vic was a liar; that he used women to get what he wanted and then discarded them like they were nothing.

They deserved to know. Anna. Monica. Maybe even Lola was at risk.

At that thought, I knew I had to do something. I also knew I wanted to hurt Vic, hurt him as badly as he had hurt me.

"Vic isn't rich," I said flatly, still staring across the auditorium at them. "That's just what he tells girls to get them to sleep with him. He pretends to be the kind of rich sugar daddy every girl fantasizes about."

Anna was staring at me. "What?"

"He's a liar. I saw through him the first night we met, and it made him so mad..." I trailed off, not sure if I wanted to tell them about our first scene in the Chamber.

"But..." Anna was trying to understand. "Victor travels around the world. I've seen the photos."

"Everyone has," Josh agreed. His eyes were narrowed at me, not believing me.

"He's a pilot for a charter service," I explained. "That's how he gets to those places."

Now they were both looking at me like I was crazy. "Are you for real?" Anna asked, her tone sharper.

"He fooled me, too. For months. He confessed last weekend after the Masquerade."

Anna glanced at Josh. "I thought you weren't seeing him anymore. That's what you told Josh, right?"

His eyes were still narrowed. "That's right."

Surprised that they would turn on me so quickly, I said, "Let's go ask him, if you don't believe me."

"That's a very good idea," Josh said. "Victor should hear this himself."

Josh led the way over to Vic. I felt like I was the

guilty one, running after them. It wasn't fair! I was telling the truth.

As they approached, Vic saw me. His eyes lit up and he took a step towards us, completely ignoring Monica.

My stomach did a flip at the way he looked at me, and I instantly regretted telling Josh and Anna. My body yearned to melt into his arms at his tender look. Even though I knew I should smack some sense into myself instead.

Then Vic noticed Josh and Anna, and their concerned expressions. He looked from them to me. His eyes hardened. He knew I had told them.

I felt a sudden chill. If Vic denied it, they would believe him. They would think I was a woman scorned trying to hurt him. Which was true, in a way. But I was also telling the truth about him.

In that moment, I knew exactly how horrible it was going to be. They were going to close ranks against me and I would be shunned. I might as well keep on walking out the door right now. But my feet were stuck to the floor in misery. All I could do was stare at Vic as a traitorous part of myself still wished that I could reach out for him.

"Hi, Anna. Josh," he said, hardly glancing at them. "How are you, Sierra?"

My traitor of a stomach did that flip again.

"Sierra has been telling us something odd," Josh said diplomatically.

"They don't believe me," I said, still caught in his eyes. "I wanted to warn them. Warn Monica."

"Me?" Monica asked, her hand to her chest.

Vic looked around at us, boring in on him from all sides. "It's true. Whatever Sierra told you, is true."

Anna was shaking her head. "She said you lied about being rich."

Vic looked at me as he admitted, "I did. There's no house in Connecticut, no business, no millions."

Monica's eyes opened really wide, and Josh was shocked as well. "Seriously?" Anna demanded. "Everyone thinks you're the original Christian Grey."

"I'm a pilot," Vic said. "But none of the rest of it is true."

I felt a spreading relief throughout my body. If Vic had lied again, I would have crawled off never to come back. I had been poised on the precipice of their disbelief, and he had pulled me back from the brink. Nobody doubted me now.

The others were staring at each other in disbelief, until Anna suddenly laughed. "I don't think you ever told me you were rich. Someone else did. So technically, you didn't lie to *me*."

"How funny," Monica agreed flatly, but she wasn't laughing like Anna, who was long over Victor and had a good relationship with Josh. Monica's glance at me said the same thing *I* was feeling—what kind of jerk did something like this?

I felt better than I had all week. *Finally* someone understood what I was feeling.

Vic looked at me first, as he said, "I should have been honest when I found out about the rumors going around."

Josh smacked him on the arm. "Dude, that takes some kind of Teflon balls."

"It explains so much," Anna agreed, still giggling like it was the biggest punk in history. "Tricia's going to *die!*" Then she grabbed Josh and pulled him aside to whisper in his ear.

That left me standing awkwardly alone with Monica and Vic. The way he was looking at me made me feel funny. He didn't seem upset that I had blown up his sweetheart deal, so it was hardly the revenge I had been looking for.

Why did I have the weird urge to apologize?

Instead, I turned and walked away without a word.

Chapter 35

Vic

I watched after Sierra as she disappeared into the crowd. I couldn't care less that she had told everyone. The only opinion I cared about was Sierra's.

Monica was looking at me like I was a snake—strangely fascinated, as if she wasn't sure whether she should run or come closer to check it out. Her expression wasn't much different from vanilla women when I seduced them into kink. They wanted to please me because they wanted my imaginary status and power, but they weren't sure about the whole dominance/submission thing.

"You're a real bad boy, aren't you?" Monica sounded wary yet enticed.

I shrugged. I couldn't see Sierra anymore. I wasn't sure if she had told Josh and Anna about our first scene together, how I had scared her to tears. But it would serve me right if she did. She had the right to say anything about me that she wanted to.

"Look!" Monica exclaimed, pointing at the stage where the pony girls were filing down the short flight of steps. A cluster of big-wheeled carts stood at the base. "The pony girls are going to pull the carts! Let's get in one."

I smiled but I didn't mean it. "I'm sorry, Monica. But I'm trying to apologize to Sierra. I need to go find her."

"Sierra? She doesn't want to talk to you now. Can't you see that?" Monica gestured to Josh and Anna who were still talking to each other. "Everyone can see that. She just blew you up."

I felt a pang. "That's true. But I have to try."

"Some girls don't want a guy unless he can take care of them. Me, I think pilots are sexy."

I gave a short laugh. "That's nice to know."

Her palm caressed my arm. "You're so strong, Victor."

Again I smiled without meaning it. "I've got to go. I'll see you around, Monica."

The crowd was in motion, making way for the pony girls pulling their shiny black carts, stepping high as they pranced around the old gymnasium. A couple of the girls had their arms bound behind them and were harnessed in, so a handler walked next to them to make sure they didn't stumble or need help. Other girls grabbed the pull bars with their hands and trotted along with their harness held by the seated driver.

I wandered around in search of Sierra, and at one point saw Monica staring enviously at the carts going past to the catchy Honkytonk Badonkydonk song blaring through the speakers. I also saw Josh and Anna here and there, always talking to others. I was greeted by more people than usual, and I knew it was because of the tale they were spreading. Everyone's glance was knowing, and their wry smiles said they were in on the gossip. Just like Monica, there was a new wariness in the women's eyes, not so eager to please, but if anything they were newly interested in me. Maybe because I had been taken down a few notches. I had never realized until Sierra told me that I made her feel inferior with my Victor role. I hoped nobody else had felt that way, but maybe they did.

It didn't matter that everyone knew. I had expected it from the beginning, and for years I'd been waiting for people to realize their mistake. To realize I was nothing much.

But if anything, the revelation was perversely making me more popular. I kept getting stopped by people who wanted to ask what I thought about the art show or the pony girls or if I knew about the new party in a downtown loft. After all, it wasn't like I had gone around bragging about my rich lifestyle. I had done my best to not lie directly, to evade questions and let people fill in the gaps with their own imaginations. It had set me apart, put a barrier between myself and everyone else, but at least I hadn't lied to their faces.

Now it seemed like they were willing to meet me on new ground, to see what I was really like. And I liked that. Now that I wasn't hiding who I was, maybe I could make some real friends.

It was all because of Sierra. Because she had reached out and grabbed my hand and pulled me back to earth instead of letting me float in a misty unreality.

The MC came out to thank the pony girls as they finished their last circuit of the gymnasium and trotted through the open double doors to the interior corridor with the fading of the music.

"And next up, we have Transcendence!" the MC boomed out.

I excused myself from the group I was talking to and picked up my search for Sierra. Lola came out wearing nothing but pink body paint and a tiny pink triangle over her crotch. I could see every dimple, every curve and every pucker on her nipples. She was swaying like she was excited by the watching eyes—a born exhibitionist lapping it up like a greedy girl.

She looked so much like Sierra, but was different in every way. I couldn't imagine Sierra strutting around naked on a stage, or making that come-on face to the men in the audience as she wiggled her hips. It was like a cartoon exaggeration of my sexy Sierra, and it was almost offensive.

So I ignored the suspension performance, scanning the audience instead. Finally I found Sierra on the far side, partially hidden by a St. Andrews Cross. I was weaving through the crowd to get to her when I saw who she was with.

Liam. Everything I wanted to be as *Victor*, Liam was. He was the real deal—he was co-owner of a computer software company and had a huge apartment in the East Village. Liam was always with the most beautiful, interesting women. I considered him to be a good technical top—bondage, caning, flogging—but Liam lacked the passion that I sought. I would rather get an emotional response while Liam focused on the physical. But the leashed sadist in each of us recognized it in the other.

Liam was talking to Sierra. They were very relaxed together, like they knew one another, not like they had just met. They were half-turned to each other facing the stage, with their heads confidentially close.

I screeched to a halt.

Liam absently stroked Sierra's arm through the dark filmy material that drifted and clung to her curves. It was her subtle, hide-and-seek style that I was drawn to.

As Transcendence performed, I stayed back in the line of sight of Sierra and Liam. She seemed engrossed in their conversation, glancing up at the stage from time to time where Martin suspended Lola. Her arms were together straight overhead, with one knee bent up high and thrust out to one side. Next to him Spike suspended June who was painted white and brown, into the form of a leaping gazelle frozen in the webbing. It wasn't until Lola pointed her hands down to show the backs—painted with a black triangle to form a beak with two black eyes—that I realized she was supposed to be a flamingo.

The delighted crowd clapped wildly and surged closer to see once the girls were fully suspended. A line quickly formed at the steps so people could file by on stage and get a close-up view. But Liam and Sierra stayed in their nook, caught up in their conversation.

My blood was boiling. I wanted to step in and force them apart—make Liam leave her alone. For good. The thought of Liam touching Sierra enraged me.

She belongs to me.

Chapter 36

Sierra

"I don't think Victor likes you talking to me," Liam told me.

I followed his gaze, and there was Vic, a dark cloud on the horizon. "That's his problem."

I had been doing my best to talk to Liam like a normal person, asking about his work and where he came from. The typical stuff that Vic had lied about.

"Are you sure? I don't want to intrude," Liam said.

"It's over between us." I wanted to stop thinking about Vic, to make a clean break between us. His jealousy now, and my own jealousy over seeing him talking to Monica, didn't matter anymore.

But my heart told me there was more. He felt more for me. Or he wouldn't have confessed when I told everyone about him.

Liam was still watching Vic. "What happened between you two?"

I took a deep breath. I hadn't meant to confide any details. But I was so confused about why Vic still had a hold on me that I needed to talk to someone. Liam knew this world. Maybe he would be able to separate the man from the master. So I gave him the run-down of Vic's lies and how he had played with me while keeping me at arm's length.

"But our scenes were so powerful," I admitted

blushing. "More intense than anything I've ever felt, if you know what I mean."

"Was it your first time submitting to someone?"

I nodded.

"That happens to everyone. It's a rush when you first do power exchange. Sometimes people mistake that for love. You hear stories about people losing their heads when they first get into the scene. You have to know when to say no."

"What if you don't negotiate a way to say no?" I asked, remembering my first scene with Vic.

"You can always say no. That's the law. No matter what you agree to, you can stop it at any time."

Unless you can't say no because you're frozen in fear. So it wasn't part of the kink game to take advantage of someone. That was the con man part.

"You have to trust the other person will listen to you," Liam continued. "And trust takes time. You don't give it away. It has to be earned."

I remembered how Liam had respected my boundaries at the Labor Day party last week when I was vulnerable. A lesser man would have tried to take advantage of me, hanging around in hopes that I would drink too much or that he could finagle me into talking to him some more, maybe even getting into my bed. But Liam hadn't treated me that way. He showed me that he respected me.

Vic was still lurking on the edges of my periphery vision. I felt as if I couldn't look away while he was there. "Isn't there an art show around here?" I asked Liam.

348

"In the gallery through there," he pointed. "Let's check it out."

We had to walk past Vic to leave the performance space. I managed to not look at him, nor did I turn around to see my sister on stage. If Lola wanted to paint herself like a dime-store flamingo and let people stare at her, then that was her choice.

The art show was in the converted cafeteria, with a much lower ceiling and worn industrial linoleum on the floor. Wooden room dividers had been set up to display the art, interspersed with shelving units that held steampunk artifacts and hand-crafted leather whips.

At first I kept looking for Vic to pop out from around a display, but he didn't, and I began to relax. With Vic out of the way, it was easier to talk to Liam about the paintings. Some of them were dark and graphically sexual, while others were more lyrical and sensual. There was a whole series of vibrant space-scapes with beautiful women-animal aliens that made me gasp.

"I used to read the science fiction books in the school library," I said. "I read every book they had. The military sci-fi, the cyberpunk, all that. But I liked the ones with aliens the best."

"I'm more of a mystery reader," Liam said with a smile. "Or a good thriller. I don't get much of a chance unless I'm on a plane or at the beach hanging out."

I took one last look at the alien-women and moved on, marveling at the intricate steampunk devices with little gears and vials of powders. Goggles of various types and glasses with moveable lenses were laid on the shelves.

"People made all of this," I marveled.

"It's good to be creative," Liam agreed.

"Like my sister?" I had to ask.

He laughed. "Whatever floats your boat. She seems to enjoy it. Was she always the center of attention?"

I had to nod. "She's a drama queen, always making a big thing out of nothing. My mom mostly cut and ran and left me to deal with her."

"That sucks." He watched me carefully. "I heard you got into a fight with her at Festival."

"Word does travel." Would I be forever haunted by that? "It was stupid. We yelled at each other like sisters do. That's all."

"Do you yell at each other a lot?"

"Only every time we see each other."

Liam let out a laugh, and I was glad I had come right out and admitted it. If he stuck around, he would find out the truth for himself.

If he stuck around... I was enjoying myself. I had actually managed to forget about Vic for a few minutes. It was such a relief!

Just being normal with Liam, talking like people usually did, reminded me of everything I hadn't shared with Vic. This man who I had met only a few times knew more about me than Vic did. Despite the fact that I had been Vic's lover this summer.

Cheated! Vic had cheated me out of having a relationship with him because he wanted to play some kind of mind game. He wanted to use me instead of love me.

Here was Liam, a handsome, sweet, smart man who was treating me like I was worth getting to know, like he wanted to be here with me. He was being honest about who he was and what his intentions were.

I had been so manipulated by Vic that my head was screwed on wrong. That's why I still kept thinking about his eyes—the way his eyes had pleaded with me to understand why he was so fucked up. Or when he said: *You belong to me.*

I put my hands to my head. "I think he really messed me up."

"Victor?"

I nodded. "Maybe it is the kink. Maybe it's the lies..."

"Maybe it's new romantic energy. There's always a burst of passion in the beginning, when you don't know anything about each other. So anything is possible."

"Wow, that might be the most romantic thing I've ever heard."

He laughed, so easy and comfortable. "I'm not the originator of that idea. It's commonly known in the scene. There are a lot of polyamorous people who have more than one relationship. They know that a new person can turn someone head over heels for a while until everything settles down."

I stared at him open-mouthed. "Is that what you do? Have lots of girlfriends?"

Liam reached out and gave my chin a tweak.

"I've done it. But I also do couple love."

"Are you seeing anyone now?" I had to ask.

Now his eyes were more inviting. "Not seriously. Would you like to go out with me, Sierra?"

I realized I had led him to this point. Or rather, he had waited for me to be open to the idea before he asked me out. It was super-suave. How was I supposed to say no?

"I'm sorry, I'm not in any state to date anyone right now," I blurted out. I wasn't sure why I was turning down this amazing guy, except how could I go out to dinner with one man while my heart ached for another?

"You're still hung up on Vic. Even after what he did to you." Liam wasn't asking, he was telling.

So I admitted, "Like I'm addicted to a drug that I know is bad for me."

Liam considered me. "I can help you with that. Detox you."

"What an idea! How would you do that?"

"I can have a scene with you, show you how it feels with someone else. You'll see that a lot of the rush you're feeling is the power exchange. That's why so many people are bisexual in the scene, the power role is more important than gender."

"You've played with men?" I asked, startled. I would have taken Liam for as straight as they came.

"I'm heteroflexible. I'm also an educator. I've done scenes with different people, teaching them skills or showing them what it feels like."

I was already shaking my head. "No way am I going home with you. I don't care if it's the cure for cancer. I know how dangerous this stuff can be."

"Well, you're right. But I hope you're not speaking from personal experience."

"I made a bad choice but I lucked out and didn't have to pay for it," I admitted.

Liam looked angry for the first time. It actually gave me a thrill to see that he could be shaken from his placid good-natured poise. Over his concern for me. "Nobody deserves to be taken advantage of. Do you want to talk about it?"

I shook my head, feeling uncomfortable. I still felt like a fool for trusting a perfect stranger. I was sure Liam would think so, too, no matter how nice he was being right now. And I wanted him to keep on being nice to me. It was soothing to my battered spirit.

We finished touring the art show, and drifted back toward the door. "Are you sure you want to go back in there?"

I felt emboldened by my talk with Liam. "I don't care if he's there."

"Good, the fire show should going on."

We went into the darkened performance space. Lights were flashing now, accenting the fire show that was happening on the stage. I looked around for Lola, but the place was packed. I didn't see Vic either.

Up on stage, bursts of fire shot out of the performers' mouths. I was glad we were at the back end of the auditorium instead of up front where sparks were falling down.

Liam called out a greeting to some people he knew, and he told me, "Come meet my friends."

I felt another pang at how easy it was with Liam compared to Vic. Liam's friends were a couple and two women who may or may not have been together. It was hard for me to tell. The older woman lightly teased Liam about his "full dance card."

"I'm not topping anyone tonight," Liam said with his usual smile.

"Not even you?" the younger woman asked me.

"Excuse me?" I asked, feeling that question was personal without knowing exactly what it meant.

The older woman saw my uneasiness. "There's always a play party after the last performance," she explained. "Liam usually has them lined up waiting to play with him."

"I'm showing Sierra around tonight," Liam said.

I felt better as they looked at me with new interest. They chatted easily about the art show and performances. Liam told them that the flamingo in the suspension act was my sister, and they exclaimed over how cool the show had been. The guy-half of the couple showed me his cell phone—he had taken a picture of the two girls suspended in the webbing. Lola really looked flamingo-ish, in a strange way.

I felt a stab of fear knowing that image would probably end up on the Internet. Transcendence had lots of photos posted on their Instagram already. I would have to get used to my little sister's over-exposure.

Liam told us about running into a cousin of his who was in the scene in Philadelphia, where he was born and raised. It turned out most of the others had family members who were kinky but hid it from the rest of their extended family. The older woman laughed about seeing her aunt at an event decades ago, when kink was much more underground than it was now, and they both had been completely gob-smacked by seeing each other.

I had never applied the word "kinky" to myself. But I must be or I wouldn't have kissed Victor's boots.

Vic's boots, I corrected myself. The man inside the mythical master...

"Do you like bondage like your sister?" Liam asked me.

I realized that I must have blanked out on the conversation. Lost in the memories of Vic, again. It was really becoming a problem.

His friends were talking to each other and he had turned to me alone. I was struck again by how refreshing it was to hear about his family and where he grew up. No secrets here. These friends had known him for years.

"I'm sorry, what did you say?" I asked.

"Do you like bondage like your sister?"

"I don't know. I've never tried it," I replied.

Liam seemed surprised. "You haven't ever been tied up?"

"Oh, well, yes. Once. My wrists," I suddenly remembered. How could I forget? It had all started with a short piece of rope, and I remembered thinking... *what harm can he do with rope in only a minute?*

It made me sigh. Everything had changed since then, and then changed again. I still wasn't used to this new reality.

The fire show on stage reached a grand finale, and everyone was watching the bursting flames. I was wondering if we should move closer to the exit in case it got out of hand, but the show finally stopped and there was a spate of clapping and some coughing from up closer to the stage.

"That's over," Liam said with satisfaction. "Now people can play."

As if on cue, three of the pony girls pranced past us as the cowboy touched them up with his quirt, making them dance faster. He drove them over to a cross that was being dragged away from the wall by a guy wearing a neon green vest. The two men chatted for a moment as the girls circled the cross, tossing their heads and pony tails.

"Why are her arms like that?" I asked Liam, gesturing to one. Her arms were pulled behind her and encased in black leather.

"It gives her body a certain posture, lifting her chest and arching her back. Some people think it looks more like a horse. Others like the bondage part of it. That feeling of being constrained and contained."

I shook my head. "Lola never liked to be restrained or contained in *any* way. If that's the allure of bondage, it doesn't make any sense why she's doing it."

"I suspect for your sister it's more about the audience. And suspension bondage is different—there's an endurance factor. It can be very painful so you have to be able to breathe through the process so the rigger doesn't have to take you down before the show is over. It gives you a real endorphin rush."

"It hurts? It looks so pretty when they're done."

"If you'd gone up on stage, you would have seen the ropes are fairly tight and dig into the skin. She's probably got a lot of rope marks on her right now."

For some reason, I got goose bumps thinking of ropes digging into my own skin so tightly that it left spiral rope marks. I wanted to feel something that wasn't pain that came from thinking about Vic. Maybe Lola was taking pleasure in conquering the limitations of her own body, of feeling something intense on her own terms, not anyone else's.

That sounded good right now.

Without thinking, I pulled my arms back, watching the pony girl and trying to imagine what it felt like. I couldn't bring my elbows together like the girl's were.

Then Liam reached around me, holding onto my elbows, gently steadying me. "How does that feel?"

"It's as far back as I can get."

"There's more play in your shoulders, but you can't do it yourself. That's one of the beauties of this pose. You have to be placed into it." His hands gently pressed my elbows inward. "Feel that?"

As he gently positioned my arms, my chest lifted towards him and my spine seemed to lengthen. "Wow... that's wild," I said.

Liam's hands sent a shiver through me. Being handled by him gave me a rush, exactly like with Vic. He held me there for a few moments, and I looked up at his eyes. He wasn't smiling now. He was intently looking at me, in control, deciding when I'd had enough.

As he slowly released me, I shifted my shoulders and let my arms drop. I felt confused and excited, conflicted by how many emotions his touch stirred inside of me. Maybe Liam was right. Maybe it was the kink and not Vic who had turned me inside-out.

The way Liam was looking at me made me blush. "Did you like that?" he asked.

"Yes."

"Would you like to try more? I could rig a harness up each of your arms using rope, with a lace that holds them together behind you."

I hesitated. "I don't think I could do that for very long."

"I'll tie each arm separately while you're standing here like this. Then I'll lace them together. It will take a few seconds to do up and easy to get out of again."

I hesitated on the edge of a big decision. Should I try it again? This man was everything Vic wasn't—honest, caring, *safe*. He had real friends who knew him. Friends who were standing right over there. People I liked, who had a lot of experience doing this kind of thing.

Liam wasn't going to go psycho on me over some fucked up mommy-issues. He wasn't going to make me feel like I was less than him.

It might be exactly the medicine I was looking for, to rid me of the specter of *Victor*. The perfect master who didn't exist.

I looked around. I hadn't seen Vic since we came back into the performance space. Most likely he had left when I went into the art show with Liam. I wouldn't have to feel his eyes on me, tearing me out of the moment.

"Yes," I said. "I want to try it."

Chapter 37

Vic

I watched Liam hold Sierra's arms behind her. I saw how her chin lifted and her chest swelled with a deep breath. The way she shyly turned her head away from him. How Liam stood so close to her, his head bent to murmur in her ear...

It was torture. My well-deserved punishment.

I stayed well back in the shadows, knowing I couldn't hide my obsession if anyone saw me. I wanted nothing more than to take Liam down for touching Sierra. But I had no right to do that. I knew in my bones that she belonged to me, but if she didn't think so, my feelings meant nothing.

I had loved Adrianne, as only an eighteen year old could love an older, experienced woman. She had blown my mind, honed my natural need to dominate, and allowed me to master her. And she had loved me, in her selfish way, as long as I gave her what she wanted.

But this was different. I felt like I knew Sierra in a way I had never known anyone. Like I had always known her. I knew how serious she was about her work, and that she would make her life better for herself no matter how hard it was. I knew how alone she was and the set-backs she'd suffered, but in spite of that, she didn't whine about the bad things that happened to her.

Most of all, I knew how tormented she was by her sister's rejection. I never knew that family could be so loyal, but Sierra was loyal to a fault. If only my sister had been that way, my entire life would have been different. If she could have loved me a tenth as much as Sierra loved Lola, I might have been okay.

Sierra was the best person I had ever met. She was so pure that she made me believe in myself. But as I tried to become a better person, I had to reveal my shit to her.

And in doing that, I had hurt her even more. I had hurt her a lot since the night we met.

I had no right to love her. But I did. *Love her.*

Liam guided Sierra closer to the wall, out of the mass of people who were gathering around the pieces of equipment that now dotted the open floor. I shifted back along with them, staying in the shadows where I could see them.

One of Liam's friends came over carrying several bundles of white rope. The three of them talked for a few moments, and Sierra gestured to something out on the floor. The guy clapped Liam on the shoulder.

Then he left the two of them alone. With the rope in Liam's hands.

They were going to have a scene.

A wordless cry of anguish filled my head, and I had to clench my fist in my other hand, telling myself not to move. I couldn't go and take Sierra from Liam by force. As much as I longed to.

Liam stood in front of Sierra, lightly holding her hands as they spoke. Probably asking for her safeword. Would she use the one I had given her?

Now Sierra was nodding and smiling shyly. Her eyes never left Liam, as he began to weave his spell around her.

Liam pushed up her filmy sleeve and began tying the rope around her upper arm, right above her elbow. He tied it off and then made another loop underneath that one, and tied that off. Then he made another loop right below her elbow and tied it off.

Liam kept stroking her arm down to her hand between tying each knot. I could tell Sierra was being lulled by the way he handled her. Her eyes closed a few times, and she visibly trembled at one point.

I felt as if I was being flayed alive. My jealousy raged, along with my envy of Liam. It was that same old envy that had urged me to take advantage of girls who didn't think I was good enough.

I deserved every moment of this torture. For all the lies I had told, and all the women I had hurt. I was getting what I deserved.

Chapter 38

Sierra

I liked it. I liked how Liam smelled and the way he spoke to me, gentle with an undertone of command. And standing there passively while he was touching me so deliberately made me shiver in delicious anticipation.

I kept trying to blank my mind, to concentrate on the sensations. But memories of Vic kept intruding... he always used to trail his fingers down my arm to my hand when he wanted to hold it. He used to touch my face with his fingertips, and smooth back my hair... I wished Liam would do that, but he was concentrating on the knots.

Chapter 39

Vic

As Liam went to the other side of Sierra to tie her other arm, I felt something ease in my gut. I could tell from Sierra's quick glance up and around as Liam changed sides that she wasn't very caught up in what was happening. She looked down at the neat ladder of rope up her arm, fingering it, and then let it dangle by her side.

I knew what Sierra needed because I was the only one who could give it to her. She yearned for intensity. She wanted to throw herself into the volcano like a virgin sacrifice. She wanted to go all in, but Liam was carrying her along in cool baby steps. This was education, not sex. Definitely not passion.

Her posture was relaxed now, without that seductive tension like before. She was enjoying it, but it wasn't rocking her world.

I would have already rocked her world, if I had been the one wielding that rope.

Sierra stood there and smiled at Liam as he tied up her other arm. She even shivered again when Liam trailed his fingers down her arm to her hand. But that was a purely physical reaction. She didn't lean towards Liam as if she was being pulled towards him by magnetic force, like she did with me. She didn't look up at Liam with hooded eyes, as if afraid to reveal too much while she was so vulnerable, like she did with me.

I breathed easier, wiping the sweat from the back of my neck. I had almost gone off the rails there. I had to learn to control myself when it came to Sierra.

If this was what she needed to realize that I was the man for her, then I was glad she was getting it. Anything it took to get her back, I was willing to pay. Anything.

Even watching another man touch her and smile into her eyes.

Liam went behind Sierra and began lacing her arms together. She tilted her head as if she wasn't sure what she thought of it. But the pose forced her to stand up straighter, thrusting her breasts out.

Liam checked the tension on the lacing, to make sure it wasn't too tight anywhere. She nodded to something he asked her. Then she smiled when he urged her to step forward. She took a few mock high steps, like the pony girls did. She laughed.

It looked like she was having fun, a light-hearted scene. Liam took her out further to walk around, to see what it felt like.

I shifted, staying behind her where she wouldn't see me. I didn't want to bother her while she was having a good time.

But that didn't mean I was going to walk away. I couldn't if I tried.

Chapter 40

Sierra

I kept raising each knee high with every step, like the pony girls did. "It's not easy walking like this," I told Liam. "They must have some kind of stamina."

"You would too if you did it every day," he teased.

"Every day? Do they do this every day?"

"They might. If it's their thing, why not?"

"It's good exercise," I agreed.

I watched the pony girls standing near the cross where another girl had her top stripped down and was being whipped on her bare back by the quirt. The cowboy had a scarily intent expression as he flicked the quirt against her, and the girl let out little shrieks and jerked against her bonds. But she was also nuzzling the other pony girls who stepped in to soothe her skin every now and again.

Liam put one hand under my arm, steadying me as I swayed. I had worn my comfortable heels because of the subway, but they were still heels. I liked it that he was making sure I was okay. It was the best part of the scene, actually.

Shifting my shoulders, testing the bonds, I was starting to feel the strain. I could see what Liam meant about the endurance it took to do bondage, and took deep breaths to relax into it. Tensing made it worse. I wondered what it would feel like to be bound all over and hung from various points, like Lola. The ropes would dig in, like they were digging into my upper arms.

"Are you okay?" Liam asked.

"Yes. It does... kind of... hurt."

"Badly?" he asked.

"No. But you can't forget about it, that's for sure." With my chest so open, it was easy to take deep breaths.

"Now you're getting it," Liam murmured, his face close to mine. "Breathe into it."

In that split second, I thought he might kiss me. I didn't want him to kiss me.

Suddenly, someone bumped into Liam from behind, and he jostled into me. Liam had to grab onto my arm to catch me from stumbling backwards.

Steadying me, Liam turned to the guy who had bumped into him. "Hey, watch out!"

"I'm sorry," the guy was already saying. His wrists were bound together by a short chain, as were his ankles. "I lost my balance."

His Mistress jerked on the leash attached to the collar around his neck. "Apologize, Meatworm!"

The guy lowered his head and mumbled, "I'm sorry, Mistress. I apologize deeply."

I glanced at Liam. *Meatworm?* Liam was clearly trying to not to be irritated. "Okay. No harm done."

As the Mistress passed us, she struck her slave with her crop. "Stop being so clumsy!"

Meatworm flinched at that and bumped into me. This time I was knocked off balance, but Liam's firm hand was on my upper arm. I sagged down in my knees until Liam helped me stand again.

The Mistress raised her crop against Meatworm. "You sorry piece of—"

Liam was practically standing between them, and he had to deflect the crop. "Stop it! It's too crowded here for that. Find a station if you want to have a scene."

I suddenly felt like I couldn't breathe. Something about the way Liam held my upper arm, jostling me as he warded off the crop, sent panic through me. His fingers were so tight, like I couldn't get away, even if I struggled.

I tried to pull away, but I staggered and Liam held on to support me.

But in my mind, it felt like something else.

The memory flashed over me, of that awful apartment in Tarrytown next to the freeway. I was snooping around my mom's bedroom while she was taking a shower, when a strange man sat up in bed and caught me holding his jacket. I didn't even know he was there. He had grabbed my arm and shook me, pulling me back into the living room. He left bruises on my arm, but even worse was knowing that I had to do whatever he said or he would hurt me. Maybe worse than he was hurting me already.

It was everything I hated about living with my mom. Not knowing who would be there, who I would run into in the bathroom, who would look at me and Lola in that appraising way... those many nights I laid there awake, hoping none of them would hurt us.

Like that man hurt me. I could feel his harsh

grip on my arm, the way he shook me to make his point to stay out of the bedroom, feeling how he was ready to do more. That terrible pause as he looked over at the sofa bed where Lola slept. And I knew something awful was about to happen, and there was nothing I could do to stop it.

"Let me go!" I gasped. Instincts took over and I thrashed in his grasp to get away. Just as I had tried to get away so many years ago.

Liam turned back from trying to keep the Mistress from beating her slave right in our faces. But I could only see the dingy living room where I slept with Lola.

"Let me go!" I cried.

Jerking my arms, realizing they were held fast, I lost my balance again. That only made Liam hold on tighter to my arm to keep me from falling. I saw the surprise in his eyes, but I also saw that man's dark scowl as he leaned over me sneering that I would get what I asked for.

Frozen in fear, I felt the ropes tugging on my arms. "Relax, Sierra, I've got it."

It was Vic's voice!

Vic was there behind me, doing something to release me, to save me. I couldn't think, couldn't speak. I was so grateful to be held by his strong arms.

Chapter 41

Vic

I saw what was happening as Liam tried to
back off that crazy Mistress and her slave. Sierra was
hardly touched, but I could tell the instant she began
to freak out. Something about being bumped into
wigged her out.

I ran forward, pulling my black rope cutter from
my pocket. I always carried it at events; the pointy
end made for a nice scary toy with the protected blade
visible but not dangerous. I had used it on Sierra to
cut off her thong, and I used it again now. I didn't
know Liam's rigging, and the whole thing looked too
ornate to try to figure out on the fly.

With one swipe, I dragged the rope cutter down
the lacings and they separated at once.

With my other arm, I held onto Sierra as she
sagged forward, the tension on her arms released.

Liam realized what was happening and was still
holding onto her arm. "What's wrong, Sierra?"

She pulled away from him, making a warding
off motion. Her head shook wordlessly, as she
trembled in my arms.

Liam backed off, looking shocked. A few other
people had noticed and were also checking us out.

"I have to get her to a chair," I said.

I picked Sierra up, like I had picked her up
when Dick had hurt her. That night I had carried her

like a prize back to my place. And held her close all night... like I wanted to do right now. To protect her from everything that was hurting her.

I set her down on the closest chair and knelt down next to her, chafing her hands. They felt cold, but her face was getting some color back.

"Are you okay, Sierra?" Liam was asking anxiously over my shoulder. He didn't try to touch her again, probably because of the way she had desperately pulled away from him.

Sierra nodded.

"She needs water," I ordered without glancing at Liam.

Liam hurried off, and I had Sierra to myself. I rubbed her arms lightly, helping to bring the blood flow back into them. It looked like Liam had done a good job. Her circulation was good. It was most likely her sudden fright that had chilled her.

"Thank you," Sierra whispered.

"I'm always here for you, Sierra."

She took a deep sigh. "I don't know what happened. I remembered one of my mom's boyfriends... he grabbed me like that, under my arm... he dragged me into the living room."

I waited a moment, but she didn't go on. And this was no time to push a story like this from her. "Trauma can come back anytime if you're triggered."

"Trauma... I was scared, but it wasn't like he beat me up. Or anything. But he could have. He almost did. But Lola woke up. She saved me."

"Sometimes being scared is all it takes." I couldn't look away from her eyes, so dark and shining, like I was falling into her. "Sierra, I'm so sorry I scared you the first night we met. It was wrong in every way. I hate to think I've given you more trauma that will come back to haunt you someday."

Her expression softened. She was searching my eyes in return. "I can't say I understand. I wish I did. But I do know both of us were pretending to be someone we weren't that night. Asking for something we didn't really want."

I picked up her hand and kissed it. I had to feel her skin beneath my lips. "I'm not pretending anymore. I love you, Sierra. I always will."

Her mouth opened in surprise, caught by my words but unsure if she could believe me. And no wonder, with all the lies I had spread as love traps for her.

Liam appeared, out of breath. "Here's your water, Sierra."

I didn't want to stop stroking her arms, but Liam had put her into bondage. This was their scene. I couldn't force him away.

I stood up and let Liam bend over her, as he asked how she was doing. Sierra drank her water and told him it was some kind of flashback from when she was a girl. Her voice shook even as she said it, like she was still caught in an old nightmare, even though she knew it was long over. That's how it was with triggers—the emotions were the same even though years had passed. She was breathing rapidly, her skin moistened.

I wanted nothing more than to go to her and hold her tight until she didn't feel bad anymore. No matter how long it took.

That's what I should be doing now. That's what felt right. But I had ruined it and couldn't even reach out for her now when Sierra needed it the most.

She only had Liam, and he was like a wet rag. While I stood there shaking with an effort to keep myself from wrapping my arms around her, Liam was practically backing away, he was so scared to touch her again. *Pussy. If he really cared about her, he would do* something.

"I feel so bad," Liam apologized. "I'm really sorry."

"It wasn't your fault," Sierra said faintly. "I'm not good at first scenes."

In all honesty, I told them both, "I saw what went down. You couldn't have done anything different, Liam. It was one of those things that happen sometimes. We're playing with intense stuff."

Liam met my eyes, startled. "That's decent of you."

"I'm trying," I said.

Both Liam and Sierra were eyeing me warily when Lola ran up. Her face was scrubbed but pink patches still speckled her arms and legs. She actually went up to kneel next to Sierra, looking concerned. "What happened, Sierra? Someone told me you fainted."

"No, I just got knocked off balance," Sierra explained. "It's nothing."

"She's shook up," I told Lola.

"I should go home," Sierra said quietly.

With her brow furrowed, Lola said, "Martin is

getting the van. We can drop you off. Greenpoint, right?"

Sierra nodded, relief spreading over her face.

I had never seen a more sisterly moment between the two, as Sierra stood up and Lola made sure she was steady on her feet. I was so glad for Sierra. She had been waiting a long time for this breakthrough. Nobody deserved it more because nobody was more loyal than Sierra.

I led the way, breaking a path for the girls, while Liam trailed behind. Liam wasn't looking too happy. It wouldn't do his rep any good to have rumors spreading around of girls fainting on him. As for me, I didn't care what anyone said about me. I was only thinking about Sierra.

Now she knew that I loved her.

Chapter 42

Sierra

I held onto my sister's arm, desperately needing her support, more for emotional reasons than to keep me steady on my feet. I wasn't going to let go until I had to. It was the first sign of a thaw in our icy relationship in months. There was something so fundamentally comforting in having Lola by my side, wanting to help me. We had been through so much together our whole lives—this rift between us was unbearable.

Having Lola there at that moment did more to revive me than anything else could have done. Our past was in the past, and I had always dragged her along with me as I did everything humanly possible to get away from that life. My frightening flashback had shown me one thing—hearing my mom hook up had taught me that love came with pain. Those men had taught me not to question them, or I would suffer in response.

So maybe that's why I had gone along with Vic's fantasy relationship, letting him set the rules, secretly afraid to rock the boat because didn't that always end in sorrow? I had stayed away from men for so long, that only my overwhelming need to help Lola had beat back my fear that first night in the Chamber.

But I wasn't that scared girl sleeping on the couch anymore. No matter how bad the memory of it could still make me feel, I would never be that girl again. I had proven I could do whatever I set my mind to, and I wouldn't put up with anyone's shit anymore.

Behind us was Liam, who had lost his usual easy smile. Maybe it was the sight of Vic ahead of us, breaking a path with ease. Having Vic there was more comforting to me than it should have been, considering everything that had happened.

I was doomed. My questions had been answered by my scene with Liam. The entire time I had been mostly disconnected from him, but with Vic, in just a few moments as he rescued me, I had felt a rush that electrified my whole body. It couldn't be denied. I could still feel Vic's hands on my arms, soothing the rope marks on my skin. His eyes looking into mine as if he was searching out my secrets.

It was a taste of heaven.

Somehow Vic had known the moment the scene went bad for me. I barely knew something was wrong when my panic hit. But he was there instantly, cutting me free, taking care of me.

Just as he was taking care of me now, making sure we got outside without being jostled again. I wanted to wallow in that feeling of being safe. Of having Vic stand between me and the rest of the world...

"Let me use your cell," Lola said. "Mine is drained."

I dug into my purse and handed over my phone. Lola typed in a text. Later I read it: *It's Lola. My sister needs a ride home. We're waiting in front.*

"Are you sure?" I asked. "Isn't it out of your way

to take me?"

"How do you know where I'm going?" Lola retorted.

I wanted to say, *Greenpoint is on the road to nowhere, believe me I know*. But I closed my mouth and shrugged. I didn't want to set Lola off again. Things were finally going well.

"Here he comes," Lola said, waving up the street.

I turned and realized I had a dilemma. Both men were standing there looking at me. It was staring me in the face—Liam was a nice, handsome man, but he wasn't Vic. I tried not to look into Vic's eyes because I would get lost in them again and feel everything I couldn't for him.

So instead I looked at Liam and held out my hands. "Thank you for the scene, Liam. I'm sorry it ended that way."

"Don't apologize. I wish it could have been better for you."

"It was enlightening, thank you. I see what you mean about endurance..."

"Call me if you need to talk." Liam slipped me his card, which I didn't need. I sneaked a glance at Vic. He didn't seem to care that I was talking to Liam. He was devouring me with his eyes.

"Martin's here," Lola said, jolting me from his gaze.

"I've got to go," was the only thing I said to Vic. Thanking him was useless. He didn't want thanks. He wanted *me*: heart, body and soul. I could see that. Anyone could see that.

I could hear him say, *I'm not pretending anymore. I love you, Sierra. I always will.*

I turned at the sliding door of the van to see him one last time. I couldn't have told you if Liam was still there. I only saw Vic, with his eyes telling me that he knew. He knew the effect he had on me.

As the door slammed shut, and I thanked Martin for offering me a ride, my last glimpse was of Vic. I tucked Liam's card in my pocket, but I knew I wouldn't use it. Liam was very nice, but not what I wanted.

Vic was what I wanted, but he wasn't very nice.

It was a disaster.

My only distraction was listening to Lola and Martin talking. Spike and June had stayed behind to play, but my sister and her boyfriend were going home. Their conversation was so ordinary that it took a while for me to appreciate how comfortable they were together. Martin asked if Lola still itched, and Lola pointed out the deli where he could stop and run in to get his cigarettes. It was warm, homey kind of talk. The kind I had been missing with her.

But they were definitely an odd couple. Martin was fatherly with Lola, if anything, while Lola was far more respectful of him than I had ever seen her with anyone.

It didn't matter if I liked it, or the fact that Lola decided to paint herself pink. I was determined to be supportive of Lola, even if it didn't make sense.

When we arrived at my loft building, Martin let me out of the back. I told him, "I'm so glad to get to know you better."

"Uh, me, too," he said, a little surprised at my enthusiasm.

"You two have to come to our next party," I said, offering up the most enticing thing I had. "The last one was amazing." I pointed upward. "It's on the roof."

Martin grinned, showing too many crooked teeth with a gap on the side. "We'll be there."

"Sure, why not," Lola said. She hesitated, then gave me a brief hug, and hopped back in the van. I was glad that Lola was being so friendly.

It made me feel even better when Martin waited until I was inside before he pulled away. If he was that conscious of keeping me safe, maybe he would keep Lola safe.

As I went upstairs, I realized I had a lot to think about. One flashback had turned my emotions upside-down. Now I had to figure out which way was up.

...

I went straight to bed and slept soundly for the first time in a week. When I woke, it felt like my feet were back on solid ground, instead of dangling over an abyss. Perhaps it was because I had new memories of Vic, instead of *Victor*. And they were good ones.

He had taken care of me again. Like he always did. Like when I overheated in the suit. And when he saved me from Dick.

Now I felt like *Vic* had been taking care of me those times, the real man instead of the fantasy master he had created.

I worked the late shift on Sunday, still feeling strangely calm. Like my emotions were in a lull. Maybe I was tapped out, but it was a relief after the turmoil of the past months. Peace was an underrated thing, and I drank it in deep.

Over the next few days, I kept checking my phone. I wasn't expecting Vic to contact me because I had told him not to. But part of me wanted him to reach out.

Then I would shake myself. *No, I'm crazy and ignoring the massive red flags again!*

Vic was trouble—he had already proven that. I had been psychic the first night I met him and called him trouble, but despite every warning sign, I had forged ahead.

My treacherous feelings were leading me astray again.

So I resisted the urge to contact him. My biggest mistake was rushing things with him before I really knew him. I couldn't let my feelings rush me into making that same mistake.

The next morning at work I got a text, but it wasn't the one from Vic that I had dreaded yet hoped for.

It was from Martin: *Do you know where Lola is?*

When I saw those words, I knew instantly that this wasn't good. *No,* I texted back. *I haven't talked to her since you dropped me off.*

She didn't come home last night, Martin replied.

"Shit!" I exclaimed. I ducked into a changing room and hit call on my phone, listening impatiently as it rang.

"Hi, Sierra," Martin answered.

"What's going on with Lola?" I demanded.

"She didn't come home last night."

"You said that already! What happened? Did you have a fight?"

There was a noncommittal sound. "Not exactly."

"So what *exactly* was it?" I demanded. He wasn't winning any points with me right now.

"She wasn't happy with an order I gave her. But she said she would obey me."

"*Obey* you?"

"Don't be judgmental, Sierra. It's our dynamic."

I told myself to not rise to the bait. "What did you order Lola to do?"

"Does it matter?" he asked impatiently.

"It would tell me how bad the situation is."

"It wasn't that big a deal. I told her to stop talking to someone."

Startled, I asked, "Me?"

"No! Not you. Someone who isn't good for her."

Mollified, I asked, "So you told her that, and she stormed out?"

"No... she was quiet after that, but I thought it was settled. I don't think that has anything to do with her being gone overnight."

"You mean she up and disappeared for no reason?" That sounded much worse.

"Yeah, did she ever do that with you? Not come home and not answer her phone when you called?"

I gave a harsh laugh. "Join the club, Martin! The Lola Club. Cut off without a word. Left behind like we're trash."

There were a few moments of silence on the other end, then Martin protested, "But nothing happened between Lola and me."

"Nothing happened between Lola and me, either! She just up and disappeared. I still don't know where you live."

"But... you keep showing up at our events. You're always so angry at her."

"I've been trying to find out why she won't talk to me. She's avoiding me so hard that I had to stalk my own sister to get near her. I'm worried about her. You're not exactly the typical boyfriend Lola chooses, if you know what I mean. And this kink stuff can be dangerous—*believe* me, I know."

"That's more judgment, Sierra," Martin protested.

Suddenly my boss was rapping on the door. "Sierra! If you're going to take a break, then take a real break. And let me know about it."

"I gotta go," I told Martin.

When I came out, Kalisha sent me down to Lingerie to help with the big sale. It was always a mess in that department when there was a sale. I almost texted Lola on the way down, but stopped myself. I needed to think this over so I didn't piss off Lola again by interfering.

So as I refolded undies and hung bras back on their hangers, I considered why Lola might stay away overnight. Listening to Martin, he had sounded like Dick when Lola was stepping out on him *with Martin*. Now I could finally see a resemblance between the two bossy men.

It made perfect sense to me that Lola would walk out after Martin ordered her not to talk to a friend. Maybe that friend was a new guy. I wondered if Lola had found someone she liked better, and she had spent the night with him. And now Martin was jealous.

I always thought this thing with Martin couldn't last long. But the photos would be on the Internet forever... stupid Lola probably never considered that.

This was exactly what I had feared. That Lola would make a bad mistake and be out looking for a place to sleep one night.

I found myself thinking about my old bed that I had shoved under my loft bed. Lola could sleep there, if she needed to. *If* Keith would let my sister stay with me. And if my roommates didn't object. But how long could that last? It could only be a temporary thing. My cubicle was too small. I couldn't live in it with Lola.

It made me mad. I had warned Lola it would come to this if she abandoned our apartment. Instead, Lola had torpedoed our nice life together because she wanted to fuck around with a carnie for a few months.

Worry and anger went back and forth inside of me, completely wiping out the blessed relief that had welcomed me the past few days. And that made me madder at Lola. Why did I always have to take care of my little sister? I had finally known what it felt like to let go of that responsibility, of learning to not care that I didn't know where Lola lived or why my sister had cut me off. The only thing that mattered was my own actions. It was a relief, to be honest. Like a weight was off my shoulders.

But now Lola was back like a demanding child, dragging everyone's attention to her as she wrecked havoc around us. It had worked with our mom growing up. Lola made a stink whenever she could, and got the last of the energy our mom had to give. And now it was still working, as Lola got men to obsess over her. Again.

I managed to get through the day and ran a few errands on the way home, completely unable to think about anything else, but doing my best. Like I was fighting an addiction. Or a co-dependency.

Finally, on the bus ride home, I gave in and texted Lola: *What's up?*

I was afraid even that was too much and that Lola would find something to hate in those two words. But there was no response from her. At first I tried to tell myself that Lola was making me wait, like she usually did. Or that her battery was dead—like it was the other night—and that's why she wasn't answering.

Finally I texted Martin: *Did Lola come home?*

Martin replied: *No. I haven't heard from her. She's not answering my calls or texts.*

I didn't know what to say to that. It wasn't good. Maybe Lola was on a bender with a new guy and would surface in a day or two. Maybe she was staying with new friends because she didn't want to be with Martin anymore.

But as I struggled to eat dinner and talk to my roommates like nothing was the matter, I knew there was something wrong.

As soon as the dishes were put away, I texted my mom: *Have you talked to Lola lately?*

I hoped my mom wasn't on shift at the grocery store because she wouldn't be able to text back until her break. But after a few minutes, my mom replied: *Not since she asked for $500 to pay your rent.*

I felt my anger rise. My mom was implying that we both needed the money, not just Lola. I knew my mom didn't give it to Lola—she had stopped giving my sister money over a year ago, and that's why Dick's help had been so critical. But the fact that Lola had tried to get it, showed me that she had made at least a little effort. From the way Lola had acted, I figured she had walked away from me without a second thought.

I hung up. I didn't have anything to say to my mom after that. What kind of mother only texted her daughters once a month? We had practically raised ourselves because our mom was so busy with work and boyfriends. Lola wouldn't find much sympathy if she went looking there.

I couldn't believe I had no other options. But I didn't know any of Lola's friends. Lola wasn't working anywhere other than Transcendence. And the performance crew didn't know where she was.

The only other person who knew Lola was Dick. And I didn't want to go there after he had been lurking around outside of Vic's last weekend.

Then again, who was the most likely person to know what Lola was doing? If Dick was stalking me, he was still stalking Lola. At the very least, he would know where she lived. If I did have to report this to the police as a missing person, I would need Lola's last address.

Then I had a terrible thought—what if Martin had something to do with Lola's disappearance? What if Martin was trying to muddy the waters to hide a crime he had committed?

I shivered. Those ropes... if one slipped around Lola's neck... or if Martin had gone too far...

With trembling fingers, I texted Dick: *When was the last time you saw Lola?*

Dick answered fast, like he always did. *A couple weeks. Why?*

I can't find her, I texted back. *Do you know her address?*

Dick responded: *1090 DeKalb Ave. Below Broadway. Shitty neighborhood. Don't go there alone.*

I gave an exasperated sound—the irony of Dick giving me safety advice! The bruises on my arm had lasted for a week after he had tried to wring Lola's address out of me. When I didn't have it.

So Dick must have stalked Lola to find it. He followed her home from one of Transcendence's events, and lurked around outside watching her and Martin go inside.

With a shudder of distaste, I texted back: *Do you know where else Lola could be staying?*

No. You should have helped me when you could. Then this would be settled already.

Dick's response was quick. Too quick. I went back and read our exchange from the beginning. He said he hadn't seen Lola in a couple of weeks.

A couple of weeks... yet last weekend Dick was lurking around outside of Vic's place and asking me for money. Was it really possible Dick had spied on me in the past couple of weeks, but not Lola?

No, it wasn't possible. Dick was obsessed with Lola.

The whole text series felt wrong. Why wasn't Dick asking more questions? All of his other texts were filled with questions, demanding answers. And now I was telling him Lola was missing, and he had nothing to say but he hadn't seen her and didn't know where she was.

Now I was really worried. I didn't trust Dick or Martin. Either one of them could be up to something bad with Lola.

Candice had gone to work, or I would have turned to her for common sense advice. Devi was home, but I no longer trusted Devi. Jake was next to useless for anything other than casual conversation, and I had barely met Marky so I couldn't talk to him about this. Keith... no, I didn't want to bring my problems back to the loft. I was here on probation—a month to month trial basis on the promise of no-drama. And if I had to let Lola stay here for a few nights, I couldn't guarantee there would be no drama.

As scared as this was making me, I knew calling the police wouldn't get me anywhere. Lola was an adult who had been out of touch for only one night. They would tell me to wait and see if Lola turned up.

But what might happen in a day or two if I waited?

I wanted to go confront Dick and Martin, and see who was lying to me. But I wasn't stupid. I couldn't go alone. Both of them were dangerous.

So I needed some dangerous backup.

Chapter 43

Vic

When my phone lit up with the name I had been waiting to see—*Sierra*—I would have agreed to do anything she asked. Sierra said right away, "Lola is missing and I'm not sure if Dick or Martin have anything to do with it. Will you come with me to find out who's lying to me?"

"I'll be right there," I told her.

Before I left, I dug into my toy collection and grabbed an expandable police baton. It was eight inches when closed and opened to eighteen inches. A nice hard stick might come in useful. If I had to get in a fight to prove myself to Sierra, I was up for it.

I stuck it in my boot and pulled my jeans leg over the top so nobody could see it. Unless I needed it. Finally something I could do. Jersey was not an easy place to grow up. I had been a loner, and had to fight more than my fair share. I was used to taking whatever advantage I could whenever I had to face a pissed-off dude. Or two.

And I was dying to make someone else pay for their sins.

I grabbed a cab over to Sierra's place and she was waiting on the street for me. She jumped into the cab, her hair swinging loose behind her. A heavenly smell filled the air—even the cabbie lifted face to breathe deep. It was like a burst of life had joined us.

"Thanks for coming, Vic." Her eyes fastened on mine, and I was immediately lost in their dark depths. "I'm not sure if we should go see Dick first or Martin."

I had to shake myself out of the spell of her eyes. "Where was Lola last seen?" I finally asked.

"Martin's place."

"Then that's where we start. You always go back to the place where a person was last seen when you're looking for them."

Sierra gave me a sideways glance. "Spoken like a true stalker." She leaned forward and read off the address from her phone to the cabbie.

As she sat back and the cab pulled out, I cleared my throat. "Actually, I've never stalked a girl. I learned that from losing my grandparents at the store when I was a little kid. If you go back to where you saw them last, you can sometimes see where they went."

Sierra turned to me, reaching out to touch my arm. "I'm sorry, Vic."

I knew it must have sounded pathetic, because it was. Nobody had ever searched the aisles looking for *me*. I had to keep an eye on them or they would leave me behind. And the two mile walk home was a killer in the winter.

"Don't be sorry," I told her. "I just want you to know I'm not all bad."

"I know," she said simply.

I was glad to hear she wasn't as angry at me. Maybe it was because I had helped her when she panicked in Liam's bondage harness. If so, it had been worth the pain of watching her have a scene with Liam.

In the end, it didn't matter what I wanted, as long as I could help her, I felt like I was right with the world.

Maybe this was true love. My own wishes didn't matter anymore. I wanted what was best for Sierra.

I took hold of her hand. I couldn't help myself. I needed to touch her.

For a second, I wasn't sure if she was going to pull away. I was looking down at our hands as she glanced over at me.

Then she turned her hand under mine, clasping it. It was so simple, but so important. I usually didn't like to hold hands. I wasn't used to that kind of touch. That was probably another reason I kept girls at arm's length through my role as Victor.

But this felt so good, like a new strength was pouring into me. As if there were two of us facing the world together.

I didn't want to ever lose that feeling.

The yellow cab pulled up in front of a run-down tenement house in Bushwick, in a dicey area. The light from Broadway petered out near the front of the building, and it was nothing but trash and filthy streets. I had a hard time believing Lola lived here, but there was a white van parked in the fenced lot next to the building that looked like the one Martin had been driving the other night.

I paid off the cabbie, and told him, "If you wait here, we may need a ride back."

The guy looked around uneasy. "I can't promise

anything."

It was the best we were going to get in this neighborhood. I knew the cabbie would prefer a paying fare back to Manhattan, if he could get it. He might stay a few minutes.

"Should I text Martin that we're here?" Sierra asked as we approached the door.

"No. Let's check it out first." I hated the fact that Sierra was with me. That made me a lot more cautious than normal.

The glass door was covered by a wrought iron grate, and it was locked. A row of eight buttons on a silver plate had been awkwardly attached to the stone wall.

"Do you know which floor?" I asked.

She shook her head.

I backed out to the street again, looking up. A lot of the windows were open, and there was loud music coming from the third floor.

"Let's try number three," I said.

I hit the third button a couple times, like someone impatient. It worked like a charm. The door buzzed and I grabbed it.

The first floor had two doors in front and two behind the stairwell. There was an apartment on either side with dual access.

Up above, someone poked their head over the railing. "What do you want?"

"Martin," I said.

"Fourth floor," the guy pointed and withdrew.

It was not a climb for the faint of heart. Sierra was breathing heavily by the time we crested the top.

It was dirty like the other floors. I listened at the door closest to the front of the building. A man was talking inside, pausing as if listening to an answer, then talking again like he was on the phone.

"I can't believe Lola lives here," Sierra whispered.

"Stay over there, while I knock," I said.

Martin came to the door, looking expectant. Then he recognized me, turning to look down the landing at Sierra. "Have you found Lola?" Martin asked.

"No." Sierra came forward. "My mom hasn't heard from her either."

Martin looked tense and worried. "Come on in."

The apartment was nearly bare, with only a few chairs and a turquoise couch against one wall. I stopped Sierra from going near it. I could see the flecks of cockroach droppings in the corners of the walls.

Sierra was looked around as if she was in shock. Her loft was no palace, but it was better than this. I felt sorry for the girls—they were struggling to make it. It made my own situation look pretty cushy. I should have been satisfied with what I had.

But then I wouldn't have found Sierra.

I was determined to come out of this with her, and with a better future than I ever imagined.

Chapter 44

Sierra

I hated Lola's apartment. It was dirty and awful, and it made me sad to see my old couch and kitchen table living here, much less Lola.

It made me dislike Martin more, but he was acting exactly like one could expect a distraught boyfriend to act. I questioned him about Lola and who she knew, but Martin had already called everyone they knew.

"Are there any... guys she might be interested in?" I carefully asked.

Martin shook his head. "Nah, she's more into girls right now."

I blinked a few times. "Seriously? Then, who did you tell her to stop talking to?"

"Her old boyfriend. Dick. He's trying to get money from her. I told her not to talk to him. She wasn't happy about it, but she stopped."

"She *wanted* to talk to Dick?" I asked, incredulous.

"Yes. She doesn't like him. But he has some kind of hold over her."

Vic was watching Martin carefully, and he gave me a slight nod, to let me know he thought Martin was telling the truth.

"Do you think Dick might have done something to Lola?" I asked, my voice higher with tension.

"You tell me," Martin said. "I don't think Lola is scared of him. Not like that."

Vic finally spoke up. "Dick hurt Sierra. He knocked her down trying to get Lola's address. There's no telling what he would have done if I hadn't shown up and stopped him."

Martin's eyes narrowed, and he stood up straighter. "I didn't know that."

"I told Lola. Why didn't she tell you that?" I turned to Vic, putting my hand on his arm. "We have to go see Dick. What if he's done something to Lola?"

Vic put his arm around me. "It's okay. I'll make sure she's all right."

Having his support made me feel almost dizzy with relief. I could count on Vic! He would help me. When he let me go so we could leave, I almost wanted to protest. It was so comforting to touch him that I didn't want to stop.

Martin insisted on going, too, and I was glad. I can't say I trusted Martin, but he was proving me wrong in my suspicions. I didn't think he had anything to do with Lola's disappearance. The man was seriously concerned about my sister.

It was a tense drive up to Kissena Blvd where Dick lived. When we got there Martin didn't try to find a parking spot on the crowded streets. He parked in front of a fire hydrant and jumped out.

Only Vic slowed us down, urging us to get into Dick's building on the sly, like we had done with Martin. Since it was a big brick apartment building, we didn't have to wait long for someone to come out. Vic timed it so we were walking through the open front door in time to catch the second locked door before it closed.

The couple who were leaving didn't give us a second glance as we strolled inside behind them.

I had been to Dick's apartment before and I took the elevator to the fifth floor. As we approached his door, I heard something.

It was a woman's voice, yelling. I stopped.

"Is that Lola?" I whispered.

Martin and Vic were listening. "Maybe," Martin said.

Vic bent down and pulled out a short black baton from his boot. With a flick, it expanded into a sizable weapon.

"Where did you get that?" I asked in surprise.

Vic gave it a twirl and looked grim. "Hopefully we won't need it."

Martin was on his toes, like he wanted to be the one running the show. But he gave way to the man with the big stick and let Vic go to the door first.

Vic listened at the door, then nodded back at us. He mouthed: *Lola.*

I wrapped my arms around my stomach, so afraid I didn't know what to do. Seeing Vic holding that baton scared me. He had gotten the best of Dick the last time, but what if Dick hurt Vic? I had gotten him into this mess. It would be my fault.

But Vic didn't hesitate. He gave a sharp knock on the door with the stick, meaning business. "Dick! Open up. We're here for Lola. We know she's in there. We can hear her."

After a few moments of silence, Vic knocked

harder and raised his voice. "Dick! Sierra is ready to dial 911. If you're holding Lola in there against her will, it's twenty-five years to life. If you don't want your neighbors to hear the rest of this conversation, you'll let us in now."

I pulled out my phone and got ready to dial 911 on Vic's say so.

Vic was standing close to the peephole so Dick could see him. Likely his baton wasn't in view, though.

"Lola!" Vic called through the door. "Sierra is here to see you. If you don't come out, we're calling the cops."

The bolt on the door shot open. In spite of myself, I felt a deep thrill to see Vic master the situation, and make Dick do what he wanted. That was power. That was the man I knelt to.

The door opened and Dick was standing there sneering at us. "You brought a posse?"

Vic shoved Dick's chest, driving the big guy off balance. Dick took a swing and Vic swiped Dick's arm with the baton, knocking it aside. Dick let out a cry at the pain. It was quick and brutal, and Vic didn't give Dick a chance to strike.

My breath caught as Vic drove Dick back inside the apartment in a short, sharp struggle. Vic got him against a wall, holding one hand on Dick's chest to make sure he didn't move as Martin and I entered. Vic's other hand lifted the baton high, ready to brain him.

Lola was wringing her hands at the other end of the room. "Stop it! Leave me alone, Sierra—" Lola broke off to stare. "Martin! What are you doing here?"

"I've been looking for you."

Lola's defiant petulance disappeared in a flash. I was surprised to see Martin's affect on my sister. Lola turned pleading eyes on him. "I'm sorry! But I had to settle things with Dick."

"What things?" I demanded.

"She owes me fourteen hundred dollars," Dick said. Dick looked from me back to Vic, who was still holding the baton ready in his hand.

"I thought it was two thousand," I countered.

"That was yesterday," Dick said with a smirk.

Lola paled under Martin's stern gaze. "I'm sorry!" she exclaimed.

I was outraged. "Lola! You don't owe Dick anything. He gave you that money because you were going out together."

"Breach of promise," Dick declared. "She was supposed to marry me."

"You were never engaged," I denied. I turned to Lola. "You weren't engaged."

Dick laughed but it sounded sick. "Yes, we were. But Lola didn't want you to know."

"Lola?" I asked in confusion. "Is that true? Why wouldn't you tell me you were engaged to Dick?"

"Because I only said yes to get the rent money!" Lola exclaimed. She glared at Dick. "I wasn't going to *marry* him."

"That's why she owes me fourteen hundred dollars," Dick insisted. "She lied to me."

In the silence that fell over them, Vic finally spoke up. "That's bullshit."

"It's not—" Dick started forward.

But Vic stuck the end of the baton in the center of Dick's chest to stop him. "You've got something on Lola, or she wouldn't pay you off. What is it, Dick?"

Dick gulped for air as he looked over at Lola.

That's when I realized Vic was right. I turned on my sister. "Why are you playing Dick's game, Lola? What's in it for you?"

Lola blew out her breath. She looked even more contrite than she had over being caught cheating on Martin. "I didn't want you to know, Sierra."

"About being engaged?" I asked, confused.

"That... and..." Lola scrubbed a hand across her face. "I knew Dick wasn't a cop. I found out a couple weeks after he brought me home that night in handcuffs. But I knew if I told you that you would make me stop seeing him."

I took a step back, shaking my head. "You knew he lied? The whole time? You knew that he was pretending to be a cop? And you both lied to me about it?"

"I'm sorry, Sierra! At first it was because I wanted to keep seeing him, and then it turned into this huge power struggle. He kept threatening to tell you that I knew. And I knew you'd be mad that I lied..."

"So you *lied* to me for over a year?" I repeated. "Including when I told you I knew he wasn't a cop, and you yelled at me for trusting him?"

"It got so messed up, Sierra. I couldn't tell you I was using him for rent money. You would have made me stop."

"Hey!" Dick protested. "Don't be such a bitch—"

Vic jabbed his stomach hard with the baton. "Shut up."

Dick let out an oof! and clutched at his middle, bending over. He couldn't catch his breath. Vic was smiling slightly, but he refrained from hitting Dick again.

"Don't feel sorry for him." Lola told me, as she made a face at Dick. "He's an asshole. Making me do this so he wouldn't tell you."

"Why not just tell me after you broke up?" I asked, still trying to understand it.

"I couldn't stand how *disappointed* in me you would be," Lola said. "The lectures I'd get. And I wasn't sure you'd forgive me. I guess it was easier for me to leave you then to see you leave me behind again. Like you always do."

I felt their eyes turn to me. How did this suddenly get to be about *me*? But somehow Vic's eyes were the worst—he didn't blame me for not forgiving him.

"You should have told me the truth," I said to both Lola and Vic.

Vic was nodding. "Yes."

But Lola jerked her chin. "It's not easy to tell you the truth, Sierra. You expect things to be a certain way. It's hard to live up to your expectations."

I realized that Lola could be speaking for Vic. It was true, I had closed my eyes to the signs of discord between Lola and Dick, because I liked having his help taking care of her. And Vic was right that in the very beginning, I had judged him as "Jersey" and dismissed him before I saw him. I did talk to him because Monica said he was rich and successful. I was enchanted by his view and seduced by the idea of his wealthy lifestyle, and that's why I completely lost control and we had wild sex that first time.

I must have looked terribly downcast because Lola came towards me. "I'm sorry, Sierra. It's sucked big time. I feel so bad, until I feel like I can't even talk to you anymore. I know how mad you are about Martin and what we're doing. So when Dick threatened to tell you that I always knew he wasn't a cop if I didn't pay him back... I didn't want to have to deal with it. I thought I'd pay him back and put it in the past so we could finally move on."

From behind me, Martin said quietly, "The only way you can move on is to confess, like you just did. And make atonement."

Lola looked over at Martin. "What do you think I should do?"

"I think that's for Sierra to say."

Lola turned back to me. "I hope you can forgive me. What can I do to make it up to you?"

I was amazed to hear her so easily take responsibility for what she had done. I had wanted to see her do that for so long. And it was Martin who got her there.

I put out my arms to my sister. "Just start talking to me again! I miss texting you and hanging out together."

Lola hugged me back, and for a moment I felt like we were kids again, comforting each other through something difficult. We had always been there for each other.

Suddenly it felt like I had my sister back.

Over Lola's shoulder, I could see Vic, standing guard over Dick who was looking sick. His last hold on Lola was gone. And he knew it. And Vic was still watching over us to make sure Dick didn't try to pull something now that his hopes were gone. What more could I ever ask for in a man?

It sent a flush through me and made my eyes shine brighter at Vic. Maybe forgiveness all around was in order.

Chapter 45

Vic

I was almost hoping Dick would make a dick
move because then I could bust him one. But it only
took one hard jab to the diaphragm and Dick's fight
went out of him. True, I had nearly broken his arm
the last time we tangled, so Dick was being smarter
than his usual self. But it was something more—
once Lola confessed to Sierra, it was over.

I still wanted to bust him one. Imagine
blackmailing a girl into having sex. It was a new low I
had never seen before.

To give her credit, Lola bounced over to Dick
and snapped her fingers in his face. "Fuck off, dude!
If I see you hanging around my place again, I'm
calling the cops."

Sierra stalked past Dick without a word or a
look, as if he was beneath her notice. Those girls were
tough, and I knew what kind of pressure you had to
go through to get that tough. It made me feel for
them, and want to help.

Martin stepped up close to Dick, staring him
down. There was something about the appraising
glint in Martin's eyes. I got the distinct feeling that
Martin knew how to settle a score or two.

In a low voice, Martin told Dick, "You go near
her again and I'll cut your balls off."

Then Martin grinned, showing his missing

teeth. There was something ominous about it. Like he was on the edge and had nothing left to lose.

I wouldn't want to tangle with the guy. Clearly Dick didn't either.

Since no one could improve on that, I saluted him with my baton and whistled on my way out. I didn't think we would be seeing Dick again.

When I reached the elevator, Sierra was asking, "What does Dick really do?"

Lola made a face. "He drives for a car service. Bor-ring!" But as soon as Lola caught the expression on Martin's face, she clammed right up.

I was glad. Lola had gotten her sister into this mess, so she needed to take it seriously. If Dick had been a more desperate character, something bad could have gone down with Sierra in the room. I was going to make sure Lola didn't do anything to hurt Sierra.

Chapter 46

Sierra

After Lola's first burst of emotion towards me, she went quiet. She kept her eye on Martin, and took her cue from his stern expression. As we got into the van, Lola asked Martin in a small voice, "Are you mad at me?"

Martin gave her a look, then put the van into gear. "Lola, if you don't want this kind of relationship, I'm fine with that. We can work together without having this dynamic. Maybe that's for the best."

"You're breaking up with me?" Lola asked, her voice higher.

"I'm accepting the fact that I have no say in who you have sex with." He gave her a meaningful look. "So that means I'm not going to be sexual with you. I like more honesty in my life than what you've got going on."

Lola's mouth fell open. Mine did, too. Finally a man my little sister couldn't manipulate!

"What if I promise I'll do what you say from now on?" Lola asked.

"I've seen today that you're not a woman of your word. You've been lying to your sister, and to me, about what's going on. Why didn't you come to me? I could have helped you with this. I could have helped put everything right, if you trusted me."

Lola stiffened and looked out the window. I

wasn't sure if I should say anything, but I knew exactly why Lola hadn't asked for help. She hated "help" even though she relied on everyone around her. She always had to have it on her own terms, or she made a stink about it.

Now Lola asked, "Are you really breaking up with me?"

"I need time to think about it," Martin said.

For once in her life, Lola didn't nag or whine until she got what she wanted. She sat there nervously chewing the inside of her mouth, glancing over at Martin every now and again. Occasionally she looked back and gave me an apologetic half-smile. I could tell she wanted to talk to me about what had happened with Dick, but she was more worried about getting Martin's forgiveness right now.

It hurt a little to be second on her list of concerns. But I had already accepted weeks ago that Lola had moved on.

Sitting on the bench seat in the back, Vic put his arm around my shoulders. I was glad to lean into him, feeling how warm and safe it felt to be in his arms. My eyes closed. There was nowhere else I wanted to be.

Martin drove us to Greenpoint without asking. It was a silent ride in the darkness, with the street lights flashing through the front windows of the van.

With my head against Vic's shoulder, I watched Lola watch Martin. Lola opened her mouth a few times to say something. But my sister managed to restrain herself. I had never seen her make such an effort to do something she didn't want to do.

When we arrived at my graffiti-covered place in Greenpoint, Martin came around to open the sliding door of the van. Vic took my hand to help me out.

Then Martin opened up the passenger door for Lola. "Get out," Martin told Lola.

I winced in sympathy, as my sister slowly got out of the van. Lola stood in front of Martin, oddly passive and silent, looking up at him. I was reminded of the night at the Chamber when I saw Lola standing in front of Martin, listening so intently to him.

I held my breath. Their relationship was on the line over this. But I had to admire Martin for how he was dealing with it. He wasn't yelling or angry, even though Lola must have had sex with Dick a few different ways to pay off $600 of what she "owed" him.

"I'll take the consequences," Lola said bravely. "Whatever you want. I don't want to lose you over this."

Martin shook his head sadly. "I do adore you, my spunky girl. But you're the one who asked for this. You wanted to be stronger. To learn the discipline you need over yourself. Your impulsive, selfish ways are fine if that's what you choose. But it's not for me."

Lola jerked as if he had slapped her. "I want you. I want our relationship. I've never been so happy."

"Good, otherwise I wouldn't let you come home with me."

"So you're not kicking me out?" she asked.

"We live together, girl. I'm not kicking you out

just because I'm not having sex with you."

"But I want more... than working together. I know I deserve to be punished."

Martin finally smiled. "If you want to be punished, I can do that. Get in the van."

Lola let out her breath in a relieved sigh. At the last second she turned and gave me a hug. It felt so good! Then my sister climbed into the van.

I worried about Lola. "What are you going to do to her?" I asked Martin.

"Enough so she doesn't forget this," he said flatly. Then he smiled at me. "No more than she deserves."

I smiled faintly in return. As Martin got into the van with a wave, I asked Vic, "Is Lola going to be okay?"

"She needs boundaries," Vic said. :Martin gives her that. No wonder she's happy with him."

"I'm starting to understand," I agreed. "He can give her what I couldn't. Maybe I took care of her too well. I didn't give her a chance to learn how to take care of herself."

"Sometimes letting someone fail is the best way to help them," Vic agreed.

As Martin drove off, that left me with alone with Vic. Not Victor. Not my master, but the man who had rushed to save me again, and saved my sister, too.

What to do about Vic?

While I was ready to reconsider everything, I couldn't do that in a flash standing here on the sidewalk. I wanted to be with him, without a doubt. But my head was already reeling from finding out that Lola had been lying to me for over a year. I had known something was wrong, but I hadn't figured it out.

I really didn't trust my own judgment right now.

I stood there silently, not ready to say good-bye but not ready to move forward, either.

Chapter 47

Vic

I almost suggested that we go up to the roof—I could hear music coming from up there. She had said she wanted to show it to me. We could hang out together, feel more comfortable together, and start to put our past in the past.

More than anything, I wanted to put my arm around her again, like she let me in the van, and hold her so she knew she wasn't alone. So I would know that I wasn't alone. Even if it was only for those precious seconds that slipped by too quickly.

Maybe someday that feeling would last.

I wanted it so badly that I smiled at Sierra in the way that usually worked with women.

And then I stopped. I remembered I wasn't playing a role with Sierra. I wasn't trying to manipulate her into doing what I wanted, to get what I wanted.

"Are you okay?" Sierra asked, seeing my smile falter.

I nodded, smiling for real this time, albeit with a little sadness. It was tough to change, tough to be the man she needed me to be. "I don't want to go, but it's that time."

She looked torn. "I'd like to talk, but I'm not sure I can handle anything else right now."

"I get it. A lot has happened tonight." I reached

out to clasp her hand, lacing my fingers in hers. "We have plenty of time to talk. I hope a very long time. There's no rush."

I brushed her cheek with my fingers, and leaned into kiss her. For me, it was a chaste kiss. I wasn't trying to seduce her into taking me upstairs. She was soft and pliable in my arms, the way I loved her. No longer afraid or resisting me. Open and vulnerable.

Now her eyes were shining like they did when she cried, only she was glowing with pleasure.

We separated slowly, and I began to back away to leave. Neither of us said a word, not wanting to break the spell.

Until I was far enough way that her hand finally dropped from mine.

I swallowed at the sudden chill it gave me. But I had to do it. I turned to walk away.

Chapter 48

Sierra

My arm was still half-raised. I didn't want to let him go. But he was walking away. Then he glanced back to look at me one last time.

There were no lies in his clear gray eyes. I knew exactly what Vic was thinking—he loved me, like he had never loved anyone. He had proven he was a changed man when he confessed to everyone what he had done. And he had proven again and again that he would do anything to help me. Watching Vic hold Dick back had been a pure rush of guilty excitement in the midst of a bunch of nastiness. But because Vic was there, I was okay.

For the first time in my life, I wasn't the one who had to pretend to be strong so everything would be okay.

I suddenly realized I had forgiven my sister without a second thought. Despite all of the pain Lola had put me through the past year. Despite the lies and the damage it had done to our relationship. Because I loved my sister, and always would.

I would never regret forgiving Lola. And I couldn't live with myself if I didn't forgive Vic. I craved his touch like I craved the air inside of me. Like I needed him to live.

"Vic!" I called out. He was nearly to the end of my building.

Vic turned as I ran up to him. "What is it?" he asked.

"I forgot to tell you something," I said breathless.

Vic put his arms around me. "What is it?"

"Don't go. Don't ever go."

He started to smile. "If you don't want me to go, I won't. Whatever you say, Sierra."

I smiled, too. "I love you, Vic. I really do."

I kissed him, and it took only a moment for him to realize I meant it. That I was done holding back, when I knew we had to be together. I kissed him like I had never kissed him before, knowing exactly who he was, and knowing how much he loved me.

I lost myself in him. In that lovely full feeling inside of me, swelling to fill us both. Finally.

It was really happening. I couldn't wait to start our relationship for real this time.

Epilogue

Sierra

I was snuggled into the leather couch with my cup of hot chocolate, looking out at Vic's amazing view. "Look! There's snowflakes!"

Vic came out of the bathroom to see. We stood together at the window watching the snow swirl in all directions, caught in the drafts between the buildings.

"It looks like it's falling upwards," I laughed. "I'm glad I don't have to go back home tonight."

Vic's arms went around me from behind, so I could lean back into his firm chest. I was so glad he took the two days off. His boss had offered a bonus for him to do an overnight to San Francisco, but he had turned it down.

"I'm glad you're spending Christmas here with me," Vic murmured into my ear.

"Me, too," I said.

Usually I went home for Christmas Eve, but when I texted my mom that I wanted to stay in the city, she told me to have fun. Lola was also staying in the city with Martin.

We were lucky compared to Vic, who hadn't spoken to his grandparents or his mom in years, so there was no question of him going back to New Jersey for the holiday.

"This is the perfect Christmas Eve," I told him.

As long as we had each other, we would be all right.

"Do you want your surprise on Christmas Eve or Christmas morning?" Vic teased.

"Oh!" I loved Vic's surprises. He had been making me feel good since we got back together, in every way possible. "I want it now! If I have to wait, I won't be able to think about anything else."

"Me either," he agreed.

Now I was really excited. If he thought it was special, it was bound to be super-amazing.

Vic squeezed me tighter, then waved one arm at the window in front of us. "This is it!"

"What?" I asked, confused. The swirling snow spangled the view.

"I'm giving you my view." Vic turned me so he could look into my eyes. "Will you move in with me, Sierra? I want this to be your home. With me."

I stared at him. "You want to move in together?"

Vic smiled. "Most definitely. I told you this summer that I love you, and I want to be with you always. I know it's fast, but it feels like the right thing to do. I hate it whenever you leave."

My throat tightened. I wanted to cry, but it felt good. I kissed him, letting him know without words that I felt the same way.

"So that's a yes," Vic laughed, when we finally parted.

I looked around the room, my expression falling. "I hoped that one day we would move in together, but I never imagined it would be here."

"Does it remind you too much of the lies?" he asked quietly.

She took a deep breath. "No, not anymore. But you said you hated sharing this place with Adrianne, that it was too small. Won't it be the same with me?"

"It felt small because she was always complaining about it. Nothing ever satisfied that girl. If you think it's too small, we can find our own place together."

"No," I said quickly. "It's huge compared to my room in the loft. I love it here. I *love* the view."

"Yeah," he smiled. "That's why I'm giving it to you."

I kissed him again, long and lingering. "It's what I've always wanted, Vic."

"Well, I'm glad I can fulfill at least one of your dreams."

I felt blissfully happy. "More than that. As it turns out, my darling Vic, you're my dream come true."

###

For more books by Susan Wright, go to:
www.susanwright.info

Good Girl

Is it just the chase he loves?

There's always a risk when you take a walk on the wild side. A risk that you may not be able to come back. That's what Kalico Jones fears when she meets a hot sculptor who takes what he wants and gets any woman he wants. Hunter Munro is definitely not the right man for Kali. He's unstable, without a real job, and he knows how to catch a girl with his dominant ways. Kali just wants to keep her head down so she can keep her dream job in New York City, but with Hunter in the mix, that's impossible.

Hunter knows he's all wrong for Kali, but he love the chase she gives him. If it means he has to break through her defenses to free the wild child within, then that's what he'll do. Even if it shatters her world.

But can Hunter learn to love Kali without trying to control her?

Will Kali reject Hunter along with her deepest dreams?

www.ingramcontent.com/pod-product-compliance
Lightning Source LLC
Chambersburg PA
CBHW060139260626
47160CB00001B/45